THE MERCIAN REGISTER

Volume 1 Book 1

Edward and Elfwina

Francine
MEZO

ISBN-10:1478247746
ISBN-13:978-1478247746

DEDICATION

For Dale, the quiet presence so deeply missed.

ACKNOWLEDGMENTS

I wish to thank Thomas S. Donahue, Professor Emeritus at San Diego State University for making the Anglo Saxon period of England more than history.

I also wish to express my appreciation of *Death of a Fool*, the excellent mystery by Ngaio Marsh, from whence came the inspiration for the horse and the grotesque.

Chapter One

Men become heroes not only by fighting legendary battles, but also through the conduct of their daily lives.
Ceadda, prince of Middelríce, Anno 461

[817] *Cenwulf, king of Mercia, fought Ædda, king of Northumbria at Stafford and there was a great slaughter. Aedred, aetheling of Mercia, was wounded. King Ædda was forced to make a peace.*

[818] *Eadberht, with a number of men, attempted to murder King Cenwulf, but was slain along with his followers. King Cenwulf and Brihtric, king of Wessex, fought the Danes at Weogornaceaster and, good allies, met at Bath.*

[819] *King Cenwulf and Gryffn, overlord of the Welsh, made an agreement.*

[820] Mercia. His men were exhausted, his horses stumbling in the heat; the summer air was as thick as treacle, and they were no closer to the force of Danes than they had been three days ago when the chase began. Disgusted, Prince Aedred called a halt at the nearest stand of trees where there was water. Immediately the large group of warriors sprawled out by the shady spring. With mild curiosity, they watched Prince Aedred cross the road and start up the grassy hill on the other side, the Saxon prince reluctantly following him.

Aedred reached the halfway point and glanced over his shoulder. There was Edward, hauling himself up the steep ground, handhold by handhold, sweating in his dusty mail byrnie, grumbling, then regarding Aedred with a sudden grin. His figure swayed across the scene below, blurring the dusty road, the spring, and the warriors milling among the horses.

Edward All-Fair.

His warriors had given this nickname to the Saxon prince, and in this afternoon, on this hillside, with his blond hair absorbing color from the grasses and trees and gleaming greenish-gold, his damp curls creeping like ivy into his downy beard, Edward could have been a sprite. But his blue eyes were narrow with suspicion.

"What the hell are you up to?" Edward called.

Aedred turned from the image with a smile and continued

upward.

"Is there something worthwhile at the top of this hill?"

Still climbing, the Mercian prince called back, "You'll see."

"It better be good--" Edward glanced back down the steep incline "--dragging me up this hot fucking hill."

Aedred snorted and rolled his eyes. At the hill's crest, he stopped.

The Saxon prince came up beside him. "Say now!" he cried. "Will you look at this!"

Where the sloping ground leveled out a furlong ahead of them there was a pond. Beyond it the dwellings of a little village gleamed through the distant trees. In the flowered meadow between village and pond the breeze sank and rose in the lush grasses and rippled the waters invitingly. Aedred stared at the prince with raised eyebrows.

Edward said, "I humbly apologize."

"You damn well should." The Mercian prince watched a flush rise all through Edward's thin beard and mustache. Aedred slapped the prince's shoulder. "You're the best friend I have, Edward," he said. He stretched out his arm, "I give you this." And then he laughed.

Bliss enveloped Edward. Nothing about the seventeen-year-old Mercian prince escaped him. Aedred was everything a prince should be. When Edward was around him, he felt good about himself. They were not only distant kinsmen they *were* friends. Over the months he had been in Mercia, Edward's admiration of Aedred and trust in his judgment had grown. He could speak now about things in which he lacked confidence, anxieties he might never have revealed to anyone else, concerns about battle strategies he thought he should know but didn't, pitfalls of leadership he knew Aedred, being who he was, would never experience. He had even queried the Mercian about women and had been given direct, blush-raising answers. One day, needing to get something straight on another subject, Edward casually said, "They say you practice magic."

"Who's 'they'?"

"Uh, you know," Edward replied with a vague wave of his hand, "the ranks."

Aedred was slow answering.

Thinking he might be treading where he shouldn't, Edward said, hastily, "I'm Christian; we don't believe in that sort of thing. I just wondered what they meant, is all."

Aedred came over to where the Saxon prince sat on the ground drawing cryptic lines on the parchment he always carried with him. "Working on your maps, again?"

Edward looked down at the parchment and then back at Aedred.

"Look here," the Mercian prince said, squatting next to him, "magic is not something I can talk to you about. It's part of my religion--sacred, you understand."

"I didn't mean to pry into something I shouldn't."

"I know you didn't." Aedred rested his fingertips in the grass near his shoe and for a moment studied the ground. Then he said quietly, "We're not sorcerers or magicians, but Mercian Kings descend from the great Allfather Woden, the God of Magic; that gives us the ability to . . . perform certain things, to summon certain forces. It's written in our blood, so to speak. You know that." He was looking deep into Edward's eyes, making sure the prince was following him. "That part is common knowledge. That's all I can say about it."

Since he and his father converted to Christianity, Edward no longer believed any aspect of the heathen religion. In fact, he viewed it with disdain. Yet from those heathen days there lingered the memory of dark entities that stalked the night and roared overhead, and there was about his kinsman an unreachable, unexplainable *something*. That Aedred had discussed with him any aspect of this secret world made the Saxon prince feel special.

Now, on this hillside, as he gazed at the Mercian prince, Edward felt the glow of that special connection.

Aedred sighed loudly and rolled his head in fatigue. "So, what about this?" He jerked his dark head toward the pond. "Are you for it?"

They helped each other off with their mail byrnies, removed their weapons, and piled them with their clothing. Aedred stepped into the pond up to his hips, gasped, "Ah, la! This is *cold*!" He stared down through the water at his magnified feet, which looked as cold and white as the rest of him. He moved slowly forward until he stood up to his navel. Sucking in his breath, he splashed water over his shoulders and chest. He called to Edward, "You'd think the water would be warmer than this. My hnocc's shrunk to an acorn. Are you coming in or not?"

"Yes," Edward called back. He looked hard at Aedred and saw he was preoccupied with dousing himself with handfuls of water. Edward's gaze intensified. "It won't be too cold for me."

"Well, come along. What are you waiting for?" Aedred drooped forward. He frowned at the contrast between his dark brown arms and hands and his fish-belly-white torso. With his head down in this scrutiny, he was calling out, "Are you waiting for me to warm it--?" when Edward's body hit his, full force, from a dead run. Yelping in surprise, Aedred went under the water, the prince on top of him.

He squirmed out of reach and came sputtering to the surface, flinging his long hair in a violent loop of water. Edward came up crowing and staggering about in great hilarity. Howling a warning, Aedred leaped on him, wrestling him below the surface where he held him down with a malicious knee, but the prince slipped away. They came up together, spewing water and laughing as they struggled for holds.

The water churned all about them. They braced, leaned, regripped, each trying to gain a purchase over the other when, in a single moment of mutual balance, their bodies joined from chest to thigh and what had been a combative grip became an embrace. Their arms slid around each other, and their heads bent forward and rested together. Prince Aedred could feel the downy hairs of Edward's beard against his cheek. The musky tang of Edward's sweat enveloped him. A sudden, voluptuous joy swelled inside his chest and strained at his ribs. He caught his breath as Edward's warm hands pressed his bare back.

There was only that single silent sealing of a bond, and then all was contention again. They shouted and grappled and thrashed about until the pond was brown with silt; they stood apart, heaving out laughter and oaths until they were ready to drop.

As they paused to build up strength for another assault, an apparition stormed up to the edge of the pond. His hair blazed around his scarlet face and burned at his broad shoulders. His body strained at his sleeveless tunic. Across the rocks of his knees the hem of his blacksmith's apron had left a murky stain. In his raised fist he held a great hammer.

"That's drinking water you're playing in, you assholes!" he boomed. "Get the hell out of there!" He brandished his hammer.

Prince Aedred stared at him with a chalky face and an open mouth. He swallowed noisily and began thrashing toward the bank. Edward trailed after him, his eyes on the hammer.

"You bloody militia think you own the countryside," the blacksmith shouted. "You don't give a shit for anyone but yerselves. But you're not pulling that here." He paced alongside Aedred as the prince came out of the water. "Do you know how long it'll take for the mud to settle out so's even an ox can drink it? Eh? Eh?" He shook the hammer at him. "The rest of the damn day. The hottest day of the year and young nor old won't have a clean drop. That's what your mucking about has done."

Prince Aedred was standing on the bank now, his color returning. He glanced at Edward, who looked back at him as if to say *This was your idea, remember?*

Aedred looked again at the ceorl. "I am sorry."

Still carried on his outrage and expecting more resistance from these young militia men, the man lifted and regripped his hammer. "If you pissed in there . . . !"

Aedred shook his head and looked into Edward's glittering eyes.

Edward laid his hand on his bare chest and gave the blacksmith a sweet, appealing look. "*I* never piss in water I'm going to swim in."

"But you don't mind swimming in water people drink, do you? Get out of here the both of you. And tell those ones below they'd better not come up here, or I'll lay their fucking heads open with my hammer."

"I'll tell them," Aedred said, as he backed away with Edward close beside him.

They turned, and walked over to their pile of clothing and weapons. As they bent to pick them up, Aedred whispered, "Carry your clothes. We'll dress on the other side of the hill."

"Why?"

"If he sees our swords and byrnies, he'll know we're not militia. He'll die of humiliation." He giggled uncontrollably and started Edward giggling, too.

"Go on!" yelled the blacksmith.

Prince Aedred whipped his long mantle around his belongings and stood up. "We're going."

He and Edward went quickly back over the crest of the hill. Aedred slapped the prince on the head. "There was swearing to the purpose!"

Wobbling about and dipping their heads together, they sank down in laughter as they tried to give each other frantic imitations of the blacksmith.

The man roared from directly overhead, "I told you to get on!" He had come to the top of the hill and was looking down at them, his red hair flaring in the sunlight, his big fingers bunched around the hammer shaft.

Aedred looked at all the upturned, inquiring faces of the Mercian warriors. He waved off the thegns who had quickly started to climb the hill.

As they began their descent naked, Edward asked, "What are we going to tell them?"

"Why should we tell them anything? Haven't you learned yet? Princes don't have to explain. No one will dare say anything as long as we choose not to mention it. We've been checking the terrain, haven't we? We'll dress right down there in front of them, and I'll wager they'll pretend they don't see a thing out of the ordinary."

"Never! One of them will say *some*thing."

"Not one. Lay your wager."

"All right, three gold mancuses somebody says something before we can get dressed and mount our horses."

Aedred's eyebrows rose. "Three! There's confidence!"

"I am confident. I know Eorl Mawer. He won't keep quiet. Look at him. He's going to hear the story or else."

The big, fair-haired Saxon eorl stood in the grass where the hill swept upward from the road, his hands on his hips, watching them.

Aedred shook his head. "Not even your Mawer. Are you leaning away?"

"No, I still say three."

"That's half your summer allowance."

"I'm going to be half my summer's allowance richer."

"Well, you've had every chance. Done, then!"

Talking spiritedly about routes and elevations and distances, their hair dripping water down their chests and backs, they reached the bottom of the hill. In the middle of the road in front of one hundred twenty Mercian militia and Mercian and Saxon noblemen, they casually put on their clothes. As Aedred had predicted, not one of them commented, not even Eorl Mawer who stood staring off down the road throughout the performance, growling occasionally to himself.

One of the gold mancuses cheerfully handed over by Edward was delivered to the villagers in the name of Prince Aedred by Grundl, the huge Mercian warrior. Through this imposing emissary, the prince offered his apologies for the blameworthy conduct of two of his men. To the nodding, approving villagers, headed by the blacksmith, Grundl stoically reported that the offenders had been severely reprimanded.

"It's absolutely true!" Aedred told the prince. "There he was—standing on the bank, his great hammer ready to throw; I thought he was Thunor! That blacksmith scared the piss out of me." He looked at Edward from under his eyebrows. "I lied to him about that."

The Mercian soldiers nearest them looked around sharply to see the two princes collapsed together, howling with laughter.

Chapter Two

[820] Wessex. They were in sight of Exeter. The hard thumping of Edward's heart fired him inside but left his skin cold and goosey. Chills flew up and down the muscles of his back and neck; he felt his hair straighten and stand on end.

Will we never get there?

Quite calmly, he said to Eorl Mawer, "It looks the same." He glanced over at the eorl, who was hiding a smile. Edward resumed his study of the town.

It lay some three miles away from where they were descending into the river valley from the autumn-flamed woods. He contrived to look casual, almost bored.

The eorl turned his great, good-humored face on the prince. Not fooled at all, he agreed. "Never seems to change, does it? No matter how long a feller has been away."

Recognizing his home grounds, Edward's white stallion abruptly changed his drowsy gait and became a different animal. He pricked forward, shook his head. Rolling his eyes toward the river and the walled town, he belled his nostrils, pulling in Exeter and some stirring promise sent out from it on the wind.

"He knows," Mawer said, and then laughed like a great bear, hugely, baring his teeth, a ferocious revelation of incisors and gums. His horse began the same eager dance as Edward's, and he reined it in with a gruff command.

Edward turned abruptly in his saddle and called up his handthegn Tonberht. From out of the ten or so thegns and servants keeping their own animals in check, Edward's personal servant rode quickly up beside him.

"Sire?"

"Send someone down to notify His Majesty we'll be arriving shortly."

A messenger galloped away down the hill as the company moved on at a walk which threatened to break into a trot.

The prince called Tonberht again. "Another message--to Princess Elfwina."

Tonberht called a second man. Edward reached inside his purse and handed a small object to the messenger. "Tell the princess this comes with love from her brother."

The messenger raced off down the slope, and Edward checked his impulse to send his own horse flying after him. With masterly restraint he led the Saxons on to Exeter.

Alerted by the messengers, the townspeople poured through the gates. Running alongside the horses, they shouted their welcomes.

The parade wound into the center of town past the monastery where the monks watched demurely from the shadows of their cowls, and then continued up to the royal enclosure and in through the wide open gates to Exeter Hall. In the shadow of the great doors, King Brihtric stood waiting. He came forward as Edward leaped from the saddle and ran up the steps. They embraced fiercely, drew back to stare at each other, embraced again.

I have grown up, Edward thought. *I am a man now and not the same person I was when I left, and Father knows!*

As the king drew away to enter the hall, Edward swung about to meet a furious assault from his left. Magically at his side appeared a stunning girl whose serenity belied the agitation preceding her, except for her dark, feverish eyes. Her skin was soft white, her cheeks and lips brushed with vermillion. Where her mantle had slipped down, it revealed an astounding quantity of black hair that sheened blue when she turned her head.

"Elf . . . !" Edward stared at the metamorphosis which had taken place in his absence.

His sister flung her arms around him, staggering him. He stood her away with a wary glance toward the hall doors, but their father had already entered. He gripped her hand then, holding it tightly, pulling her close to his left side to hide their intertwined fingers as he answered disjointed questions from the people crowding around them.

And then their cousin Prince Cosmer, leading a pack of Edward's friends, swooped in and surrounded him. He felt Elfwina's fingers slip out of his hand and looked around to see her bobbing back, drifting away, while he was carried forward, pummeled by his friends and tossed about and deluged with a thousand questions about the year's pursuit of the Danes.

He passed happily through the feast in honor of their return, drinking ale, stuffing himself, and never once stopping his narrative except to swallow or answer questions. But his gaze kept drifting to his sister. *She's so beautiful,* he thought. From where she sat on the other side of their father she was sending him fierce looks which melted into pleas. Satisfied with this, and enjoying himself immensely, he made no attempt to go to her. Toward the end of the evening, however, when he glanced past his father, he saw that Elfwina was looking up at an auburn-haired youth whose glorious mustache glinted copper-red. Lean and muscular, the youth looked extremely handsome in his gold-embroidered tunic and yellow mantle, his finely proportioned legs outlined by yellow hose and banding.

What's Tilhere doing in Exeter? Edward thought venomously. *He's*

Mercian.

He strained to hear their conversation. He could see them clearly enough: Tilhere smiled, Elfwina smiled; Tilhere spoke, she spoke. The surrounding noise pushed the Mercian very close to Elfwina, and he made no move to straighten away, continuing to loom over her and gaze boldly down into her eyes. He took her hand and squeezed it. Edward shot up from his seat, but sank back down when his father turned to him.

King Brihtric had also been observing the scene and was not pleased with his son's reaction. Before the prince realized this, he blurted out, "What is *Tilhere* doing here?"

Brihtric's cool gaze brought Edward up short. "Mercians are always welcome in this hall. Is there a reason he should not be here?"

"No, Sire. I was just surprised to see him so far from Kettering."

"He's here with his father to beg consideration."

"Sire?"

"He wants to marry your sister, Edward." The king glanced again at the Mercian youth who still hovered over Elfwina. "It could be a decent match. He'll be eorl of Kettering, one day, and he's heathen."

"She's only twelve!"

Brithric smiled, leaned over to say in his ear, "Your mother was thirteen when we were wed."

Edward stared at him.

"But sixteen, I think, for Elfwina. Nothing has been settled yet. There are others to consider."

"What others!"

After a long look at his son, King Brihtric replied, "Others I have chosen," and he leaned away to speak with Eorl Peohtwine.

Beneath the tabletop, Edward's hands closed into fists as he stared at Tilhere.

Chapter Three

[820] Wessex. Edward stood outside the door of his sister's chambers, glancing uneasily down the empty hallway. His father was at the benches, and Edward hoped the whereabouts of his son would not be on his mind. Fretting and unhappy, the prince hesitated, but he had to see her. He had to do *something*. But what?

Marriage! Can I stop it? How can I stop it?

He resented his father's plans and that man who would know her in all the ways he could not. The thought was unbearable. That interloper had at first been Tilhere, but now there was a threatening crowd of suitors. He felt stripped of control and aggrieved with his father for moving events in such a blinding way. Now everything was *assumed*. He and his sister had obligations--it would happen one day, it was inescapable. But *one day* seemed much too close now.

He knocked on the door. It was promptly opened by Elfwina's personal servant, her thegnestre, Edyth. She closed the door quickly behind him. Once Edward was in the seclusion of the anteroom the woman's eyes swept him with critical interest.

"Is she here?"

"Welcome home, Sire! Yes, she is." She took in Edward's amber beard and mustache. Seeing approval in her scrutiny, Edward blushed.

"Not in bed, I hope."

"She has been waiting for you." She lowered her voice. "But you understand, Sire; only a few moments, please. You know--"

He flipped his hand, silencing her. "Announce me."

She swept through the doorway to the main chamber. "His Royal Highness, Edward, Prince of Wessex!" Hiding a laugh, she stepped back and watched as Elfwina came running to meet her brother.

"So you were sure I was going to come," he said.

"You didn't speak to me once!" she cried. "Not once! Even though you could have with propriety if you'd wanted to--" she paused on an indrawn breath. "No one saw you in the hallway, did they?" This always had to be established.

He shook his head.

"Father . . . ?"

"Still at the benches."

Her breath rushed back out. "I shouldn't be nice to you at all. I should do what you did and not speak to you. But I'm kinder than you by a long stroke. I'm not going to let you go until you tell me *everything*!"

Her reprimands given, she flung her arms around her brother, bouncing joyfully against him. Suddenly ill at ease, he took her arms down. He glanced at the open door of the next room and saw Edyth walking about, talking with other servants. Elfwina looked at him curiously. Then, grabbing his hands, she tugged him across the room.

"Where do you want me to go?" Freeing himself, he walked behind her to a window thrown open to the night. They sat down on the bench beneath it. She leaned against him and looked inquiringly into his face. The faint smell of rosemary oil from her hair tingled his nostrils. He looked into her face and shifted position.

"Tell me about it," she said. "Every little thing."

So he told her about the year in Mercia, and she listened closely, absorbing all he was saying, putting herself inside him as she always did, her dark eyes never leaving his face. While he was speaking he was seeing her looking at Tilhere with that same concentration, and he hated what their father had planned for her.

He told her about the blacksmith who had chased him and Prince Aedred out of the pond and how terrified the heathen prince had been when he thought the man was a God.

Elfwina shuddered. "I would have been scared, too! Thunor! And with his hammer . . . why wouldn't he be scared to death?"

"He's no coward," Edward said quickly. "He was the first man into every skirmish. No one is braver. He's an excellent horseman, too. He trains his war-horses himself."

"Is he handsome?"

"Handsome?" He was amused. "All the girls think so."

"What color hair does he have?"

"Dark brown." He was giving her a quizzical look.

"Is he pleasant?"

"Why are you asking me? You've met him."

"I have? When? I don't remember."

"At Bath--when Father met with King Cenwulf."

"I don't remember," she repeated. "He can't have been *very* handsome."

"You were a little girl," he replied, looking her over. He smiled. "Everyone likes him. He has a temper, but you don't see that often. No one ever spoke ill of him." She was still listening closely. "He's very devout. There are certain prayers he says to his gods before battles. Sometimes he consulted runes. He believes he is descended from their god Woden--"

"So are you, Edward."

He had been rambling. "I'm a Christian, now, Elfwina."

"That doesn't change your ancestors."

His look held a warning. She made a face at him.

"I respect his beliefs, and he respects mine." With conviction, he said, "He is going to be a splendid king."

"You'll be better."

"I wasn't comparing--" He was.

"Were you afraid when you went into battle?"

Edward paused. There was an ethic forming in the new person he thought himself to be. Honesty seemed crucial. He tested himself. He had not thought Aedred had been afraid.

"Yes," he said finally, able to admit it to her. "The Danes are fiercesome and ugly--"

"Did you kill any?"

"No, thank God!" She was the only one to whom he would ever admit this reluctance to kill. "I got in some good strokes, though."

"I'm so glad you didn't kill anyone, Edward," she said. "Not this time, anyway." It was his feeling exactly. Killing needed to be approached obliquely, over time, in careful steps. One needed to develop immunity to that final act.

"I was afraid you wouldn't come back," she whispered with her face close to his, her eyes wide open and so reflective of that fear it took his breath away.

"Look!" she said abruptly, and held up her right hand. A large gold ring, flashing with gems, spun on her bent thumb. It was the gift he had sent by messenger.

"Do you like it?"

Her eyes told him yes. She gazed down at it, and then back at him.

"It belonged to Offa, our great, great, great grandfather--"

"Much too many greats," she laughed. With reverence, then, she asked, "Really? Offa?"

"King Cenwulf let me take it from the Mercian treasury. It's way too big, but I'll have the goldsmith size it for you. It's a bracelet the way it is now."

"I think I would like it on a chain," she said. She twisted the ring this way and that, tilting it so the torch burning on the wall above her head sparked over the jewels. "He actually wore it? Offa?"

"Yes."

"Then I absolutely do not want it changed. I'll wear it around my neck. Will you have a gold chain made for it?"

"If that's what you want."

"Yes, I do." She rose up and, putting her arms around his neck, kissed him at the corner of one eye, and then rested her forehead against his temple. "Thank you, Edward," she murmured.

Edyth came in then with a cup of ale for Edward. Elfwina sank quickly down and Edward leaned away.

"The ring belonged to King Offa," she told Edyth.

"Offa! Imagine! Only a few more minutes, Sire," she cautioned the prince.

When the woman left the room, Edward reached for his sister's hand, glanced toward the door, then rested her hand in his palm. With a sudden shy eagerness, he told her, "The gems each have a special meaning. Shall I tell you what they are?"

"Yes," she said, in a low voice, her eyes wide. She murmured, "What could they be?"

"It applies to us, Elf." He slipped the ring from her thumb to her index finger. With their heads bent together, they looked down at the ring. He moved it slowly, with two fingers, and they silently watched the play of light over the stones, their heads touching, long strands of her black hair caught by his thick curls.

"Is it magic?" she whispered.

"It seems like it could be, doesn't it?" he said kindly, smiling at her.

She wiggled impatiently. "Go on--what does this one mean?" She touched the large center stone.

Their heads bowed together again. "It's a ruby. It stands for faithfulness--faithfulness of blood and heart."

This was partly true, told to him by King Cenwulf, but he was also improvising from his own desperation. "Our blood is the same, Elf," he said solemnly. "It binds us together. No matter how far away we are from each other, even if the sea were between us--"

"I don't want you to go away anymore, Edward," she said gravely.

"I--I'll have to go when the levies are called. Before too long I'll command the army, and you will marry one day--" He stared at her, and then looked back at the ring, tipped it from side to side.

"I don't want to marry."

He stopped moving the ring and looked up. "You don't? What do you want to do?"

"Nothing. I mean, stay here--in Exeter."

"Yes?"

"With you . . . and Father."

"But you like Tilhere, don't you?"

Elfwina's eyes widened. "Tilhere? He's quite nice. And sooo handsome--that glorious hair! All the serving girls love him." She laughed, doubling over. "But he'll be an eorl one day. Eorls do not marry serving girls."

"No, but they can marry princesses," Edward said, with a dark look. "What is so funny?"

"You." She mocked his frown. "What princesses? Why are you so annoyed? Don't you approve of Tilhere? He's very respectable." She started laughing merrily again but watched him closely.

"I won't be marrying him."

"Indeed! Queen Edward Tilhere! That would be a topic!" She bent over again in laughter.

Edward leaped up and stood glowering at her.

Her laughter stopped abruptly. She said, "What is this about Tilhere? Do you think I am going to marry him? You're being silly. I am never going to marry. Are you?"

"Of course, I'll marry. She'll be a beauty, too; although, naturally, I'll select her for her importance to the kingdom."

The words had fallen out of his mouth like ugly toads and left their awful taste. He was surprised at his lie. He did not want to marry. He didn't know why he had said that. "I must, you know. It's my obligation." Now he felt bad. "But I won't like it. Some dreadful cow I'll hate." He sat down again. "We'll both have to marry. You know that, don't you?"

She turned her head away.

"I'll make sure Father chooses someone special for you. Not just anybody. I'll make sure that man is worthy of you." He leaned toward her so she would look at him. "Whoever he is, he will never be closer to you than I am. He will never come between us."

"I know."

"Look here at the ruby, Elf. Blood is faithful. I will always be faithful to you. You must be faithful to me."

"Yes," she sighed. A shudder ran through her. In a sad voice, she asked, "What meaning does the amethyst have?"

For a moment he looked away from her to the stone. "Sincerity. We must never be false with each other. No dishonesty or untruthfulness." His eyes turned a deeper blue as his gaze returned to her face. "No one could ever take your place with me. No silly wife, that's for certain." He hesitated. "Could a husband take my place?"

She leaned toward him, drawn by his whisper and his eyes. "No, not ever."

"Will you swear that on Offa's ring?"

"Will you?"

"I swear on this ring no wife will ever take your place."

"I swear on this ring no husband will ever take your place."

"This will be true as long as we live," he whispered.

"Yes . . . ."

They looked at each other and each believed this was true.

Edward took a breath.

There were three center jewels: a ruby, an amethyst, and an emerald. Surrounding these three was a small ring of emeralds. Edward ran the tip of his finger around that circle. "The emerald is the enemy of all impurity, and King Cenwulf told me that if it were to touch the skin of an adulterer, it would break. It's strange that a stone would know, isn't it?"

They looked at each other solemnly. Edward carefully placed the ring back on her thumb.

"An emerald most of all represents tolerance." Edward grinned suddenly. "Just to remind you that your brother has the patience of a saint, and you so often try it."

She leaped up with a startling growl, and then her laughter pealed out. She wound her arms around his neck again and pressed against him. He felt her round little breasts mashing into his upper arm. When he turned his head to look at her, she placed her mouth firmly on his and pushed. As her dry warm mouth pressed his lips uncomfortably against his teeth, a sensation passed through his entire body and focused at his loins.

The different man he now imagined himself to be shoved her away, not roughly, but firmly. He looked quickly toward the other room and then back to her. "You mustn't do that."

She looked bewildered. "Why not? Do what? Kiss you?"

"Yes. You're getting too old to be kissing me. It isn't proper. Don't do it anymore."

She stared at him in confusion. Then the confusion turned to injury, and then to distress; he watched it all flow across her face. "I won't," she said, sadly looking down, her shoulders slumping. She twirled the ring around and around on her thumb.

He slipped it off. "I'll have a gold chain made for it. Don't be angry with me. There are just certain ways you must behave when you begin to grow up. Kissing me like that is--is just not done. You're not a little girl anymore."

His eyes slid to her breasts. They were clearly outlined by the long, close-fitting gown she was wearing. Small, firm, they were somehow defiant. She looked down, too, and then both their glances came up together.

"Jesus," said Edward, "you're so . . . different somehow." And it carried such bewilderment that she laughed and reached up with both hands to pull at his new beard, which had gotten thicker and more darkly amber by the end of summer.

"And where did you get this?" she cried, still laughing. "But it makes you look so handsome! Don't ever take it off!"

He decided he never would.

Chapter Four

[820] Wessex. "Now then, Prince Edward, you don't look like a Mercian, but I'll wager your language sounds like it. A few months with the Mercian militia would smudge the speech of a saint. But the question I want to ask you is, Did you kill a Dane?"

All this was being said by Eorl Teownor, just joining the group of the king's retainers. With an affectionate grin, he clapped Edward on the shoulder, and then smiled slyly at Brihtric. Teownor did not let the prince answer his question. Instead, he dismissed it with a flip of his hand. "No, you'll tell me Mercian military fables and extol that heathen kinsman of yours. Tell me; rather, how it was you managed to leave your sister for so long?"

His cheeks burning, Edward glanced off toward the water's edge where Elfwina pranced in and out of the foamy tide, her gown trussed up between her legs and tied to the thin metal girdle at her hips. Her mantle had been blown back by the wind (or thrown back, he suspected) so that her shiny black hair hung loose and rippled with her movements. He frowned. Earlier he had started to tell her that she was too old now to bare her legs in that way or to let her hair show, but his father had stopped him, "No--look how carefree she is. Let her be." He had gazed fondly at his daughter, and Edward had said no more. Now, with the heads of the men turned toward where Elfwina danced through the water, Edward felt extremely uncomfortable about the appearance she made; at the bright, abandoned way she was racing through the foam.

"It's a good thing you're back, Prince Edward," Eorl Sigeric said. "Your sister gave us no peace after you left."

Edward glanced at his father and then looked at the eorl with a slight frown. "How is that?" he asked.

"She may have had it in mind to join her brother in the field--one can't always tell with young girls--but whatever her reason, she persuaded our good Eorl Teownor to teach her how to use a sword. Now that she has beaten all your young friends at swordplay, she's looking for other challengers. I can tell you it is hell to be followed about by a young girl with a sword in her hand."

The laughter was subdued and friendly. Although Edward flushed again, he looked into the eorl's eyes and said, with an angelic smile, "That can't have lasted too long--once she'd beaten you, who was her next challenge?" He heard Mawer's laugh.

Sigeric smiled and answered gallantly, "I declined the challenge and was spared defeat. I suggested Peohtwine of Bosham as a more able competitor."

"She's already conquered us a hundred times over," Peohtwine replied smoothly. He turned his lean face toward Edward, and smiled. "The princess spent most of her time gazing toward the north. I would suspect she missed her brother. For her sake, Prince Edward, you should remain in Exeter or take her with you next time."

"For all our sakes," Eorl Teownor added.

Through this exchange Brihtric had remained silent. Edward looked uneasily at him.

The talk moved on then to other subjects, and Edward drifted away from the group. He sat down in the sand with his back against the warmth of a small dune. On its crest long, tough grasses sighed with the velocity of the wind. He listened to their soft hiss as he watched his sister picking up little bits of drift from the darkened record of the tide and imagined her missing him, knowing he had missed her in spite of all the exciting and sometimes dangerous events of the campaign. He wondered if she had felt the same aching in her chest, the same tightening of her throat as he had felt in Mercia when he'd held her in his thoughts.

Crooking his arm under his head, he gazed up at the sky, at the deep and brilliant blue of these late days of autumn. Small white clouds very close to the earth churned toward land, repatterning endlessly. He could hear the low drone of the men's voices, the near, soft measure of the wind, and the benevolent breathing of the sea. Then, over that collective murmur, came a high, ringing voice. *"Edward!"*

He straightened as she ran up to him, her bare feet showering sand over his clothes. "Watch out!" He laughed, flinging up his hand to protect his eyes.

She dropped down beside him and leaned heavily against his shoulder. He braced himself.

"Go down the beach with me."

Her request puffed against his cheek and tickled his ear. He flinched, his head tilted toward his shoulder, but she leaned still closer to speak, and her lips danced over his ear. He winced with pleasure and did not try to move away again.

"There are so many shells I can see just above the tide line. Much better than these--" a little cascade of shells filled his hand.

"How can you tell from here?"

"I can tell. Go with me, please."

She glanced over at the group of men, and then back at Edward, breathless, her dark eyes wide, her cheeks blazed from the wind.

He looked at her with the same wonderment he had felt on his return. "I'm resting--you go. I'll watch you from here."

"I would like you to go with me," she insisted, her bright gaze threatening disappointment.

"Did you miss me when I was gone?" he asked abruptly.

Her slender body sprang upright on her knees, and her hands slapped around his face. The suddenness and ferocity held him stationary. "I knew Father was going to send you away. I was so unhappy. But it was unkind of you to stay away for so many months!"

"We were following the Danes." He took her hands down, but held them in his where they couldn't be seen. "I wanted to come back." In a low voice he asked, "Did you cry?"

"*Did* you want to come back?"

"Yes. While I was gone, did you cry for me?"

"And you--did you miss me so much you cried?"

"I was sad."

Her arms came tightly around his neck. "Don't go away again--give me your oath you won't!"

Conscious of the groups of men all around them, Edward pulled her arms down and pushed her gently back from him. "I told you--I can't do that. I can't promise I won't have to fight. I would promise I'd always come back, if you'll be waiting here for me." He was looking intently into her eyes, his own eyes anxious and sincere. "Will you promise me that?"

"I want to go with you. Eorl Teownor even taught me to use the sword--"

"You know you can't do that," he said. "But you could promise to always be waiting here for me." That promise was suddenly very important to him.

She recognized it and gave her oath as he wished, although her own dream ran more to fighting with him side by side.

A sudden whirl of emotion left Edward confused, He gave his oath in return, an oath which now had the mystic properties of a vow. Looking quickly back toward his father, who was looking at them, he came to his feet. "Come along--let's look for your shells."

He walked along with her, stopping and starting, as she picked up shells and little bits of sea-polished wood and exclaimed over each of these treasures, insisting he note every detail. She had him sit down with her in the dry sand to reexamine them all, one by one. In the distance the men of their father's retinue strolled together, relaxed in the sand, or stood talking, their mantles rippling and folding in the cool breeze.

Edward looked back at his sister. She was bending over the pile of shells in her lap, one bare leg in front of her. It glistened with sea water. The fine dark hairs flowed down in a pattern fashioned by the water and were starred with sand grains. He reached out and slowly brushed the grains away, his fingers lingering to feel the silky hairs and the warm roundness of her calf muscle; his hand stroked the soft skin under her knee. She looked at what he was doing and then up at him, her eyes large. Her lips slowly closed together, and she drew the leg beneath her. He was suddenly embarrassed. He stood up and looked out over the ocean, his hands resting on his scabbard belt.

"You have enough shells," he said. "It's time to go back." He started away up the beach.

Elfwina stood up slowly, letting the shells fall away into the sand. She unfastened her gown from the girdle and shook out the folds of material. Adjusting the mantle around her head, she ran to catch up with her brother. They walked back together to join the others, both looking ahead, a small confused distance between them.

In this year the Danes harried into Mercia. Aedred aetheling and Edward, prince of Wessex with Mercian levies and other men from both kingdoms opposed the force at Staines and had the victory. They fought again at Bergentford and again at Fullanhamm. At the end of summer the force was driven back into East Anglia, and Prince Edward returned to Wessex.

Chapter Five

[821] Exeter, Wessex. Elfwina rested on her knees in the middle of a great map representing Exeter and one hundred square surrounding miles. Up until now, Edward had been creating his maps on parchment, maps used by all his father's commanders. This one, however, was being constructed in clay. The idea had slowly evolved, become exciting, and now hovered at reality, a miniature representation of their Devon piece of Wessex, with the river and the coastline, the rich red soil of the lowlands, the rising ground of the moors, the combes and streams, the walled town itself. Convincing the king that assisting with the construction of the map would be an appropriate study for Elfwina fell on her tutor, and he had been eloquent. So she had been allowed one hour during her daily study time to spend in her brother's chambers at this pursuit, with her tutor and Edyth and Tonberht in attendance, of course.

The map was being assembled on the surface of a large table, and Elfwina was in the center, her hair loose and tumbling out of her mantle. She kept pushing the hair back, until Edyth made her come to the edge of the table where she could secure it again.

Holding her gown expertly out of the way, Elfwina thumped impatiently over to her. "I don't have much time," she said crossly.

"It will only take a moment, Princess," Edyth said soothingly. "Then you won't have to fight your hair to see what you're doing."

As Edward watched his sister's hair being bound, he was thinking her thirteenth birthday was only days away, and his gift was going to be a perfect match. He drew in a quick breath.

With her hair once more confined within the mantle, Elfwina waggled back to where Edward was kneeling on the other side of the River Exe.

"This is our kingdom, Elf," he said. "Yours and mine."

They were two giants forming their realm. A third giant stood at the edge of the kingdom--Elfwina's tutor, a young Mercian monk of the cult of Woden. He had a round merry face beaming enthusiasm. He was waiting to help them build up the level of the terrain to the scale agreed on by brother and sister.

With wet hands slick with clay, Edward and Elfwina leaned inward, molding and reforming, their eyes shining at each other with pleasure. She had gently persuaded Edward that the combe they were now impressing into the clay slope above the river was at a slightly different angle and elevation than he had originally designed. It faintly stung his pride--his accuracy was well-respected--but he was soothed by the upsurge of delight that she shared and understood this passion for precisely demonstrating given stretches of land. She, too, expressed this gift; the sensitive eye and impossible-to-describe sense of terrain and elevation, correspondences and distances and the point at which those many dimensions converged.

She alone in the entire world shares this with me, Edward thought in wonder. He looked at her with love. Seeing her dark responding gaze, he slid his clay-slicked hand over hers, and the yearning that would not go away expanded and filled him with pain.

Edward sat through dinner in the company of his sister and their friends. Once the meal was over, the group settled near the center hearth to play a game of knucklebones. Edward sat away from the table quietly watching Elfwina's hands. They moved gracefully, hypnotically as they held and shifted the small sheep's knucklebones with which the game was played. Each time she tossed the bones up and caught a number on the back of her hand the guests would gasp and applaud. Because she was so skilled she usually won. The boys complained loudly to fate; the girls laughed; Elfwina collected pennies as she always did.

Edyth came up to Elfwina's chair, and the princess looked up at her with a plea. Receiving no response, she rose and glanced around apologetically. Everyone protested, Eadric loudest of all. While he was leading this futile clamor, Elfwina's eyes sought her brother. He smiled at her, and then, unnoticed by the others, strolled across the room and through the huge doors.

He came out into the starry night and walked quickly along the front of the building past the guards, who saluted him. Breaking into a trot, he cleared the linden grove and cut across the grounds toward the pasture. The stars were so bright he had no trouble finding his way to where the pale base of a stone rose from the dark grass. He sat down on the stone and looked up at his sister's glowing windows.

In the blackness above the roofline the shoulders and a portion of the bow of the hunter wheeled slowly over the dark line of the hall. Edward arched his neck back, searching out the Wain in the glittering sky and, finding it, followed the tongue of the wagon to the North Star. Here, at this very moment in Devon, from the groove he had carved in this stone rose an ascending and arcane line leading to that star and into the firmament beyond, a line on stone and parchment shooting outward, out over the hall, across Devon, Somerset, all of Mercia and Northumbria, out across the cold sea and off the end of the earth to the pivot point of all creation. He knew that line existed; she knew that line existed, and Edward believed to the depth of his soul that within that vastness the line described, time stood still, incasing him with her in everything existing and which was yet to exist, now spreading backward and forward to the past, to the future, encompassing all, and as he sat there believing these things, within the black outline of the hall, where his sister's windows glowed, the lights went out.

She has been undressed and gowned for the night. She will be in bed. He imagined her lying there, not yet asleep, looking up into the darkness.

He raised his arms and whispered, "I am north and you are south; I am east and you are west; those lines join us forever." As if he would embrace the earth and the air, he stretched his arms wide. "Come down to me," he said softly, "Come down to me." He closed his eyes.

Her gown brushed over the grass; he heard the scrape of her shoe on the stone as she rose up in front of him, spreading her arms, pressing her palms against his. They stood face to face, breast to breast, belly, thighs, all touching, skin annealing to skin, growing into one flesh, one becoming the other . . .love . . .love . . . .

It was a glorious June morning, perfect for a birthday party. Not one small cloud diminished the dazzling blue sky. The slight breeze moved a small wave through the linden trees, drifting their heavy perfume and fluttering the colored ribbons strung throughout the enclosure glade.

Smiling with delight, Elfwina danced among her guests. Earlier, in the town, the people had honored her with a pageant and nearly smothered her with flowers. She had graciously thanked as many individual townsfolk as possible before her escort whisked her back to the hall. Filled with pride, Edward had observed the show of affection shown her by the people, and because he was not allowed to touch her, the sudden pain from his need to be next to her, just to breathe the air she breathed had been nearly overwhelming.

Now, as he waited for the last gift from the huge pile of presents to be acknowledged, he lifted his hand in a signal to a nearby servant stationed to pass word along to the stables.

"Just a minute," he said, as the young men and women of the party swooped in. He smiled down at her. "I've one more gift for you."

"Another? But where is it?" She looked about her as if it might have been left in the grass.

He laughed with a little gasp and reached out to take her by the shoulders so she couldn't turn but then quickly drew his hands back. "You won't find it there. It's coming. But you mustn't look yet."

"No? What is it?" Her lips curved, as she looked into his eyes.

There were sudden exclamations as everyone else saw what it was. If Edward had not stepped close to her, she would have turned. "Oh, let me look!" she begged him, laughing.

"Don't anyone call out what it is," Edward warned.

From behind a hedge came a groom, grinning widely, as he led a magnificent filly so black her coat drew light into it, and then flashed it back in blue streaks along her flanks and arched neck as she pricked forward. She was fine-boned, with a small, beautifully formed head and intelligent eyes. She had a long mane, and her tail swept the ground. Tricked with silver, the black bridle and saddle shot sparks as she passed through the dappled light of the glade. There were exclamations and excited laughter from the guests as they waited to see the reaction of the princess.

"Edward!" she pleaded.

"Stop there!" he said over the top of her head. The groom halted and grinned all about him.

"Stand still, now, Elf. Don't move."

"I won't--I won't!"

"Don't move, now." He smiled down at her.

"Yes--yes, I'll do what you say, only *let me see!* You're so cruel."

Edward stepped back where he could see her face when she turned. "You may look," he said.

She spun around. Her eyes grew huge and round, her hands flew to her mouth. Then she sighed and approached the filly with small, light steps. She smoothed her hand in a long caress down the gleaming neck.

Edward's face glowed. He was laughing silently.

Elfwina turned to look at him. "Oh, Edward! She's so beautiful!"

She decided to ride the filly and, with an entourage of young women, flew to the hall, returning in the billowing trousers women wore to ride. Edward stood about with his friends, watching his sister pace the filly around the pasture, up and down, all around the enclosure. Since the guests were not there to ride, they began to interest themselves in other activities, and gradually the crowd sifted away from Elfwina.

Edward followed her to where she had halted near the stables, preparing to dismount and rejoin her guests. His approach delayed this. Her face still shone with pleasure as she looked down at him. "I like your gift best of all, Edward," she told him softly.

"I was matching your hair. Did you notice that?"

"Really?" She ran her hand along the filly's neck. Her eyes met his. "Was it difficult?"

"Yes. But I wanted it to be a perfect match." He looked over the filly again and then up at where Elfwina sat watching him intently. "It is perfect."

"Yes," she said, almost a whisper.

"Would you like to ride out with me beyond the fields? It would be a better test than riding around in here."

"Right now?" Her eyes swept over the guests who were moving through the linden grove and came back to him, intense, questioning.

He replied, "No one will mind. They're all busy."

"Just the two of us?"

"Would you like to invite someone else?"

"No! But is it all right? What about Father?"

Edward laughed. "I asked his permission." *I will deal with that later,* he thought.

She suddenly smiled at him, her cheeks flushing.

He stepped back and called out quietly. A groom came from the stable leading Edward's horse, a white stallion fitted with gold trappings. The stallion tossed his head and shook his mane in a show for the filly. Flaring her nostrils delicately, the filly arched her neck. Edward mounted the stallion and turned him out at the side gate. Elfwina followed, and the gate was closed behind them. They rode side by side into the fields that stretched like green silk toward the beech woods beyond. The princess looked over at her brother with a long inquiring gaze. His smile trembled and then vanished as they rode on.

Chapter Six

[821] Exeter, Wessex. For weeks Edward had wakened with the same uneasiness, the same lack of interest in the day ahead. He didn't want to throw back the covers; he didn't want to go to the trouble of putting on his clothes. He wasn't hungry, he wasn't thirsty, and he didn't know why he was still on the earth.

Because there was no way to avoid it, he did get up and allow his handthegn to dress him. With dragging steps, he followed his father and Eorl Teownor into the hall chapel for Prime. Later he went in for breakfast and was glad to be the only one at the benches. He had almost finished eating what tasted like straw, when Eadric and Bass showed up. They greeted him and then scrambled noisily into their seats, yelling out instructions for their meal. They started throwing bread chunks at each other.

"Oh, grow up!" Edward said furiously when a large piece hit him on the cheek. He stood up, brushing crumbs from his beard. "You act like you're still in the nursery."

"They wouldn't allow it in the nursery," Eadric replied, grinning at Bass.

Edward scowled at his friend; he wanted to hit someone, but neither boy rose to him. He stalked across the room and left the hall.

Coming down the stairs, Tidfirth saw the prince leave and ran after him. "Where are you off to?"

"Riding," Edward snapped.

"Wait, I'll go with you."

Edward spun around and walking backwards, called out in a shrill voice, "Why can't I be left alone for just ten minutes!"

Tidfirth stopped and stared at him, open-mouthed. Edward stomped away toward the stables.

A groom barely older than the prince came quickly out of the stables and bowed.

Edward told him crossly, "Saddle my horse."

Seeing the prince's mood, the groom said uneasily, "Which one, Sire?"

Edward was pacing angrily. He stopped and glared at the groom. "I don't care--the bay mare. And hurry up!"

He rode his horse out of the gate at a gallop, which was forbidden, gouging his heels into the mare's flanks and not letting her slacken until they were up on the higher ground that opened onto the moor. He looked out across the sweep of land, trying to release himself from all his gnawing thoughts.

For a time he wandered his horse among stone buildings once

inhabited by an ancient people, dwellings tumbled and roofless, melancholy in their ruin.

What was it like for them? He wondered. *So long ago. All of them dead now. They looked out on this moor, too. At that outcrop of rocks, the very same one. Were the men brave? They must have been. Was everything impossible then, like it is now . . . ?*

Edward turned his horse aside and rode out of the shallow basin that had sheltered the empty dwellings from centuries of wind. A small combe lay ahead. It was thick with bracken at its entrance and heavily wooded within its steep walls. He tied his mare near the narrow stream that tumbled from the mouth of the combe and stood looking around. Behind him was the wood, to his right--north toward Exeter--lay rolling ground; to the west and south, the windy moorland. Nowhere in that great expanse was there any sign of human life.

He made his way deep into the bracken, decided that was no good, and came back toward the edge of the stand where he would be screened to anyone approaching yet still be able to command a view of the countryside.

He tramped out a space, spread his mantle over the crushed fern, and sank wearily down. He stared up at the milky sky, the fleeting, shredding clouds framed by the bracken.

Should I confess? He pictured the priest whispering into his father's ear, the look on his father's face. *They're not supposed to tell, but he's the king. O God! Heavenly Father. . . .*

He groaned, knowing he was being foolish. It must be confessed to a priest. It must be an act of contrition. God knew, as he knew, that deep, deep inside him, he was not contrite and he did not think he would ever be. Even as he was thinking this, he groaned again and came to his knees. Clasping his hands above his head so hard they shook, he cried out, "Please, Merciful Father, Almighty God, Creator of the earth and all the stars in the heavens--" he stopped abruptly, his eyes squeezed tight, his mouth open and sucking air into his lungs. He let his hands fall to his sides.

Edward lifted his head, his eyes still shut. "I couldn't help it!"

He sank forward on his hands. His head bent down and almost touched the ground.

He stayed in that position for several moments. Then he rubbed his forehead hard across his arm, opened his eyes, and came upright again. He knelt there, blinking in the bright sunlight, his hands on his thighs. After a moment, he bowed his head into his hands and, gripping his hair, howled, "Oh, God--I am damned!"

He swayed to his feet, uneased, and retrieved his mantle. Mounting his horse, he made his slow way back to the royal hall.

Tonberht intercepted him at the top of the stairs. "Your father has been calling for you," he said.

Edward stared at him, his lips parted. "Did he say why?"

"Is he going to tell *me*?" Tonberht's tendency was toward impudence; in this instance he was anxious.

Edward was too uneasy to reprimand him. "Where is Father?"

"In his chambers."

When Edward was seated before him, King Brihtric said, "I was told you and your sister rode out from the enclosure on her birthday. Is that correct?"

Edward struggled to look directly at his father and speak without gasping for air. "Yes, we did, Sire. I thought it might be a better test--a run to show her strides. You saw the filly yourself, Father. Isn't she a beauty? I wanted Elfwina to see--"

"Who was your escort?"

"I . . . didn't think one would be necessary, Sire, for that brief time."

"How brief, Edward?"

"I'm not sure. It wasn't very long."

"You were not only in the fields; you went into the beech woods."

Edward swallowed, took a casual breath. "For a little time, Sire."

"I think for a longer time."

"We walked around some before we started back."

His father studied him for a long moment during which Edward tried to think how he would be acting if this were a normal conversation. He couldn't remember. He sat very still under his father's scrutiny and thought he was going to suffocate.

"What has been your charge regarding your sister?"

In a low voice, Edward replied, "Never to touch her, Sire. Never to be alone with her."

"You disobeyed me again, Edward." It was said quietly, as his father always spoke. It elevated the fear that was rapidly engulfing him.

"Father, there wasn't anything--"

"We will learn that. The bishop is at the monastery. Go to him."

"Please, Father--"

"Go now, Edward."

The prince rose, bowed to his father and, with heavy steps, left for the monastery.

The interrogation lasted three days. It was not the first time he had endured it.

When Elfwina was nine and he was twelve, he chased her

through the soft early grasses of the enclosure orchard, catching up to pin her against a small plum tree. The blossoms in the low branches poured down their perfume, engulfing them. Tiny white petals stormed in the thick air as, laughing, she struggled to free herself, her face burning with the effort. She cried *"Edward!"* in three different warning tones as she pounded at his chest, and when her pink lips drew together the third time over his name, he leaned forward and kissed her. It wasn't a very long kiss, and she laughed again when her mouth was free. But in leaning forward, he stretched his body against hers, causing him to stiffen, grow tight, and it felt so good shoving against her, he didn't want to let her go. But she pulled free and, still laughing, raced away. He followed her about that day, from space to space in the great hall, up and down corridors, needing to feel that sensation again. She would look back at him from the servants always in her wake, her dark eyes brilliant and teasing.

When she was eleven and he was fourteen, they were playing *Cyningstæfl* and for a brief time they were alone. To tease her, he cheated. She caught him out and flicked one of her pieces at his chest, and then snatched up his king and leaped away from the table. He grabbed her, and they stumbled together and fell on the rug with him sprawled over her back.

With a high trill of laughter, she managed to squirm free, crabbing away on her hands and knees, but he caught her hips and hauled her back against him. He held her there, his erection hard between her thighs and snagged in her skirt. His whole being concentrated on that sensation and without being able to stop, he ejaculated into his clothing. He fled. Finding a vacant room, he took off his undergarment, wiped himself with it, rolled it into a tight ball, and jammed it behind a heavy chest in the darkest corner of the room. As before, he dogged her footsteps, going from place to place and room to room; at any brief space of time they were without eyes watching them, he would touch her, press against her, or just gaze at her, with a terrible yearning.

One dreadful morning he learned that Elfwina's tutor, a Christian priest, was striking her with a rod during the course of her lessons. When the prince saw the bruises, the broken and bleeding gashes on her back, he chased the tutor from the enclosure. On a galloping horse and gripping a lowered spear, he caught up with the running priest and nearly beat him to death with the shaft. Returning to Elfwina's quarters and examining her injuries again, guilt overwhelmed him; because it had been he who had talked his father into employing the priest as her tutor.

Elfwina sat gazing at her brother in wonder, and that wonder in her eyes filled him. Her gown draped down to the small of her back and lay loose in front. He knelt and touched his lips to her bare shoulders, pressed his mouth against the back of her neck and on each of the small bones he counted as she bent her head. He could see the small formation of her breasts within the folds of her gown. His hand slid down under the garment, and she held his hand there, looking over her shoulder at him, her dark eyes filled with love. At that moment their father had walked into the room, and their fear poured one into the other, filling them with silence as they stared into his judgment. They were never allowed to be alone again. That incident occasioned the first time Edward was led to the secret room beneath the monastery. He did not confess to anything but what their father had seen. Shortly after, he had been sent to King Cenwulf's court in Mercia for a year.

Edward knew what to expect here in this stony tomb. He was forced to kneel on the cold stones for hours at a time, naked except for the device wrapping his loins, the metal points stabbing at his testicles, jabbing his penis whenever he moved. Blood ran down his legs and pooled around his knees. When he wasn't being questioned he was led in prayers by a series of monks who prayed with him. He was not allowed to sleep. He swore to innocence, did not confess. At the end of the three days, when it was determined he had nothing to confess, his father embraced him, and Edward thought he was safe.

He was wrong. Within days their father announced Elfwina would be leaving for Kent. He told Edward the princess was to be given the advantage of a year or so in the court of Baldred, king of Kent, Brihtric's brother. King Baldred's plans included a journey which would take her and their cousin Prince Cosmer to the Continent. They would visit the courts; meet people who would be an advantage to her; they would share an audience with the Pope.

Edward had been stunned by this decision, and then physically ill. He had coiled up in his chamber with a fur wrapped around him, staring out the narrow window, unable to stop crying. When he had seen her leave for the ship, he had buried his head under the fur and had not looked out again until he knew the ships escorting her to Kent had disappeared into the fine haze that stretched all the way to Canterbury.

Chapter Seven

[821] London, Mercia. The coronation ceremony was over. From the Thames, the night mist smoked up and caught in the thickets along the bank. Finger by finger it crept over the south wall and into the lighted streets of London, haloing the torches burning every fifty feet at the late King Cenwulf's command, a measure against theft and violence.

The royal hall stood on a gravel terrace west of Walbrook and within a ten acre, high-walled enclosure. From the open gate a double row of torches curved to the hall. Men and women on foot and mounted riders shared the lighted path. The hall was large, rectangular, with high narrow windows that diffused a golden light through the fog now immersing the building. Doors wide enough to allow four horses to pass abreast opened on the night and the mist that groped around the people making their way in and out of the building, clinging briefly to those entering and encircling those who came out.

The huge area inside was crowded and noisy. All around the walls guests sat on wide benches or stood about those seated, talking in small and fluctuating groups, or listening to the musicians strolling through the room with pipe and harp. Some of the guests watched a juggler tossing five silver balls in a rapid circle, the warm up for a command performance.

At either end of the enormous room giant hearths gaped, dark and empty. Taking up the center of the room were a series of tables and benches covered by richly embroidered cloths; place settings glinted with gold, and delicate glassware caught the light from the great lamps hanging overhead. Gleaming on every table, silver bowls brimmed with ripe fruit. Around these tables, male servants stood motionless, their eyes glancing along the display in front of them alert for small defects of arrangement as they patiently waited.

At one spot near the supper tables, the crowd was thicker, more animated. On the group's periphery, two men of different religions unknowingly approached on a collision course. Strolling in opposite directions, they encountered the bulge of guests and met face to face. The stout heathen priest of Woden, clothed in a lavishly blue mantle and long tunic, looked into the eyes of the portly Christian bishop, garbed in elaborately embroidered robes. They regarded each other in a moment of silent struggle. By some mystic ritual of assertion, dominance was established. Exchanging nods and meager smiles, they passed on.

A nobleman entered through the wide doors, noted the group

causing the confrontation, and hurried over.

"What have you to tell us, Eorl Leodwald?" a woman's voice called out. "Will he be coming soon, or should we attack the fruit bowls?"

She was plump and short. Her tone twinkled, but her eyes beamed annoyance. The people around her tittered. She was Leodwald's wife and an intimate of the king's sister, so she permitted herself these kinds of remarks. Leodwald did not like it. He knew the young king cast a tolerant eye on the power movements taking place since his accession, but he also could run short of patience and display a fearsome temper. Leodwald, a man of considerable temper and little patience, did not want his wife causing any problems for him through her efforts to firmly establish her position at court.

He flicked her a sour glance. Then, speaking to no one in particular, he said, "The king wants Prince Edward. Has anyone seen him?"

There was a general stretching and survey. "Near the east hearth," someone replied at the same instant Leodwald caught a glimpse of the prince's curly head and gold diadem. "I see him."

When Edward arrived at the royal chambers, he found the thegns of King Aedred crowded into the sitting room, all talking at once, everyone in high spirits. Edward walked slowly around the edges of the press and was let into the inner bedchamber by Grundl, the king's captain of the guards.

Surrounding the king, his retainers were chatting amiably with him and receiving humorous answers. Although the king appeared to be enjoying himself, Edward detected impatience. Aedred still wore his coronation robes, and the gold trefléd crown still encircled his dark head.

His handthegn stood by with three other servants, waiting to help with the removal of his outer garments. "No," Aedred was saying, smiling an answer to someone's question, "but let me get this monstrously heavy thing off my head, and then we'll—" He saw Edward then, standing just inside the room gazing intently at him, and his whole face lit up. The men gathered around the king drew aside so Edward could approach.

With the news that King Cenwulf had died and Aedred had succeeded to the Mercian throne, Edward had been struck by uneasiness and depression. Like so much that was happening to him in his sixteenth year, he feared this, too, would have endless and unforeseeable repercussions. How would this affect their relationship? Would they have a friendship? If they did, would they still be as close?

On his arrival in London, Edward found the newly crowned king inaccessible. At the hall, Edward had not been able to get near him. But then, in his anxiety, he had not tried very hard. Worried about how he would be received by Aedred, he had been dreading the summons. Everything so far had magnified that uncertainty and dread.

So now he gazed at the king, and then did his obeisance with downcast eyes.

"Well . . . !" the king exclaimed, with a short gust of surprised laughter. When Edward was again standing, Aedred turned slowly from him. Then, all impatience, he told the men around him, "Get these things off me—I'm sinking into the floor!"

Stripped of all the ceremonial trappings except for a plain gold circlet around his brow, Aedred linked arms briefly with the prince. Then, with Edward walking directly behind him, he led the train of retainers back into the hall quite as if everything was unchanged between them. It was and it wasn't. The difference was too subtle to measure with any certainty, the difference being as much in Edward as in the fact that Aedred was now king of Mercia.

Edward was within a day's hard ride of where his sister was living at Canterbury. Torn by his intense yearning to see her and the fear of threatening whatever contact he and his sister would be allowed in the future, Edward hesitated. But in spite of this fear and his father's warning not to visit her, the slow undertow of his unhappiness brought him to the London-Canterbury road. He traveled for some ten miles along that way with a fractured plan to snatch her up and make an escape to the Continent, until he grimly recognized the futility of it and turned back. Rejoining his puzzled companions, he returned to Exeter.

In this year King Cenwulf passed away. He had ruled for twenty-five years. Aedred received the kingdom.

Chapter Eight

[822] Mercia. By the unfolding of events, his sister was placed beyond his reach, and Edward labored to create emotional distance from the cause. The distance was from his father as well: he couldn't face him day after day, fearing with a holy dread he would give himself away. Receiving his father's consent, he threw himself on the hospitality of the king of Mercia, engaging himself in the activities of Aedred's kingdom and gaining a respite from his sense of guilt and dispossession.

One autumn morning, after months in Mercia, Edward took the king aside. "What's this game everyone's talking about? This Rollypig thing. What kind of game is *that*--rolling a pig?"

"'Rollypig'? You mean *áwyte sé fór?* Roll-the-Pig, Edward."

"Roll-the-Pig, then. What is it?"

"It's rough and tumble. I doubt a Saxon has the stamina for it."

"Did *you* play it?"

"With a passion."

"If you can play it, I can play it."

"You think so, do you?"

"I know so." His gaze narrowed as he looked at Aedred. "Is the pig alive?"

Aedred laughed. "No, the pig is not alive. It's a stuffed pig skin, about the size of a weaner pig." Aedred spread his hands about eighteen inches, and then brought the measure down to a foot. "This much through the center. The ends are tapered."

"Makes it a little hard to roll, doesn't it? It would go this way and that."

"We Mercians like to play to a challenge. We don't go for the easy rolling kind of ball you Saxons use."

"What's the object of this game?"

"Winning! What's the object of the games you play in Wessex?"

Edward ignored the question. "I'd like to play this game, since you're so timid about describing it."

"I don't think so."

"Afraid to let a Saxon show you up?"

"No fear of that. You couldn't stand up to it. This game's too rough. You'd be carried back to Wessex on a litter. I wouldn't want to see that happen, or try to explain it to your father."

Edward was smiling and shaking his head. "You're bluffing. How do I get in this game?"

"If you're really fixed on this . . . ."

"I am."

Aedred gave him a doubtful look. "You have to understand, competition is stiff. We have some stellar players on our team we couldn't do without, but you might be able to buy your way in through the others."

"What? I don't believe this. I have to *buy* a spot on the team?"

"And it won't come cheap. Players covet their membership. Occasionally, one has pressing business at game time and can't participate, but there's always a waiting list." He studied the prince. "If you seriously want to expose yourself to the dangers, I'll see what I can do."

"You do that." He looked more closely at the king. "What dangers?"

Aedred shrugged. "All kinds of dangers--maiming, broken limbs, drowning, adder bites." He drew an imaginary bow. "You could get elf-shot--"

"Elf-shot!" He couldn't help the smirk. "I don't believe in elves. How are they going to shoot me?"

"Better not laugh, my friend, elves lie in wait for tender youths like you." Aedred was only half-joking. "I can't protect you all the time from such things."

"*You* protect *me*!" Edward was slightly offended.

Aedred had not meant to reveal that. He did incant charms to protect Edward against elf-shot. "I'm not going to be able to protect your purse, either, not in this instance," he said, getting away from the subject of magic. "Before you buy your way in, you'd better understand the purchase."

"Right," Edward said. "Are you going to sit down so I can sit down?" Edward bent his knees several times, grinning at the king.

"Since when has propriety ever stopped you?" Aedred replied, but dropped into a chair.

"I'm being extra proper so the king will aid me. So, what are the rules? What do you do?"

"It's simple--one team tries to reach a goal, the other team tries to stop it."

"And . . .?"

"There's no 'and'; that's what the game's about."

"All right. You roll the pig toward the goal. I got that. Where's the field this game is played on?"

"It depends on the goal. It could be all of Mercia."

"Huh?" The prince cocked his head.

It was a slight exaggeration. "And it's hard going all the way. No niceties. You get battered. Anything goes--no weapons, of course--"

"So this pig gets rolled all over Mercia by one team, and the other team tries to stop it from reaching a goal. How do you know when the game's over? Everyone falls on the ground with exhaustion, and the last man breathing wins?"

"There is a time limit."

"And that is . . . ?"

"Seven days."

"*Seven days!* One game lasts seven days?"

"The teams need time to move thirty miles."

"This is a joke, isn't it?"

"Not a bit. Oh, another thing--when the game starts, privileges end. No titles. Everyone takes their knots equally. No complaints, no reprisals. Think you can deal with that?"

"You haven't heard me complain about battle knots, have you? It's not likely a game is going to be more of a threat to my health than a battle."

Aedred just laughed.

With the king's help in the background, Edward had been able to buy a place on the team from a thegn from Repton for eight gold mancuses. The prince was flabbergasted, but gave it over willingly because he was now so curious he actually would have paid considerably more to join the game.

In the last few days, most of the time had been spent preparing strategies. Aedred was grudgingly conducting the kingdom's business, and then rushing back to the strategy sessions. He finally dumped the administrative duties into the lap of his hall-reeve Ceolric, and then devoted the rest of the time to planning the game.

It was serious business. Edward was feverishly making notes. The team Edward had bought into was the Wild Boars. The captain was a ceorl from Stafford named Pegg, whose talents were respected. He was a wainwright by trade. His speech was uneducated, but he was a master of the game.

The opposing team was called the Rowdy Bears. Their captain's name was Nail. The prince compiled a list of both teams' players and their nicknames, except for his and the king's. He discovered he knew most of the men on both sides.

PLAYERS—**Wild Boars**

Captain		*PEGG (wainwright)*
Wedge Driver		*WECG (tanner)*
Runner		*STAG (Eorl Aethelred)*
Kicker		*HEDGEHOG (Ceawlin, king's thegn)*
Blocker	?	*(King of Mercia*
Blocker	?	*(Prince of Wessex*

Blocker	*EEL (leather worker)*
Plus six other players	

PLAYERS—**Rowdy Bears**

Captain	*NAIL (Eorl Aldhune)*
Wedge Driver	*QUOIN (Farmer)*
Runner	*SQUIRREL Eorl Leodwald)*
Kicker	*FOX (Tilhere, king's thegn)*
Blocker	*OTTER (Ricsige, king's interrogator)*
Blocker	*BLUE WOLF (Baldan, Chieftain of the Hwicce)*
Blocker	*HARE (king's beekeeper)*
Plus six, two of which are Hwicce	

The Boars had won the rotating trophy the last time the game was played, which was a year and a half before. When the planning began, the trophy was brought out and proudly set on a table in the king's chambers.

Edward choked back a laugh when he realized that all the players, including the king, looked on this item with reverence. It was a silver sphere six inches in diameter with figures at the top. It rested on a gilded, rune-incised base that added another ten inches to the trophy's overall height. When everyone had gone back to the planning table, Edward closely inspected the figures and found them to be a wild boar riding the back of a bear and pricking hard.

Shaking his head, Edward went back to the planners.

Each team had thirteen members, all seasoned players. Edward was concerning himself only with the Boars. In addition to their star Pegg, was a tanner named Wecg. He was a man of average height with an ox's neck, an axe handle's breadth of shoulder, and a plow horse's haunches. He was the all important wedge driver. If the boars won the toss, he would be the leading edge of a formation driving the action forward when play began.

The players were now using their nicknames. As it was explained to Edward, nicknames were essential to preserve anonymity once the game was progressing through the countryside. The list Edward had compiled did not yet include the king's sobriquet, or his, for that matter. When he did learn Aedred's nickname it turned out to be *Badger*. Edward was puzzled; the name hardly seemed suitable for a warrior king.

"Why, 'Badger'?" Edward asked, interrupting a deep discussion over possible goal sites.

Everyone stopped talking and looked at him. Then they started laughing.

"I don't know, Edward," the king replied. "I've been trying to figure that out myself."

The company went back to their discussion, leaving Edward without an answer.

Aedred's chambers now were less a king's quarters than the site of a campout, with all the Boars spread through the rooms with their bedrolls and personal items and rarely leaving. Occasionally, some would go down into the great hall to eat. Most of the time meals were brought up to them, and they would eat and plot. They did very little drinking, the subject was so serious. That part, they told Edward, would come later.

Because he didn't want to miss anything, Edward abandoned his own chamber, dragged his bedding up the corridor, and dropped it on the floor next to the king's bed. He rejoined the group at the table.

"We gave you a name while you were gone," Aedred said.

"So, what is it?"

"*Grouse*."

All the faces around the table were waiting.

"Grouse." He looked back at them. "I guess I don't have a choice." He shrugged. "All right, *Grouse*. But I don't, you know."

Aedred slapped him on the back. "You're a real team player, Grouse."

"Damn, Edward! It's game-start tomorrow! We need to sleep."

"All right, all right. Just one more question--"

Aedred sighed. "*One* more."

"Who is the judge for this game? You do have a judge."

"We don't call him a judge. The term is *Cudgel*. Our cudgel is Grundl."

"*Cudgel*? I don't like the sound of that."

"Nevertheless, that's what he is, and his word is law."

Edward thought about it. He decided Grundl probably was the best man for that job. But he was curious about the term. If no weapons were allowed . . . ?

"Does the Cudgel have a weapon?"

"No! Grundl has a fist. Now, if you say one more word, Edward, I'm going to kick you out in the hallway. *Go to sleep!*"

Edward threw the covers over his head and hunkered down into his bedroll. This was a new and different Aedred. He could see he was going to have to make some adjustments.

The morning of game-start was clear and crisp. It was Wintirfyllith in Mercia--October. The trees were turning from gold to russet. South of the royal hall, the rising sun was disturbing the mists pooled in the low-lying areas near the old Roman road known as Cyninges Street. The teams had assembled on the paving. They were standing around a reddish circle of stone some two feet in diameter, which had been set into the surface of the road. Edward had noticed that circle before on journeys up and down the Street. He had idly wondered about it, and then dismissed it as a Roman decoration.

He was informed with reverence that this had been the starting point for generations of Roll-the-Pig players. Edward had been going along with all this game silliness, laughing about it to himself. The whole thing had gone so far to the absurd that the teams even had special tunics.

"Well, we need to tell each other apart, don't we?" Aedred had told him, as if it were the most reasonable idea in the world.

The Boars had sleeveless tunics of rough gold cloth. A wide blue stripe stretched from left hip to right shoulder. A race of boars decorated the stripe.

The Bears had similarly made garments but with a color reverse: their tunics were blue, and there was a large gold bear dead center. This caused a disturbance among the Boars. These tunics were new for this game and were not what the Bears had been wearing in previous games. From what Edward could glean from the disgruntled players was that the Bears were using one of the symbols of their god Woden--the golden bear. Since it was not against the rules, the Boars had to accept the change. *Not a good mental start for us,* Edward thought.

"They'll need more than a golden bear to save their sorry butts," Badger said loudly.

Edward turned to him in astonishment.

Grundl's voice boomed out, "I'll hear the Boars' goal."

Pegg, the captain of their team, followed Grundl a distance down the paving. With their backs turned, Grundl and Pegg conferred. Grundl nodded. Then he called out Nail, captain of the Bears. The two captains exchanged narrowed glances as they passed each other. Grundl was informed of the Bears' goal.

"Aren't the goals going to be announced?" Edward asked the Badger.

"No reason to. We know where *we're* going with the pig. Their goal isn't important."

"I would like to know, anyway."

Badger gave a little snort, and turned his attention back to Grundl. The big warrior had come back to the red circle. He drew a silver coin from the purse on his belt.

"Last game's loser, chooses," Grundl instructed tersely. "Heads or tails?" he asked the Rowdy Bears' captain.

"Tails!"

Grundl balanced the coin on his thumb. "Tails, Bears' goal; heads, Boars' goal." He flipped the coin high, and they all watched it turn over and over and come down with a chime on the stone. There winking up at them was the profile of *Aedred Rex.*

"Nice looking *head* that fellow has," Badger said, leaning over Leodwald the Squirrel's blue shoulder.

Squirrel gave him a hard glance and took a launching breath, but before he could say anything, Badger cocked his head, raised his eyebrows, and smiling close to Squirrel's contorted face, said pleasantly, "Bears lose again."

"Let's have the pig," Grundl called.

A young man came running in holding the pig. He gave it to Grundl, who felt it all over, squeezed it with his big hands, and set it onto the circle with the tapered ends pointing north and south, the traditional alignment. He straightened. Running his gaze over both groups, he said, "No weapons. No touching the pig after sundown. Play ends seven days hence. Boars, form your wedge."

"North!" shouted Pegg, and all the Boars moved possessively around the pig, shifting and sorting themselves out, until they had shaped themselves into a spearhead pointing northward, Wecg at the point. Ceawlin the Hedgehog was at the center with the pig, guarded by Grouse on one side, and Badger on the other. The Bears had lined up opposite them in the same general formation, the Bears' burley Quoin faced off with Wecg.

Grundl mounted his big roan. He looked over at the horn blower. Edward, glancing at the faces around him, wasn't sure he recognized these men, especially Aedred. There was in the king's face and in his stance a savage intensity, a predatory focus new to Edward's knowledge of his kinsman; a focus unlike any he had witnessed in battle or in Aedred's preparation for battle. It was an entirely new aspect of character being revealed, and for the first time, Edward realized there were facets of the man he was yet to discover.

The horn blew, and the wedge began shuffling forward. At its protected center, Ceawlin the Hedgehog poised, his eyes first on the pig, and then on the force arrayed against them. With a sudden burst, Wecg pounded forward into the front line of the Bears. The men immediately behind him drove into the opposing wedge with him, and there was a free for all as the Boars slammed into the Bears. Two of Edward's teammates, Stag and Eel, swung out from the rest of the pack and around the melee to a point behind the Bears. At that moment Hedgehog, waiting and eyeing the men struggling toward him, kicked the pig in the air.

It sailed high and far. Stag and Eel were swinging into position, the pig coming down closer to Stag. The Bears were not taken by surprise. The ferocious Hwicce leader, Blue Wolf, had been in the back field and now hurled himself at the man providing defense for Stag as the runner's hands reached for the pig. Another Bear player was moving to cut off Stag, but an opponent threw his arms around the Bear and brought him to the ground. Stag switched directions and now raced off with the pig in a westerly slant toward their distant goal.

The Rowdy Bear players began a charge after the pig carrier. Grouse was picking himself off the ground. He had shuffled forward with the rest of the wedge, according to the first plan, and was whacked in the chest and kicked in the shins. Before he could respond, someone shoved him over a player on the ground, and he went down. He was stepped on, kicked, and trampled as the melee passed over him, moving farther downfield.

He pulled himself together and staggered off in the direction the players had taken, vowing he was not going to be caught off-guard again. This was indeed serious business.

The game had reformed where Aethelred the Stag had been finally overtaken and dropped. The Boar runner still held the pig wrapped in his arms where he was curled under two Bears rolling around on top of him, trying to take it away. A number of Boars yanked and cursed at them, and then swiveled about to meet the rest of the attacking Bears. Grouse caught up and hauled back on a Bear, who turned out to be a blue-haired Hwicce. He spun around on Grouse with his teeth bared and toppled him backwards.

Badger appeared. Slamming the back of the man's knees, folding him, he fell on the blue body, pinning the man face down. Close to the Hwicce's ear, he said, "That blue stuff--you comb it out of your women's ruffs. Is that right?"

The player roared, but Badger kept him in place with a knee hard in his back. He looked over at Edward. "Been taking a nap, Grouse? Pegg needs you over there where the game's being played. Think you can manage?" He dropped his knee hard again against the back of the struggling Hwicce.

Edward picked himself up again, very irritated. "I can see now where you get your nickname," he said. "But you should have been called Ass."

"Ho, *Grouse*! Do a better job of keeping *your* ass up."

The Cudgel appeared at that moment on his horse and said--meaning the length of time for a player to be held on the ground--"That's the limit, Badger."

Grouse said, "That's a fact," and stalked off toward where the players were reassembling.

"This is early for you to be thrown out of the game," the Cudgel said.

Badger exhaled, "Oh!" as if he had just realized there was someone beneath his knee. He got up with an extra push off the man's back, and gave Grundl a guileless look.

"Go back to the game," the Cudgel told him.

They formed up again, this time wedge against line. Grouse was ready when they shuffled toward the Bears. He slammed into the Bear called Otter, and gripping him around the chest, lifted him up and would have flung him to the ground, but someone's foot kicked Edward hard between the legs. He dropped the Bear and went down clutching his testicles and moaning. Again, Grouse was left alone on the field.

Grundl rode up and appraised him from the saddle. "Are you calling out of the game?"

"No!" Edward gasped. "No, I am not!"

"Then get on your feet and go back to your team."

"Jesus!" Edward said, and managed to stagger upright.

He went back to the team, noticing that the whole parade had only made it about one hundred feet from the starting point.

How in the hell are we going to make it thirty miles to our goal at Saltwic in seven days? he thought.

But at least they were heading in the right direction.

Chapter Nine

[822] Mercia. Not only players held the field; half the countryside had turned out to watch as the game moved across the terrain. Noisy with their support for the team of their choice and vociferous with abuse for the opposition, the spectators encroached on the field. Cudgel acted swiftly and harshly. After that, the spectators stayed out of the immediate field of play.

The Rowdy Bears managed to get the pig and had now recrossed the starting point and were heading due east toward their goal. The Wild Boars were in a riot to get back the pig. Knowing the rules clearly now, Grouse kicked a Bear savagely and threw him down. He dove into the pile of bodies, clearing the way for Badger and Hedgehog to leap on Squirrel and wrest the pig away. With a triumphant shout, the Hedgehog started back across the red circle with the pig and had a clear field to race up the slight incline from the Street, leap a brook, and make it to the woods before Tilhere the Fox, running belly to the ground, caught up and, flying at his legs, crashed him to the mast.

They were rolling around in the leaves and acorns in a fight for possession of the pig, when Boars and Bears arrived and joined in. There was a furious assault. Fox squeezed out of the heap and started running back down the incline in the eastward direction of the Bears' goal, but Badger was on top of him in an instant, and they rolled down the grassy slope and out onto the paving of the Street. Badger rose from a crouch, leaped at the auburn-haired man, but Fox caught his point of balance with both feet. Badger was lifted in the air and hurled far enough away that Fox was able to scramble to his feet and begin running with the pig toward the east again.

By this time, the teams had untangled themselves. The Boars were now in pursuit of Fox and the Bears were moving to halt that pursuit. At that moment, the Wild Boar captain ran up to Grundl and yelled, "Confrunce!"

The Cudgel immediately signaled the horn blower. When the horn sounded twice, everyone stopped in their tracks; the pig was placed on the ground, and with Tilhere the Fox straddled over it, the Bears formed a tight circle around him and consulted in low tones.

The Boars, meanwhile, grouped together around their captain, Pegg.

"Them fellars are running stripes over your asses. Twict they got the pig and weor barely off the rosy circle. If yeor planning to hoist at Saltwic, you do better than I seen so far." He looked sternly around. As Edward scanned the circle of faces, he saw sullen embarrassment.

"It wasn't all bad, tho," Pegg said, relenting. "The wedge moved good. Stag did some smart running, and Hedgehog took us into the woods. The newtie, here--" he was referring to Grouse "--and Badger saved it so's that could be done."

This odd praise elated Grouse. All of a sudden the whole prospect of the game seemed brighter.

"We need more hard play," Pegg went on. "When they form thur wedge, we do a half-arc shift with a four-man carrier chase. Let's get that pig and get it over the hill by the end of play today!"

The horn sounded, and the players got into position. This time, when the Bears' wedge shuffled ahead and then plowed forward, the Boars' line dissolved and swept around the sides of the wedge to attack before Fox could kick. Understanding this maneuver, and hearing a shout from his captain, instead of kicking, Fox grabbed up the pig and in a break made for him dashed out into the open field. His auburn hair and mustache caught the sunlight as he glanced back over his shoulder to judge the troop hard at his heels. He put in another burst of speed. From the side came his teammate Squirrel. The Fox shoveled the pig to him, continued a short way, and then swung off and back into the oncoming Boars. Hurling himself across their path, he leveled three of them. They all went down in a heap.

Badger, coming headlong onto the pile, made a leap that would have cleared it, but at the last instant, Fox reached up and caught him by the ankle. Badger crashed down full length, the impact knocking the breath from him. It was not enough for Fox. He leaped up and, forgetting his job was to help run the pig, would have placed his heel on Badger's neck in a show of victory, but Badger rallied enough to knock him off-balance and then fall on him. Boar and Bear wrestled and swore at each other, exchanging angry blows, until Grundl dismounted and, grabbing each by the collar, drew them up and slammed their heads together.

"No personal fights," the Cudgel said, holding them upright while the stars cleared.

Badger shook his head several times. His nose was bleeding down the front of his tunic. He wiped the back of his hand across it, smearing his cheek. Fox's eye was swollen and starting to close, but it could see well enough to glare across at the enraged Boar. Badger glared back.

"You lost the pig," Grundl said to Fox.

"Shit!" Fox saw the pig now being carried back across the Street and up the western incline by Stag.

Badger laughed.

When the two combatants rejoined their teammates, the play had moved far into the woods. Grouse, staying close to the pig, had now taken up the role of escort, and was rather proud that it had been Pegg, in his unique patois, who had suggested it. He had also noticed they had now lost most of the spectators, which meant they really were putting distance between them and the starting point.

They had no sooner reached the top of the hill, however, when Ceawlin the Hedgehog, getting off a kick too fast, had the pig caught by the Blue Wolf. This Bear player was immediately joined by his fearsome blue kinsmen, and their downward plunge back off the hill was unstoppable. They crossed the Street at a point some two hundred feet south of the circle, pursued by a race of Boars, with the Bears breathing fire at their backs.

The spectators who had drifted toward their huts, quickly reassembled.

Grouse was getting frustrated with the progress of the game, and he was getting irritated with the Hwicce. It was at this point the horn sounded, the pig was put down, and everyone broke for lunch. Grouse looked around unbelievingly.

By custom, the alternate players, who accompanied the game anyway, were charged with feeding the starters, providing them with water, and setting up their tents at night, if there were no village accommodations available. These men now moved through the players where they lay scattered on the ground catching their breath and examining their injuries.

"Over here, Grouse." It was Badger, calling from where he had sprawled back on the grass propped up by his elbows.

Grouse dropped down beside him. "What happened to you?" he asked, taking in the bloody front of his tunic.

"Nose bleed."

Bread was handed down to them, and they each took a chunk of cold meat from a bowl.

"Where's the water?" Badger asked the alternate.

"Coming up," the man answered and moved on.

"This game is getting nowhere," Grouse complained.

"This is just the first day," Badger replied, looking up as Aethelred the Stag joined them.

Stag sat down beside him. "What happened to you?"

"Nose bleed."

"I saw you wrestling with the rusty fox. That was good when Grundl smacked your heads together. You both were hanging there like dead chickens." He was laughing hard.

"I missed that," Grouse said.

Badger waggled his eyebrows and smiled. "Tilhere lost the pig on that one."

Ceawlin the Hedgehog appeared with the other Wild Boars. He

was chewing on a large piece of bread. He shifted it to one cheek to ask Badger, "What happened?" He pointed at the bloody tunic.

"Tilhere bled all over it."

Hedgehog chewed thoughtfully. "Doesn't look like Tilhere's blood."

Stag started laughing again. "Did you see the Cudgel work those two over?"

Hedgehog wrapped his fists around the necks of two imaginary geese. He shook them. "That was good," he said, and everyone laughed.

"Tilhere lost the pig," Badger said.

Wecg and Pegg came up, and they all turned to the two leaders.

"Yu think yu deserve to eat?" Pegg demanded. "It's noon and yeor two rods from the start. Yuv lost your eye. Yeor sheep are bolting. Pull yeorselfs togeder." He crouched down, and they circled around him. "Wur taking a differnt tack."

He began laying out a new maneuver. Badger had come to his feet and was leaning over to see. He rested his hands on the shoulders of Stag and Grouse. Edward glanced back at him. The old, familiar Aedred squeezed his shoulder and gave him a slow smile.

This time, when the play started, the Boars dominated. Hedgehog got off a kick that sailed into the wooded hillside without hitting branch or twig and dropped neatly into the arms of the waiting Stag. This time the pig was taken up and over the hill and headlong down the other side as Stag recklessly leaped bushes and careened through the wood to jump a small brook and stumble on up its uphill bank. There the Bears snagged him. But the Boars were on the spot to protect him and fought off the opposition.

Somehow, Grouse had gotten the pig, and now he was scrambling up the hillside, gasping with exertion and the wild necessity to get as far as he could. He knew now just where he was going. The map in his head had kicked in--that gift for terrain and land contour, the unerring sense of direction. He cut toward the southwest, running along one of the deer trails that criss-crossed the grassy hillside.

He heard someone pounding after him. Glancing over his shoulder, he saw the blue hair and blind white eye of Blue Wolf, as heart-stopping as a specter, loping in and closing fast. Grouse put on a burst of speed, heard Blue Wolf's harsh growl close to his ear and felt his paws slap his back. As he went down, Grouse gripped the pig against his stomach and rolled into a ball. Blue Wolf fell on top of him, grappling for the pig, but Grouse held on.

"Good lad! Good lad!" he could hear Pegg shouting, and Edward put a death grip on the pig.

Help and the opposition arrived at the same time. There was a riot over Grouse's head, jamming his ear in the dirt. Hoof beats vibrated the ground; the players retreated, and Grouse opened his eyes. Bears and Boars were all looking down at him.

" 'e 'umbled the pig," Quoin said.

There were sighs and a general noise of resignation from the Wild Boars. The Rowdy Bears cheered. Edward looked down at the deflated skin he was holding against his chest and the thick trail of sawdust down his tunic.

"Take a rest," the Cudgel told them, "while we bring up another pig."

"Sorry," Grouse said, coming to a sitting position. He held up the limp skin. "I wasn't going to let Blue Wolf get it."

The Hwicce chieftain was laughing. "Is that what you do to your women?"

Badger was leaning against a tree with his arms folded, looking at Grouse with amusement.

"Lord, I hope not," he replied, turning red.

Water was being passed around, and Grouse took a long swallow, still holding up the pig skin where he could look at it. "Ugly," he said, making a face. "It stinks, too." He tossed it away from him.

"You weren't worrying about the smell when my hand came down on your back."

"How did you gain on me so fast?"

Baldan glanced at the two blue-haired men who sat on either side of him. "We live in the forest, Grouse. This is our home. Our babies run up these hills faster than you did."

"I don't want to meet your babies."

Grundl's horse brought him up the hillside to where the teams lounged on the ground. The players came slowly to their feet.

"Team humbling the pig, forfeits its turn." He tossed the new pig to Nail. "Rowdy Bears' pig."

"No!" Grouse cried. "No! Damn it!"

Grundl turned his head toward him.

"I mean, we've finally got this far. What kind of rule is that?"

"Next time you get the pig," Stag said cheerfully, "don't try to fuck it."

Edward could see his complaint was going nowhere. "I still don't think it's fair," he grumbled.

"Naow," said Pegg, when the Boars had all gathered round again. "Thair going to take away some rods from us, but thaets all right. It means we'll have to take this hill again, but we've done it onct, and we'll do it twict. That Bear, Squirrel, is going to beeline down, and we need to be there when he starts up the other side. Onct we get the pig it goes to Stag. The Grouse and Hedgehog protect his back." And

Pegg went on describing their strategy.

They heard Grundl's deep voice call out, "Ready!" They broke up to reassemble on the hillside as the Bears prepared to start. It wasn't easily managed on the incline, and the Boars weren't fooled by their attempt to kick. Squirrel ran down pell mell just as Pegg said he would. Some of the Boars were in pursuit, and some were running and sliding straight down, trying to get to the bottom before Squirrel. Two of them ran head on into the Bear runner, and the pig squirted out, immediately scooped up by a Boar, who, without breaking stride, tossed it uphill to Badger, who relayed it up to Stag. There began a frantic run to gain the hilltop.

Grouse and Hedgehog were scrambling behind Stag, their eyes on the oncoming Bears. Fox was gaining, and Edward knew he had to take him out. He swung around and dove straight at him, and they both rolled a distance, and then slid together, leaving a wake of golden leaves churning behind them.

As he was sliding, Grouse was looking back up the hill and saw Stag disappear over the top. Grouse jumped to his feet and was promptly knocked back to the ground. He wrestled out from under Fox and got to his feet again. Not interested in fighting, he wanted to get up and over the hill to make sure play kept moving westward. But Fox was determined to hang on to him.

"Let go, you stupid fucker!" Edward yelled, trying to shake him off.

Badger flew in, knocking Tilhere over, and they bowled along until they both smacked up against a tree. Grouse leaped up, saw them grappling with each other, and scrambled up the hill after Stag.

Fox had Badger pinned, until Badger hooked the Bear's leg and flung him over. They rolled around on the ground, grunting and swearing and trying to get handholds. A huge shadow suddenly loomed above them, and a horse's hoof came down next to Fox's red head. Badger's head bumped up against the chest of Cudgel's big roan. The smell of a sweating horse engulfed them.

"Mother!" Fox gasped, staring up past Badger's shoulder.

Badger released his hold on Fox, but made no other move.

"Climb out slowly," the Cudgel told them.

Badger moved carefully over Fox and away from the horse. Then Fox crept backwards on his elbows and heels, like a spider. He stood up alongside Badger.

The Cudgel stared down at them from the roan. "This is the last warning you get. Next time you're both out. Understand?"

"I understand," Badger said.

"Yes," said Fox.

"Go find your teams."

Keeping a distance between them, both players started climbing the hill. Grundl watched them briefly, and then urged his horse on ahead of them. He stopped at the top of the hill and looked back. The two young men were still a distance apart, ignoring each other as they climbed. A faint smile tilted the corners of Grundl's mouth before he went on over the crest and down the other side.

Chapter Ten

[822] Ercesdene, Mercia. As the sun lowered to the western horizon, the teams stumbled out into a small valley bisected by a shallow stream. Thirty or so modest dwellings lay grouped at one end, with four or five at a distance from the main village. Supper fires had been lit and smoke lifted from the chimney holes. The villagers had emptied their houses and poured out on the green, cheering as the players came careening onto the meadowland.

The Wild Boars were stretched out behind Aethelred the Stag, who was stumbling along with the pig under his arm. Two Rowdy Bears were closing the distance. The horn sounded. Stag came to a ragged halt and fell on the ground, panting and clutching the pig. The rest of the players staggered forward and dropped to the grass. The Cudgel rode up with two auxiliary players in tow, one from each team. He declared play ended for the day and posted the two on their oaths as guard over the pig. The villagers swarmed in on the prostrate teams.

Grouse lay full length with his arms stretched out, calling for water. One of the alternates ran up with a skin and held it as Edward drank. The prince fell back, staring up at the sunset's afterglow. He closed his eyes. Every muscle in his body ached; every bone rang with pain. Through his misery he heard the chatter of the villagers as they talked excitedly with anyone with strength enough to speak. He was glad no one approached him.

The villagers knew the progress of the game. They knew all the rules of the game. They knew the nicknames of the team members--not always who they were, but if knowing who they were did not violate the rules by saying so. Through some mysterious process, they knew which players had done something of merit and were lavishing praise accordingly. The Boars had determined the goal, but the villagers knew the Bears could prevent them from reaching it and still win. Praise was spread over both teams.

Aedred lay on the grass not far from Grouse. He was soaking wet. Sweaty and ground with dirt from skirmishes with Fox, he had jumped into the river to wash himself off and now lay with his wet head propped on one hand, surveying the general scene.

This was the first time he had been to this particular village--or the area, for that matter. It was his plan to visit all regions of his kingdom at sometime during his reign, but it would take years. This game allowed him to make an unofficial visit, one which did not count, of course, for to honor the village properly, he would need to appear in his presence as the king. Still, being anonymous had its benefits; a truer picture might emerge than one a scheduled visit might present. He rather liked the idea.

A short distance away, Blue Wolf and his Hwiccans were holding court to an older group of men from the village. These men were discussing the game in excited terms and comparing it with games of the past. From the way it was going, Badger could tell they all knew one another, although they were not using real names. It was no surprise to Badger that they were acquainted, since this region bordered on the lands of the Hwicce. As he was idly watching this group, he saw three young women cluster around the prostrate form of Grouse.

Edward opened his eyes and found a trio of fresh faces leaning over him. He smiled his heart-turning smile, and they giggled. Two of them seated themselves. Grouse sat up and looked around at them. All three had dark hair and eyes of varying degrees of brown. If they were not sisters, he thought they must be cousins. The youngest looked perhaps thirteen. She was the one who remained standing. The other two were Grouse's age. All three were very pretty in the fresh, plumpish, farm girl way, suggesting a healthy diet of milk and cheese.

"So," Edward said finally, "am I sitting on your turnips?"

They all laughed, and the one nearest him said to the others, "See? Didn't I tell you he was a Saxon?"

"And how would you know that?" Grouse asked, admiring the sassy dimple in her cheek.

"Your accent, silly. And your hair." She reached over and actually touched his curls. Edward resisted his instinct to draw back. "We've never heard of a Saxon playing Roll-the-Pig before."

"What's your name?" he asked her.

"Jewel, tonight. What's yours?"

"Grouse."

The girls laughed merrily. Grouse had no other option but to laugh with them. "I didn't think it described my qualities," he said. "I would have preferred Lion, or maybe Dragon, but--" here he lifted his hands and gave them such a charmingly resigned look, they took his hands and tugged him upright. His smile was puzzled.

"Come with us!" they cried together.

He resisted their pull. "Where? What do you want? Where do you want me to go?"

The two oldest girls took his arms in theirs. "Come and find out."

Grouse glanced around and saw the interest on the faces of the nearby players lolling on the ground. He saw Badger's half-smile. Stag had dropped down next to Badger, and the Hwicce had ambled up to where Badger was lying stretched out comfortably, leaning on one elbow, his ankles crossed. His head rested against his left shoulder, the long dark hair hanging down his bare arm. He was watching Grouse with amusement. There was also a challenge in that subtle expression.

Grouse pulled free of their hands and put an arm around each girl. When Jewel looked up at him in surprise, he kissed her lightly on the mouth. "Let's go, then," he said, with a swift look at Badger. The youngest girl danced ahead as the group made their way toward the village.

Badger observed, "It's that curly blond hair and those blue eyes. The women always go to him first. Bees to nectar."

Blue Wolf said, "I think he is going to be disappointed."

"Oh? Why is that?"

Blue Wolf told him. Badger threw back his head and laughed. Stag fell against the grass, whooping, "He just knew he was going to get something else."

More seriously, and with a tone of respect, the Hwiccan chieftain said, "I have here, Elhmund . . . ." Baldan brought forward a stocky man in his fifties. His short hair was black from the nape of his neck and over his ears, but grey on top. He was husky and had the healthy look of a farmer, a farmer of means.

Taking Blue Wolf's cue, Aedred immediately got up. Looking into the man's eyes, he said, "Good evening, Elhmund. I'm Badger. This is Stag. I am afraid we've crashed in unannounced. I hope there's been no damage."

"No damage, Badger," he replied. "We welcome you. This is the first time the game's come through here, and we're proud it's on our ground. There's a modest supper and some of our home ale to share with all of you, if you care to join us."

"That's very kind of you."

As they started toward the village, Stag waved back at the players observing this, signaling for them to follow.

"Our ale hall is just over there."

Dusk had fallen, and the meadow had darkened. In the village the windows of the houses shone with golden light. Smoke from the supper fires lay fragrant in the air. Larger than most of the dwellings, the ale hall was also older. Its low door had been thrown open, and the light from inside streamed warmly out into the growing night.

Villagers crowded the large room. They all cheered as the players entered, led by Elhmund and the Hwicce. Badger deliberately dropped back, ducking in behind them through the low door frame. He looked around.

The thatched ceiling was low, giving the room a cozy feel. In the old style of architecture, the supporting trees ran down the center of the room, their stout upper branches forked to hold the rooftree. Scattered about the room, benches and tables offered seating, and one sturdy table along the wall held a row of ale barrels that was drawing a crowd. Bowls and horns, presumably the individual drinking vessels of the community, lined the long shelf above the barrels. But an assortment of vessels had been gathered and stood ready for the guests. Seeing this and the food being laid on the tables, Badger was pleased with the villagers' hospitality. He found a bench toward the back of the room and sat down to enjoy the interaction of the people and the players.

"Aren't you having any?" Squirrel asked. He had a glass of ale and a loaf section jammed with a chunk of meat. "It's good . . . tender."

"I'll wait a bit."

"This ale is really fine." Squirrel held the glass up, checking the liquid's glow. "You want me to get you some?"

"Not yet."

Squirrel sat down. "This is the best I've tasted in a long time." He took a long swallow. "Did you hear what Grouse was in for?"

Badger chuckled. "Not what he was expecting." He surveyed the room a little more closely. "Do you see Stag anywhere? Did he get in here?"

"I saw him talking out front to a couple of the local girls."

Badger rose, and Leodwald had to check his impulse to come to his feet. He looked up inquiringly.

"I'd better keep him out of trouble." Badger made his way back outside.

His brother-in-law stood just beyond the square of light from the doorway, the attention of a group of five young women centered on him. Badger sauntered up and put his hand on the eorl's shoulder. Stag stepped back. "Here's Badger," he said. "Maybe he can tell you."

"Tell you what?" Badger scanned the faces.

A honey-haired girl with dark eyes leaned forward to say in a low voice, "We've heard the king is one of the players."

"Yes," said another, with rosy cheeks and stunningly white teeth. She glanced back over her shoulder. "We know what he looks like," she said.

"You do?"

"Why, yes. He is young and handsome, and he has dark hair and dark eyes."

Stag said, "I told her that just about describes all of us."

"That's true," Badger offered. "I have dark hair--" he held up a strand for her inspection. He leaned closer. "My eyes are brown."

She struck his bare arm with her palm and shoved. "You're

common like us," she told him, acceptingly. "What's your name?"

"Badger."

"What's your trade?" She looked at him closely, considering.

"My trade?"

"Yes, Badger," Stag said. "What *is* your trade?" He looked over at the girl. "He's a little slow. He comes from over near Lindsey. The dull wits leak over the border there."

Stag stood back and waited, grinning over the top of the giggling girls. He reached down and laid a sly hand on the butt of one. She huffed at him but didn't move too far away.

"Why don't you guess," Badger told the honey-haired girl. "I'll wager you can't come close."

"Gimme your hands," she told him, and reached down for them before he had a chance to move. She looked them all over on both sides. The other girls leaned in. Stag grinned broadly at Badger.

"It is a neat occupation," she said to her friends. "See his nails?" they nodded.

"He's not a farmer, that's for sure," a girl with a lovely combination of black hair and blue eyes said firmly. "What do they do over there by Lindsey?"

"I knew you couldn't guess," said Badger.

"Naow!" the girl with the white teeth cried. "I'm not through." She dropped his hands and took one of his arms and examined it. She let that one fall back and took up the other. "Here's a scar," she said. They all looked at the diagonal scar on his left forearm. "That's from a sword," she pronounced. She looked up into his face. "You're a warrior."

"On the basis of one scar? I'm called out with the fyrd. Every man has one or two scars."

"But you wear an arm ring." She held out the arm into the light from the door so the wide band of white skin could be seen against his tanned arm.

"She's got you there, Badger," Stag said.

"I've been practicing with a cloth on my arm so the other players would know what team I'm on."

Stag laughed.

"He's probably a thegn," the black-haired girl said.

"No," the girl who still held his arm said. "He's common as dirt. Listen to his 'eths'. He'd probably like to be a thegn. He's a ceorl."

Stag threw back his head and laughed and couldn't stop.

"This could go on all night," Badger said. He gently took his arm from the girl's hand. "I work with horses," he said. "My family has always trained horses."

"You're a horse-thegn," the black-haired girl exclaimed. "See?

Didn't I say?"

"I tell you on my life," Badger said, "I am not a horse-thegn. But, look here, I'm hungry and I'm thirsty and I'm going in there where the food and drink is. You're welcome to join us, if we can still get to the benches."

He had moved around to where he could get a grip on Stag. He threw his arm around his neck and towed him back to the doorway and pushed him inside. Stag laughed all the way.

The girls did not follow them in, as Badger guessed would be the case. The men squeezed their way into the noisy room and found a bench near the back.

Stag was still laughing. "'On my life, I'm not a horse-thegn'. You do know how to tell the truth."

"What's so funny?" Leodwald the Squirrel asked as he sat down with them.

"My brother-in-law," Stag said, flinging his hand toward Badger, "he just swore he was not a horse-thegn."

"It's a long story," Badger said, rising. "I'm going after some of that ale you've been touting."

They watched him stroking his way through the crowd, pausing with a word or touch to anyone turning to him as he passed.

Squirrel looked back at the eorl. "Horse-thegn? What was that about?"

"Some village girls wanted to know what his trade was."

Squirrel laughed. "So he's not a horse-thegn."

"He didn't let them pursue it any further than that. Did you see that little one with the snow white teeth? Unnn, I'd like to have her gnaw my--"

The Fox slid in next to Stag. "You don't mind, do you? This is the only seat in the house. I thought you were going to die before the horn blew, Stag."

"You weren't moving so fast yourself. I hear the Cudgel planted his horse over the top of you and Badger."

"You heard? Can you believe he did that? I almost shit! You should have seen that roan's big cock snapping at the back of Badger's head. If the horse had pissed, we'd both been drowned."

At the barrels, Badger had been handed a bowl of ale. As he took a grateful swallow, he was listening to the conversation of Otter and Wecg. He looked down at the bowl. The ale really *was* good. He finished it off and turned back to the barrels. One of the villagers cheerfully poured him another. Badger lifted his bowl to him.

When he looked back into the crowd, he saw that Tilhere had joined the group at the far end. He decided he'd had enough of the red fox for the day and looked around to see who was where. He did not see Grouse. It had been some time since the trio of girls had taken him off, and Badger decided he'd better do some reconnoitering in case Grouse needed rescuing. He stepped outside the ale hall and looked about, wondering where to begin the search.

Chapter Eleven

[822] Crecsdene, Mercia. The air was cooling rapidly, and Aedred wished he had grabbed his mantle. At that moment he spied one of the helpers and called him over. "I don't suppose you know where my mantle is?"

"It shouldn't be too hard to find."

Badger looked at the man's cloak. "Loan me yours, and you can wear mine when you find it."

The man took off the brown cloak and handed it over. Badger pulled it around his shoulders. It was of light wool and reached his knees. He left the hood down. "Did you happen to see Grouse?"

"I did. I don't know the exact one, but he went into one of those houses over there." He pointed to three houses grouped beneath a huge tree luminous with golden leaves.

Aedred walked slowly toward the dwellings. The windows of all three were lit. Deciding not to disturb the tenants until he found the right house, he approached the first one near enough to peer into the interior. There was only one room and it was empty of people. He stepped away, and then strolled over to the second house, his eyes on the lighted window. Next to the window was a small porch surrounded by poles entwined with leaves. In the soft light, the leaves were red and gold.

He moved forward to look inside, and a voice quietly said, "I am hoping you are looking for the blond boy and not up to some mischief."

Hearing the voice so close to him, Aedred jumped and reached for a weapon he didn't have. He aborted the movement.

A woman was sitting on a small bench by the door of the house. The light from the open doorway lit her brown hair and brightened the embroidered shawl thrown over her head and shoulders. He could just make out her face; a woman in her late twenties, with pleasant features and a calm bearing.

"No mischief intended. Is my blond friend here?"

"No, he's next door. But--" she added as he started to leave "--you might want to wait a few minutes. My father-in-law is talking with your friend and will fall asleep very soon. If you could wait . . . ?"

The plea was politely made and the kindness it implied, the respect to that father-in-law, held Badger. "I'll wait," he said.

"Would you like to sit down? There is a stool just there beside the vines."

Badger found the stool and set it where his legs could stretch down the steps.

"Your father-in-law likes the game, then? I understand he sent his daughters to find a player who would discuss it with him." He had the grace not to laugh.

"He played the game a long time ago, when Cenwulf was king. He never tires of talking about it. It was a very important event in his life. He actually played alongside the king."

"Did he? What's your father-in-law's name?"

She smiled at him. "Naow, you know real names aren't allowed."

"Of course." He looked down.

"Your friend--Grouse, isn't it?--he has been very patient. I do appreciate that. My father-in-law--" she smiled, relenting "--his name is Wulfgar--he is severely confined, and an evening like this means a great deal to him."

The name was not familiar to him. "Were those your sisters?"

"Sisters-in-law. I married into the family."

"Then your husband must be in that merry bunch over there." He nodded toward the noisy ale hall.

"My husband is dead."

"I am sorry," he said, looking closely at her.

"It has been awhile. He died in the service of the king."

"King Cenwulf?"

"King Aedred."

"Which campaign?"

"Campaign? He went with the fyrd to Northumbria."

For that campaign the casualty list was small. Three deaths in two skirmishes before the Northumbrian king submitted and the treaty found agreement. All deaths had been honorable, one in the first skirmish, two in the second. He could not remember their names. He felt bad about that. But he did remember their faces. He would always remember their faces.

There was nothing he could say to her without revealing his identity. Even then he wasn't sure what could be said. But he continued to look at her, trying with his eyes to convey something of the feeling he had for all his warriors, the living and the dead.

"He was proud to serve him," she said.

"I'm sure the king was grateful," he murmured.

"My husband was a farmer, although farming hasn't gone well for the past few years." She said, more brightly, "But his first love was for brewing ale. I don't know if you had any over there--"

"Yes, I did. It's excellent."

"The recipe has been in his family for generations. My husband perfected it. He improved the flavor. And it doesn't go off as soon as other ales."

"Is that right? Two days is the usual limit of our ales. The pigs get it after that."

"That was the way with our ale, too, until my husband struck on a better combination of ingredients and brewing method. It lasts over a month now, without going off."

"A month!" His head tilted down thoughtfully. "A month . . . ." His eyes swiveled up to her face. "What is the name of this village?"

"Ercesdene. You didn't know?"

"No. We piled in here because that's the way the pig rolled."

She laughed, a low mellow laugh of genuine amusement. He thought she probably did not laugh often.

The laugh became a pleasant smile. "I think the gods were kind to Ercesdene, today."

"They were certainly kind to us." After a pause, he said, "This ale of yours--how much is brewed annually?"

"About four tuns."

"Is any included in the feorm?"

"No. That is a strange question."

"I suppose it was. I think the question I was really trying to ask is, with farming not going well, how do you get by? Does the ale provide a living for your family?"

"You are a rare pig player! What was the connection between the king's feorm and how we get by?"

"I guess I sometimes think like a merchant. Ale as good as your family brews and that holds for as long as you say it does would sell easily in London, or anywhere for that matter. I was thinking a sample at the royal hall there would find potential customers. That's what the connection was."

"We don't make it in enough quantity," she said. "But thank you for taking an interest."

He thought that over. "*Could* you make it in quantity?"

"No," she said slowly. "To make quantities, quantities of ingredients are needed. And barrels and all the elements of brewing." She lifted her hands. "All that takes a large treasury."

He went silent, a silence she did not try to break. "Do you ever dream?" he asked her. "Dream of possibilities, I mean."

"Doesn't everyone?"

"Let's consider a dream." He got up and, bringing the stool with him, placed it in front of her and sat down. He leaned forward. "If you were able to buy all the supplies you need, would you be able to brew in quantity?" He added, "Would the rest of your community want to be involved?"

"Some of them, possibly. But, we are after all, still farmers. This is our land. This is what we do. This is what we have done as long as this valley has been here."

"You do both now."

"What a strange man you are to have dreams of ale brewing."

Badger decided it was time to back away. This was the kind of enterprise that whetted his curiosity. He knew nothing about the making of ale, but he did appreciate the drinking of it and to think he could learn something new, excited him. He made up his mind to look into the process when he had more time and to file this village away for future reference.

"Not so much the brewing," he laughed, "but I truly dream about the drinking."

Both turned their heads when they heard the door in the next house opening.

"There he is," Badger said, coming to his feet. He set the stool aside and walked down the steps to intercept Grouse. The older girl was accompanying Edward.

"Hallo, there Grouse," Aedred said.

"Do you know Blossom?" Grouse had his arm around the girl. She looked up at Badger. "It's not her real name. This is Badger."

"Hallo, Blossom," Badger said politely. He glanced back at the porch and lifted his hand in farewell.

"Goodbye, Badger," the woman called.

As the three were walking away, Grouse looked toward the voice and back at Badger, who said, with a grin, "Have a good conversation?"

"Actually, yes. Wulfgar is a nice old fellow. He played the Pig with your--with your King Cenwulf."

"That's what I understand."

"Oh? Were you waiting for me?"

"Just checking. You could barely lift your head not too long ago."

"I'm flattered."

"You should be."

They had reached the ale hall. They ducked in and were immediately enveloped in the steamy warmth generated by the crush of bodies. The noise level had risen significantly.

"I am very behind," Grouse exclaimed, looking around.

A hand slid up Badger's arm. The honey-haired girl danced at his side, laughing. "There's a place over here, Badger," she said. "They all want you to come over." She took Badger's hand. "Come on." She included Edward and Blossom in her invitation, as she pulled Badger along.

"Come on, Grouse," Badger told him.

It was a table with a crowd. There was the Hwicce, four villagers, Squirrel, Nail, and Stag, with a girl on his lap. When he saw Badger coming, Stag moved the girl with the white teeth off his lap and onto the bench beside him.

Blue Wolf made room, and Badger sat down. Squirrel grabbed the girl with the honey-hair. She laughed and threw her arms around his neck.

"You lost your woman," Baldan said, casting his baleful eye on him.

"Happens on a regular basis," Badger replied. "I'm used to it." He laid his hand on Blue Wolf's shoulder. "What do you know about brewing ale?" he asked.

Chapter Twelve

[822] Creesdene, Mercia. Badger was hoarse from trying to shout over the noise level. With a roll of his eyes, he shook his head at Nail, got up from the bench, and made his way outside.

He walked away from the ale hall and the noise, and looked up. Stars were splashed brightly across the black bowl of the sky. The air was cold and refreshing, and for some moments he stood there, breathing deeply, enjoying the peace of the valley. He glanced down the meadow at the shadowy forms of the pig guardians at their post; he smiled.

He pulled the cloak around his shoulders and started to return to the ale hall but noticed there was still a light at the house of Wulfgar's daughter-in-law. He hesitated, and then he strolled over on the chance she might be open to some more conversation.

When he stepped up on the porch, she appeared in the doorway. "Is this too late for a visit?" he asked.

"Not on this night," she said. "Please come in."

It was a small house, one room furnished with two chairs, a bench and a table. An alcove with a curtain drawn across it he supposed held a bed. A sconce burning on one whitewashed wall and a large candle on the table provided light. Autumn branches of gold and red decorated a table beneath the window. The room was pleasant, inviting. He took the chair she offered.

"May I get you something to eat or drink?"

"No, thank you. Your good neighbors over there were generous. If I'm going to be in the game tomorrow— " He spread his hands.

"Then you'll be playing through?"

"If we can keep the pig from the Rowdy Bears."

"I'm sorry," she said, with a laugh she choked into a smile. "I don't understand why you all beat yourselves up that way. What do you get out of it?"

Under the mantle, her hair was very straight and followed the strong contour of her face. Her brows were dark and held a natural angle suggesting kindness. Not a beautiful face, yet it held honesty, especially in her eyes. Her gaze was direct, and he responded to that openness.

"If you're asking what I personally get out of it, I would say freedom to enjoy myself. Freedom from constraint."

"But there are rules . . . ."

"I don't mean that kind of constraint. Naturally there are rules." He smiled at her. "It's a week where I am free to be a badger and not be concerned with being anything else."

"Do you live up to your name?"

He laughed. "I think I do. They tell me I do. But look--my tale is dreary. Let's hear about you. How long have you lived in this valley?"

"Eight years."

"I didn't think you were born here."

"No, I came here after I was married."

"May I know your name?"

She hesitated. "My friends call me Robin."

"I certainly want to be counted among your friends, Robin of Ercesdene." He smiled at her again. "Robin-of-the-Valley."

She smiled back.

He said, "It's beautiful here. Peaceful. I was out there a while ago, looking at the stars, listening to the river, getting a sense of the place."

"Yes, it is peaceful."

She fell silent. He sat looking at her. "What do you do in this peaceful valley, Robin?"

"What do I do . . .? I take care of Wulfgar. I provide some guidance for the girls. I cook, clean, preserve. I help with the brewing. I milk cows. I make cheese. I do anything and everything that is the work of women. I do not freely chase pigs."

They smiled at each other.

She asked, "Was your fyrd called out to the border last year?"

Badger considered a moment before he responded. He answered with a simple "Yes."

She looked down where her hands rested in her lap. "I know it's unlikely, men were fighting--for a time so short it didn't seem possible for someone to die--but could you have seen my husband?"

"I didn't know the names of anyone outside my . . . immediate group. I could have seen him. Describe him."

She took a breath. "He was a little taller than you and heavier. His hair was reddish, not as long as yours, just below his ears." She paused and searched his face.

He shook his head slightly. "There were over five hundred men there during the campaign," he said kindly. "Can you tell me anything more?"

She looked off to the side. "He was very handsome and such a good man." She looked back at him. "Everyone respected him."

"I'm sure they did," he murmured, not finding any clue in those descriptions. "What weapons did he carry?"

"A billhook--" she stopped, seeing the expression on his face change.

He had already eliminated the man killed in the first skirmish because that man had been middle-aged and balding. The two who had fallen in the second clash could have matched the description she had given; the weapon identified him. A heavy stroke from a sword against his protective leather cuirass had driven a broken rib into his heart.

"I never spoke with him, but I can tell you he died honorably. There was more than one Northumbrian attacking him, and he fought bravely."

He felt her distress and was disturbed by her tears. He took her hands and looked into her eyes. "There is no compensation for the loss of a husband. Take some comfort in knowing that because of the sacrifice he made, and the others made, we have a peace with Northumbria. That peace protects all of Mercia. His was not a death in vain."

She drew her hands slowly away and wiped her cheeks and her eyes with her fingertips. "My husband was a good, an honorable man. He went willingly to fight with the king. He believed there should be a peace because he was a peaceful man. He had faith in King Aedred. He believed that even though he is young, he has a good heart. 'His heart's instinct will guide his judgment.' That's what my husband said before he left . . . ."

Badger listened as she talked, filling in a picture of a man who had been an unknown until these moments. He looked down and took a breath. The battle had not lasted twenty minutes. Aethelred's men had come in on one side, the fyrds Aedred had brought up with him on the other side. They came together, clashed briefly with the Northumbrians, drove them back across the border for the second time that day, and this time surrounded the Northumbrian king and his army on his own ground and forced Ædda into a peace on the spot. But two men whose names he did not know had died in that skirmish. Now he knew one more intimately than perhaps he ever wanted to know the legions who answered when he summoned them.

He let her talk as he leaned forward in his chair, his forearms across his knees, his eyes sharing her grief. When she had finally poured it all out, she said, "You were kind to listen to me. I thought I was getting over his death."

"I don't know that you ever get over losing someone. The pain is less over time."

"You've lost someone?"

"My father not too long ago. My mother in years past."

"That is hard."

"But we go on."

"Yes, we do." She smiled at him. "I am glad you came back."

"I am, too. More than you might know. But now, I think I'd better be searching out my teammates." He stood up. "At the rate this night is going, no one will be able to lift the pig tomorrow, let alone carry it." He stretched his back, giving her a wry smile. "I might not be able to lift it."

He walked to the door, where he stopped and turned to her. "I'll remember this evening."

She smiled, but did not answer. They stood looking at each other. There was an upwelling of emotion in him, a sense of something not completed, a need yet to express his understanding of her grief, his own grief. He put his hand out and touched her arm. She moved forward. He put his arms around her. Leaning back against the door jamb, he cradled her full length against his body. It was at first a gesture made in kindness to ease another human being, a need to share what he could not voice. But, at some point, it changed.

Her arms went around his waist, and he pulled her tighter against him. Her face turned up to him. He bent his head to kiss her, and then stopped. In that instant he became aware of something that had never crossed his mind before: he had a responsibility for maintaining his integrity at every level. This woman was his subject. This woman was offering herself to a fiction. He knew he would one day come back to this village, and he would come back as who he was. And she would see that person and feel diminished. His sacred oath as king bound him to protect her. He suddenly understood that his oath demanded adherence in all his actions however large and public, however small and private. He could not gratify his desire at her expense.

He took her face in his hands. His fingers stroked her temple and smoothed back her hair. "I want this," he told her softly. "But, it's not possible for me. It is not something I can explain to you. I have . . . obligations that prevent me from acting on what I want at this moment. Will you understand that? Please?"

She closed her eyes and tilted her head down within the warmth of his hands. She sighed and rested her forehead against his chest. "I understand." She thought, then, that he must be married and, although feeling this attraction as strongly as she, was not allowing himself to dishonor his wife. She believed that wife a very lucky woman and immediately thought of her own, loving husband.

She drew away from him, reached up to briefly touch his hair, marveled at its softness.

He straightened away from the door and stood silently for a moment. Then he took her hand. "Goodbye, Robin." He placed his other hand over hers. "Better days are coming. I can promise you that."

"I hope so, Badger."

He stepped off the porch, looked back once, and then walked

away to find out how the Boars and Bears were faring. But he changed his mind before he reached the ale hall and instead went out into the great meadow and located his geteld among the other tents that had sprung up in the grass like mushrooms.

He pulled his bedding out of the tent and unrolled it on the grass. He sat down and looking around saw the sentinels still at their post, talking quietly, the murmur of their voices barely distinguishable from the purling of the river. The stars spilled overhead. He unwound his leg bands and took off his shoes. He rolled his borrowed mantle into a pillow, climbed under the covers, and then lay with his arms crossed under his head, gazing up at stars so brilliant it seemed a great burst of sound should have emanated from them.

He needed to think. Truths had been revealed to him tonight. He marveled that wisdom accumulated like snow, one small flake at a time. And coming unexpected, it was always possible it could be missed. He praised the god who had given him the grace to perceive it. The fleshing out of a man who had simply been a tally had affected him profoundly. It wasn't that he didn't know the men who answered when he called out a fyrd had lives beyond their military obligations; it wasn't that he didn't feel grief when they died; it was that he had never before been projected into one of those lives.

The husband's words had taken him unaware. And the wisdom, the faith embodied in those words, had brought the man who had spoken them directly before his eyes and into his heart. But that had not been the only lesson he had learned on this cold, crisp Wintirfyllith night. He had also learned that self-indulgence was not a corollary of freedom, and integrity was not always a public expression.

As he lay considering these gifts, the night began to speak. The uproar of stars blazed on overhead, the river slid murmuring through its grassy banks, and the laughter from the ale hall brought its human note to the music around him. More than at any time in his life he recognized his place in the world, accepted it, and was finally comfortable in it, assured now he was not drifting alone, but had guidance to help him become the king he wanted to be.

He became gradually aware of other sounds in the night. From one of the tents near by, he heard low voices; little squeals and moans that he slowly translated. It was Edward's tent, and he had two girls in there with him. Badger groaned, rolled his eyes. Keeping the pillow jammed over his ears, he was finally able to sleep.

Chapter Thirteen

[822] Saltwich, Mercia. During the night, clouds had moved in and the morning was drizzly and cold. The players stood shivering near the pig, waiting for the signal to begin. None of them looked very lively. Not having drunk much and getting some sleep, Badger was probably the most alert of the entire company. He had scanned the villagers gathered to cheer them off, but he did not see Robin. He accepted that and understood why she might not have wanted to come to the field.

The Wild Boars' strategy was to get the pig west across the river and beyond the valley. To that end, and because Badger had the clearest head this morning, he was stationed closest to the river. Ceawlin the Hedgehog got off a spectacular kick, farther than Badger had anticipated, and he had to splash knee deep into the frigid water to receive it.

His fingers closed on the pig with just enough time to draw it against his body before he was slammed face down against the pebbly bottom. He twisted, tried to surface, but a knee held him down. He kicked savagely, got his nose into air, but the knee pinned him again. Released abruptly, he staggered to his feet.

The Bears and Boars were thrashing about in the water. With the pig clutched against his chest, he made for the far bank and stumbled free of the river, glancing back to see Otter and Squirrel making for him and moving fast. Farther back he glimpsed auburn hair and knew who had held him down. Grundl was thundering up through the water toward the bank. His horse surged forward and gained the ground.

Squirrel was drawing closer, but it was one of the Hwicce that brought Badger down. Squirrel had reached them now with the rest of the Hwicces. Quoin grabbed the pig. Badger staggered up and looked around. Quoin had plunged back into the river and was plowing toward the east bank, but the Boars were closing fast with Wecg out in front, an excellent match to the bull-like Quoin. Fox, however, was coming purposefully out of the river toward Badger, his long auburn hair in wet strands, his mustache drooping with water.

"Come ahead, you red-haired son of a bitch," Badger called, his eyes glittering. He lowered his stance and was so completely focused on Fox; he didn't see the Cudgel riding up until the big roan was squarely between him and Tilhere. In one motion, Fox switched directions and strode back into the river toward his teammates. Badger looked innocently up at the Cudgel, raising his arms and turning his palms toward Grundl. The big man swung his horse away.

Grouse was in a chase after Squirrel, who now had the pig and was back at the starting point. Grouse tackled him, allowing Hedgehog to sweep in, grab the pig, and head back into the river. Aedred ran at a diagonal, ready to receive. Hedgehog cleared the water and handed off the pig to Badger, who plunged into the woods. Stag was waiting to run it farther to a small rise marking the western edge of the valley.

When Badger reached the top, he paused to look back across the valley, at the lush, meadows, the silvery river, the little village; a scene to remember.

By the middle of the seventh day, they were still in the woods but closer to their goal. There had been minor infractions in the antagonism between Fox and Badger, halted in all instances by the appearance of Grundl. But in the late afternoon as the game had come within sight of the salt springs and the hut of the chief waller, whose door was the goal, an unfortunate altercation occurred. It wasn't clear how it started, but it was a fight which was not going to be easily stopped.

Everyone left Fox and Badger rolling around on the ground. Stag and the other Boars drove toward the pit hut door. A Rowdy Bears' man, the chief waller would not open the door for Stag to throw in the pig, thereby winning the game for the Boars. Now for them to win, the Boars had to keep the pig touching the door until the horn sounded at sundown. There was a ferocious struggle with only moments remaining. The Boars and Bears boiled against the sides of the hut, threatening the wattle structure, while the man inside kept the door barred and yelled encouragement to the Bears.

Meanwhile, the Badger and the Fox had battled their way down to the brine troughs and pits. The Fox crowded Badger down the lead steps of one pit, preparing to kick him in, but Badger braced himself on the timbered sides, hurtled forward, and planted his head in Fox's belly. The man bellowed and fell back with Badger on top of him. Straining upwards, his fists wrapped in the collar of Badger's tunic, Fox was choking him. As Badger's hands slipped on the man's sweaty arms, he got knocked off.

Badger slid backwards to the timbers of the pit, but managed to get up in time to grab his opponent. They struggled. Badger slowly forced him backwards toward a salt ship, but the Fox made a quick move, reversing their positions and now had the upper hand, pushing Badger backwards on the slippery ground until his back pressed on the salt ship's gunnels. Inside the ship was a thick grey slurry of brine.

Badger gained some leverage and turned the Fox so they faced each other against the rail. It suddenly gave way, and they both plunged full-length into the brine.

They came up gasping and howling. Thrashing about, they swore, dug slurry out of their eyes, and then flung themselves out of the ship and onto the ground. Instantly, they flew together, slid about, and then fell, with Fox on top. He had his fist drawn back, when Blue Wolf took hold of it. The Fox looked up at him in surprise.

"The game's over, Tilhere. We won, they lost. Immunity is expired. You might want to get off His Majesty."

Tilhere looked around. Grey brine clung to his auburn hair and dripped in clumps off his mustache. All the players of both teams were laughing. Grundl sat on his horse, watching dispassionately. Tilhere looked down at the king, who was in the same sorry state as he. Fox rose and stepped to the side. He reached his hand down.

Aedred had been looking around, too. Before he took Tilhere's hand, he asked Grundl, "The game's over?"

"Yes, Sire, it is. The Wild Boars lost."

The king blew air out of his cheeks. Taking Tilhere's hand, he came upright.

"Your Majesty," the perfidious chief waller said, "I would advise you to wash the brine out right away. If you leave it on much longer your skin will shrivel permanently. Over there's the stream--"

The Badger and the Fox glanced at each other, leaped into a dead run, and threw themselves into the water.

A month after everything returned to normal, Aedred called in his hall reeve Ceolric and discussed ale brewing with him. He set him the task of finding out all he could from successful merchant brewers and to report back to him. When Ceolric accomplished his mission, Aedred and the reeve worked out a proposal to offer Robin of Ercesdene and her family.

As Ceolric and a small escort prepared to leave, Aedred was busy at his writing table with quill and parchment. When Edward came in, wondering where the king had been all day, he found Aedred at a table littered with scraps of parchment on which he had apparently been trying to draw the picture of an animal.

"What is that supposed to be?" he asked the frustrated king.

"Does your ability for map-making extend to drawing animals?"

Edward shrugged. "I don't know. I guess so. What are you trying to draw, anyway? Is that a vole?"

"No, it's not a *vole*. It's a badger."

"Badger? You got it all wrong. Look here--" Edward took the pen "--the body is like this . . . the tail . . . this is the snout . . . and this--" he looked straight at Aedred "--is the evil little badger face."

Aedred held up the drawing. "By the gods, Edward, this is excellent!" He looked approvingly at the prince. "You do have a gift." He laughed with pleasure as he gazed at the picture.

"Thank you. But what's it for?"

"I just wanted a picture of a badger."

From the way Aedred answered, the prince had a pretty good idea he was not going to hear the real reason. He looked down at the littered desk with its badger attempts. "I can see that." He shrugged and went on his way.

Ceolric sat in the tidy home of Wulfgar. A man in his fifties and ravaged by a stroke, his body was paralyzed, but his mind was clear. Sitting with him were his widowed daughter-in-law and his young daughters.

Ceolric was offering them this proposal: if they would brew a steady supply of ale, develop markets for that ale and arrange transport to the buyers, the king would loan them the currency to run the operation until it was self-sufficient. Repayment of the loan would be necessary only if the enterprise succeeded. If it did, which the king had every confidence it would, then the repayment would be five pennies on every tun sold plus two tuns of Ercesdene Ale delivered to the royal hall at Ceolworth on the sixth day of Wintirfyllith of every year the brewery remained in existence.

Once offering this proposal, Ceolric stayed to answer questions and to steer the discussion in ways the king had instructed. By the time Ceolric was ready to leave, the family had decided to involve the rest of the village and form a guild which would distribute profits among the members. Ceolric had given them a list of merchants' names whose advice might be useful.

It was clear to the reeve that the daughter-in-law was a cohesive force in the family, and he was impressed with her practical approach to the project, once she had gotten over her shock that their sovereign had made them this proposal.

"I don't understand how this came about," she said to Ceolric. She was unclear how a conversation with the player of a game had gotten back to the king. "Was he an eorl's thegn? Who was that Badger?"

"I'm sorry. I'm not at liberty to say."

She had accepted that, and the meeting had gone ahead. When it was over, Ceolric handed her a parchment envelope carrying the crown and serpent seal of the king. She looked at him with a question, but took the envelope and turned it over. Ceolric offered her a small blade, and she carefully broke the seal.

She looked inside and picked out a silver penny. On the obverse was a head in profile and the legend, *Aedred Rex.* "What is the penny for?" she asked Ceolric, puzzled, but thinking it might be some legal way of acknowledging a contract.

"There may be an explanation inside," he suggested.

And there was a smaller piece of parchment. She took it out. On it was the drawing of a badger. She stared at it, lifted the penny, and looked at the drawing again. She dropped her hands in her lap. "Oh," she said, staring helplessly up at the reeve.

Ceolric understood the symbolism, but did not know the complete story. Without betraying it, he was enjoying her astonishment. And from what he had observed (and drunk) this day, he thought the young king had not only been generous, but had also made a very wise investment.

Chapter Fourteen

[822] Mercia. King Aedred and Prince Edward withdrew their combined forces from East Anglia, bringing with them the treasure of the Danish king they had slain, retribution for an incursion into Mercia and payment for that insolence. The chest bulged with silver coins and ingots, gold arm rings and collars, silver chains, and gold brooches and bowls. Armor and weapons from the fallen Danish warriors had been distributed on the battlefield. The prisoners had been marched ahead to London to be sold on the banks of the Thames.

At the first hall inside the Mercian border, Aedred halted the army. He and the prince paid off their warriors and disbanded the levies. They rewarded their retainers from the booty, divided the balance into their treasuries, and then settled down at the noisy benches.

Their host was the thegn Ecoberht, a jolly, rugged man who had served Aedred's father in his campaigns. He had four strapping sons, all in the county fyrd. This particular fyrd had not been called out for the engagement with the Danes.

"We're always ready to leap in, Sire," the eldest son told him. "The messenger summoning us must have taken a wrong turn." It was said with a jovial wistfulness. Aedred laughed.

The mead flowed at the benches, carried in pitchers by Ecoberht's three handsome daughters. Prince Edward riveted his attention on the youngest. As she went along the benches merrily serving the guests from her large pouring vessel her eyes were on the prince.

Throughout the evening Aedred observed the progress of this romance and was amused that Edward, in a fever, was prudent enough not to dishonor his host--or endanger his own life--by seducing Ecoberht's daughter. Instead, Edward quietly disappeared with the lovely wife of a thegn who was a neighbor to Ecoberht. This thegn had arrived with several other men and women of the countryside to join in feting the king and his company and had drunk too much ale. Rolling senselessly into a corner of the room, he slept while his wife entertained the West Saxon prince.

Edward returned to the hall with the flush of exertion still on his cheeks. His glance to Aedred was so filled with self-satisfaction that the king sprang from his seat, grabbed the prince, and, scattering people from their path, spun him along the floor.

Aedred shouted in his ear, "Have you enough energy left for this?"

"For this and ten times more!" Edward shouted back.

Aedred roared a challenge.

They came to a halt at the far wall. Bracing their hands on each other's shoulders, they grunted out a first cadence. They cross-stepped and stamped and whirled all up and down the long room, sensing their course only at the corners of their eyes and by the shouting and whistling and rhythmic slapping of hands. With their eyes locked, now laughing, now breathlessly concentrating, each trying to outlast the other but both captured by the perfect measure they kept as their silent commands flashed back and forth between them, they flew in their wild dance.

Aedred suddenly broke step. With one arm tight around Edward's neck, he brought them to a whirling, staggering stop. He swung himself around on that arm, kissed Edward roundly on the mouth, and then hung laughing at his side, his arm still gripping the prince's neck.

"Ale!" It was the only word he could manage.

Edward stood grinning at the king, his chest heaving and his arms limp. Someone handed them each a horn of ale, and they drank, their eyes locked in pleasure, their bond reaffirmed.

[822] Mercia. "Something going on?"

Edward had been observing the king for over fifteen minutes, after a comment he had made remained unacknowledged. Aedred was sitting forward, staring into the coals of the campfire. They were alone. Everyone else had given up for the night except for them and the watch.

Aedred straightened, tilted his head toward the prince in a side glance. "There's a legal matter I must attend to tomorrow. Not one I relish."

"Sounds serious, if it's fallen into your lap. Where at?"

"The Ivel Valley."

"That's in the province of the Gifla folk, isn't it?"

"Yes. I don't like dealing with these kinds of matters. I don't like being the court of last resort."

"It's an appeal?"

Nodding, Aedred compressed his lips and exhaled through his nostrils. Edward waited. He made himself comfortable, stretching his legs out and crossing the ankles.

"What do you know about the kingdom's administrative history?" Aedred finally asked.

"Not nearly as much as the administrative history of Wessex. Am I going to get a lesson?"

"A short one, if you're interested."

"Oh, I'm interested. Go ahead--enlighten me."

"I'll make this short," Aedred said, noting the prince's relaxed posture. "As you know, we don't use the shire system, as does Wessex; we're a grouping of peoples, like the Cilternsætna, Herefina, Hwicce, my own Myrcenes, etc.; provinces, as you said. Which is why our borders are a little fuzzy and sometimes disputed--" he paused, looking at Edward from under his brows.

"By my ancestors, not me. Not yet, anyway."

"I'll keep that in mind," Aedred replied, with a half-smile. "Well, for generations the Mercian kings have been overlords of these provinces, but originally each tribe had their own king."

Aedred swung around on the stool to face the prince. "The chiefs of some of these groups can still trace their lineage back to those early kings. The Gifla leader's line is ancient; it doesn't trace back to Woden, of course."

It always took the prince off-guard--this conviction of Aedred's that he was descended from a god. Knowing Aedred was intelligent and a realist in most things, Edward was always amazed that his kinsman could seriously entertain the hocus-pocus of his heathen religion. But, unlike his own fraudulent practice of Christian religion, Edward had to acknowledge that Aedred was a devout practitioner of his. And there were certain dark things surrounding Aedred, things not seen, only felt sparking along the skin--

"As a sign of respect," Aedred was telling him, "Mercian kings have always referred to the Gifla lords as *subregulus.*

"Sub king."

"That's right, Edward. You remember your Latin."

"I was always a good student." He grinned at Aedred. "But what has this to do with tomorrow?"

"Patience, Edward; I said I'd make this short. Now, *I* may refer to the leader--his name is Bieda--as a sub king, but his people view him as a king in all matters, and he does conduct himself as a king, except for events that coincide with the interests of the kingdom as a whole, or when he feels an impartial authority needs to be called in."

"And he's called you in."

"That's about it."

Edward waited again, and then finally raised his hands in a question. "Do I get the end of the tale?"

"It's a case of adultery."

Edward thought about it for a minute. "That used to carry the death penalty, didn't it?"

"It still does, Edward."

"No? Really?"

Edward had not heard of the penalty being exacted in all the time he had been coming to Mercia. "It must not be common. The penalty,

I mean."

He knew of some ongoing cases of adultery in the kingdom which had not occasioned anything more than raised eyebrows, including his own occasional participation, the remembrance of which now brought a little chill to his neck. "But it seems a common practice."

"Every culture has it's tacitly ignored prohibitions. Until there's a case that can't be ignored."

"And this is one of those."

"It appears to be."

Aedred leaned forward again on the stool, his forearms across his knees. "Bieda's wife, Ælfgifu, was found in *flagrante delicto* by a number of witnesses. There was no question of what they saw, and she admitted the relationship had been going on for some time. The offense couldn't be ignored, so charges had to be brought. I'll listen to the evidence, of course, but . . . it doesn't sound good."

"You could grant clemency, couldn't you? You are the king."

Aedred looked at him in surprise. "I still work within the framework of the law. And the custom." He lifted one hand. "Well, perhaps I might in another case, but this involves a king and his queen. What the king symbolizes in the eyes of his subjects dictates scrupulous adherence to the law. If the case is proved, there's no other way for me to rule. I'm an instrument here, Edward. And this final judgment had to be delegated to the authority outside the community, for the reasons I just gave."

"It doesn't look like she has much of a chance."

"I'm afraid it is going to be a joyless undertaking," the king agreed.

"Mind if I go along?"

"No, of course not. It will be good instruction for your future kingship. It's not all feasts and heroic battles."

"You think I don't know that?"

Chapter Fifteen

[822] Ivel Valley, Mercia. Edward had thought their return route from East Anglia into Mercia was round-about, but he hadn't questioned it. Then, when a number of the king's men from London had joined them as they crossed Ermine Street, Edward had assumed the king was strengthening his numbers for the ride home, and thought no more about it. Now there seemed to be a connection with the appearance of these men and Aedred's side journey into the land of the Giflas.

The army was left in camp as the king's company began their march into the flat expanse of the Ivel River Valley. Spread near its center was a community of over three hundred dwellings. Aedred had sent couriers ahead the day before, so they were expected. People were gathering in front of their houses and along the road, watching quietly as the king's company slowly advanced down the lane toward them.

Aedred's standard was carried before him, the gleaming blue silk with the gold crown and serpent rippling back toward the king. He rode his war-horse, his eorls flanking him; accompanied by the Saxon prince of Wessex with thegns from both kingdoms, all riding solemnly toward the hall of Bieda of the Giflas.

The sub king was a short man in his fifties. His hair was white and thinning at the top. In some battle his arm had been broken and had not healed properly. He held it crooked, the knob at the elbow not permitting the arm to straighten. His face reflected the serious aspect of the villagers and of the nobles surrounding him. He was dignified and gracious, but it was apparent he had been shedding tears. He took Aedred into a side room for a private interview.

Edward, the rest of the king's company, and the Gifla noblemen took their seats at the benches. In the death-watch gloom of the hall, the king's company sat drinking and speaking in low tones, glancing about the large room, uncomfortable with the melancholy pervading its atmosphere and with the grim demeanor of the Gifla lords and the servants.

Eorl Mawer was too soft-hearted and too easily moved by emotions such as the ones draining the air out of the hall. "I think I'll check the horses," he rumbled to Edward, and rocked himself out of the bench. Edward affectionately watched him go.

It was a half hour or so later that Grundl, stationed at the side room, opened the door, and Aedred emerged, his face grim. He came over to where his men had risen from the benches. "We'll be doing this at the hundred's site." He motioned to one of his thegns. "I'll need that chest. See that it's brought along."

The meeting place of the Gifla hundred was a large grassy area overspread by an ancient elm. Benches facing the dais were placed firmly into the earth and were weathered by decades of storms and sun. The benches were filling, and those villagers not arriving in time to get a place were standing nearby or seating themselves on the ground.

Edward now understood why the men from London had been summoned. Hearing of the need for his judgment at the Ivel Valley while still on campaign, Aedred had sent for the trappings of his authority; he wanted to indicate to the people both the seriousness of this court and his respect for the sub king.

Now the people of the Gifla stood as the young king of Mercia took his seat on the dais, the folds of his gold-edged scarlet robe draping heavily down around him. The jewels in his treflέd crown caught the sunlight shining through the leaves overhead and the gold beamed into the eyes of the observers. He looked out over the assemblage, which, never loud, grew silent. In that silence, he struck twice on the planking of the dais with the end of the gold scepter he carried.

Standing next to the king's standard, Aldhune, Eorl of Beorhhamstede called out, "Hear now! Comes Aedred, king of Mercia to review the charge of adultery against Ælfgifu, wife of Bieda subregulus."

An imposing man named Crida, the one chosen to present the sub king's charge, came up to the dais and genuflected. Then, in a resonant voice, he began to speak. But before he proceeded with the charge, Aedred held up his hand.

"Bring Queen Ælfgifu before us."

Edward and the other members of the king's party had been given seats in a newly placed array to the right of the dais and facing the assembly. Through the aisle created by this arrangement, the queen, surrounded by a guard of warriors, was brought before King Aedred.

Considerably younger than her husband, she was no more than eighteen, with a nicely rounded figure, grey eyes, and brown hair tucked neatly within her dark blue mantle. She had a wholesome look about her. Although normally she would have been pink-cheeked, she was now very pale. She curtsied, and then stood twisting her fingers slowly as she looked up at the king.

"Would you like to sit, Queen Ælfgifu?"

"Yes, Your Majesty."

A chair was brought for her, and she sat down, her shoulders bent slightly, her hands in her lap.

"Continue," Aedred told the man reciting the charges.

As Edward listened with keen interest Aedred threading his way through the complexities of the charges, the story began to emerge.

She was a second wife, the first having died a number of years earlier. She had been married to Bieda for two years. At some point in the marriage, the half-brother of the sub king had become a resident of the hall. Over a course of time, the queen and the half-brother had begun an affair. The affair had been uncovered and made public by the angry wife of the half-brother. This brother had brought in his men with the idea of taking queen and hall but was killed on the stairway by the nobleman now presenting the charges. Although there was no proof of complicity by the queen in this misadventure, she was undeniably an adulteress, as the witnesses brought before the king testified. The evidence was clear to Edward and everyone else, including Aedred.

The king listened to her spokesman and then heard her out, asking questions which Edward knew were designed to find some point on which to pass a more lenient judgment. It simply was not there in the testimony. By her bearing and her tone of voice, the queen knew it, too.

"Queen Ælfgifu," Aedred said, "we have heard the charges against you. We have listened to the evidence and the witnesses. Do you have any further words for us to consider before we make our judgment?"

"No, Sire, I do not."

"Then, from the evidence and the testimony and your own admission, it is our judgment you are guilty of the charge of adultery."

There was a reaction from the people in the assembly. Subdued, without protest of a verdict which had been expected, it was a response to the reality of the awesome legal machinery being put into motion. They quieted as the king pronounced the sentence.

"You will be taken to the place of your execution at sunrise tomorrow, and at that time you will be put to death. This is the final judgment. There is no further recourse." He stuck the scepter three times on the floor of the dais.

The young queen, held up now by the arms of her guards, was taken away through the silent crowd. When she was out of sight, Aedred rose, bringing the whole assembly to its feet. He came off the dais with a glance at Edward. Shortly after, Edward was admitted to the king's room. The heavy crown had been lifted from Aedred's head and was being secured in a silk-lined leather bag. The prince watched as Aedred rolled his neck and arched his back, and then shrugged out of the robe. The gold scepter lay on the bed. Merefin was directing the packing of all these items into the chest. Throwing himself into a chair, Aedred stared at Edward.

"I don't see how any other verdict could have come out of it," the prince said, taking a chair close to the king. "But I was wondering why banishment was not an option."

"We're not Arabs, Edward. This is not a polygamous society. If she were banished, she is still the queen, still Bieda's wife and a potential threat, and he can take no other wife as long as she is alive."

"Couldn't he put her aside?"

"That's an option for everyone but a king. The standards are set higher for us, Edward, as you will one day find out. We reap fabulous rewards, but we also have serious strictures."

"I don't know about that; kings are always having affairs, with no punishment at all."

"I'll have to admit it's unjust, but it is the way it is. And no doubt always will be as long as kings rule. But then it largely depends on how discreet a queen is with her affair. Some have managed it over years with no consequences. If few people know and are not inclined to talk about it, and the king, who always does know, is tolerant, then she is safe. This queen was reckless. She disregarded her husband's role as ruler of his people by her total lack of indiscretion. That disrespect is why she will die tomorrow."

"A sad case," Edward said, sincerely, shaking his head. He exhaled, slapped his knees with his hands. "So--we're leaving this afternoon, then?"

Aedred frowned at him. "No." The frown smoothed out. "Not until after the execution."

"You're staying for it?"

"I've always felt if you sentence someone to their death, you should be a witness to their execution. To my mind, it is the best arbiter for careful judgments."

In the first silvery light of dawn, Aedred, wearing a dark cloak, walked from his horse through the wet grass to the area of execution. Grundl followed him on one side, Prince Edward on the other. There were six men now grouping near a copse of trees bordering the field. These were witnesses. Bieda stood with them, his face severe.

They were standing at a pit dug into the marshy ground. It was six feet long, three feet wide, and four feet deep. From the walls of the excavation water had seeped in, leaving two or three inches pooled at the bottom. A freshly dug ditch ran back from the pit to a small reservoir where two men holding shovels waited. The final foot or so from the lip of the reservoir had not yet been dug out. Balanced on one side of the pit in a harness of ropes was a large flat stone. Leaning against it was a withey hurdle.

Deciphering this set up, the prince looked over at the king, aghast. Aedred remained expressionless, only the tightening of his jaw giving Edward a clue.

Bieda stood pale, his lips bloodless. He said to Crida, "There's water in there. She can't be put in muddy water." He was clearly disturbed at this. "Have them put some boughs down. She can't lie in that muddy water."

The man looked at him as if he might be joking, and then he called to the men standing at the head of the ditch, "Get some boughs to line the pit!"

The light had grown by the time the men had dumped in enough branches to make a bed above the water seepage. The sub king, barely controlling his distress, nodded to his spokesman. Crida stepped back to signal to a group standing at the headland near a wattle fence. In the increasing light the figures were now visible as they came slowly forward.

Two warriors half-carried the young queen, who moved limply between them, her head swaying loosely. A guard of three followed them, and two women brought up the rear. The witnesses standing at the pit watched silently as they approached. Far off, the villagers had gathered. When the bodyguard with the queen reached the pit, there were a few moments of consultation among Bieda's men. Bieda himself did not join in or look at his queen. He stared straight ahead toward the woods beyond the fields.

"Lower her in," Crida said.

One guard stepped down into the pit and reached up as the other guard, lifting the queen off her feet, handed her down. Very gently, the guard in the pit laid her onto the pad of boughs. She looked at him with drooping eyelids, her head lolling back into the leaves. Then she raised her head slightly, looked dazedly at the walls of the pit, and then dropped her head back down.

The guard was hauled up with a grim backward glance at the queen. He stood aside. The three warriors forming the rest of the body guard now waited by the stone. Kept back by the gestures of the men, the women stood sobbing and clasping their hands.

At a signal from Crida, the warriors lowered the withey frame into the pit. It had legs that held it a few inches above the queen. She put up her hands as it came down, and the witnesses saw the sticks bend upward where her hands were pressing, but the frame was heavy enough and her attempts so weak the hurdle stayed in place.

Now Crida nodded to the warriors. They took up the ends of the ropes wound around the stone. They tossed two of these ends to the warriors positioned on the other side of the pit. The sub king had stepped back and was being supported by two of his thegns. The women began to wail.

Edward breathed, *"Dear Jesus,"* softly, and crossed himself. Aedred had not moved and neither had Grundl.

The warriors were lowering the stone carefully, not allowing it to drop suddenly onto the frame. It came to rest. They could hear the withey frame creaking as it gave but did not break. There was a muffled cry from under the stone. Bieda drooped forward, and then straightened and shook off the hands steadying him.

The spokesman waved his hand sharply at the men standing at the pond. They began to quickly shovel out the remaining barrier, and the water shot from the reservoir into the ditch and down the earthen walls. There was a strangled scream from the pit. The women rushed forward, shoving their way through the men to drop to the ground, wailing and calling the queen's name. One tried to stop the flow of water with her hands, but a nobleman yanked her to her feet and flung her away. The warriors took the women off, still screaming.

When the water level had reached the lip of the pit and begun to spill over into the meadow, Aedred turned and walked back to his horse. Grundl and Edward followed close behind. They mounted and rode to the hall where they silently waited for the return of Bieda. The sub king was close to collapse. But he had the document brought out and all the witnesses, including Aedred and Edward signed it.

They left the valley without looking back.

In this year King Aedred and Edward, prince of Wessex, rode out with the fyrds from London and Winchester and all the surrounding counties of both kingdoms and harried into East Anglia because the Danes had ravaged Heortford and Hæthfeld. They slew a Danish king and one hundred fifty of their men and carried off the treasure hoard of the king. In this same year Queen Ælfgifu of the Giflas was put to death for adultery.

Chapter Sixteen

[823] Mercia. "Why are you being so insistent about this, Edward?" Aedred was having none of it, knowing that guileless look. "Come out with it--why do you want me to go to Exeter now?"

They were bivouacked at Dyrham, having routed a force of Danes out of Pringslea. They sat on stools across from each other in Edward's tent.

"I want to repay your hospitality. It's no plot. Lord, I can't stand a suspicious man! Look, you're always entertaining me in London and at your other vills. Let me return the favor; we're only a day's distance. Really, I do insist! You don't have anything pressing at the moment, and my honor's at stake here--"

"Your honor!" Aedred was laughing.

"Yes, my honor. As a host. Is that so far-fetched?"

Aedred cocked his head at the prince.

Edward smiled the disarming smile that melted hearts and objections. "Disband your fyrds and come with me. Father would be glad to see you, you know that."

When Edward saw that Aedred seemed to be considering his invitation, he fell silent and watched his face.

"All right, I'll go--"

"Splendid!" cried Edward, leaping to his feet.

"Wait a minute--wait a minute! On one condition . . . ."

Edward looked at him sharply. He sat back down. "What condition?"

"Tell me what this is all about. I know you too well, Edward All-Fair. Something's in the wind. Confess it now, or I'm for London. I want no surprises."

For a long time Edward just looked at him, and Aedred was puzzled by this uneasiness in his manner. "Well? What's it to be?"

Starting somewhere in the middle of the reason for his discomfort, Edward began, "Things change . . . . How long has it been since you visited one of our halls?"

Aedred said nothing.

"You needn't look at me that way. How long has it been since you've seen Father and my--my sister?"

Aedred leaped on the faint stammer. "Your little sister?" He stared at Edward, baffled. Then he laughed. "Is she what this is all about?" He laughed again.

"No, she is not what this is about. I told you; I want to repay your hospitality." Edward frowned at him. "She's hardly little."

"No? How old is she now?"

"Fifteen."

"Fifteen. Didn't you train her to the sword? To the *sword*! Listen to this!"

"I didn't train her; Eorl Teownor did. It wasn't to be a warrior. She had an . . . exploratory interest. Her nature is gentle really. And she is . . . quite beautiful."

"Gentle and beautiful. This sounds like the daily subtleties I get in London, Edward." His smile remained amused, but his voice held an edge of annoyance. "I'm not taking any fifteen-year-old girl to wife," he said lightly. "I'm not ready to marry anyone, yet."

Demoralized that Aedred thought he was taking advantage of their friendship to find his sister a husband, the prince ran his fingers through his curls, a mannerism Aedred noted. *But that is exactly what I'm doing,* Edward thought grimly.

He had been summoned to his father's quarters. He had known what it was all about.

The search is not going to be prolonged, Prince Edward.

No match has been good enough, Sire. I . . . just want the best advantage for Elfwina.

The best match has always been the king of Mercia. You will approach him, and you will do it before the month is out.

He had gone to Elfwina. His behavior with her since she had returned from Canterbury was scrupulous, distant, and even severe. Her responses were tentative, unsure, and sad.

Father isn't pressing you to marry, she said, with downcast eyes. You are the one who will be ruling the kingdom.

That is why he isn't pressuring me. The marriage will be one that will best serve Wessex. I am not the subject of this conversation, Elfwina.

Edward knew he could not survive her being taken from Angelcynn. Although jealousy burned in his heart, he would make the appeal to the king of Mercia. It was the only way he could keep her close and have some measure of control over her.

In a quiet voice the prince answered, "I didn't say anything about marriage."

"So you're presenting me with a mistress."

Anger flashed out of Edward's eyes. Aedred stared back, chastened.

"That was an outrageous thing to say. I am sorry. Forgive me. I meant no offense to your sister. I remember her as a charming little girl. The truth is you're embarrassing me, Edward." He sighed, and stood up. "I'll go as I promised. But please understand, I am not looking for a wife at this time."

"I know. I understand." He looked sadly up at Aedred, thinking, *I've gone at this stupidly. Elfwina can speak for herself--if I let her."*

In this year there was an eclipse of the moon on Modra Nect. King Aedred and Prince Edward fought with the Danes at Pringslea and had the victory. In this same year, King Aedred took to wife Elfwina, daughter of Brihtric, king of Wessex. She is a descendent of Offa, king of the Angles.

Chapter Seventeen

[825] Ceolworth, Mercia. Prince Edward had sent a message ahead that he and his entourage would arrive at the royal hall at the end of the first week in May (Thrilmilci, according to the heathen Mercian calendar). But the weather had been excellent and because the roads were in good repair, all bridges intact and no rivers to be forded or detoured around, they arrived a week early. They assumed that was the reason there was no official welcome for them at the gate.

"You see, Eorl Mawer, what comes of a steady peace," Edward said to the big Saxon riding beside him. "We could walk right in and take over the hall without lifting a spear."

As Mawer well knew, this was not a criticism but a proud affirmation that with only minor skirmishes with the Northumbrians, Aedred had kept the peace in Mercia for four years.

"I doubt that," Mawer dutifully replied.

Although there had been no greeting party at the gates, there were villagers about who recognized the prince and the eorl and the other members of their party. They waved and called out their welcomes. Edward waved back enthusiastically, glad to be back at Ceolworth after six months in Wessex.

They all reined in their horses at the open doors of the hall. Edward glanced up at the window of the queen's chambers. Where the casements had been thrown open to the sunny air, two grey doves paced the wide ledge.

"Something's going on down there," Mawer said. His face was turned toward the south end of the building. There, a number of workmen were moving to and from a center of activity not visible to them.

Edward peered into the dark mouth of the front entrance. "There's not much stirring here. All right--let's see what's down there."

The workers were hauling lengths of ancient lead pipe through the doorway leading into the space beneath the hall. Edward and Mawer and the twelve thegns with them dismounted and went over to watch. Coils of rope were descending into the darkness along with the pipe. Several house servants had also been called into this labor. Voices could be heard under the hall.

After watching this for some minutes, Edward turned to the man who seemed to be in charge of this sunny end of the conveyor line. "What's going on under there?"

"His Majesty's project, Sire."

"Ahh!" said Edward. "What is it this time?"

The man frowned and looked perplexed. "I'm not altogether sure, Prince Edward. Something to do with speaking through walls. Ceolric would know. He's down there."

"And His Majesty . . .?"

"Down there, too."

Edward laughed. "I'll ask His Majesty, then." He turned to Mawer.

"I'll see to the unloading," Mawer said hastily. He added, "The ceiling's too low down there."

"Oh, the ceiling, is it?"

"I'd be bent over double for hours, the way this thing looks to be going." Mawer swung his head like a disgruntled bear.

"What on earth do you think he'd have you doing?"

"I don't know," Mawer growled. "But when he turns out the whole hall like this, no man's safe."

Edward raised his eyebrows. "I'll have to learn his secret. You never quail over my activities."

"He doesn't abet *you,*" the eorl replied.

"Oh, go along, then. Being your good lord, I'll abet your cowardice."

"Humph." Mawer turned away and began giving rough orders for the stabling of the horses.

"Have Tonberht unpack those gifts carefully," Edward called after him, grinning.

Mawer waved his hand and fled with the rest of the party.

Edward paused at the low doorway to let through a length of pipe, and then ducked down and followed it in. He stopped just inside to let his eyes become accustomed to the darkness. From where he was standing near the doorway a line of men wound back through the heavy supporting timbers of the underpinning and around the caches of wine, mead, and ale barrels to a far lighted corner.

He squeezed along the line, stooping as the others were forced to do in the five foot clearance between the bare earth and the thick planking of the floor above their heads. In the light thrown out from an array of candles and oil lamps, he could see the tall, thin form of Ceolric. The reeve was hunched forward uncomfortably, the back of his hand resting in a tired attitude on his hip as he craned his neck to carry on a dialog with the king.

His Majesty lay on his back on a narrow stone ledge, his face inches from the stringers above him. He was cradling a pipe in his hands, the other end of which was suspended from the flooring by a piece of rope and attached to another section of pipe by a sleeve beaten out of a thin sheet of brass. A brass sleeve lay close at hand on his belly. Ceolric was holding another, which had a right-angle curve.

"Soon as we finish this section," Aedred was saying, "We're ready to go up through the floor. Did Wiferth bore that hole, yet?"

"Yes, he did, Sire." Ceolric looked up, apparently in the direction of the hole. He saw the glow of Prince Edward's fair hair as the prince came into the light, smiled recognition, but Edward signaled the reeve not to give him away. Ceolric eased his features into a bland expression and looked back at the king.

"Where the hell's that last pipe?" Aedred asked him, not able to move to look for himself.

Edward took the end of the pipe being maneuvered past him. Coming up to the ledge with it, he put his knee up next to Aedred's head to brace himself and slid the pipe forward over the king's shoulder.

"Hold it," Aedred said. He slipped the brass coupling over the end of the pipe Edward was holding. "That's got it--now, ahead with it . . . slowly . . . ."

At once, Edward aligned it to the end the king was cradling.

All Aedred could see of the man helping him was his hands. "Well done!" he said. "Now, keep it steady while I make sure it's tight." He twisted and shoved the coupling over the other pipe.

"Tight and dry," Edward whispered into his ear just as Aedred was registering that the finely embroidered linen sleeve swaying near his nose was not the sleeve of a ceorl.

He howled with surprise, "Oh, fuck!" The connection fell against his chest, and he grabbed Edward's wrist. "I wanted to have this finished before you got here!" He laid his head back on the dusty ledge and whooped with laughter. "But you popped in too soon!" He lay there gasping.

"The roads were good. What is all this, anyway? You've got the whole hall working on it, and no one's at the gate."

"Well, wait a minute, and I'll tell you. But as long as you're here and so willing, hold that pipe again while I string it to the plank." He proceeded to do this. "Did you see Elfwina?"

"Hell, no. There wasn't anyone in sight. Not at the gate. Not at the hall doors. You have everyone down here."

"Well, not *everyone*. Elfwina's doing her accounts. She wanted to get them out of the way before you arrived. She probably didn't see you coming. How's everything in Wessex?" He was still chuckling. He began wrapping the pipe with a length of rope handed to him by Ceolric.

"Uneventful. Father sends his love."

Aedred glanced over at him with a smile broadened by a residue of mirth. "We heard about how uneventful it was. Well, we'll have that story later. How is he?"

"His health? Excellent." Edward was following the course of the pipes with his eyes, trying to figure it out.

"Still working on his scholarly pursuits?"

"When he's not pursuing Danes." Edward was looking at him from above, so he was seeing Aedred's face at an angle of forehead, fine dark eyebrows, and straight nose. The king's lips were tightening and relaxing with the labor of his hands and the strain on his arms. He was sweating profusely, and the rich odor steamed familiarly into Edward's nostrils. "He's been doing some translations."

"What's this about you and Lady Aebbe?"

Edward grinned. "You heard about that, did you?"

"Well?"

"Father keeps pushing."

"And you keep resisting. Marriage isn't all that bad. He's going to clip your wings before too long."

"We've had this conversation before."

"You never did heed anything I say. Tie off that end for me, will you?" Aedred dropped his head back against the ledge, breathing heavily. "Not much space to work. Ceolric?"

The reeve bent forward. "Sire?"

"I think the three of us can finish down here. We won't need any more pipe. Tell those men to go back to their duties."

"Am I being called into service?" asked Edward.

"I knew I had a craftsman when you lined up that end so well."

Chapter Eighteen

[825] Ceolworth, Mercia. The king eased himself out from the ledge and dropped to the floor. "Come here," he told Edward and gave him a violent hug, awkwardly, because they were both stooping. "Early or not, I'm glad to see you." With his arm still around the prince's shoulders, he said, "Now, see what you think of this," and led him back along the sections of pipe which had already been attached to the flooring.

"This is what I've been waiting for. Where did you get this pipe? Some old Roman dump?"

The pipes did have a cast off appearance: dark, almost black with age, but with a whitish bloom in the scars and dents. They were in eight-foot lengths and about two inches in diameter.

Aedred looked at him from the side. "Could be. My father had it hauled in from somewhere and had it stacked out behind the stables. I've been eyeing it ever since I was a boy, wondering what use I could make of it. The other day, after I'd sent someone running down here three different times for a particular barrel I wanted, I thought, Now, if I could just talk to him while he's searching, there wouldn't be all these trips up and down, and I wouldn't be in danger of dying of thirst. Then I thought of the pipes."

Edward was silent.

They had reached the point where the sections of pipe disappeared through a hole bored in the stone foundation. "This portion leads on to the kitchen, another problem area, I need not remind you. Those delays from kitchen to hall will be remedied by better communications, too."

Edward was puzzled. "You've got enough servants, haven't you? If the messages aren't getting through, send four men on your errands. One of them is bound to get it right."

Aedred snorted. "Modernize your thinking. There are things that can be more efficiently done than by a relay of servants."

They started back up the pipeline. "The principle is simple, really," Aedred said cheerfully. "When you were a boy you've taken reeds and connected them, haven't you? So you could blow seeds through them? Or inch them up to where some girl was sitting, and blat out a disreputable noise? You've done that haven't you?"

"Never."

"Oh, never *you*."

Edward started laughing. "What are you going to do? Sit up there in the hall and blat through the pipe at the kitchen wenches?"

"This is a superior insight, here, Edward. Give it the respect it deserves. If I'd only had it in place when you came. But, ah well. You have the imagination of a Dane." His hand slipped around to the back of Edward's neck, gripped it, and gave it a hard shake.

He released Edward and turned to the reeve, who was coming up to them out of the gloom. "Grab that end there, Ceolric. Let's put this last section in, and then we can get out of here and straighten our backs."

Together they lifted the heavy lead pipe and carried it forward and attached it in the same manner as the preceding sections.

"The idea is this, Edward: whenever I want to talk to anyone down here, or if instructions need to be given to the kitchen, all that must be done is to speak into the end of the pipe--which will soon go up this hole that was just cut in the floor--and it's done immediately. No running to and fro. There's the beauty of it."

Edward peered up through the hole and suddenly started back, laughing. Someone was peering down from the other side.

"Wiferth?" Ceolric called, crouching beneath the hole.

"Yes, Sire!" a muffled voice answered cheerily. "Ready for the pipe?"

"Send it through."

The end of the pipe appeared.

"Hold it there!" shouted Ceolric.

The pipe hung suspended.

"Now, this is the tricky one," Aedred said. He and Ceolric consulted while Edward stood aside and looked back along the pipe, shaking his head and laughing to himself.

A treewright was called in and a brace made to hold the bottom section of the brass elbow where it joined the two pipes at right angles. Then the treewright went upstairs to devise a support for the upright pipe. They followed him.

As they stood at the corner of the south wall watching the treewright and his helpers working where the pipe emerged from the floor, the king said, "You see, Edward, this funnel the metalsmith made for the purpose will fit neatly down inside the end of the pipe."

He held the funnel out for Edward's inspection. "What ever needs to be communicated is spoken into it and thence to the person who needs to hear it. The task is efficiently carried out with no needless running about." Aedred beamed at him. "We'll try it out in a minute."

He eyed the workmen impatiently. "There we have it! They've finished. Good--good!"

The workmen stepped away and then stood watching curiously.

"Well!" Aedred cried, grasping the funnel with a triumphant look at Edward. He stuck it into the end of the pipe. "We'll address the kitchen first." He stared meditatively at his brother-in-law, seemed to be at a loss for anything to say now that the moment had arrived. He blew into the funnel, listened, then yelled, "Bring up mutton!" and began laughing. "What does one say to a kitchen?"

"I guess mutton is as good as anything. Although I would have said beef. Will they answer?"

"I don't know," Aedred said musingly, staring into the funnel.

"You have too much time on your hands," Edward said.

Queen Elfwina had been most of the day bringing up her accounts on the estate she held in Wessex and the six in Mercia which had come to her as marriage gifts from her husband. She was doing this now, because she wanted no nagging administrative duties to interfere with her brother's return. Since the day of her marriage to the king of Mercia, Edward's behavior toward her had changed. The stiffness in his manner, the coldness that had met her on her return from Canterbury had evaporated. Now in his resumption of the long ago relationship they had shared there was warmth. For each half year Edward spent at Ceolworth, Elfwina basked in that warmth, affirming herself in the security of her brother's love.

So it was that in her efforts to get things done, she had neither seen him arrive, nor heard he was in the hall until, descending the stair with her clerk Leofgyth, a servant passed them, carrying up various packages and bags. He bowed low to her and continued on his way. She had gone several steps farther, when she suddenly stopped, turned about, and exclaimed, "Tonberht!"

He hurried back down to her and bowed again.

"Where is Prince Edward?" she asked, with a wide, wondering gaze.

"With the king, Your Majesty."

"And where is that?"

"By the south wall, Ma'am."

"Did you have an easy journey?"

"The roads are in excellent condition, Ma'am," he answered.

She smiled. "Thank you, Tonberht."

Tonberht bowed again and went on his way.

She dismissed Leofgyth and hurried to the bottom of the great staircase and turned toward the south wall, her eyes gleaming and her cheeks bright with color. The prince and the king were standing together with several workmen in the far corner of the hall.

"Edward!"

The prince turned, his whole expression changing to joy. He rushed forward a few steps, halted, and opened his arms.

Elfwina flung herself at his chest. "You're early! We didn't expect you this soon!" She hugged him fiercely and tried to look at him at the same time.

"The roads--"

"I know--Tonberht said--"

"Before I got a chance--?"

"Things are half-done--"

"What needs doing?"

"But here you are--here you are! How I've missed you!" She leaned back in his embrace.

"Here I am--here I am," he mocked delightedly. "Thrilmilci to Blotmonath, every year, reliable as a solstice." Then, glancing toward Aedred, he pulled back, disengaging himself with a slight frown, and Elfwina felt that faint, disturbing echo of a hundred withdrawals, that dreadful sinking of love away. She took his hand. He looked at their hands, tightened his fingers, and smiled at her, dispelling the echo.

Aedred came up from behind and put his arms around them both, beaming at them in turn. "Welcome home, Edward," he said warmly, and lay his forehead briefly against the prince's curly head.

Chapter Nineteen

[825] Ceolworth, Mercia. The horse reared. Fire exploded from its eyes; the flames whipped down the gashes in its cheeks, rolling in sparks over its beak-like nose to pool in the terrible nostrils. Its hanging jaw suddenly clanged shut, flapped open, cracked hard again, and then flopped back against the dull black hide of its throat.

Snapping at the crowd reeling away from the roaring bonfire, the horse charged. The crowd surged back toward the bonfire, dissolved before it, and reformed in a nervous circle around the horse. Flagging its tail, the horse pawed the ground and tossed its iron head threateningly at the nearer figures, most of whom were young women. They poised for flight, breathless and round-eyed, keyed to the creature's every move.

The horse's hide was mounted on a frame that surrounded the man inside and hung from his shoulders by leather straps. There was a narrow horizontal strip cut from the neck, which allowed a limited view. Running down inside the neck from the moveable jaw of the iron head was a leather cord. Pulling it snapped the jaw. When a lower string was pulled, the stiff, plumey tail swished back and forth.

Inside the horse the air was hot and smelled of rude tanning and sweat. Because of the heat, the man wore only a pair of thin trousers. A thick sweatband was wound around his forehead to hold back his streaming hair, but it had soaked through long ago, and the sweat rolled into his eyes. From time to time he would manage to work his hand up near his face and by shrinking his neck down into his shoulders wipe his eyes so he could see. In spite of his discomfort, he was swearing good-naturedly and laughing to himself. He was casually making choices about which girls he charged based on a formula comprising roundness of figure, manner of flight, and into whose arms the girl would fly, since he knew who was who in the host surrounding him.

While he was engaging in these antics, he was not only scanning the restless crowd of young people directly around him, but also the large group of older villagers on the other side of the bonfire and a third assembly, residents and guests who had sauntered down from the royal hall to drink ale and watch what was going on.

The horse pawed again. The girls poised, quivering. The young men behind them laughed and shouted taunts at the creature, their eyes shifting expectantly from the fearsome horse to the girls.

At the fringes of this assemblage and at an angle slightly to the rear of the horse was another grotesque. It was taller than the tallest man in the vicinity and represented the male and female principles conjoined. It was, however, a man. He had hanging from his shoulders a huge skirt over a withey basket. The skirt began just below his armpits and belled to a diameter of four feet. Its thick woolen folds swept the ground.

A green mantle draped his head, completely covering his hair. His beard was not concealed. It was jet black, and the charcoal which had been liberally applied to it had smudged the section of the frame rim just below it and also marked the front of his tunic. Several girls in the crowd also bore these smudges on their faces.

His left arm was covered to the knuckles with a delicately embroidered woman's sleeve, while his strong right arm was bare, except for a man's gold arm ring measuring his bicep. Wooden risers attached to his shoes added to his awesome height.

Like the horse, he was scanning the crowd. Focusing on a small boy dancing at the crowd's edge trying to see the horse, the grotesque let out a wild, falsetto shriek. The people immediately in front leaped away with loud cries, and then surged back to look as the grotesque rolled after the boy, flung up its skirt, and swallowed him screaming under the folds. They whirled away, swept half the circle; the skirt whipped up again, and the boy shot out with an ecstatic shriek and plunged into the crowd of elders.

The horse had taken this moment to dive at the nearest girl turning her head at the diversion. He cut her out from the group, brought his head down, and with a tender contact, closed his jaw over the nape of her neck. Her mantle pulled away, revealing corn-silk hair. She twisted around to look at him, her mouth a rosy O.

The bottom edges of the horse's hide were saturated with bird-lime, ashes, and honey. With a flip of the frame, he swished the edges of the hide over her gown. It left a dark and sticky trail. She huffed in mock indignation. He laughed, neighed victoriously, and then chased her squealing into the arms of a blond-haired boy. The boy grinned, squeezed her against his chest, and swung himself between her and the horse. The horse retreated.

Meanwhile, the grotesque had cornered a shrieking girl against a line of palings. With no place to go, she put her hands over her head and squatted like a hen. The skirt belled down over her. The grotesque bent his knees so his arms could hang comfortably over the skirt-frame, and looked down at her. She crouched, her face turned up to him, red with exertion and suppressed laughter.

"Ah, now," he said, "there's only one way out of here."

"And what is that?" she replied, sucking in the words.

"You have to put your arms around me."

She glanced swiftly about at the woven walls of the basket and back to his face. He straightened his legs and stood upright so she could also stand.

"Or then, you might like to stay in here all night."

She put her arms around him.

"Tighter than that," he said.

Her face pressed against his chest. She squeezed and giggled, a high, delightful trill that made him grin. He rotated his hips over her belly. "Now lift the latch," he told her throatily, and laughed when she pulled back.

He swiftly kissed her on the mouth, tilting his chin as he drew back, leaving a long smudge along her cheek. He lifted the skirt and spun away from her.

At the edge of the shifting crowd around the horse, there suddenly appeared a handsome youth dressed all in green. He wore green shoes, green-banded hose, green tunic, and a wide leafy hat made of elderberry twigs. The headdress was starred with tiny white flowers and hid his hair. Some green substance had drawn delicate tendrils at the corners of his mouth, sprouted around his eyes, and entwined with his dark eyebrows.

He was slender and moved with a graceful step as he looked about with bold, dark eyes. He strolled unnoticed to a tall pole freshly denuded of its branches except for a leafy knot of greenery at the top. Garlands of flowers lay twisted around its base. The ground around the pole was heavily trampled, the site of an earlier event.

That morning, the first day of Thrilmilci, the month when cows gave milk three times a day, the villagers had spiraled out from the pole in an intricate dance, stomping their feet as they wove in and out in an ancient pattern, swaying and stamping without breaking the links of their hands or the chain. The whole village participated down to the youngest child.

The king and queen and Prince Edward had come. They wore crowns of greenery and were all three clothed in purple and gold. Most of the nobles had accompanied them, and they had all joined in the dance, stamping as hard and as energetically as the villagers to wake up the spirits of spring. They had eaten cakes and drunk ale, and then returned to the hall for their own entertainments.

At this pole, which had been set deeply into the ground near that edge of the village bordered by the wood, the young man in green now took up a stance. He folded his arms, crossed his ankles, and, with his head tilted toward the horse and the crowd encircling it, rested his shoulder against the wood and waited. He did not wait long.

Running arm in arm from the corridor between the young crowd around the cavorting horse and those elder villagers stationed near the ale barrels, two girls came to a dead halt several feet from the figure lounging against the pole, and stared. They hunched briefly together, and then approached him boldly. He gave them a smile of exceptional sweetness, but did not move except for a slight inquiring twist of his head.

The bolder of the two girls was about thirteen and lovely. She had soft hazel eyes and straight brows which touched hazily across the bridge of her nose, giving her, in spite of her daring manner, an expression of supplication which would have been difficult for any man to resist. Her mouth was charmingly bowed. Her soft lips parted as she gazed at the young man. Even now, he did not move but remained leaning against the pole and smiling, his eyes touching both girls in a friendly, including manner.

"It *is* the Green Man!" the girl with the hazel eyes said.

"But a wild and foreign one," said the other girl. She had a long, narrow face and brilliant red hair. "Where are you coming from, then?"

The Green Man smiled, but said nothing. He saw that a crowd of girls, with two or three boys at their heels, were running over to see what was happening. They gathered close, trying to hear over the clamoring of the horse and the falsetto cries of the grotesque and the squeals of their victims. Above his gentle smile, the Green Man's eyes seemed to be gauging these gathering numbers around him and the force of the inquiry being put to him. He seemed to be considering possibilities.

"Tell us now," the first girl said, "you're not from Stafford, either." She said it as if she knew everyone in Stafford.

The Green Man shook his head and grinned so infectiously, everyone watching grinned, too.

"Tis secrecy, don't you think?" the red-haired girl said, with a bright chirp in her voice.

He nodded emphatically.

"He's got no tongue, that's for sure," the first girl added, with a darling smile.

The young man grimaced and stuck out his tongue. With crossed eyes, he gazed at it as if to prove it was still there. He laughed silently with the boys and girls.

"He be an elfin form," one of the boys said. "Watch yourself." The others laughed and made little warning noises.

The Green Man straightened abruptly, unfolded his arms, and nodded. Frozen by his sudden animation, the group stared. He made a low and graceful bow before the girl with the hazel eyes.

Swallowing a little laugh of pleasure and uneasiness, she looked vaguely at the faces around her. "Naow!" she said. "Naow, look at him!"

The Green Man straightened as gracefully as he had bent. Plucking a sprig from his headdress, he gallantly offered it to her. She looked at him in warily, and then reached for it, checking the movement as he slowly drew the sprig back toward him. Nobody moved. A little sweep of disappointment disturbed her features. The Green Man's hand remained in mid-air; his smile encouraged. Her hand came slowly forward and just as circumspectly his drew back. Her hand followed, causing her to step toward him. He beamed and nodded and brought the sprig all the way to his lips. Her beautiful eyes widened. From around the two figures there came a sough of approval. The youth held her gaze as he trembled the sprig against his lips.

"He wants a kiss for it," said one of the boys on a high note of excitement.

"Go on--go on!" the girls cried.

A flush darkened the girl's cheeks. She glanced all around.

The Green Man's lips closed from their broad grin, but a smile lingered at the viney corners. His eyes flicked beyond the girl in front of him to where the horse stood remarkably still, the awesome, bird-like head turned toward them. His eyes came back to the girl. Her head pecked forward in decision. The Green Man pulled the sprig away just in time. There was a sudden release of energy as the Green Man surrendered the sprig. The boys whooped and jumped in the air, while the girls cried, "A sprig! A sprig! Green Man, a kiss for a sprig!" and danced about him.

It was at this moment, the horse charged.

Those on the outside edge of the crowd heard the snapping jaw and the dangerous neighing and leaped away before they saw the peril. The girls screamed and ran. For an instant, the Green Man stood with his head back, laughing, and then it became clear to him just who the horse was charging. With a startled look, he sprang from the horse's path. The iron jaw cracked at his ear with a ferocity that dimmed his hearing and rang inside his skull. Before the horse could turn about, the Green Man sprinted across the ground, hurdled over a bench, and plunged into the wood.

Sensing the chase, the boys and girls scattering to leave the horse a clear charge at the Green Man, swarmed together again and would have followed the bulky figure as it lunged purposefully in the direction the Green Man had taken, but at that moment a horn wound; sticks beat in rhythm. The crowd trailing the horse and its quarry hesitated, and then swerved back to gather where the contests of strength were about to begin.

Moving slowly around the perimeter of the thickening crowd of elders, noblemen, and youths pushing for places at the site of the games, the grotesque disappeared along the footpath leading between the thatched huts to the wood beyond the village.

The Green Man was crouched behind a tree, trying to catch his breath and adjust his eyes to the darkness before going deeper into the wood. He looked toward the village. The light from the bonfire glowed into the woods, and he could see figures and movement beyond the trees. He closed his eyes and leaned his forehead against the rough tree trunk. But his eyelids flipped opened at the crackling of trodden sticks and the whipping of shrubbery. Not far off was the horse, moving with care. With a strangled laugh, the Green Man leaped up and ran along the dimly visible path. The horse snorted and clanged forward, gaining on the Green Man, who was laughing himself into near collapse.

"Kissing the maids!" roared the horse, hard on the Green Man, now. "We'll see--we'll see!"

The Green Man made a swift dodge to the right, hurled himself through some bushes, which tore the leafy hat from his head, ran a little way on, and then stopped and looked back, gasping with the need for air and silence. Some of the fastenings holding his hair had been pulled away, freeing thick black strands that fell to his waist. He peered out between the branches of an elderberry.

Not ten feet from the Green Man's hiding place, the horse stood in the path, swinging his head from side to side. He snorted and snuffled. The Green Man put his hands over his mouth and bent double but could not prevent laughter from escaping. The horse shuddered, flung himself in the air in wild upheaval. The iron head clanged against a rock with a bell-like stroke. The hide crumpled to the ground, and Aedred sprang forward after the lithe figure darting away ahead of him.

With a deep, triumphant laugh, he dropped a heavy hand on the green shoulder, growled, "No Quarter!" and bore him to the ground. He sprawled over the smaller figure and began kissing and berating him. "You can't get away--I have you now--stop struggling! I'll toss you green on the fire, and you can throw your kisses to the damn girls from the smoke!"

Elfwina flung her arms around his neck. "I surrender! I surrender!"

"Well, yes you do," he said. He kissed her more gently several times. "You have me up," he murmured huskily. He settled his hips. "I was up before I got into the wood." He kissed her again.

"How did you know it was me?"

"At first? That ring you wear around your neck."

"Unnh!" It was an exasperated little grunt.

"Let me in," he murmured.

"On the path--?" But she was responding. She giggled.

"Ah . . . ." He got to his feet, pulling her with him. They swayed and strained.

"You've nothing on under your tunic!" he said in surprise, then bowed forward to clutch her bare skin in both hands. "You *are* a wanton sprite!"

"And you're a randy stallion," she laughed.

"That's true enough." He gripped her hard around the waist and towed her off the path. He laid her down and fumbled with his trousers. She sighed.

A dark form blotted out the glowing leaves above their rocking bodies. A still and looming figure invaded, hurled out cold and ice and froze her passion to its center. And then it was gone. No movement, no sound, just there and then gone. She gasped.

Aedred, spent, kissed her eyes and sucked gently at her lips with his wet, sweet mouth. "You wanton Green Man, that was good! Was that Edward?"

"Yes, I think so."

Aedred's chuckle was low and fruity. "Well, he could have guessed when I went thundering after you."

"I don't think he realized."

"He'll get over the shock."

Elfwina, shocked, wondered.

Aedred swayed, pushed gently at her.

"Again," he said, and spreading his mouth over hers, became all hot and active.

The horse and the Green Man walked back into the village and parted their separate ways, the Green Man inconspicuously to the hall, the horse to a brief, ferocious caper through the crowd before trotting docilely to his stable.

The grotesque stayed on and got roaring drunk.

In this year the Danes devastated Sceapig. In this same year there was a strange glow in the sky for many nights. Then came the high priest of Woden from his seclusion at Wodnesweoh with warnings to King Aedred to prepare for war, for this was the portent of it.

Chapter Twenty

[828] The Wash, East Anglia. His responsibilities had driven him back inside his tiny dwelling, back among the bladders and bags, the shelves littered with jars and tiny vials, the table stacked with scrolls, all the clutter from months of disregard. A column of plates and ladles and other such utensils leaned awkwardly on a stool in the center of the room. A wooden bunk, barely wide enough to hold a man, hung from one wall. Bedding lay rumpled over a mattress ticked with successive insertions of tough grass. The room was warm, the air hung with dry, exotic odors.

The warmth came from a brazier thoughtfully set away from the spilling tinder of the bed. The man stirred the coals in the brazier and set a pot of seawater to boil. With each addition he made to the pot from various containers along the shelves, he spoke uncommon words. He ladled the final liquid into a wide bowl. After studying it, he paced to the door and stood looking out on the silent marshland. To the east the tidal marsh gave way to a beach cobbled with smooth black stones. The ebb tide foamed along the shingle.

The man turned back into the room. Pouring the liquid off the dregs into a bowl, he drank the bitter potion. He wiped his beard and stared into the empty bowl. With a sigh, he added the bowl to the careless pile on the stool, walked over to the only window in the hut, and took up a ragged fur from the wide sill. Draping the mantle over his shoulders, he left the hut and strolled out onto the marshland along a track of fragrant sea grass.

When he reached the shingle, he turned north and walked slowly along, listening to the ebb tide sizzling through the stones as it drew away the sand. He moved with a supple stride, his body flowing forward in an easy motion. He gazed now at the pebbles gliding under his feet, now at the marsh where his thatched hut grew out of the reeds, now at the birds wheeling and piping above the frothy stones.

His stride lengthened. He floated, sinking and rising on his fluid legs, his arms stroking the air. His head turned, his body following in a slow spiraling curve. He balanced on the wind.

"What do you want of me now?" he asked the sky.

The wind eddied and sighed around him, shifting through his hair, pressing softly at the folds of his mantle, touching him everywhere, like a lover.

When he returned to his hut, he packed some items into a leather sack with some belongings, and lifted out a stout pole from behind the door. He secured the sack to one end with a small hook, and then leaned the pole against the outer wall of the dwelling. He went back inside to douse the embers of his fire. After a last glance around, he pulled the door closed. He raised his arms and chanted a protective web around the dwelling and its dangerous contents. Then he took up his pole and set out.

[828] Ceolworth, Mercia. From beyond the Northumbrian border and to the southeast where it crossed Fosse Way and continued on to London and beyond, Cyninges Street lay across Mercia like a rod, as straight and as uncompromising as the Romans who built it centuries before. Along one section of this royal highway lay the gently rolling countryside, with its sere grasses and melancholy thickets, its ancient bare oaks.

The man stood where a road intersected with the Street. Leading eastward through the scattered oak trees, it disappeared over the swelling ground. In the distance rose a dark and secretive forest. Between the near hill and the dark background of trees, smoke lifted in thin columns. A heavy sky finally obscured the sun, and a cold wind moved fitfully over the paving, bringing with it a flurry of snow.

The man stood motionless gazing toward the north. Then he pulled his fur cloak more closely about him, lifted his carrying pole to his shoulder, and adjusted it so the leather sack was balanced well.

The wind gusted suddenly, blowing his dark hair around his face and catching some of it in his grey-streaked beard. His free hand came up to drag the hair away. He had wrapped strips of cloth around his palms against the cold, and an end had flapped loose, but he ignored it, his attention fixed on the forest, which was slowly blending into the growing darkness and falling snow.

He started down the road. As the snow began a steady fall, he stopped briefly to draw the edge of his cloak up over his head and trudged on. When he had gone about a mile and had reached the top of a hillock, he paused for a moment to get his bearings.

The snow had been falling in thick flakes and had now accumulated on the bare trees and the ground. Just beyond his vantage point lay a valley. Where he stood the fields began, stretching to a shallow river that meandered along the valley's eastern rim. Through the snowfall he could make out a small village across the stretch of water. The road continued down the slope to a stone and timber bridge spanning the river. Beyond the bridge approach the road forked, one fork continuing to the village, the other toward a rise of ground where a great hall stood, the forest looming behind it. To the south of this hall was a vast, snow covered meadow bordered by a wood.

The smoke he had noticed was from the village supper fires. Wisps of it curled up from the thatched huts and the few larger wooden dwellings. His glance moved from the village to the hall again. It was a long, massive structure narrow in relation to its base. A second story projected from the main building, an imposing later addition to its original dimensions.

The hall was constructed of stone and immense timbers and was enclosed on grounds covering over half a hide. A high timbered wall secured the entire area. Within this enclosure a number of smaller buildings clustered around the hall. A wide ditch encircled the entire exterior wall of the complex. Where the road sloped upward to the hall a double gate and a gate tower overhung it at the enclosure wall. From the upper story of the hall, light shone warmly from a few narrow windows. The man smiled faintly, a grim movement of his lips. He did not continue down the road, but stood beside it, waiting.

The snow had covered his shoes when he heard the sound of creaking leather and of hooves padding quietly through the snow. Sifting darkly through the oak trees, a group of mounted warriors rode silently toward him. As they gained the road and passed close by where he stood, one of the horsemen looked dully into his eyes, and then with a growing alertness. When the horseman had gone a few paces farther, he suddenly raised his gloved hand. The warriors stopped.

"Come forth!" he called, in a weary voice but one accustomed to being obeyed.

The man at the edge of the road walked slowly forward. Two of the warriors came up on either side of him. He stopped. For a moment the horseman gazed at him with dark, tired eyes. With no hostility or challenge in his voice he asked, "What is your name? Where are you coming from?"

"I am Ceadda," the man answered. "I have no particular home. Most recently, I lived in that part of the fens ruled by the Danes."

A horseman with fair hair leaned forward. "You're Ceadda the Magician."

"That is how I am known, Prince Edward," Ceadda answered politely, watching him closely.

Aedred turned to the prince. "You know this man, Edward?"

"I've never met him, but he was a friend of my father's. He's no enemy, whatever his reason for living in East Anglia."

"You are seeking enemies, Sire?" Ceadda asked the king.

"I hardly have to seek them," Aedred answered. "They announce themselves as regularly as the seasons. And occasionally out of season, as you can see. I am Aedred, son of Cenwulf. I am sovereign of this kingdom. And this, as you have noted, is Edward, son of

Brihtric."

"Your Majesty," Ceadda murmured, and bowed his head to the king. To Edward, he said, "You bear a strong resemblance to your father, Sire. Although it has been a good many years since I've seen him. How is His Majesty, your father?"

"In good health, God be praised."

Ceadda smiled. "That is the Christian god?"

"Yes, I am the Christian. My sister, Queen Elfwina, follows Woden."

Ceadda sighed. The tips of his fingers where they were exposed in the unwinding rags teased his beard. He could feel the weight of fatigue in the men around him.

Aedred shifted in his saddle. "What's your destination, Ceadda? It's still a way to the village, and the snow's getting deep. It will be hard going afoot."

"To Stafford, Sire. But, with the storm coming, I thought possibly a warm fire at Ceolworth."

"We can accommodate you in that." Aedred glanced behind him and lifted his hand. A rider moved up, a huge man with a scarred face. "Mount behind Grundl."

They followed the road, clattered over the bridge, and took the right fork up the slope to the gates. The watch called out a challenge from the tower, and the big warrior sharing his horse with Ceadda bellowed an answer. The iron-sheathed gates began to swing open at the center. A man came quickly forward as they entered. He wore a sword over his fur outer garments, marking him as a thegn, but the fur was shabby and the tears unmended. He had obviously been sheltering in the gatehouse. He lowered his head respectfully.

Aedred was swinging his horse in a quarter turn to avoid blocking the entrance of the men coming up behind him and was paying scant attention to the thegn. When he was clear, he looked back at the man. "Yes? What is it?"

"Your Majesty, Queen Elwina is in the far guesthouse. May it please you; she left word for you to join her immediately on your arrival."

Aedred sighed. As he looked down at the thegn, he was holding the rein tight against the saddle bow, curbing his horse's tendency to swing toward the stables. The gear of the animals around him fretted and chimed as their riders held them in check, awaiting the outcome and as impatient as the horses to find food and comfort.

"Do you know if Eorl Leodwald has returned?"

"Yes, Sire. He arrived shortly after Her Majesty returned. He should still be in the stable close."

"Her Majesty left the enclosure?"

"Yes, Sire."

"Where did she go?"

"Sire, I do not know that. I was not one of those chosen to accompany Her Majesty."

Aedred heard the petulance. *You sulky bastard,* he thought as he stared down at him.

Prince Edward drew his horse alongside Aedred and frowned at the thegn. The man shifted his weight uncomfortably as he looked around at the disgruntled semi-circle of riders formed behind the king.

Aedred turned to them. "Go on--settle your horses and warm yourselves. Eorl Heafwine," he said curtly. "Escort Ceadda to the hall."

As Aedred turned away, Heafwine inclined his head, murmured, "My pleasure, Sire." His eyes slid away from the king's back to where Ceadda sat behind the warrior. He nodded to the magician.

The horsemen began heading along the enclosure wall toward the lighted stables in the distance. They had only gone a few paces when Aedred called out, "Grundl!"

The big warrior stopped his horse at once and began negotiating a turn through the riders, but the king shook his head. "Follow us later." The warrior lifted his hand in acknowledgement.

Aedred glanced at the prince, and Edward reined his horse about and fell in beside him. They moved off in the opposite direction from the warriors, heading obliquely from the gate to pass behind the northern end of the great hall.

"Did he say Elfwina had been out of the enclosure?"

"That's what he said."

"For Christ's sake! Did he say where?"

"No."

Edward burrowed his chin into his fur collar and stared ahead into the white gloom.

Is there going to be more of this to put up with? wondered Aedred.

He was tired and already irritated by a four day hunt with no trace of the outlaws rumored to be in the area. Suffering the tension of the lightning quarrels running in the air between Edward and Elfwina for the past several weeks was something he was becoming less prepared to do. He had no idea what was sparking their bad humor. Proximity? Edward had stayed longer than he usually did. Was it too long? If so, it was something new. They never before found each others' company tiresome. He wanted to wring both their necks. Out of long experience he said nothing to them. He had learned early not to interfere in that close relationship, that love. But the closeness was not in evidence lately, and the quarreling was getting on his nerves.

Should he try mediation? A separate approach, one to each? Easy, smooth--*just quit it?* Please.

"Shit!" Edward said.

Aedred clamped his jaws together.

They pressed their reluctant mounts into a trot, passing through a scattered grouping of thatched wooden buildings; all guest houses built at different times and from the instructions of kings long dead, yet built to last and kept in good repair.

A wide, snow covered field lay beyond these dwellings and beyond that a clump of trees where two more buildings humped in blurry outlines in the dim light. There were horses in the shed attached to the larger house and more tied outside. Light spilled cheerfully onto the snow from the windows of the larger house, and smoke billowed from the hole in the thatched roof. A short distance behind the two structures the high enclosure wall loomed like the rim of the world.

"The gates were to remain closed," Edward growled. "That was made very clear before we left. What was she up to? Where the hell would she go?"

"Edward, I don't know."

The prince turned his head to look at him. Aedred's face remained in profile. His peaked cap was pulled low so the dark fur merged with his brows, disguising a possible frown. Plumes from his nose were white in the frosty air. His mouth was closed, the lips firm, but a growth of beard smudged his cheeks, obscuring any tightening of the jaw muscles. Edward, however, was not trying to read his expression; he was too agitated to notice signs.

"The whole damn countryside's under alarm, raiders on the loose, sitting all around Ceolworth, for all we know. What was her idea?"

"Give it a minute, Edward, we're almost there."

Edward sank his chin back into the furs, not subdued by Aedred's curt reply and priming his anxiety into anger.

As they pulled their horses up outside the dwelling, the low door was pushed open and light streamed out in a smoky billow. They could hear the crackling of a fire being fed with pitch. The smell of burning boughs sharpened the cold air.

A Mercian warrior emerged and seized the horses' reins as Aedred and the prince dismounted. They had not touched ground for several hours, and Aedred hesitated as his legs jellied, and then hardened. "Leave the horses here," he told the warrior, and then led Edward into the building.

The guest house had one large room and an alcove with a large bed. In the main living area, a fire roared in the fireplace. The walls were richly hung with rugs. There was a heavy table with ornate legs and figures incised on the single, beautifully grained slab that formed the top. In one corner of the room was an intricately carved chest. Chairs and benches were placed around the room. In one of these chairs a man sat with his arms tied behind him. Five Mercian warriors guarded the prisoner. Another turned back to tend the fire, after bowing to the king.

The queen was standing near the wall to the left of the doorway. She was dressed in a fur-lined cuirass and leathern stockings wrapped with fur from her ankles to her hips and bound with leather thongs. She held a man's fur cap in her hand. Strands of her glossy black hair had come loose from their bindings and were tangled about her face. Her clothes and hair still glistened with melting snow.

"This is an odd welcome, Madam," Aedred said, glancing at the man in the chair.

"Not a welcome, a gift--from the Hwicce."

"Oh?"

Edward stood to one side, staring hard at his sister.

"The Hwicce captured this man and two others. Baldan and his sons came onto a force in winter setl below Tewkesbury." She glanced at Edward, sensing his anger.

"A force?"

She looked back at her husband. "A considerable force, Aedred. Some two thousand, they estimate."

In complete amazement, he swung around to look at the man in the chair.

The prisoner glared back at him through a half-shut eye. His face was bloody from a gash running from his forehead to the corner of his mouth. He had a heavy mane of blond hair stiffened with dried blood and a full beard rusty with the seepage from his wound. His thick winter tunic was ripped down one side, revealing filthy undergarments shredded at the tear. The bandings on his right leg were gone and the woolen trouser sagged limply, leaking blood and melting snow into a cut running across the leather upper of his shoe.

"He's a Dane!" Edward said, as astonished as Aedred. He approached the chair and stood looking at him in disbelief, his hands on his scabbard belt.

The Mercian warrior called Ricsige, preparing to question the prisoner, moved uneasily, flung out his hand in warning, and then grabbed for the prisoner. He was not quick enough. The man in the chair jerked back his head and then forward again, as he shot out a gob of bloody mucus at the prince, aiming for his face. Edward made a lurching quarter-turn, and it landed on his shoulder instead. Ricsige clutched at the Dane's head, caught one ear instead. Edward had swung back with his heavy boot off the ground, slamming it into the prisoner's chest with a loud crack, hurling the man backwards. The chair screeched along the plank floor before it reared up and over against the fireplace, toppling sideways. The Dane's head crashed into the hot grate. He screamed.

Edward swung completely around. He ripped off his mantle and flung it away from him. It kited toward the rafters, fluttered down into a corner. He turned toward Elfwina with a look of outrage.

Aedred was watching his warriors rescue the Dane. He made no comment to Edward, and the prince, still heaving with passion, knew the lack of comment was disapproval. At that moment, he didn't care.

"You said you had two more prisoners," Aedred said to the queen. "Has Ricsige gotten anything from them?"

"No," she answered, looking away from her brother. "He wanted this one first, since he appears to be their leader. He believes they'll be more forthcoming if this one's questioned first."

The man had been hauled out of the fire, and the flames were being roughly beaten out of his hair and tunic. He sat with his head lowered, his breath whistling thickly in and out of his open mouth.

"He's a jarl?"

"I don't think so. His weapons didn't indicate it. And he was never addressed as jarl."

"The others are next door?"

"Yes."

"No one was to leave the enclosure," Edward began angrily, but Aedred moved to close them from the rest of the room, saying, "Drop it, Edward. I want to know why the hell two thousand Danes are sitting inside my borders."

Edward kept his eyes on the man in the chair. He said nothing further.

"They came up the Severn," Elfwina answered. "They raided the countryside, and then moored their ships below Tewkesbury. Baldan says Tewkesbury has made a peace with them. Some silver, evidently, and the promise to keep them supplied with food and fuel through the winter. The village has seen no destruction. According to Baldan, the force has quieted down, and he expects them to stay put for the rest of the winter."

She nodded toward the prisoner. "These men wounded one of Baldan's sons rather frightfully. He didn't want to move him. That is why he sent a messenger to the hall asking for a man of rank to meet him and accept the prisoners. There was no man of rank to send."

Aedred knew she was addressing this explanation to Edward. Annoyance coiled inside him like a snake. He stood very still, controlling it as he was keeping in hand his outrage at this incursion into his kingdom.

There was a flurry of activity at the fireplace. The Dane had slumped forward, bleeding now from his nose and mouth. Air was not getting through. Ricsige was trying to keep the prisoner's head upright. "We'll lay him on the floor," he said to the men beside him.

He looked at Aedred. "I think he may have something broken inside him." He glanced at the prince.

Aedred leaned over his shoulder. "Did you get anything out of him?"

He stepped aside as two of the men dragged the Dane out of the chair and laid him on the floor. Ricsige squatted beside the prisoner, and then rocked back on his heel and looked up at Aedred. "No, Sire. I didn't expect to out of this one. I was going to work on the others through him."

"The son of a bitch is not going to live long enough," Edward said.

Aedred swung toward the warriors standing around him. "Bring those others in here. Hurry up--*run!*"

Chapter Twenty-One

[828] Ceolworth, Mercia. The men leaped away. One of them threw the door back, smacking it against the wall, and they ran out, leaving it open.

The man on the floor gaped and moved his mouth, but no air moved down his throat. Ricsige came to his feet. Turning his head away from the Dane, Aedred looked hard at the prince. A furious sound rolled in Edward's throat. Walking off a few paces, he swung around and stood glaring at the man on the floor.

Elfwina remained near the wall, her face expressionless. She did not look at her brother.

"Come *on*!" Aedred said between his teeth, his eyes on the door.

There were angry shouts from outside, a stumbling rush of footsteps, a yell of pain and fury. Ricsige sprinted to the door and grabbed the first prisoner staggering in, wrenched him forward by the hair, and swung him in a savage arc that lifted the man's foot above the floor. He yanked the prisoner's head back then thrust it forward again, screaming into his ear in Danish.

Ricsige flung the prisoner to his knees, half-sprawling across him as he shoved the Dane's face down toward the dying man. He continued to shout in Danish, a violent, guttural repetition. The prisoner's head was twisted, his torso bowed with the force of Ricsige's knee in his spine.

All at once there was a cessation of movement. The man on the floor lay still; the warriors did not move; the man in Ricsige's grasp froze. Then the prisoner cried out, *"Haddr!"* strained forward to look at the dying man, the veins in his neck ballooning. Then he screamed, a cry that came from his bowels and stopped the breath of everyone in the room.

He rose straight up, his neck stretched like a goose, rammed himself toward the ceiling, dragging Ricsige with him, his mouth still wide with his scream, lips flat against his teeth, the scream still coming, his eyes bulging and sightless. He lunged, and then reared back, loosening Ricsige's hold at his throat. The Mercian clawed at his back, trying to keep from being thrown, but the Dane charged at the wall, dropping his shoulder and slamming Ricsige into it with his full weight. Ricsige's breath went out in a shrill howl, and he slid to the floor, immobilized.

The Mercian warriors rushed at the Dane, but he spilled them aside, bellowing and snorting like an animal, turning to strike anything within his reach. His bonds had broken. He thrashed forward. Leaping away, Elfwina ran along the wall, slammed into the open door, staggered back, and then grabbed its edge and swung behind its protection. Two Mercians jumped on the Dane's back, slowing him, but he rolled and heaved, turning again and dragging them along the floor.

Prince Edward collided with a third Mercian the Dane had spun toward him. The prince flung out his hand to the wall to catch himself. Diverted from the queen, the Dane came running at Edward and rammed his elbow up under his chin, snapping the prince's head back and cracking it against the window sill. Edward went down in a heap, blood pouring out of his mouth.

The Dane shook off the men on his back, flailing his arms wide as he wheeled around bellowing and spraying froth. He hit Aedred in the chest as the king came up from a crouching leap at his belly, sending Aedred sprawling into the heavy table to slide down on one knee before his hand hooked the carved leg, and he caught himself.

The warriors went crazy. They fell on the Dane in a howling mass, their sheer weight bearing him back from the king. They toppled with him, beating at him in a frenzy, fear and anger unleashed and unstoppable. A warrior bit into the Dane's arm, the only part exposed to him, and with his jaws locked and spewing blood and saliva from the sides of his mouth, he went down with another warrior sprawled over him.

The other prisoner had been hurled away and was crouched in the fireplace corner, his hands tied behind him, staring in horror as the Mercians mauled over the crumpled form beneath them.

Aedred clawed himself upright, yelling, "Don't kill him--don't kill him!" But he knew it was impossible to stop them; they had gone as berserk as the Dane. He picked up a chair and swung it down against the men boiling over the prisoner. *"Don't kill him!"* He cracked the chair down again. "You stupid bastards!" The legs broke and shot out splinters.

A force exploded through the door and slammed down on the pile. One of the Mercians went bowling across the floor followed quickly by another. Aedred staggered back out of the way. He threw aside the broken chair and stood gasping and trying to work saliva back into the desert of his mouth. He thought he had never been so glad to see Grundl in his life.

He stumbled away to where Edward lay on his side, unconscious, Elfwina crouched above him. She had his head against the soft fur padding on her thigh and was swabbing inside his mouth with a piece of cloth.

"He was choking. He bit his tongue when that creature attacked him." She glanced over her shoulder, saw Grundl making order out of chaos, and briefly closed her eyes.

Aedred squatted beside her. "He wasn't convulsing, was he?"

"No!" she said sharply. Anxiety, he knew, and forgave it. She forced the swab between Edward's teeth with fierce concentration.

Aedred curved his hand around the back of Edward's skull, feeling the stickiness. He leaned over, saw the curls were saturated and dripping blood down Elfwina's fur legging. The scalp was cut. "He's had worse wounds," he told her.

"Can we get him over there on the bed?"

"Just a minute."

He stood up and looked around him. *What a disaster!* He thought. *One Dane nearly wipes out eight of us. What are we going to do with two thousand?*

The berserker was dead and not in pretty shape. The Mercians who had accomplished it were in a rumpled group looking at Aedred, shamefaced and uneasy. Grundl was standing next to Ricsige, his big hand gripping the man's arm to steady him as he wavered, his face pallid. But Ricsige had recovered enough to be showing anger at the warriors who had killed the second of the prisoners he was supposed to interrogate.

The prisoner remaining alive was still huddled against the fireplace, his knees drawn up to his chest, his head lolled forward, his eyes closed.

"Are you doing all right?" Aedred asked Ricsige.

The Mercian straightened and drew away from Grundl with a stricken look. "Your Majesty, I beg your forgiveness--"

"You were doing the task put to you. The thing needs to be finished now with some benefit to us. Take that one across the way. We'll be using this place awhile. Prince Edward needs attention. Can you manage with two men?"

"Yes, Sire. Thank you. Two is all I need." He glanced at the Dane cowering against the stones. "Or one--to hold him up for me."

"Take two and leave the others here." He turned to Grundl. "Let's get Prince Edward on the bed."

Ricsige and the two men hoisted the inert Dane to his feet and hauled him off. Aedred directed a man to lift Edward's feet, while Grundl took his head. They carefully moved him to the bed. Elfwina took over immediately, and Aedred retreated.

Taking Grundl aside, he quietly told him, "Take these bodies all the way out to the Street and hang them from the oak at the junction of the road. When Ricsige has finished, hang that one, too. When their bones have been plucked clean, have them scattered. And see no bone touches fire. There'll be no pyre for them."

"I'll see it done, Your Majesty."

"Whatever Ricsige gets from the Dane, I want to hear it

immediately. I'll be at the hall. And I want those men reprimanded."

"Yes, Sire."

Aedred looked directly into his eyes. "You were a welcome sight," he told him.

"Sire." Grundl bowed his head. He straightened; the king had turned back to the bed. Grundl signaled the waiting men to lift the bodies. His eyes rested on the queen, and then he followed the cortege into the snowy night, closing the door softly behind him.

"Wina," Aedred began, concerned about her.

"It's cold in here. Can you build up the fire?"

He took his hand from the nape of her neck where hairs pulled loose from the coil webbed her white skin. He wanted to put his lips on the hair that was as fine and soft as down. But he lifted his hand away and walked over to the stack of oak limbs next to the hearth, laid several on the stone and, pulling his scabbard out of the way, knelt to prod the coals around in the grate until he had uncovered a satisfactory bed. He threw in some kindling, and when that was blazing, he tossed on several branches. Moving back from the heat, he watched the fire's progress for a moment before going back to Elfwina.

Edward was still unconscious. A basin of red water was marring the fine wood of the small table next to the bed. Elfwina had washed Edward's face and beard, placed a thick pad against the back of his head, and wound a blue cloth around his forehead to hold it. She fussily tucked the furs around him.

"Has he stirred at all?"

"No."

"I'll send someone down."

"Tonberht and Edyth. And some more bedding."

"You're staying here with him?"

"Of course."

Of course. One of them had to attend Edward. Always. Depression crept toward him. *What the hell is the matter with you?* he asked himself. *I'm not thinking right. I'm too angry, too tired to deal with this.*

"I need to hear the whole of this adventure, Elfwina. The eorls need to hear it."

"Before Ricsige is finished?"

He thought about it. "Ricsige may not get anything of value out of him for hours, if at all. On the other hand, you were there. Questions may be asked only you can answer."

"I've told you everything that happened. There is nothing to add. Baldan sent a messenger. I responded. With admirable control, he gave the prisoners over to me instead of killing them. You should have seen his boy. *I* felt like killing them. We brought the prisoners back. You came before Ricsige began his questioning." She was impatient. "You can see--I'm just reiterating. The Danes are at Tewkesbury, and so forth. That's all I can tell you. I can't add a thing to it. Perhaps Ricsige could give you a different perspective, but the basic information will be the same. I think the prisoner will talk. You saw him. He seemed compliant enough."

He could see she would not easily leave Edward. The little flame of resentment sparked and twisted. He looked at Edward lying senseless within the storm center.

"His color is good," he said, giving himself time before he responded to what she had said. "His breathing is easy."

He bent past her to pull back the furs and lay his hand flat on Edward's chest. "Heart beat's strong." He took his hand away, and Elfwina immediately settled the furs around him again. "He has the constitution of an ox, Elfwina. He'll come around. All the signs are good."

"I think we should send for Lady Pen."

Aedred was gazing at the prince. The signs are good. He'd seen enough wounds to know when a man was dying of them. *Damn you, Edward, you couldn't hold your temper. It's your own damn fault you're lying there unconscious and Elfwina has to tend to you as if you were a child. Has to? Hardly. All right, you're jealous,* he thought, unhappy with himself. *Why? There lies the best friend you have in the world--the brother of your heart! And you are no physician.* Still, he did not think Edward's head wound was all that serious.

"Before we do that," he replied, "let's give him a chance to come around on his own. You know your brother as well as I do. How pleased would he be to wake up and find the hall in a fret because he was cold-cocked by a mad Dane outnumbered eight to one?"

"Tiw be praised!" Elfwina burst out, and ignored Aedred's frown. "Naturally, the odds of eight Danes to one Edward would have been better."

"Much better," he said, holding on with both hands to his equanimity. "As Edward himself might tell you if he were able, and if you dared to ask. Peace, Wina. I know you're worried."

And he did know that. He felt himself relax. "Head wounds are the worst of the lot. You're right to be concerned. But he'll survive. All he needs is rest. He was dead on his feet before it happened. When he wakes up he'll have nothing more than a sore tongue and a headache."

She was not altogether placated. She lifted the furs again, tucked them up to Edward's chin, and anchored them under his shoulders. Like the carcass of a freshly killed stag his body responded with a warm suppleness drained of volition. She stilled her hands, resting them on his chest as she peered into his face. Then she straightened and clasped her fingers roughly together and stood motionless, her eyes still on him.

"The quarrels hardly seem worth it now, do they?" Aedred said softly, the thought forming as the words left his mouth, opportunistically, with a lack of kindness he did not in any way regret.

She jerked her head around, the ferocious points of her eyes beaming out the boundary warning. This time, he did not honor it. His gaze was sympathetic but unyielding. He waited for her to speak, and she finally did, looking away from him and down at Edward.

"I don't know why we have been quarreling."

He felt relief. He tentatively explored the possibilities. "He's stayed longer than usual. You've had more time to get on each other's nerves."

He watched self-recrimination grow in her expression. Guilt pricked all around his heart. *Leave it,* he thought. *It's enough to plant the seed. Take your little victory and be satisfied.*

"That's not it," she replied, and Aedred felt the hairs rise slowly on his neck.

She looked up at him.

"What is it, then?"

When she didn't answer, he said, "Then I don't know the reason either. But the quarreling would be better ended now, don't you agree?"

"Yes," she finally answered. She was not looking at him, and the answer seemed distracted. But, he hoped, not meaningless.

"Well." He was prepared to leave her now. "I will send Tonberht and Edyth. When they have settled in, you will come up to the hall and speak with the eorls." He was not suggesting anymore. His voice had changed when he said it, and she had heard. "When that's finished, you can come back and tend him."

She accepted without comment.

He leaned forward and because he had four days' stubble on his face he only brushed her cheek gently with his. It was a touch of affection and restraint, for if he had acted on his own needs, his ardor would have been unacceptable here, under these conditions, in front of that unconscious brother. Knowing his wife and loving her deeply, he left her staring down at the prince, and went on about his business.

Chapter Twenty-Two

[829] Ceolworth, Mercia. Ceadda dismounted in the stable yard with the rest of the group. A number of horsemen already there began to head toward the hall. The magician stood out of the way, watching as a number of warriors standing before the open doors to the stable carried on a tense discussion. Unsaddled horses were being led around the group, heat steaming from their bodies as they crossed into the light. The aroma from piles of dung melting into the muddy snow drifted pungently on the cold air.

The chief of the group of warriors gestured and stamped as he spoke. Planted stolidly nearby, Grundl listened with his arms folded across his massive chest. Then he broke away, remounted his horse, and rode back toward the north end of the hall.

Eorl Heafwine also left the group and came over to where Ceadda quietly waited. In his husky voice, he said, "Shall we go inside?"

They tramped across the snowy expanse of the enclosure to the great hall. A short flight of stone steps led up to an arched entryway. Heafwine opened the heavy wooden door, and stood back for the magician. They proceeded down a long stone passage way, their shadows flicking back and forth under the burning torches set into the walls.

The eorl glanced over at him. As Ceadda met his gaze, the handsome warrior's face softened and smoothed. His eyes glowed with a golden light. Within three steps the man walking beside Ceadda had morphed into a beautiful woman, and the magician understood the rejection he had witnessed earlier and the distance other men kept from the eorl: Heafwine was elf-touched; a particularly malicious and complex spell which Ceadda recognized. He knew that whatever agency had worked the spell Heafwine was innocent of its origins; it was evil directed at someone else through the eorl; an enchantment of an old order, in place for many years, perhaps from Heafwine's birth, the instrumentality spinning it no longer abroad, or simply having forgotten about it once satisfaction had been exacted from the real target of its malice. That sometimes happened. It was unfortunate for the one spellbound, for that kind of enchantment was almost impossible to break. Only a sorcerer or sorceress, one with greater powers than his, could break it.

"How long have you lived in the fen?" Heafwine asked, as his features dissolved and reformed into the masculine.

Ceadda's answer bounced off the walls. "Not long. I was in Alcluith these past ten years."

They were coming out of the bitter cold of the passage into a large area of light and warmth. Fresh straw lay thick on the floor. At intervals down the long hall, three enormous brass and leather lamps, bristling with candles, hung out of the smoke that obscured the ceiling. Huge timbers, blackened by centuries of smoke, supported the brooding upper structure of the hall. A great staircase richly carved with the figures of tormented animals led up to the chambers.

Around the walls under the lower part of the ceiling formed by the second story, torches leaned into the haze. At a hearth in the center of the east wall, two servants were throwing a log onto a blazing fire. Even with that warmth, a constant river of cold air flowed knee-high along the floor. In front of the great hearth, tables and benches were being pulled into place to make one long surface, and people were beginning to move in that direction. Ceadda smiled, comfortable in this heathen hall.

Food was arriving at the benches, carried in by a stream of servants. Women were coming into the room to meet the warriors, some of whom already stood near their places. Their loud mingling of greetings and questions rang in the smoky air, while their offspring ran up and down the hall and in and out of the parade of servants that dodged each rush with supple, practiced movements. It was all familiar to the magician.

The king arrived, assured the company the hall was safe, and then they all sat down to a noisy, tumultuous meal. At a point during the long supper, the king signaled for the magician to come up and take a seat across from him.

"Are you thawed out, Ceadda?" he asked, opening a conversation which then meandered pleasantly through a broad range of topics to end at a discussion of the styles of certain jugglers with whom they were both familiar.

"They're all independent as hell, you know," said the king. "Fulco was at London awhile. What an artist! Those silver balls--they were made by--" and he mentioned the name of a silversmith of the Continent whose work was done only for the court of the king of the Western Franks. "The process is quite complex."

For Ceadda and all those sitting close enough to hear, the king described in detail a method using heat, glass-blowing, and delicate welding to produce the perfectly balanced silver spheres. "The balls are very light for their size." He made a twirling motion with the tips of his fingers.

Making an assessment of the man in front of him, Ceadda knew by the manner in which the king had guided the topics that an assessment was being made of him. And he was impressed by his skill at this and amazed that Aedred was only twenty-five.

The king was looking at him from under his brows. "I wanted

Fulco to stay in my hall, and I am embarrassed to tell you I offered him almost as much as I gave in marriage gifts to my wife. Independent bastard. He went on to Rheims. I nearly wept."

The magician had heard of the brilliance of Aedred's London court--with or without the great juggler Fulco. Now he had an understanding of how the king had been able to gather around him the people who created that reputation. Looking about this friendly hall, he saw a trader from Persia, another from the Continent; a priest of Woden he recognized, a wise and learned man; a scholar from Wessex; a well-known minstrel, all perfectly at home in this cordial atmosphere.

Knowing the true measure of a king, Ceadda observed how his subjects reacted to King Aedred. In this hall children were not intimidated by him. They spoke to him, and he answered readily. He knew all their names. Women approached him; he responded graciously, yet with a restraint not carried over to his interactions with men; these subjects he touched or wound his arm around as the mood and his affectionate nature dictated.

It was a long meal. After two hours with no sign of an end to it, the fatigue of his journey bowed Ceadda's head. To his embarrassment, King Aedred caught him at it. With good humor, the king summoned a servant to guide the magician to his bed. As Ceadda was being led up the stairway, he glanced over the heavily carved rail to see Aedred rise and leave the hall with his eorls. The magician continued up the stairs.

Chapter Twenty-Three

[828] Ceolworth, Mercia. Elfwina paced about, avoiding the gory section of the floor as she measured out the room. She set chairs upright. One had a splintered leg. She carried the chair to the fireplace, found it too large to throw in whole, and put it to one side for the servants to break down into firewood. She placed more oak limbs on the fire. Each time she performed one of these tasks she made a circuit of the room, ending at the bed to check her brother and, finding no change, to veer off again. She was thinking of what Aedred had said and how senseless it was for her to quarrel with Edward. She didn't know why they were quarreling; she had been honest about that.

The lamps lighted earlier had now gone out one by one until only the fire illuminated the room. The alcove was to one side of the fireplace wall, so the bed lay in shadow. She did not know where the lamp oil was kept.

For some moments now Edward had been gradually coming to consciousness. He was totally disoriented and had no idea where he was. He could smell wood smoke. The glow from the fire and the dancing shadows crept under his eyelids. He felt warm, which seemed important, and the snap of the fire was pleasant. But his head and tongue hurt. He attempted to roll his tongue and was agonized. He lay very still, monitoring his body. Why was he in pain? He didn't know. He listened for intimations but heard only the crackling fire.

I'm in bed, he thought, pleased he could figure that out. *Not my bed. Whose then?*

He considered, drifted a little, his consciousness still tentative.

A graceful form glided toward him.

"Who . . . ?" His mouth was burdened with a tongue too large.

Elfwina heard his voice and came swiftly to him. "Edward." She touched his face.

"Where is this place?" his tongue managed.

"The far guest house."

"Are we alone?" He was thinking, *Father! Father will find out--no . . .wait. That's not right. I don't have to be afraid of that. Then what? Aedred!* "Where is Aedred?"

"Where's Aedred . . . ?" She was concerned. His confusion disturbed her; he should not be like this. "Aedred is at the hall. He was here, but he's gone now. Don't you remember? The Dane . . . ?"

His expression told her no. "Edward," she said, speaking calmly, "can you remember going with Aedred to hunt the raiders?"

It was slowly coming back. The hunt. The cold. Elfwina haring off into the countryside and away from the protection of the hall. The Danish prisoners. He remembered.

"Let me up," he said. She was not preventing him, but he had to throw out words that would push her away.

"You can't be steady enough, yet," she cried, certain he was not himself.

"I'm all right." He shoved back the furs and raised himself, and then hung in a blackening roar, panting, as it slowly diminished.

Elfwina was standing in front of him, her hands gripping his shoulders. "Please don't rush it."

"For God's sake, Elf! Let me be!"

She released him and stepped back one pace, two. He swung his feet down to the floor and sat on the edge of the bed, propped heavily on his arms. He looked around. His head was hurting like hell, but he could manage it. His tongue was the problem. He realized his head was bandaged. He pulled off the cloth and threw it on the floor. Pushing his fingers into his hair, he felt the break in the skin and the bump.

"Did everyone go back to the hall?" he asked, and then looked toward the door. Footsteps crunched toward them through the snow.

Elfwina answered, "All except Ricsige and two warriors. They're next door with the last prisoner. Are you sure you should be sitting up like this?"

The door opened. Edyth and two servants carrying bedding crowded in followed by Tonberht. His keen face remained carefully composed, until Edward said, "Oh, Christ!" at which moment Tonberht, with disdain, took over.

Seeing Elfwina's relaxed features and the brilliance in her eyes, Aedred felt relief. Relieved, too, to see Edward on his feet, his hair and beard freshly scrubbed, his garments changed.

He watched the prince carefully taking a seat beside Heafwine. Edward stretched his legs out slowly, one at a time, as if his hips were arthritic. He mauled his greetings to the others, and then slumped in his chair.

Aedred was slumping, too. They all were. Four nights in the cold, sleeping in rain and snow, none of them rested, this night already entering the second quarter, and the Danes were threatening.

Whatever Ricsige can pull from the prisoner, he thought wearily, *it won't need action in the next few hours. We all need sleep. Aldhune's half dead. Even Leodwald has run down.*

Leodwald had reseated himself next to Eorl Guthuf and was twisted toward him, his energy frozen: Leodwald, for once, was still.

I'll let them ask a few questions and then send them all to bed.

Elfwina had wrapped herself in a long magenta mantle that covered her hair and reached to her feet. The color flushed over her lips and cheeks. Suddenly, intensely, he needed to touch her. He pressed his hand on the white fingers. She turned her head, her gaze moving into him, and his throat went thick. He looked away, out at the men waiting now for him to start things going.

"Madam," he said, turning back to her, "everyone has been informed of the threat at our border and of your meeting with the Hwicce, so there's no need for that to be restated. We don't intend a lengthy discussion, but there are a few questions . . . ."

The eorls and Prince Edward were grouped in a loose semicircle in front of the king and queen. Five or six thegns stood against the wall behind them. Eorl Aldhune was staring blearily at the king. There was a silence. Then, as Aedred would have been willing to wager with anyone, Leodwald took the initiative. He snapped forward and stood to bow to Elfwina.

"Thank you for allowing these questions, Ma'am. My problem is in reconciling a force of two thousand Danes moving about in winter. Was Baldan absolutely certain of the figures? Did he observe it himself, or was it a report from his men?"

"He did observe the force, Eorl Leodwald," her soft voice answered. "Two of his sons and their men confirmed it. He assured me he had taken great care to get an accurate count. His experience as a battle chief is well-known. I am satisfied his information is correct."

"Thank you, Ma'am," he murmured, and sat back down.

Her eyes moved calmly over the faces of the men. "Eorl Heafwine?"

"Thank you, Your Majesty. Was--?"

The question was never completed because Grundl came into the room and charged the sudden silence. His feet pressed over the rug, the leather of his shoes making a stern crackle. They all felt the vibration of his footsteps as he approached the king.

"Let's hear it, Grundl."

"Sire, the three Danes were from a detachment of three hundred sent out at various times over the past two weeks to rejoin in Northumbria. A combined attack with the Northumbrians led by King Ædda is to be mounted in the spring."

A collective gasp was followed by silence, and then all glances swung from the big warrior back to Aedred. He was staring at Grundl, reading those stoic features, reading the light glowing in the deeps of the thegn's eyes.

"Let me live that long," Aedred said to him, answering that glow. "Go on--what's the rest?"

"They were taking advantage of the earlier mild weather, Sire. All members of the detachment reached Northumbria but the one group. They were caught by the storm and spied out by Baldan. All but the three were killed by the Hwicce. The Dane killed by Prince Edward carried a verbal message--" When Edward swore quietly, Grundl glanced at him, and then went on, "The prisoner thought the message was important, but he didn't know the content. He said there were rumors Lindsey was expected to aid King Ædda. That was all of it, Your Majesty."

Aedred silently grappled with his anger. But Leodwald, looking like he was going to fly off the bench, cried, "That treacherous bastard!"

Grundl turned his head toward him as a bull might an intruding shoat, only assessing.

"The filthy sod! Bringing in the Danes!" Leodwald's voice cracked with violence. For a few seconds he focused the outrage flashing through the room. The intensity flared, then eased; no man there could equal it, except Aedred who was containing his anger.

"Where did they decide this?" Leodwald's brother Aldhune asked the company. "And when? How could Ædda make an agreement like this, and we not get wind of it?"

Guthuf said, "We only have this one man's word for it, and he wasn't even a leader. All he knew was hearsay--"

Leodwald shouted, "It wasn't hearsay that he was on his way to Northumbria, Guthuf--"

"Maybe! Maybe!" Guthuf flashed back. "We need that confirmed. What's the gain? If you're going to ask questions. What's the gain for Ædda?"

"How can we know what gain?" Heafwine said, leaning forward. "What sensible man can understand Ædda? He deposed his own father and then had him murdered. Patricide! How we can ask what gain for a man like that?"

He spoke intensely, in a marvelous contralto which suited his dark, androgynous beauty. His velvet eyes swung to the king. "Shouldn't we be asking what it means in terms of the numbers we'll be fighting?"

Trying to quench his own hot responses, Aedred resented Heafwine appealing to him. He had never found the Eorl of Onlinden compatible and his changes were thoroughly unsettling. However, the eorl's question to him was reasonable and one he would have readily accepted from any other man in the room. Aedred remonstrated against that unyielding faction in his heart: *cool yourself. The man deserves to be treated with respect.*

But his silence had forced Heafwine to speak again, a

reassessment that diluted his question, because the king, by his lack of expression of approval or disapproval, lessened its importance.

Heafwine sank back in his chair, diminished. Unreasonably, Aedred was irritated with him for back-tracking.

Aldhune had been looking at the prince with curiosity. "How did you happen to kill that Dane, anyway, Prince Edward?"

Edward, who had all this time been sitting slumped in his chair, raised his head so his eyes could met the eorl's over his clasped hands. "He spat on me," he said, his battered tongue rolling over the words.

The men in the room turned to look at him.

Elfwina's cool voice drew their attention to her. "East Anglia may have a role in this, Sire."

"And the Norse in Ireland," Edward added quietly, on the pause of her breath and in a rhythm so like her speech pattern he might have been completing the thought from her skull. Without looking at her, or speaking directly to her, Edward illustrated the intimacy of their bond.

Aedred nodded, not saying anything himself, because he wanted the others to take it up.

"It takes a better pack of dogs than the lot combined to do us any damage," Leodwald said hotly. "Osward thinks he's going to march his fleas in here again. How many times has he tried that? Ædda is a raving lunatic if he thinks he can pull this off. His grandfather tried it, and King Wulfhere drove him back. His father tried it, and King Cenwulf stopped him. The man's a fool. There's only one way to deal with a dangerous fool: I say kill the son of a bitch, now. We'll take on the Danes in the spring."

On Leodwald's heat, the mood in the room blew into conviction. There was no disagreement with Leodwald's headlong boast. The same belief he uttered was now swelling every rib cage in the room.

He knows I won't do that, Aedred thought. *He's too emotional, a frenzied engine as usual. Come on--come forth!* he willed, looking at the faces of his eorls. *Temper this into something constructive.*

It was old Guthuf who crystallized Leodwald's emotion into useful substance. "I'd like to know if these three hundred sent north were the only ones."

The question had been addressed to Grundl. "It was possible there were others, Sire. The prisoner could confirm only the three hundred."

Grundl was standing with his hands clasped at the small of his back, his feet comfortably apart, a solid stance, his posture erect, but not strained. His whole demeanor encouraged confidence in his assessment. He could have been a firmly rooted tree subject only to the wind at its crown.

Aedred looked at him with approval. *Good man! You can't be drawn into useless emotion.*

Grundl continued, "Total count, Eorl Guthuf, including those on the Severn, is twenty-three hundred, with an unknown additional number. It did not seem the number exceeded that of the earlier group of three hundred."

"How can you be sure?" Heafwine asked, venturing to speak again now that the question he had first posed to the king had resurfaced. "I don't see how the prisoner would not know the full numbers of the force he was with."

"The man responded to Ricsige's questioning, Sire. His answers clearly indicated a force of that size. His ship was one of the last to moor. They had been joined by several ships. Ten, he thought, from East Anglia. He never knew exactly how many."

"Maybe he needs to be questioned again on that point."

"He's dead, Sire."

"Oh."

"You were on to that East Anglia connection, Prince Edward," Aldhune said.

It had been Elfwina's suggestion but the two statements, one from her, the other from Edward seemed like one, and Edward was given attribution.

Aedred listened to the discussions. The comments had taken on a circular flow. Beside him, Elfwina stirred restlessly. He stood up, and everyone rose. "Well, this is enough for now. Go to your beds and sleep well. We'll meet here mid-afternoon tomorrow and make some decisions."

They all filed out of his chambers.

Blessed Gods, I'm tired, he thought, and glanced toward his bedchamber. He raised his head and turned as he heard Merefin approaching to help him disrobe. He tilted his head back, straightening every bone from his skull to his heels. The small of his back ached. His handthegn stood patiently.

In a sudden decision, Aedred said, "No, I'm staying in the queen's chambers tonight."

Chapter Twenty-Four

[828] Ceolworth, Mercia. Elfwina had finally gone to sleep after a restless effort filled with battle strategies and a resolve to stop quarreling with her brother. She was awakened by Edyth, standing by her bed with a candle in her hand, the light gilding the ample contours of her body. A rug had been hastily thrown around her shoulders.

"His Majesty is on his way over," she said, her teeth chattering as she bent over Elfwina.

Elfwina pulled herself up in the bed and smiled. "Is he, now? Light the lamp, please, and the fire. And then go back to bed before you freeze!"

When Aedred entered her chambers, he found Elfwina propped up in the bed with a fur cover tucked around her chin and her hair surrounding her like a black mist. He wanted to plunge into it, swim his way to her neck and nuzzle in the soft downiness there, feel the hairs slide against his lips, do what he had wanted to do--how many hours ago? Only now he thought he was too tired.

"Do you mind my coming here, now? I won't be much good for anything. Maybe a warm log to wrap yourself around."

"Get in then, and let me wrap myself around you."

He gave her a tired smile and began pulling off his clothes. He tugged his kirtle off over his head and dropped it on a bench. He said carefully, not looking at her, "You know that was a dangerous undertaking."

"Nothing happened to me," she replied, the quiet tone a warning. "I think you know the information was critical."

He pulled off his thick woolen undershirt and dropped it on a chair beside the fireplace. "I do know the value of your information. Can I say I value you more without provoking you?"

"May I say that every time you put on your mail and your sword I worry about you? But I would not offend your honor or question your judgment by forbidding you to go."

"I wouldn't be so reckless as to forbid you anything."

"I've always believed you to be a wise man."

"Wise, eh? Wise enough to leave the subject."

He sat down to pull off his shoes and unwind the bands around his trouser legs, all of which he left in a pile on the floor. His movements were slow, weary. "I'm still trying to understand Ædda's motives, Wina."

"What difference would his motives make?" When he turned to her, she could see how haggard he looked.

"You're right; what difference does it make? He's set the course now. But it still baffles me. He has benefited from the peace as much as we have. His kingdom prospers. Like Guthuf asked--what's the gain?"

"You could ask him."

"I just may do that."

He carried her basin and water jug to the hearth and knelt down in front of the fire. He began sponging his face so liberally the front locks of his hair were drenched. "Uh! This is murderously cold!"

"You don't have to do that now. Bathe in the morning, or let me call someone to heat water for you--"

"No, don't bother. I'm almost finished. We've been wallowing on the wet ground for a week. I smell like a boar. I'm too ripe even for myself." He sponged water into his armpit in a cascade that ran down his side. "Cursory," he muttered, "I should be dunked."

She laughed. "You look dunked. You *are* going to dry off, aren't you?"

Water stood deep on the hearth and steamed at the edges of the fire. He looked down at his feet, grunted, paddled thoughtfully, and then raising his foot high, brought it down with a smack that splashed water halfway across the room.

"Aedred!" The queen giggled into the edge of the fur tucked around her chin. "Pretty little Getle will come in at daybreak, and you'll be frozen there with a leg up like the village dog."

"It won't be my leg she'll be looking at." He resumed his liberal sponging.

"Oh, la!"

He grunted impatiently. "We'll need to move on this latest information. I'm going to convene the witan. We'll let the council consider the question of Ædda's perfidy."

"Ah, yes. At the same time you can tell them taxes will be raised. It will save sending out all those messengers to inform the provinces."

"Taxes--?"

"When will you call the witan?"

"Couriers go out in the morning."

"And the schedule?"

"Mid-Solmonath."

"A winter council!"

"The situation calls for it, wouldn't you say?" He had finished his bath and was vigorously drying himself.

"Of course. We'll pray they can all make it."

"Yes. Now let me in. My feet are freezing to the floor!" He burrowed under the fur skins and quilts, ignoring her little yelp as he wrapped himself briefly around her warm body and then flattened out on his back with a deep, contented groan. "Don't let anyone near me until noon tomorrow."

"Oh, I won't!"

After a while, he said, "Wina? I'm lying here half-dead and can't even lift my arm, but he's as hard as iron. Come hold him for me."

"Umm--standing to the challenge."

He reached up and drew her head to his and kissed her long and deeply, his hands moving her head slowly as he probed her mouth with his tongue.

"I thought you were a log," she said breathlessly.

He rose up. "One part of me is."

When Elfwina awoke late in the day, the snow was falling in small beads, thickly, steadily. Aedred had gone. She had not been aware of him leaving.

Toward evening, when Edward found his sister was finally ready to receive visitors, he came to her chambers and informed her of what happened, that Aedred left with a troop of men and supplies for the holdings of Eorl Gyrth, thirty miles to the west at Wenlock. Raiders had struck there. Most of the eorl's stock had been herded off and a number of his buildings burned. His hall had been sacked, and three members of his household had been wounded, including his eldest son.

"I was *given orders* to stay put. No point in arguing with him." Edward's annoyance was clear.

He hunched into his chair and stared at his shoes. He frowned, slouched back, lifted his left foot and laid the ankle across his knee. He rubbed at the shoe, smoothing at a rough patch, until the nap lay in one direction. Elfwina watched him silently. "Aedred plans to return by Friday." He shot a glance at her.

"Don't be annoyed."

"I'm not annoyed."

"Yes, you are."

He snorted, and sunk deeper into his chair.

In a white dressing robe, Elfwina sat in a chair by the fire with her hands in her lap, listening quietly to her brother grumble at being left behind. Her long braid lay coiled into her lap, her fingertips buried in the thick interlacing. Her dark eyes held on Edward, absorbing everything.

"Your tongue seems mended," she said. "How is your head?"

"My head is fine." His gaze hardened, slipped away, and then snapped back to her face. "There's all this concern about my head. I know he thought I wouldn't be able to keep up the pace. That's ridiculous. I'm all right. But no use trying to argue with him; when he's mad, he's single-minded. Nothing can change his course."

"I agree with him," she said firmly. "He was right to leave you here. It has only been a few hours since you were injured. Recovery isn't certain in that length of time."

"Oh, come on." He snorted again.

"No? Remember Botwine? The next day after he was hit on the head, he went to lift a wheel and fell dead of blood on the brain."

"Christ!" He looked squarely at her. "I am perfectly sound."

She dropped the subject.

Neither of them said anything for a while. Then Edward took a preparatory breath. She looked up at him. "I was just thinking about Gyrth's oldest son. He's a lot like the old man must have been in his younger days. A good fellow." He grinned widely. "Wild as a boar." He abruptly quit smiling, not wanting to encourage her to ask questions. "If he dies. . . . ." He shook his head. "He's the old man's favorite."

Elfwina had read his smile and knew women were its origin. Her stomach tightened. Her fingers worked through the braid. She said, "Aedred was wise to go himself."

Edward cocked his head at her.

"Concern must be visible. Gyrth is our most important defense against the Welsh."

"Are we going to be serious?"

"One of the most important. In any case, Aedred depends on his eorls. How else can a kingdom remain strong? When he acts in their defense; he's strengthening their loyalty."

He waved his hand, giving her the point. "You were equivocating just now when you said 'Welsh.' You meant Gryffn."

"I am certainly not as confident about Gryffn as you and Aedred."

At first Edward was not going to reply, thinking it a waste of time. But he couldn't let it pass. "I don't understand what you've got against Gryffn. In all the years since his agreement with Cenwulf he has never given one sign of hostility--unlike Ædda, who's always trying to stir things up at the border, like this latest treachery. And Gryffn's never refused to fight a common enemy, has he?"

Elfwina gazed silently at him.

"What is it you have against the man?"

"Oh, you'd discount it. It's something instinctive. If I had fur, it would rise up all over me when he's around. He's treacherous. I feel it in my skin." She looked at him with annoyance. "I really don't know what's so funny."

"You--with fur. There's a picture." He waggled his fingers at her. "A cat jumping back from a shadow, all doubled in size with its tail straight up like a plume. Oh, yes, that's you." He laughed at her sour expression. "But look--be rational. He's done nothing to verify your instincts. And for how many years now?"

"Twelve. Nevertheless, the feeling persists. However my fur stands." She smiled when he laughed again.

"Maybe you need to reexamine these suspicions."

She waved her hands, giving the subject over. Edward studied her, and then sat back. He smiled. "All right. To hell with this. Let it rest for now."

"Yes, to hell with it. I'm weary of the whole thing. Let's agree not to speak about Northumbrians, Danes, or the Welsh for the rest of this evening."

"Fine with me. I give them far too much of my time as it is.'

"Were you going to have supper here with me, or were you going to eat downstairs?"

"When I have the choice, with you--always."

She rose and came to his chair. She hesitated, and then touched his hair. He glanced up at her, his face expressionless.

"Good," she said. "I wanted you to stay." She called Edyth in to arrange for their meal.

They talked pleasantly throughout their supper and on into the evening. Outside the high narrow windows, the snow silently increased on the wide sill.

"There must be two feet lying by now," she said.

"That's likely. Don't be worried about Aedred getting back."

"I'm not worried. He'll manage as long as the raiders have cleared out. You don't think they were still at Wenlock, do you?"

"No. And Aedred took a force large enough to meet any challenge they could put up. They were probably long gone with their booty."

Without help, Edward had emptied a pitcher of wine. Elfwina was sipping at her wine the level of which had not dropped much since he had first filled her cup. He did not notice. He lifted his own cup. "Here's to the king," he said. "A toast from his loyal subject, Edward." He drank. "I'm always willing to play his subject when I get to stay warm and comfortable and he's out there freezing his royal ass."

"Were you really so annoyed he didn't let you go with him?"

"Maybe. But the evening's borne me out, hasn't it? I'm fine. Just like I told him. You haven't seen me collapse, have you?"

"You're scarcely on your feet, now."

"Yes, but not because I was struck on the head."

Halfway through the second wine pitcher Edward threw down some fur skins in front of the fire he had built up to a roaring blaze and, with hand gestures and wobbly nods of his head, insisted that she sit down. Once he saw her settled with her back against a big chair and a wine cup in her hand, he very carefully positioned himself in front of her, his legs stretched out toward the flames. Just as carefully he lay back and propped his head against her hip. He heard her intake of breath; she said nothing.

"There!" he said, and quickly emptied his wine cup. He refilled it, spilling some down the side of the cup. He brushed the drops into the fur.

Elfwina was testing her reaction to this closeness he had arranged. It was, she thought, uncomfortable, this closeness. It was seldom they were alone like this. They were never alone like this. The discomfort, she believed, came from the rarity.

She set her cup on the floor beside her, held it loosely. With her other hand, she touched his hair. Then, very lightly, she combed her fingers through his curls. She had done that when she was a little girl and he was a little boy. She thought she may have done that often, the sensation was so familiar. She watched dreamily as, gleaming and golden from the firelight, his curls sprang back into shape and she knew this was what she remembered. She rarely touched him and this was suddenly wonderful, this easiness with him.

"Have you been keeping track, Edward? Do you realize how long you've stayed this time?"

"Mmm . . . eight months. Why? Is it time for me to leave?"

"Of course not. You could stay here forever, you know that. I was wondering why Father hasn't sent for you. He usually begins his stream of messages by the fourth month."

"Don't know. Don't care."

She gripped his hair and felt him shrug. She rested her head back and mused her fingers through his curls again. He took her hand and let it fall against his chest. He placed his hand over it. She could feel his steady heartbeat and thought *This is the way it should be. No quarreling, no unhappiness. How good it is to have him here like this.*

He lifted his head and looked around. "Where's that girl with the wine?"

"You sent her away."

"Did I? Whatever for?"

"You were being considerate, I think. It *is* late. Here, drink the rest of mine." She handed him the cup. He took it and drank deeply.

"Why do you think Father hasn't sent for you?"

He tilted his head back to see her face. "Am I straining the hospitality at Ceolworth?"

She gave his beard a sharp pull.

"Ouch! It's the truth. Didn't you just point it out?"

"You could build a Ceolworth of your own."

"There you go--desperate to get rid of me. My oath, Elfwina, you sound like Father! I'm not home a month when he's singing his marriage themes and bringing in lady minstrels for accompaniment." Wine had loosened him, and his annoyance rang unimpeded in his tone. "You heard about Lady Aebbe?"

"You escaped that."

"Fourteen, for God's sake! What's he thinking of? My God!"

"Her mother is--"

"I know, I know--sister to the king of the Franks. I heard that enough." His voice dropped and flattened. "What the hell would I have in common with a fourteen-year-old girl? I'm not that eager for heirs."

"But Father is."

"I know." His chin sank on his chest. "It all comes down to it, doesn't it? It will happen."

She leaned over him. "What are you complaining about? Look how long you've held out. Far longer than I was allowed. But then, why should you hurry to make up your mind about one single one when the process of selection is so engaging?"

There was that adder's tongue that had been jabbing at him for weeks sprung again from its concealment and then retracted. Irritated, he decided to pretend ignorance of the strike. But he bit her finger hard, and when she sucked in her breath, he quickly kissed the pale skin and his teeth marks. His irritation receded. He laughed against her knuckles.

Her serious face appeared above him. "Why don't you want to marry?"

His head bent forward, and he stared into the fire. He regretted that he had drunk so much wine. All at once, he wanted to speak truths. *Lord God, what are the truths?*

"It will undoubtedly happen one day."

His eyes appeared closed to Elfwina. But the lashes flickered slightly, and she saw he was staring at the hearth. "Why are you so reluctant?"

Drawn as tightly as a bowstring the question sprang out, an assault. He heard the tension and thought he should know what it meant, but he couldn't pull up the meaning. "I haven't found anyone I wanted to be shackled to for the rest of my life."

It was a curious, dully-spoken answer. Strangely thrilled by it, she pressed him. "What are you going to do now that Father is becoming insistent? You can't weasel out as deftly as you did with Lady Aebbe, and you know what will happen if you don't make a choice for yourself--Father will make it for you"

"I know that."

"So, then?"

"Why all these questions?"

Why indeed? She really didn't know, she just had to ask them. He was drunk, and the barriers he often imposed were now composed of different stuff. She could dare at this moment. "I want to know, Edward. You were quick enough to find me a husband."

"What is this? Do you want me to marry? Whom do you want me to marry? Name her--I'll propose tonight and make everyone happy. And what is your complaint about my choice for you?"

She was not pleased with the way things were going now. His tone was belligerent, partly because of the wine, partly because she had pushed too far. But she found it beyond herself to stop. "Provide the name yourself. How would I know all you've sampled?"

"You couldn't, could you?" His heart was beating furiously. "But that's my business. A prospect doesn't have to come from that lot. Just about any woman you could name would consider becoming queen of Wessex a fair bargain."

"Bring on the parade!"

He sat up, laughing. "Leave off, Elfwina, please. This is too pleasant a night to ruin by quarreling. What do you say? Truce?" He held out his hand.

After a brief hesitation, she slid her fingers into his.

Chapter Twenty-Five

[828] Ceolworth, Mercia. It was a relief to now carry on a conversation and discard the debris of their lightning quarrel, to smooth away the gouges, restore the love. She spoke of Wessex, of Exeter, and of the memories they shared, the good memories of when they were young in the Devon reaches of their childhood.

He listened to her, at ease now, drifting on the sound of her soft voice, his eyes on the dancing flames.

"Remember the combes around Exeter? The way the fields looked in summer? The woods, too. Those beautiful little glades where the flowers twisted through the grasses? The little streams that flowed under bluebell and fern . . . Do you remember, Edward . . .?"

A memory emerged from the flames, the danger in it unheeded in her soft narration.

Shadow and light, coolness and warmth, a pattern on their faces . . . her birthday. An escape. A ride without retinue through the wood.

". . . the filly you gave me . . . ."

Sleek, spirited, raven black.

I was trying to match the color of your hair.

Across the warm, early summer yardlands and into the cool woods.

"Your horse was snow-white. The trappings were gold. You looked so brave on your snow-white horse . . . ."

Across the rolling warm green fields and into the cool woods, through the dappled grasses and flickering sunlight patterns.

Over your raven hair.

"Over your snow-white horse."

Into the cool glade and by the stream where the horses drank with their noses just touching the water. Where the sky was blue through fathoms of leaves and each vein on each leaf was clearly outlined in golden-green and the horses trailed their reins in the tall, flowered grasses and grazed the blossoms.

"The blossoms were so fragrant."

Where light and shadow brushed the bending grasses.

Your hair was so black against the green grass.

Where the shadows were cool and deep under fathoms of leaves and the scent of crushed grass heavy and thick. It filled her nostrils and throat like smoke. She was suffocating with distress and fear and love as he kissed her with a shaking mouth. The silken hairs of his mustache brushed her upper lip, intimately, unbelievably. She opened her eyes. His eyes were closed, the lashes curved into the hollows above his cheeks. His lids tightened and the lashes fluttered, but his eyes did not open.

With a sigh, he was carefully lying down on her, swaying as he pressed down, a stranger breathing hoarsely and whispering assurances she didn't understand. His frightened eyes now opened above her face, crystal blue. His lips were swollen and wet, sliding down over all her mouth. Something was sweeping through her. Love--love for him, vast overpowering love for him . . . .

Edward felt her shudder. He lifted his head very slowly from her hip and got up from the fur skins, twisting as he rose unsteadily, looking down at her dark head as she came to her feet and stood stiffly, not looking at him, but off to one side, her face white and blank. He felt himself collapsing inward.

She abruptly walked away from him.

He followed her. "Elfwina, listen. Please."

She shook her head violently and walked ahead of him about the room. They went from table to chair, all around the furniture, covering the space two, three times. Edward kept a distance, confused, stumbling drunkenly after her, propelled by his fear.

He came to a stop and she did, too, turning to him, but still not looking at him. He realized he was quite drunk. As long as he was moving, he could manage. But to remain still without toppling he had to lock his knees and even then he swayed dangerously. His brain was sluggish, as if it had swallowed a fat rat. It rolled and squeezed and tried to digest, but the mass remained, formless and heavy.

I feel so sad, he thought, staring at his sister. *I'm dying of sadness.*

He said, "Adolescents sometimes do . . . improper things when they love someone--"

"You didn't love me, not like I loved you."

"What?"

They stared at each other. Her cheeks were flushed a dark maroon. Redness flared and diminished in a rapid pulse down the center of her throat, leaving white pillars at either side of her neck.

Acid and wine boiled in Edward's stomach and backed up into his throat. He swallowed hard. "I did love you."

"No, you didn't. You *made* love to me, and then you *abandoned* me. I wanted to die."

He did not know what he could say. He was trying to maintain his balance. His hand groped for support. Meeting the surface of a table, his fingers rested there. "That's absurd. I didn't abandon you."

"No? After the beech woods, you hated me. You couldn't even look at me. What a *cruelty* that was."

"I didn't hate you. I was . . . confused."

"I see. And in your confusion, you sent me away to Canterbury for *two years*."

"I didn't send you to Canterbury! That was Father! Don't you remember anything right?"

"Oh, I remember. Did you protest? No. You didn't even say goodbye to me. It was all right with you. "

"No, it wasn't! But what could I say? I did *not* want you to go. I never wanted you to go to Kent. God, when you left I cried for two days!"

"I never *stopped* crying, waiting to hear from you. And there was nothing--not one word of concern or love. What an agony! Why did you put me through that?"

"Lord," he cried, "It was a hundred years ago!

"And that makes it all right? What you did?"

"No, of course not. It doesn't make it right. But it was a long time ago." He dug one hand into his hair. "We were just children--"

"*I* was a child."

"I wanted to send you messages, but Father might have intercepted them. That wouldn't have been good for either of us."

"You could have found some way to get a message to me, if you'd wanted to. All I wanted was some small word of comfort. Anything to tell me you might have suffered, too."

"I did suffer."

"Why didn't you come for me?"

"How could I? For Christ's sake, Elfwina, I was only sixteen! Father would have--I don't know what he would have done." But he had been deadly afraid. The fear welled in him now.

"You could have taken us somewhere."

"Are you saying we should have run away?" He had thought of it, but had been powerless to act on it. "Where would we have gone? How would we have lived? This is nonsense you're talking. Can't you see that? Plain nonsense."

"It was nonsense to you all along, wasn't it? I was just an irritation you wanted as far away as possible. Packing me off to Kent was the perfect solution."

"You keep saying that. I had nothing to do with it! You've mixed everything up."

"You *liar!* You are a liar in everything you say!"

"Wait a minute—wait a minute!" he said. "Calling me names won't get us anywhere." He was thinking they could speak about this rationally. "Jesus, Elf, I didn't want you to go. But what do you think I could I have said to Father that he wouldn't have seen right through? And—God!—what would have happened then? Think of that."

"Oh, stop it! You were relieved when I left. You were able to go right on with your life as if I had never existed, and you are a *liar* if you deny it."

"I do deny it! God look down on me--I deny it! I deny it! I loved you--"

"Let me speak! For once, listen! I will tell you what it was like for me."

He put up his hands, not able to stand their proximity a moment longer. He stepped back unsteadily. "I'll listen. I always listen to you. Go on; say what you have to say."

He swayed over to one of the windows, drawn by the peaceful dark. Small, pebble-like snowflakes swirled and struck the pane. He avoided looking at her reflection emblazoned on the wavy glass. Instead, he stared at the snow piling up on the deep ledge and wondered where the doves had gone. *To the dovecote,* he thought. *Where else would they go in a storm like this? Can I leave this room? Walk out so I won't have to listen to what is coming?* He didn't think he could. He didn't think his legs would bear him to the door. *I have to listen. Truths are going to be spoken. I wanted to hear those truths. But not now. Not tonight. I am not ready. I am not ready for all this hatred. Has she hated me like this all along? Under the love?*

He heard her moving about, her soft footfalls on rug and bare floor as she paced, and he was suddenly afraid she would touch him.

Don't come near me! Yes, come near me. Touch me. Put your arms around me. Stop buffeting me. Forgive me.

He felt very cold. He began to shake. Tremors ran up his shins, shuddering his kneecaps and rolling to his thighs. His buttocks quivered and jerked uncontrollably. Nausea swelled his stomach and made it taut and threatening. He was powerless to stop her from speaking.

Her voice was low, very hard, with none of the emotion earlier riding there and without the softness that had always been implicit love.

"I know it doesn't matter to you, but I got through all those months in Kent only by believing you were going to come for me. You were going to ride up one day and take me off against all protests. As you say, how unrealistic. Oh, I know all the ramifications, the impossibility of it. But you didn't even try. You just . . . left me to Wyrd."

"I didn't leave you to fate," he murmured to her reflection. "There was nothing I could do."

"When they finally let me go back to Exeter--"

She was standing very still, remembering how joyously she had entered the walls of town. She had scarcely been able to breathe as she had run up the steps and through the wide doors of the royal hall. She had been weak with joy seeing him standing with their father. He had been courteous, distant, and she had understood the reason. But later, when the excitement of her return had moderated and she had come down into the great room to seek him out, he had treated her in an off-handed way, getting reluctantly up from a game he was playing with his friends, looking back to see the way the bones fell even as she was approaching with smiles and tears. His friends, having stood at her approach, laughed as he muttered an oath because the bones had rolled against him. Giving her an obvious dismissal, he had gone immediately back to his game.

She was suddenly so struck by that remembered humiliation it was a moment before she could speak. Edward waited throughout this silence, knowing her thoughts and helpless to justify his behavior because he had done that; he had deliberately done that. He had done it because of fear, fear of his father and what he might glean from any contact between brother and sister, fear of seeing her again and uncovering two years of denial. What he had found was the same blind yearning, the same impossibilities. But he couldn't explain that to her, even now.

"Everything that had gone on with us you put out of your mind as if it had never happened," she said. "We never spoke of it or anything else except for my marriage arrangements. You were finally able to put an end to that long, long irritation."

She was sobbing out the words, but there were no tears.

"That is not true," he said.

"Why did you treat me that way? What had I done to make you treat me like that? I loved you, trusted you, and you cast me away when only one kind word from you--"

"To what purpose?"

"To let me know--" Her arguments had become circular, and the composition of his phrase struck down her reply, its cold logic suddenly and profoundly revealing, an echo of that long ago indifference. Her heart drove the blood into her throat. She felt suffocated by old misery that was astonishingly fresh.

"Let you know what?" He could hardly breathe.

She walked about, and then halted with her back to him. "Like you said, it was a hundred years ago. Who cares what happened then? Not you."

"Of course I care."

"It doesn't matter. I don't want to talk about this, anymore. Please go. Now."

Edward turned back to the window. He knocked his forehead against the pane. He felt like putting his head through it. The wine had blurred his tongue. He couldn't bring his thoughts into order. There were things he could have said, proofs he could have offered, if only he could have formed the words. No words came. Air rushed through his nostrils. He dropped his hands to his sides. "All right. I'll go, if that's what you want."

"Yes. Go." The restraint in her voice made it shake. He did not fool himself that it was a sign of capitulation. He went blindly from the room.

For a long time, Elfwina paced about her chambers, weeping. She refused Edyth entrance, shoving her back into her room. She spent the night pacing and sobbing, while Edyth, loyal and perplexed, sat stiffly on the edge of her bed, listening to the queen and feeling anger at Prince Edward.

Panicked, they had left the woods aware now of the dangerous passage of time, not speaking, running their horses back through the trees, back across the fields. They had pulled up their foaming mounts at the stables. He could not look at her as they parted each to go to their own chambers. He had gone straight to his rooms, ordered his servants away, torn off his clothes, and burned them in the fireplace. He had bathed himself until his skin was raw.

He had committed a mortal sin. He had never confessed it, and over the years he had compounded it by taking communion. He had been afraid not to, for if his father would have asked why, he would not have been able to lie to him. It was easier to suffer estrangement from God, risking the peril to his immortal soul, than to face the earthly judgment of his father.

Now, as a man, Edward was so far from a state of Grace that the distance seemed irrelevant to anything in his life. There was no comfort from any quarter. He rolled on his bed and moaned and gripped his hair. Sliding to his knees onto the floor, he buried his face in the spilling bedcovers, trying to smother his sobs in goose-down and fur, while Tonberht stood silently watching from the shadows. When the prince had fallen into a drunken, exhausted stupor, Tonberht put him to bed.

Chapter Twenty-Six

[828] Ceolworth, Mercia. Elfwina did not sleep that night. She either paced the floor or sat numbly in her chair, staring at the fire.

Morning came. The world was deep in snow with snow still falling. She continued to alternately pace and sit. Later in the morning she pulled herself together enough to confer with Ceolric on business of the hall, and then arranged so she would not have to leave her chambers. People came and went. She surrounded herself with a barrier of women, although she knew Edward would not come unbidden to her chambers. But still she was afraid he might. At every knock on the anteroom door, her heart squeezed into a knot. He did not come.

There had been no word from Aedred. She became apprehensive about what that might mean. The world shook beneath her feet.

The following day, wrapped in a mantle which hid her face, Elfwina left the hall on horseback, letting the animal pick his careful way down the snow-packed road toward the village. Just before the first dwellings, she turned aside into the forest. The horse plunged through the deep snow and came out into an ancient grove. She halted him beneath the bare oaks and looked up at the dark flakes sifting through the branches. She dismounted and tethered her horse.

She made her way through an arch of snow-ladened branches into a small clearing. This was the first time she had been to the sacred grove in winter. In spring and summer the processions wound through the blossoming grove; in autumn the festivals were held beneath the flame and yellow-gold of leaves vibrant in the twilight. But now the vitality, the joy was erased and a great sadness lay over everything.

The simple and unadorned altar of blue fieldstones was at the center of the clearing. Across it the snow lay in an unbroken sheet. Next to the altar was a life-size stone figure of a woman, no detail defined, a figure seen at night or in a thick mist, the Great Mother of all humankind.

There were rituals to be observed and offerings to be made, but the queen could manage none of these. She wrapped her mantle closely around her, sank into the snow at the feet of the Earth Mother, and rested her head against the stone.

"O Mother Erce, help my sovereign. Place your arms around him, protect him from his enemies and bring him safely to hall and hearth." She spread her hands on the cold surface of the form. "Help me, Great Mother. I am afraid. You know how it has gone with me. Direct your servant Elfwina. Tell me what to do."

It was growing dark when the queen reached the gates. She left her horse with the head groom and went back to her chambers, seeing no one but Edyth, who was relieved at her return. She went to bed but did not sleep, as restless and worried as she had been before she had visited the sacred grove. There had been nothing--no response, no indication her prayers had been heard.

She sat on the edge of her bed, her mind a river in spate flowing misery out of the darkness. She had heard his indifference to that old pain and knew without a doubt that what had motivated him in the heat of his youth had burned out long ago. She suddenly cried aloud. She sat wailing and hugging herself and rocking in distress.

By evening, Elfwina had gathered the scattered pieces of herself together. Knowing the court was already unsettled by the king's absence and by the threat against the kingdom, she decided she must make an appearance in the hall. She descended the great staircase for the evening meal. Edward was not there. Feeling neither relief nor disappointment only unrelenting tension, she sat at table, carried on normal conversation, made reassurances, pushed food around in her plate.

Edward had not known what to do. He wanted to offer some explanation, but he knew there was none. It had all been there in the memory, in the realization to both of them of what underlay all his attentions to her. It had seemed to him that in that instant of revelation they had been shoved to opposite ends of the earth and there would be no regaining their closeness or their innocence.

If he had been within a hundred miles of a Christian priest he would have sought him out and thrown himself at his feet and finally made his confession so the burden could have been lifted and his soul made pure again.

There was only one answer to all the questions and the agony: he would have to leave at the first opportunity and never again live at Ceolworth.

I will leave, but—please God!—with dignity.

Ceadda the Magician finally presented himself to the queen. She had been unaware of his presence at supper, unaware he was in the hall. She had risen, freeing everyone to follow their own pursuits, and had gotten as far as the stair when she saw him approaching, a tall man of indeterminate age with a sad, haunted face. He had black hair and a silver-streaked beard. His brows were heavy, his eyes dark but with a kindly warmth. She paused with her hand on the head of the savage creature that formed the newel post..

When the queen turned to face him, Ceadda was surprised by her somber expression and the dark circles under her eyes. He had been observing her discreetly throughout supper, but he had been seated far down the hall. The remarkable resemblance she bore to her late mother, Queen Eadburh, was even more apparent as he looked at her now. Her pale skin had the same soft texture. Her mother was there, too, in the intelligent and patient gaze and in her extraordinary beauty. Ceadda felt his heart quicken and forgave its blindness.

"You wish to speak with me?"

"Your Majesty, I am Ceadda," he answered, with a deep bow. "I am a traveler King Aedred found on the road. He most graciously invited me to stay out the storm."

"Then I welcome you, too, Ceadda. It's bad enough to be on the roads in winter. But this storm--have you ever seen anything like it?"

"Farther north, sometimes."

"You are traveling from the north?"

"No, Ma'am, I have been living in the fens."

"An extraordinary address. Where in the fens? Not with the Danes, please!"

"No, Ma'am, not with them, but on their territory. It was an isolated spot. They didn't know I was there."

"Then you are one up on them. It's usually the other way round."

"That is what I have been hearing, Your Majesty." He shook his head understandingly.

As he was speaking, she had been reappraising him. "You did say, 'Ceadda'? Are you the magician?"

"Yes." He bowed again. "I am Ceadda the Magician. I had the great honor of knowing your father and your mother."

"This is amazing, Ceadda! Your welcome is doubled. When I was a child, my father spoke of you often. What a pleasure this is after hearing all the stories about you and your magic. Father always said it was the best kind." She smiled.

He was warmed by her perception and directness. So like her mother, he thought. His heart turned foolishly. He reproved it: *Blind animal! She is gone.* But his heart wouldn't believe it.

"His views on magic have changed, naturally, since his conversion to Christianity," she was saying in a familiar, soft voice. "Christianity does that. But he allowed your wisdom--wisdom being the greatest magic of all."

He smiled. "Ah, your father would recognize that."

"I am so glad you are here," she said.

The strength of her statement revealed to the magician more than the kindness it expressed. He inclined his head.

"Yes, I am pleased you are here at this time. Perhaps it would be a relief to everyone, if you could read the Glory Twigs for us. Would that be possible for you to do tonight? It would be a great favor to me."

He held her gaze. Her brain had a sensation of gentle entry, a standing at the threshold, and then withdrawal. She stood motionless, her lips parted, her eyes bright and disturbed. "Of course, I will, Your Majesty," he replied. "It would be my great pleasure and my honor." He paused. "You do understand the Twigs speak only the truth. It is not always what is hoped for."

"Oh, we are prepared to hear the truth," she breathed, her lips barely moving. "We would welcome it."

He bowed then, and said, "If you would have the branch of a fruit tree brought to me . . . ."

By the time the bare branch was brought in, everyone in the hall had heard the Glory Twigs would be read and were pressing around Ceadda. No one had been aware he was a magician. Once it was announced, it was hard for those watching to equate the sad-faced, quiet man with his reputation and the powers at his hand. Their mood was uncertain, more as if he had been announced a juggler or an acrobat: there was an air of expectancy, a tone of good humor, and some skepticism.

The spectators watched closely as the magician turned the branch in his hands. He slowly broke away nine twigs from the stem. He was not a showman. The very lack of showmanship spiked their curiosity. He ignored his audience, going about his work as if he were alone.

He had chosen to stand by the great hearth, and now he reached forward and without ceremony laid the stripped branch on the coals. As he stepped back he was groping inside his tunic. The people were watching this search with interest, when the ones nearest the hearth suddenly leaped back with loud cries; the branch had burst into flame with a thin shriek and burned a bright green and purple, the colors so brilliant eyes were momentarily blinded. Ceadda stood alone in the broad semi-circle their retreat had opened. He held his hand edge-on as he made a smooth revolution, and along the line he described, a cold tongue of blue flame miraculously rose from the stones and sped around the circle. The flame encircled him, flickering and shifting fretfully. The crowd pushed farther back with an uneasy murmur. The movement left the queen isolated beside the circle of blue fire. She was watching the magician intently, unaware of the receding crowd.

He had pulled a jeweled knife from his tunic. He carefully stripped the bark from the twigs, his movements observed now in complete silence. On each pale stick, he carved runes, speaking each one into the wood in a deep chant as the knife engraved the figure. Then he held the sticks cupped in his hands and at last looked into the crowd.

His voice was low, but it resonated clearly in the smoky room.

"*Hwæt!* The future will be revealed. The runes will speak to three. *Hwæt!* You will hear the truth!"

He flung the twigs high into the air. They spun upward, end over end, rising toward the roof beams and up into the smoky haze above the great hanging lamps. The faces below swiveled to the ascent. The silence was absolute. Then the thick smoke suddenly boiled downward, and the sticks plummeted toward the floor, blackened and changed, wood no longer but rods of iron, heavy, dangerous, aligning as they plunged, hurtling like spear points to pierce the hearth and stand ringing in the stone.

"The truth is immutable!" Ceadda cried out in anguish, because he had no power to alter it.

Leaning forward, the people watched as the magician reached down to pull at the first rod. It would not move from the stone. He tried the second; it would not move. The third slipped easily into his hand. He turned it slowly in his fingers. A voice came from the rod, low and sweet. Only Elfwina understood its song.

A second crown will bow your head.

She was suddenly deaf, unaware of the rush of whispers behind her as the crowd gave way, and Aedred stepped through, his clothes wet, a dark stubble smearing his cheeks. He saw the magician and Elfwina standing motionless. He said nothing, but walked slowly to the circle of fire and looked down.

As he lifted his head, his eyes met Ceadda's, and something passed between them. Then the magician bent down again and put his hand around the fourth rod. It was tightly embedded in the stone. His hand moved to the fifth and was unable to pull it free. Nor the sixth. Beyond the silent ring of noblemen and women, the servants had gathered and were trying to see what was going on at the hearth.

The seventh rod leaped into Ceadda's hand. It sang in a deep, harsh tone. Members of the crowd looked questioningly at one another. But no one responded. The eighth rod remained firmly held, but the ninth and final rod spoke with a sad melody. The king looked up at Ceadda with an inquiring gaze, and then he turned his head slightly as if he were puzzled. Ceadda placed the rods on the hearth and stepped back.

"You who have understood the words have been given the course your lives will take," the magician said quietly. As he spoke, all nine rods, those still piercing the stone and those lying beside them glowed white-hot and fell to ashes. The circle of blue flame vanished without leaving a mark. Ceadda bowed to the king and queen. Then he wrapped his ragged fur around him and backed respectfully away.

"By the Gods!" someone cried, and the hall was suddenly filled with confusion.

"Did you hear them speak?"

"I heard them, but what did they say, those iron sticks?"

"Wood into iron--"

"Could you make it out?"

"Did anyone understand the words?"

"No, but that was a real magician!"

Suddenly realizing that the king stood in their midst, and remembering the reason he had been away, the people shifted and closed in on him. Ceadda, like a good magician, had disappeared like smoke; or rather, he took the moment of changing priorities to walk unhurriedly across the room and up the stair.

Elfwina stood transfixed, her gaze on the stone where a pile of ashes had now disappeared. Then she looked up and saw Ceadda on the landing. She jerked back from the hearth and moved away, skirting the crowd as she followed him up the great staircase.

Mystified by her behavior, Aedred watched her for a moment, but then his thegns milled about him, pressing for an account of Gyrth, and he turned his attention to them.

Because the queen still appeared dazed, Ceadda led her into his room and seated her by the fire. He pulled up a chair for himself. "May I?" he asked politely. Realizing she was unable to hear him, he sat down. She stared at him.

"It will take a moment or two," he said, kindly, and waited.

Presently, Elfwina nodded to him, and he asked, "Do you have a question, Your Majesty?" He watched her face in the firelight, that beautiful, haunting face. Even in the ruddy glow, he could see her pallor.

"I need . . . clarification to understand what I heard."

He asked gently, "What did you hear?"

"Didn't you hear it? It was spoken very clearly."

"The message was not intended for me."

Her gaze passed over the textures and planes of his face. "I understood the words the first rod spoke, but the other two were in a language I'd never heard before. I don't know what they said. I want you to tell me."

"I can't do that." He paused. "What did you understand the first rod to say?"

"It said, A second crown will bow your head. What does that mean? I wear the crown of the queen of Mercia. There is no other crown I can wear."

"The voice--what was its quality?"

"Low. The tone was low and gentle."

Ceadda nodded. "Your Majesty, you heard those words because

the message was for you alone. The other two messages will be understood only by those for whom they were intended. What the meaning of yours is, I cannot say. I cannot interpret its meaning."

He was lying, but it was the prerogative of a magician to lie when it suited him, like now, when truth could be dangerous. "The significance will be revealed as time spins out. I can tell you the quality of the voice indicates a sympathetic attitude; it was not a hostile delivery. There is one other thing--there is often a hidden meaning. What seems obvious is not always the whole truth."

"It doesn't seem plain to me on any level. It is like . . . nonsense."

"No. Forgive me, Your Majesty; you must not dismiss this foretelling. It is clear and truthful. It only seems obscure because it is projected from a future point in time; the events preceding it have not yet unfolded. As time goes along what seems obscure now will lose its mystery. Your arrival at that point you have only just glimpsed will be taken in the most logical steps."

"I must take your word for that."

"Gracious Majesty," Ceadda murmured.

"The other messages--who were they for?"

"King Aedred, for one. The other I cannot say. No one claimed it."

"I see . . . King Aedred."

"Yes, Ma'am."

"Then the words would have been lost, if he had not come in at that moment."

"He was meant to come in at that moment. He was meant to hear the message of the runes."

"And you can't tell me what that was?"

"No, Ma'am."

"And the other? Who was the other?" Her gaze was dark and compelling. He could not look away from it. Suddenly, he felt her power, the authority coming from the dark aura around her. "The meaning of the runes connects the destinies of the three who heard them, doesn't it, Ceadda?"

He wanted to lie, but under the force of that gaze, he could not. He nodded slowly.

Elfwina came swiftly to her feet. "Tell me who that other was, magician. *Tell me what it means!*"

Ceadda pushed himself from the chair, his mouth open to answer her question. Beneath his feet and along the planking of the floor, up through the massive stones of the hall, from the earth lying under the snow, he felt a deep vibration run along his bones and ring in his skull. He groped for his chair. "Forgive me."

"Are you ill?" She laid her hand on his shoulder.

"No, no, thank you. I am all right. I just need to sit for a moment."

"Shall I send for someone?"

He shook his head. "You are gracious, but no." He looked into her beautiful face, and his heart began a dull leaden beat.

"If you are sure, then . . .?" She put out her hand, and he took it carefully. "The Great Mother returned my king safely. I did not think she had heard my prayers. The rest doesn't matter. Goodnight, Ceadda."

"Goodnight, Your Majesty."

When she had gone, the magician rested his head against the back of his chair and stared up at the smoke-darkened ceiling.

Chapter Twenty-Seven

[828] Ceolworth, Mercia. Aedred's clothes were wet. His nose was cold. Stubble bloomed darkly on his face, which he kept scrapping with his knuckles in an irritated pawing. He was dirty, miserable, and he had not understood what was going on with the magician and his wife.

Penned in on all sides following that exhibition, he was reassuring the men around him the Danes would not be attacking Ceolworth, when Edward appeared. Flinging his arm around the prince's neck, Aedred would not let him go until Edward had helped ease him away to the staircase.

As they jogged up, Aedred asked him, "What was all that with Ceadda?"

"A little heathen show, as far as I could see. Where are we going?" They slowed to a walk when they reached the top.

"To hold a minor witena in Elfwina's chambers before I tackle the rest of them. What's wrong? Would you rather meet somewhere else?"

"No, of course not."

They stopped at the wide entrance to Elfwina's rooms. Aedred pounded on one of the heavy doors.

"What happened at Wenlock?"

Aedred shook his head. "It wasn't good."

Edward stood to one side, wondering why the door wasn't opening. "So Thyrdfurth died."

"He died. Gyrth went crazy. If we hadn't held him down, he would have beaten his brains out against the wall. With good cause." Aedred was looking hard at the door, his mouth grim. He frowned. "They did the bloody eagle on Thyrdfurth."

"Ah, Jesus!" Edward's face went white. He crossed himself swiftly, automatically.

Aedred shook his head. "Sickening. Far beyond anything I've ever seen. There was little we could do for Gyrth, but we finally got him quieted down. He wouldn't leave Wenlock, and I was uneasy about staying away from the hall any longer. We're in for a fucking hot summer, Edward."

He pounded on the door again. "What's going on here?" He gestured at the door. "Every time I do this myself I have to stand around and wait. I should have sent a servant; they seem to know how to get a response."

As he hammered at the door, this time it opened. Edyth's calm, broad face appeared. She curtsied deeply to Aedred. "Sire, the queen is not here."

"I've been a long time waiting for that information. Where is she?"

"She was reported to be in the great hall, Your Majesty."

"The report was wrong. I saw her mount the stairs myself. Send someone to find her. Her king wants her immediate presence in his chambers."

He swung away as she curtsied again. Edward followed him up the corridor, glancing blankly at Edyth, his brows drawn together.

As they entered his chambers, Aedred started flinging off his wet clothes, and then let Merefin finish the job. Edward lowered himself into a chair and sat watching.

"Nothing right now," he told a servant who was approaching with a cup.

Aedred was helped into a silk gown. "Fill the biggest vessel you have there with ale," he called.

The servant stationed at the table plucked a jar from among the pitchers and flasks and began filling it. Aedred pulled his gown around him and sat down, his eyes on the prince.

"My throat's so dry I can hardly squeak." He yanked his gown up to his knees and lifted his feet to a bench. "They're frozen," he said, holding up one foot and then the other as Merefin, clucking and shaking his head, rubbed briskly before he slipped woolen socks on each foot.

"That's better--where's that ale? Did you warm it?" When he had it in his hands and had taken a long, deep swallow, he lowered the cup to look at Edward.

The prince sat with his elbows resting on the chair arms, his fingers linked across the gap. It was a deceptive pose. Aedred sensed tension. He wondered.

Edward was now regarding him with an unreadable expression. Aedred noted the shadows darkening his eyes, the lack of vitality in the full mouth. He smiled at him.

"You look as though you were the one staggering through five-foot drifts for the last several hours. In fact, you look like hell. Is it your head wound, or too many nights on the hnocc?"

Edward drew himself together, gave Aedred a crooked smile. "You always credit me too much. What's this 'five-foot drifts'? " He got up and walked over to the table.

"I'm minimizing," Aedred laughed. "And why shouldn't I credit you? You're more profitable than a toll! I've won wagers on how fast you move from the battle-field to a woman's bed. Like a plunging hawk. You're my treasure, Edward."

"If I respond to that, you'll brand me either a liar or a braggart. I'm condemned no matter what I say." He indicated mead to the servant, who was restraining a grin. He took the brimming bowl.

"Ah, here she is," Aedred said warmly, his irritation evaporating as the queen came into the room.

"A council, Aedred?" Elfwina said. "Welcome back." She did not look at Edward.

Aedred was sitting with one leg thrown over the arm of his chair, the skirt of his gown folded along his thigh and piled modestly in his lap. He reached up and pulled Elfwina into the chair with him. "I hope to be welcomed by you, finally! Where have you been?" He kissed her with a loud smack.

Edward returned to his chair and sat looking into the bowl in his hands while his sister and the king worked out their misconnection. Finally, when they had left off the particulars of Elfwina's anxieties and returned to nuzzling, Edward said, "I hate to break this up, but we do have a situation, and a disaster."

They both looked at him.

"Gyrth's son has died," he said to his sister, "and the old man is out of his head with grief."

Elfwina glanced at Aedred. He closed his eyes briefly in agreement. She rose from his lap and said to Edward, "Tell me what happened."

The result of a mixture of emotions, Edward's eyes filled suddenly with tears. He was unable to continue.

Aedred told her, "They struck in the middle of the day. About sixty Danes--"

"Danes!"

"--coming up so fast there wasn't a chance for Gyrth to mount a defense beyond what was at hand. Who would have suspected an attack in the middle of a damn snowfall? They put up a fight, but it was no contest against that pack of wolves."

As Aedred spoke, Elfwina moved a few paces to the table and stood there with her arms folded, listening to him.

"They took the cattle, slaughtered the rest of the livestock, and fired the outbuildings. They found Gyrth's hoard. Gyrth resisted. The Danes fell on Thyrdfurth." Aedred had been debating, but he said, "They did the bloody eagle."

There was a shocked gasp from Elfwina. Then she said, "This cannot go unpunished, Aedred."

"My oath on it," he replied.

"And mine!" Edward said hoarsely, finally able to speak.

There was a long silence engulfing the servants as well as their stunned glances were exchanged around the room.

Elfwina's eyes moved from the stern set of her husband's face to the alcove off his bedchamber. There the form of Woden was enshrined, the wood of its base glowing with the oils from Aedred's hands. She said, "Did you bring Gyrth back with you?"

"He wouldn't leave the site where his son died."

"You should have insisted."

He shook his head. "He was where he wanted to be. They had shelter, and we had brought supplies. We'll send more when the weather lets up. They'll manage till then."

"And the Danes? Where did they go?"

"That is the grand question," Aedred replied. "We don't know. We trailed them for a distance toward the north, but the snow covered the trail. We came back to Ceolworth as fast as we could with our hearts pounding." He looked at Edward.

The prince was watching his sister launch from the edge of the table to drift through the room in her thoughtful, absent manner, touching this, picking up that. He briefly closed his eyes.

Aedred said, "If you pass near the table, Wina, will you take my cup along?" He winked at Edward.

"To get rid of it, or fill it up?" she took it from the hand he had raised over the back of his chair.

"Fill it up, of course. I just made twenty miles dragging my horse through six-foot drifts. All the liquid's burned out of my body."

Edward snorted. "Your drifts have accumulated a foot of snow in the past hour."

"It does continue to pile up."

"Something's piling up, but I don't think it's snow."

"If it's not, you'll smell it in the thaw."

"I smell it now."

Aedred lifted his arm and sniffed. "Well, you probably do," he said. "I've been a hellish long time on the road."

Elfwina handed Aedred his cup. "That's very amusing, my lord stablemucker. Do you plan on sleeping with the horses tonight?"

With the sound of Aedred's uninhibited laughter, the weight of tragedy that had been crushing the room shifted, lost its center, and became diffuse.

Aedred said, "I want to go over this before I call the others in. So, let's do a little summary of the way things stand right now--make sure we can give them a clear grasp of the numbers."

Edward settled back with his legs stretched full length. Elfwina, drawn by Aedred's hand, took a seat next to him, and they began discussing the looming crisis.

The Danish force, nearly two thousand strong, was in the south, in the lower Severn Valley. In the north, with the Danes already committed to him, the Northumbrian king Ædda could assemble his own sizeable force. To the east was Lindsey. Osward, an easy foe in usual seasons, needed careful reevaluation now, with the possibility he might be reinforced from the Danish settlements in East Anglia. It had to be faced: given only her own resources and without substantial aid, Mercia would not be able to resist over an extended period of time the numbers assembling against her. Any strategy for survival would depend on the help of Brihtric and Gryffn.

"Let's consider the first move will be from the Severn," said Aedred. "What counter do we have?"

Edward was now leaning forward, staring intently at the king and concentrating on his reply to him. "All right, let's assume the participation of Father and Gryffn--" he glanced at Elfwina "--if their armies were to join at Tewkesbury, they could contain the force in the Severn Valley, and you and I could throw back Ædda and any polyglot group Osward and that degenerate son of his can arrange. The whole lot combined couldn't make up much over a thousand."

Elfwina asked, "Why are they going to all this trouble coming up through Mercia in the winter? Why not just sail up the east coast and come in Osward's front door at the Humber?"

Both men sat considering this.

"Probably thought the Humber chancier in winter," her brother answered.

"This has been an unusual winter," Aedred said. "We can't discount that they had intended coming in at the Humber. For a time-directed assault, going up through Mercia may have been an alternate route. They could as well be coming in at the Humber. There may be a force gathering we have not encountered in all our history."

"Why all this attention on Mercia?" Elfwina wondered. "Wessex is easier to get at."

"Since when?" cried Edward.

"Geographically," Aedred answered, and was pleased that for once he knew where she heading and Edward didn't.

Edward grunted and, for a long moment, sat regarding Aedred. Then he suddenly leaned forward and brought his fist gently down on the king's knee. "We have to inform Father immediately. He's the only one equipped to watch the coasts. If there's a force coming in longships along the southern coast, the beacons will probably inform him. But, in any case, he needs to be aware of our suspicions."

"Off go the messengers," Elfwina said drily.

Edward took a breath. "Look, Aedred, I'm the best one to go to Exeter with this."

Elfwina had bent slightly to run her hands slowly along her thighs, smoothing the soft material of her gown. She paused to look at her brother.

"There are advantages to your going," Aedred answered, thinking about it. "You could handle any questions that come up, and you could help formulate plans, knowing what our position of the moment is, but unless you're dead-set on going, I'd like to have you stay at Ceolworth. At least for the time being. Nothing's certain yet. What we know now may be insignificant tomorrow. All we really know for actual fact is that we have two thousand Danes on the Severn and an undetermined number heading toward Northumbria. Everything else is phantom rumor . . . conjecture. While the thing's still fluid, I'd like you here."

Chapter Twenty-Eight

[828] Ceolworth, Mercia. Edward stared at the floor. "All right," he said, slowly, lifting his head. "I see the sense in that. Do you want me to draft the message and see that it gets off?"

Aedred gave him a grateful look and heaved a long sigh. "That would be a hell of a favor. My brain's gone numb. And I'm in no shape to lay the thing out to them downstairs beyond a simple outline. They can sleep on it, and we'll tackle it tomorrow. I'm dead on my feet."

"Hell, yes. Nothing can be done about anything tonight, except send the message."

Edward stood up and glanced at Elfwina. She was standing beside Aedred, her fingers resting on his shoulder. "Any word you'd like me to include for Father?"

"Send him my love," Elfwina said, not looking at him but down at Aedred.

"You can tell him his old friend Ceadda is staying here," Aedred added.

"There--I'd forgotten Ceadda," Edward said.

Elfwina stepped around in front of Aedred, trailing her fingers along his shoulder to rest at his neck. He looked up at her inquiringly.

"Ceadda said one of the rods spoke to you." Her cold hand pressed the side of his throat in a little spasm.

"I understood one of them," he said slowly.

"What did it say?"

He tried to assess the tension that emanated from her like heat. The anxiety he recognized made his skin contract. "Were you not able to understand any?" He felt her fear now and took hold of her arm without realizing it, catching that fear and multiplying it.

As Edward watched this, a strong sense of revulsion overcame him and he said, "Oh, for Christ's sake, everyone understood those voices, even me. It was a trick, don't you know that? A trick. Cleverly done, but a trick. He's a famous magician. He has to put on a good show."

They both looked at him with such guileless and shocked faces, he was suddenly angry. "Good God," he muttered. "You are a pair of innocents!"

"You were there?" Elfwina cried.

"Yes, I was there. I wanted to be entertained like everyone else. Were Christians excluded?" He was thoroughly angry, now.

"Don't be ridiculous," Aedred said, without fervor, his lips bloodless.

"I didn't see you there," Elfwina said so breathlessly Aedred grabbed her hand in alarm.

"I was there."

Elfwina rushed up to her brother. "Did you understand them all? All three?"

"No, not all," he answered, his anger curbed by the hands resting on his forearms. "The second one, I believe--yes, the second one. What does it matter? The whole thing was a show."

"What did it say? You must tell me what you heard!"

Aedred got up quickly and took hold of her arm. "Elfwina--"

She paid no attention to him. "What did it say?"

Edward's mouth went dry. "It was nonsense. Gibberish." He shot a glance at Aedred's white face, and then pursed his lips and answered, "If you must--it sounded like All will not be enough. Some rubbish like that."

What sorely annoyed Edward was the implied greed. He had never in his life imagined himself to be greedy. And then he was angry with himself for being annoyed for so foolish a reason, and he was incensed that Ceadda would have attributed greed to him when Ceadda knew nothing about him. And then he thought it implied comparison and in the comparison he, Edward, had failed. After all, Ceadda had been a confidant of his father and had known his uncle, King Baldred. His spirits began to sink.

"It could hardly be taken seriously by anyone," he said. "Although he might not have made me out a selfish tick."

"Don't make the mistake of taking it lightly," Aedred told him.

"Oh, how the hell else can I take it? It's absurd. All will not be enough. What's that supposed to mean? Anything in the world could be said and as many interpretations put on it. It's anything you want it to mean."

"Like your Bible," Elfwina said.

Edward rounded on her, but before he could speak, Aedred told her, "That's enough, Elfwina. We're not going to battle religion, here."

"It isn't I who is behaving uncivilly. I know the blessings that stream from Mother Erce. You know your body and shield are protected by Tiw. Every child in Mercia knows what moves in the darkness and hunts the sky. Even the Danes know who to worship. It was the misfortune of Edward's life he was torn away from his religion. He does not believe, but disbelief has never changed one fiber of the truth. What the rune predicted will come about, and Edward will know it when it happens. May the AllFather he disclaims forgive him and protect him as the son he truly is."

Aedred was astounded at this reprimand. The prince was shocked, too. His cheeks went suddenly scarlet as he stared at his sister. He seemed, at first, incapable of a reply. And then he bowed his head to her. "I apologize. I shouldn't have made light of this." Then he gave her a formal bow. To Aedred, he said, "I am sorry."

"Accepted," Aedred said. He looked at his wife.

"Yes, accepted." Two vermillion spots burned in her cheeks.

"Well," said Aedred, "for being here such a short time, Ceadda has claimed a fair measure. That was not the message I heard."

"Then, what was it?" Edward asked.

"Remember, we can't assign meanings with any certainty. We can't jump to conclusions." He sighed. "It can sound dire when it really isn't. None of us have the gift of interpreting signs, so let's keep our minds open." He could see that these preliminaries were causing Elfwina distress, so he just came out with it. "The message was, You will be pierced to the heart."

Elfwina's face went dead-white. He took her quickly in his arms. "It could mean several things that have nothing to do with spears. You mustn't worry about this. Not yet."

But he was fearful, too. *My Father Woden, I am your son. Let me die in your glory . . . .* He could feel Elfwina shaking, and it raised the flesh on his arms. "Was the third rune for you?" He was aware of Edward standing like a statue. "What was it?" he asked gently.

He had her repeat what she had heard. He had no conscious understanding of its meaning, but his blood knew and could not translate. He kissed her closed eyes. "Stay here with me tonight."

"Yes, if you want me to."

"I've a letter to write," Edward said, and moved toward the door.

Aedred glanced up at him. "Thanks, Edward."

Edward lifted his hand in response and quietly left the room.

Long after the meeting with his eorls was over, and he had returned to his chambers and the candle beside the bed had burned down, Aedred lay in the darkness, trying not to think of the future. Something half-formed and monstrous stirred in the deep. He could almost make out is shape. But it was a thing too dreadful, and he drew back, closing it off. In the moments when sleep was finally descending, he felt Elfwina's hair fall all around his face. Her whisper made rapid, soft percussions in his ear.

"I love you--I love you so dearly. I have never once regretted being your wife. I want to be with you for the rest of my life. I love only you in all this world . . . ."

He listened to her, amazed, touched by the words which ceased only when she bent to kiss him. He reached up to put his arms around her, but she took his hands and made him explore and probe. She guided his mouth to taste all the silky soft saltiness that he knew, but never before like this. She took control of him, engulfed him, made him move in rhythms she created by sheer physical strength. And when it was finished, he murmured the things always somewhere in the back of his mind but rarely voiced.

"You've given me such joy. You can't know . . . ."

His hands stroked back her hair, and he pressed his mouth against her forehead, pressed hard, because he was overflowing and it confused him. He wanted to give over *something*, and he didn't know what it was and he felt like crying because he had no idea what it was or how to give it. So he pressed her forehead with his lips and he squeezed his eyelids tight and pulled air into his lungs and prayed with his blood, because there were no words for the fear that ran with joy. He didn't want to imagine what dark thing the runes had suggested, not now when happiness was as bright and wide as the sky, and there were no dark corners anywhere.

"Aedred?" It was a dreamy prompt.

He lifted his head and felt the blood rush back to his mouth. "I was just thinking what a fortunate man I am." He smiled, shifted his weight to his forearms and laid his hands along her face. "Do you realize we've never been angry with each other?"

"Really? No, I don't think we have."

"Is that normal?" He chuckled. "It could be a record--five years married without a quarrel."

"It has been wonderful, Aedred. You have been wonderful."

"Am I? I think I can be damn self-centered at times." He thought he was, but maybe not too bad. But what he wanted was a refutation, and he had cannily let it slide up into a question. She denied his self-centeredness, and he was pleased. "I want you to know I recognize what the gods have given me."

"Mmmm." She stretched her fingers over his cheeks. He slid off her and lay on his back with one arm holding her against his side, the other cushioning his neck. He stared at the ceiling through half-closed eyes. "You were the gem of Wessex."

Her laugh was sleepy, more a growl, like a small bear. "The gem! Naow!"

"Edward had to drag me to Exeter, but the moment I saw you, I knew. I tried every trick I had--"

"Tricks?"

"Oh, yes. I plotted and schemed and then I was scared to death you wouldn't accept me, because--" it was always difficult for him to speak of it "--with no child from the union, you would have to bear the blame for it." He turned his face toward her when there was no response. "All the whispers . . . has it been hard to endure?"

She rose slowly, winding her hair out of the way as she looked down at him, knowing she had to quench that tiny, burning doubt which could never be fully extinguished, which he could not conquer.

"You allowed me the choice. You might not have, but you did--in that honesty that so marks you above other men. That is why whispers don't matter."

"Honesty? Is that what it hinged on? I almost wasn't--honest. The risk seemed too great."

He had been wavering--should he or shouldn't he? His pride in that honesty, the purity of motive it allowed him in all other things, in this had been rapidly losing its importance, for how important was honesty if it lost him the thing he wanted more than anything he had ever wanted or would ever want in his lifetime? Balanced on the sword's edge, he had sought Edward, and Edward had told him, "If you don't let her know, the effort to keep it a secret will poison your marriage. Ultimately you will have to blame her, you know; a king can't be infertile. She will give you all her loyalty and love, and if she thinks she has failed you in any way, it will destroy her. You will see it, and you will hate yourself for it and eventually hate her, too."

When he had still wavered, Edward told him from his own desperation, "All right--this is the most serious wager you've ever made in your life, and you think the odds are against you, but I am your friend and I am her brother and I know her better than anyone ever has, and I tell you she loves you and it won't make the slightest difference to her as long as she knows you are happy with her. It's your decision, but from the bottom of my heart and the faith I have in the integrity of my sister, I urge you to tell her."

"Friga must have guided me." Aedred caressed her face. "A strange wound, isn't it? To leave my hnocc active and destroy my seed . . .?"

His father had arranged it in secret at the sanctuary at Wodnesweoh--nine slave women, put under the charge of the high priest of Woden and the priestess of Friga. Kept in confinement to record their menses, kept in separate rooms. He had charged in like a stallion to perform the duty his father had commanded, an erotic dream turned nightmare, for they were all just girls, most barely beyond puberty, their eyelids sewn shut, afraid in the darkness, terrified of him, and he was not allowed to speak and ease their fear.

The schedules were inviolable; the positions strictly prescribed and recorded by observers whose presence shrunk him. No love-making, only acts of procreation that became a task so grim and dehumanizing it was a year before he could feel desire.

A year later, he was finally a man again, but not all a man, for not one of the nine young women had ever conceived by him, although some had later by others. But the priestess had offered his father a faint hope. The readings are not clear, she had told him, but there could be a future possibility. Not one Aedred believed, for in five years Elfwina had never conceived . . . .

"But that's the way of it," he said, dragging himself out from the misery of that time. "I was luckier than most men skewered like that." He lay back, cupping her head against his chest. "Your father's disappointed though, isn't he? No heirs with Wessex blood forthcoming."

"He loves you too much to be seriously disappointed. And he's never spoken of it to me."

Aedred smiled on a sigh. "Well, if Edward ever settles himself to one woman, the heirs will pop out like lambs in the spring. More than enough to keep the bloodline till the end of time." He began to chuckle deep in his chest at the thought of Edward surrounded by babies.

In the curve of his arm, Elfwina lay staring bleakly into the darkness.

A great force of Danes made winter setl at Tewkesbury. As evil men do, the Northumbrians, Lindsey men, and the Danes made a pact against Mercia. Thyrdfurth, son of Eorl Gyrth was cruelly killed by the invaders. King Aedred and his trusted men rode in pursuit of the Danes but the force escaped.

Chapter Twenty-Nine

[829] Ceolworth, Mercia. The snow had begun to melt, leaving the roads and tracks muddy. Snow still lay deep in the shaded areas and in thin slices in the fields. But wherever the sun touched or where the warming air moved steadily, the snow had receded and left a shimmer of water. In the village, household linen and clothing lay over drying frames. Racks had been thrown down on the muddy streets, allowing people to cross without stepping in the mire. On this early morning the breeze moved chillingly over the ground, but the sun steamed the long incline to the gate tower. Everywhere mist wafted up from the warming earth.

Edward pounded into the hall from the passageway at a dead run. He spun onto the staircase by the head of the creature that formed the newel post and, taking three steps at once, nearly collided with Aedred sauntering down. Edward pulled up breathing hard.

"Do I award a prize for this?"

"I see . . . you're ready . . . for the morning's activities," Edward panted.

"Not nearly so ready as you."

Edward fell in beside him, moving at Aedred's sedate pace.

The king gave him a side glance. "How many times have you run these stairs this morning?"

They reached the bottom step and started across the floor. Aedred's course was set toward the benches, but Edward slipped behind him to the other side and easing close, altered the king's direction with a springy stride that struck sparks. Curious, Aedred allowed the detour.

"Do *you* feel like taking a little exercise this morning?"

"Running up and down stairs? No."

Edward was still controlling his direction, bearing him toward the back passageway.

"This isn't going to delay my breakfast by much, is it?"

"That will be up to you. How about a little skirmish?"

"With you? What's the game?"

"You're up to a challenge, then?"

"If it's worth my while."

"Are thirty Danes worth your while?"

"Thirty, eh?" Aedred was not going to let Edward ruffle him. He was still suspecting a joke. "Not before breakfast."

"Danes are better on an empty stomach. It shouldn't take long. We should be back by lunch time. They're only a half-mile the other side of the Street." His glance was sharp, without humor. "Three miles to the south of us and heading steadily northward."

Aedred's eyes had gone black. "Set to the purpose, are they?" His face had drained of its tolerant good humor. "So the bastards are going to try it again. Are they afoot or horseback?"

"On foot. I sent word to the barracks. They should be rousted by now. Leodwald's down there . . . ."

They crossed Cyninges Street and gained the top of the hill beyond. Where the hillside swept westward to the level ground, they could see the Danes about a half-mile from their position. As the riders came up around the king and the prince, the foot-soldiers spread out around the mounted group to stand with their spears leaning at their shoulders or to squat with the butts of their spears dug into the patchy snow. They were all watching the body of warriors moving northward at a normal pace on the downs below them.

Leodwald leaned forward in the saddle. "Have they seen us?"

The forward movement of the Danes stopped. There was a glittering confusion of spear points, a pause.

"Now they have," said Waltheof.

They watched silently. There was another flicker of spears as the group resumed their march.

Penwahl had been quietly assessing the movement of the Danes. He turned his handsome white head to the king "If they reach that copse," he said to the king, "we'll have a harder time of it."

About three-quarters of a mile ahead of the Danes' line of march the open land was intersected by a straggle of bare trees that followed a rise in the land. "We'll be at a disadvantage if they reach it before we can close."

"If we ride ahead we can turn them back into our foot soldiers," Edward suggested. Mawer mumbled an agreement.

Aedred twisted in the saddle. "Split into two groups--Pen, you take one, I'll take the other. Grundl, you bring up the foot as fast as you can." He pulled on his gold-banded helmet, looked around to see they were ready. "For the glory of Tiw!" he shouted and plunged forward.

They moved swiftly down the long gentle slope and onto the downs, where the ground, still partially swathed in a grainy layer of melting snow, made the earth spongy beneath it. Aedred and Eorl Penwahl led the way, with the other horsemen split behind them and moving alongside the foot soldiers. The Danes were still going forward; almost as if they were unaware they were being pursued. None looked back, but their pace quickened and almost imperceptibly they were widening the block they presented to the Mercians.

"Don't let them do that!" Aedred shouted. He adjusted the mask of his helmet so his vision was completely clear and, with his prayer beginning, drove his horse ahead.

Great AllFather, if this is the day of the runes foretelling, welcome me to your hall. I am your son. I will die with honor . . . .

Because his horse did not have a bridle, his hands were left full play with his weapons and shield. His saddle was specially constructed to his own design, allowing him freedom to instruct his war-horse with his legs and feet. He repositioned himself in the saddle and got a firmer grip on his shield. He glanced back at Grundl and got a hand signal indicating the big warrior knew what the Danes were about.

Aedred nodded to Edward. To Penwahl, who was just breaking away with his men, he called, "Keep it wide!" Penwahl lifted his spear in acknowledgement. Signaling his riders, Aedred touched the flanks of his white horse with his heels, and the mount went forward into an easy lope. The following horsemen swung away from the widening line of Danes and beyond the reach of their spears. But the Danish archers were drawing their bows. The Mercians came into a storm of arrows as they rejoined with Penwahl in front of the force and swung about to face them.

The line which had been widening now squeezed back together, jammed by the Mercian foot soldiers coming hard into the force from the rear. The archers howled for room to draw their bows but were jostled by the rear of the force as it turned to defend itself, and the group in front that had been balked by the horsemen. As Heafwine, Penwahl, and Waltheof spun into place around him, Aedred pulled Cwellere from its scabbard. The high, descending battle cry of the Mercians split the air. His horse lunged forward.

For the first few seconds his moves were consciously directed, but the need for instantaneous response became too critical to be thought out and the battle became a pattern he followed, a roaring rhythm his body was swept into in one flow of skill and concentration and fear.

They had swarmed the Danes, and now the Danes were rallying against them. His bodyguard was flung back. Ahead of him, he glimpsed Edward's horse going down and the Danes pressing in. He plunged his horse forward, maneuvering it in a close circle around Edward, side-stepping the animal into the main group of attackers as he sliced down on them with his sword. With one arm holding his shield, the other wielding Cwellere, he guided the horse with the pressure of his legs, fish-tailing the animal, still describing the circle around Edward, until he saw the prince was on his feet and heavy into his own defense. Mawer swung in like a reaper to Edward's side.

Aedred had to look to his own safety as a rush came on him, forcing him to slash indiscriminately, protecting his side with his shield as he legs worked at the horse's middle in the second by second need for direction change. He was exposed, his eorls held back and bawling in fury as they tried to reach him. He swung the horse about. And then, an instant before he could react, he saw a warrior run at him, sag abruptly, and thrust his sword upward with both hands, his arm muscles bulging with the strain as he buried the sword in the horse's belly.

The horse screamed and reared, and then went down with its legs flailing. Aedred leaped free and landed awkwardly, tumbling through bloody snow toward the opening he had glimpsed. His shield cartwheeled under him, twisting his wrist. He hauled up on one knee and could rise no farther, held by the blows coming down on him. He pulled his shield close and slashed out furiously with Cwellere.

There was a roar of outrage, and then the warriors were attacked from the rear by Edward and Grundl. From the side, Heafwine and Penwahl staggered in and swung their bodies heavily around, like draft horses, and faced the attackers. The Danes fell back. The rim of Aedred's shield struck the ground and bounced as his arm dropped. Looking up at Edward, he leaned into the shield, drafting in air, reviving. Edward leaned down, his face close to his. His blue eyes glittered behind the face mask. "While you're down there on your knees, you might mention to Mighty Tiw that a Christian just saved your ass."

"Even!" Aedred gasped.

Edward hauled the king to his feet, and then he was gone, running up a slight grassy rise to where the battle had reorganized itself with a small remainder of the Danish force.

Aedred stood with his shield resting against his leg. His head was lowered as he looked out on the battlefield, his eyes black and violent. *"No prisoners!"* It was a piercing cry repeated all over the killing ground.

Edward heard. He was in a clear space, but he saw three Danes running toward the trees where a number of Mercian horses had come together and were placidly grazing. Their heads came up as the men stumbled toward them.

"Ho! Get them!" Edward shouted at four of his thegns who were making their way over to him. They spun around and took after the fleeing Danes and brought them to the ground.

To either side of him the battle was suddenly, quietly over. Edward lowered his shield and his sword and heard Aedred yell, *"Behind you!"* An explosion cupped deafeningly in his helmet, and then he knew nothing.

Chapter Thirty

[829] Ceolworth, Mercia. Furious he had been so close to being killed by an enemy arrogantly invading his own province, Aedred commanded their slaughter. He had torn off his helmet and stood watching while his order was being carried out. He had seen the running Danes and heard Edward send his men after them, then realized by Edward's posture he was unaware of the warrior rising up from behind him.

Aedred shouted, rushed forward, but was not quite fast enough to completely stop the downward chop of the battle axe striking the top of Edward's head. Edward dropped like an ox. With both hands knotted on the hilt of Cwellere, Aedred sliced through the Dane's mail and into his ribs. The warrior bowed sideways, lifted off his feet by the impact. He folded to the ground, spewing blood from his mouth.

Aedred scrambled to Edward, and sank to his knees, his breath sizzling through his clamped teeth. He ran his arm under the prince's shoulders and raised him up. Edward's head fell back, and Aedred carefully drew it up into the crook of his elbow.

There was a long crease in the helmet. He unstrapped it and set it on the ground, and then ran his fingers into the thick, curly hair and gently over Edward's skull. He grunted, found a ridge along that portion of the bone which had been under the dented metal, and got a better idea of the extent of his injury.

Mawer landed hard on the other side of Edward, slamming his shield on the ground. "Mother of God!" he groaned. "How bad is it?"

"I don't know. He took a clout, but it was through his helmet."

Edward's eyes fluttered open and locked on Aedred. For a brief instant, his face held a look of absolute terror. Then there was recognition. He moaned and lifted his hand to his head. "What am I doing on the ground?"

"Must be the way you fight. You might think to look behind you. You already took a hit on your hard Saxon head; you can't take many more. Feel that knot on his skull, Eorl Mawer. He outdid himself this time."

Mawer reached toward Edward's head. Edward looked up at him, moaned, "Watch out . . . !" He pushed himself out of Aedred's arms, lurched across Mawer's big thigh, and vomited in the snow.

As Mawer balanced in surprise, Aedred came up in a crouch to hold Edward's shoulders. "Wished you'd waited on breakfast?"

"Just let me hang here," Edward said raggedly.

"You're sure?"

"Yes." It was an irritated croak. "Eorl Mawer, see to the others."

Mawer shifted away, steadying the prince with one big hand as he rose to his feet. "I'll be back," he said.

He looked at Aedred and gave his head an anxious shake. Aedred nodded, and Mawer picked up his shield, hesitated, and then lumbered off to do the prince's bidding.

Aedred squeezed the trembling shoulder under his hand and stood up. "Don't try to get to your feet too quickly."

Edward answered with a grunt of misery. He listened to Aedred's footsteps go off, to his voice calling to Heafwine, and to the fading dialog as they moved farther away. High above him, he heard the raucous gathering of ravens. Without moving his head, he looked about, his eyes rolling painfully in their sockets. Finding a patch of clean snow, he scooped out a mound with one hand and dumped it over his head, holding the bulk of it on the swollen ridge as he winced and sucked in his breath. He brought his legs under him. Moving by degrees, he got unsteadily to his feet, dragging up his helmet with him. He wavered there, blinking, testing himself, before he straightened all the way up. He brought his helmet to eye level and examined it. "Christ!" he muttered and crossed himself.

"Are you all right, Sire?" It was Cedric, with a background of Saxons.

"Just a smack on the head. Everyone make it through?"

"Yes, Sire. No serious injuries."

"Praise God for that!" He crossed himself, as his men did, and then gestured to the field. "Help strip those bastards. Leave the bodies for the crows. Do whatever you have to do. Ask Eorl Mawer."

"Yes, Sire."

Speaking was nauseating him, so he waved his hand in dismissal and went back to staring at the damage to his helmet. He clumsily pulled out the padding and let it fall to the ground. Where the helmet was creased outside, it projected inward like the keel of a ship. Swaying, he gazed at it, thinking if he was to wear it again, it would have to be pounded out. He bent down carefully and picked up his sword. The world whirled, and he jerked to keep his balance. He stood still, breathing deeply. Everything steadied.

Aedred appeared. "What the hell are you trying to do with your helmet?"

"Beat the son of a bitch out so I can put it on my head."

Aedred looked him over carefully. "With your sword? You'll wreck the pommel. Why don't you use this?" He stooped over and pulled a Danish battle axe out of the snow. "Here, let me have it."

He took the helmet, held it against a stone, and began hammering it with the metal haft of the axe. Between blows, he told Edward, "We didn't lose a single man to those bastards. Five wounded, but they can all travel. That includes you in the casualty count. Are you expecting to wear this right away?"

Edward was staring at the helmet with dull eyes. "Why did I take it off?"

Aedred was not sure about him. He held up the helmet, stared at it critically, pounded on it a few more times, and scrutinized it again. "Not seeing double, are you? You sound a little foggy." He sighted along the top of the helmet.

"Double? No. I've a roaring headache, and every time I talk I feel like I'm going to vomit, but I'll live this one out. You don't have to worry about that." Edward dropped his chin to his chest with a heavy, unsteady sigh.

Aedred told him cheerfully, "Here you go. Want me to strap it on for you?"

Edward gingerly slipped the helmet on his head, winced, and pulled it off again. "No. I don't think I'll be able to keep it on after all."

Aedred watched his slow movements with amused concern. "I didn't think so."

"I feel like I've grown a fucking horn."

Aedred laughed. "You're never with one woman long enough to be cuckolded. Well, if you're ready, we'll be on our way."

"On foot, it looks like."

"It won't be the first time."

The warriors returned to the hall in the afternoon, their numbers swelled by the people who had come out to the hill overlooking the battlefield to watch. They jammed the road as the foot soldiers pressed forward shouting victory and striking their shields with knifes and spears. The whole noisy conglomeration of women and children and warriors and horses wound into the enclosure and slowly dispersed toward the hall as armor and weapons were shed and the horses stabled.

Edward's head still ached. Although his curly mass of hair hid it, he could feel the ridge on his skull. With any quick movement, he became dizzy. Otherwise he felt all right. He decided he needed food more than he needed ale. He parted with Aedred at the stable and went on into the hall with a group of warriors who scattered out along the benches to their places. There was nothing on the tables yet, but when Aedred dropped into his chair a short time later, the queen at his side, and shouted, "Ale!" the servants came running.

Edward saw the expression of joy and relief on his sister's face as she looked at Aedred. That damned magical nonsense of the runes. He sank down on the bench. Mawer settled his big frame in beside him with a lurch of the bench and a mumbled apology. He looked expectantly all up and down the table, and then grabbed up a cup of ale Heafwine slid toward him, and drank half of it in a swallow. He nodded at Edward with satisfaction, drained his cup, and dragged his fist across his broad, clean-shaven mouth. A cupbearer leaned between them, refilled it, and withdrew.

"Swearing off?"

Edward touched his head. "Waiting awhile." He cast a furtive glance at his sister. *You don't even know I've been wounded,* he thought sadly.

Mawer rumbled into a conversation he had started and frequently interrupted as they had marched back, Edward and Aedred on foot, Mawer riding beside them, because in Mercia anyone losing a horse in battle, even if he is the king, is obliged to walk.

"Of all the war-horses you've trained, that roan was the best. I hated to see him go down." Mawer shook his head.

"He'll be hard to replace," Edward agreed gloomily. He had brought only two war-horses with him to Ceolworth. "My bay pulled up lame in the paddock."

He would have to train another. None of the other mounts he had brought with him were suitable for the arduous moves demanded by Aedred's form of training. *Do I really care?* He thought.

Mawer was nodding, his big face glum with commiseration.

You good man, Edward thought warmly. *You are all I have in this world.* He felt tears hot behind his eyes.

Suddenly, the eorl's eyes widened. His teeth came together, his lips drew up, showing the gums and his long incisors in that unmistakably bear-like and uncouth grin. "Here's your ale," he said.

Edward turned to refuse and made no further movement. A brimming horn was being held out to him, the liquid bulging at the rim, but steady in the hand of Eorl Aldhune's daughter, the Lady Ella. She was smiling at him, a curious, enticing smile. Her mouth curved slightly more at one side than the other, giving it a subtle boldness. Her pale gold hair was pulled back beneath her mantle, emphasizing the clean, strong bone structure of her face. Her creamy skin was blushed delicate pink. Her eyes were darkly lashed. And it was the marvelous color of her eyes beneath those lashes--so green, and yet swarming with gold flecks--and their frank appraisal of him, which made him pause, and then accept the horn, putting it swiftly to his lips to prevent his spilling it as she gave it over.

But his hand was still unsteady from his injury, and some of the ale ran down his hand and wrist. "I wished I'd seen you cross the floor with this." He smiled at her, wondering how she had managed it.

"If you had been watching, my hand might not have been as steady." She smiled again, warmly. "It was a necessary risk; you are the only man who has not quenched his thirst."

"And me so dry."

Mawer lurched on the bench, and Edward gave him a startled glance, then frowned at him and looked back at Lady Ella.

"You were gracious to notice," he murmured, staring into those surprising eyes with their curious color, the irises so large they nearly enveloped the eyeball. "Ah, Lady Ella," he said, and drank again, looking at her over the rim.

She smiled her bewitching crooked smile. "Ah, Prince Edward."

Behind Edward, the king and the men nearest him were exchanging looks. Elfwina was sitting very still.

"Your eyes are a most extraordinary color, Lady Ella. All bright speckles of gold . . . ."

She leaned forward, speaking to Edward, but also to the wider audience following this exchange with rapt attention. "It isn't only my eyes that are extraordinary."

Her mouth curved again, and she glanced up briefly, casting it out as well to the noblemen whose low calls encouraged her.

It was a challenge Edward rose to automatically. Both were now speaking for the benefit of the listeners. Edward leaned toward her. A few inches closer and their lips would have touched. "Your modesty is even more extraordinary."

Her eyebrows lifted delicately. "Modesty is something I've neither claimed nor practiced, Prince Edward. I've observed the exercise of it wastes valuable time which could be spent so much more profitably."

"You must be a wealthy woman," said Edward, with his sweet, outrageous smile.

"The Great Mother has been generous with her endowments," she agreed, smiling down at him, her fingers clasped lightly at her back now, allowing her body to bow away from him, her ample breasts tilted upward in lovely conformation. The volume of her voice increased slightly, yet kept its soft serpentine cadence. "If you should want your horn refilled, good Prince Edward, do please call out for me."

She swiveled around and moved unhurriedly away. Edward laughed for having been bested in such style. He watched her glide off through the appreciative crowd, her body speaking within the folds of her gown in a natural sensuality.

He swung back to the table to find himself the intense center of interest. He saw Aedred's grin and gave him a look of protest.

"Better empty your horn," the king said.

He did. Of all its ale in a contest with Mawer he had no business entering and which he knew he was going to lose, but couldn't imagine how badly.

While Edward slowly drained the horn, getting encouragement from his thegns and Waltheof and the king, Mawer waited patiently. Edward cheated a little, letting some of the liquid stream down his beard. Pretending not to notice, even when there were cries exposing it, Mawer sat gazing reverently at the prince. For a breath or two, as he gulped at the horn, staring at the big eorl, his eyes bulging, Edward thought it was genuine.

"By the Holy Virgin," Mawer sighed, shaking his head as if he might have to forfeit the contest. It was then Edward knew his folly for certain. Mawer squinted, his eyes wicked. Taking up Eorl Heafwine's full horn and his own, he held one at each corner of his mouth, the great show-off, and drained them both at once without taking them from his lips and without spilling a drop. All the while, the men crowding around roared *"Down and down and down . . .!"* with each mighty swallow.

Mawer tossed the empty horns on the table, belched grandly into the applause, and exhaled mightily. He held up his hand for silence, and then laid the hand heavily on the prince's shoulder. Giving him a moue of pity, the eorl said loudly, "You fight like the true son of Brihtric, good Prince Edward, but you drink like a hen."

Edward accepted the laughter amiably, having nothing else he could gracefully do, knowing he had brought it on himself in full knowledge of Mawer's capacity. He could only blame his lunacy on the thump he had taken to his head.

The laughter gradually died, although Aedred now and then looked at him in wicked amusement. Elfwina ignored him, and he began to feel like a fool.

The general conversation rolled back to the battle. The alcohol he had drunk so recklessly hit Edward with a jolt. His head began to throb in earnest, and his stomach burned and boiled upward. He looked over at Aedred. He was deep in conversation with Penwahl. Elfwina was gone; he had no idea where, he hadn't seen her go. Mawer, too, was missing. Unloading two horns, Edward thought maliciously.

His stomach cracked and burned. His symptoms were becoming urgent. He rose and made his unsteady way across the hall, feeling more ill with every step and trying to get to his chambers before he either fainted or vomited or both.

He started up the staircase, his hand grasping the heavy carving of the banister, concentrating very hard on pulling himself along and keeping everything swallowed. The sound of his own breathing filled the space around him. His cheeks turned icy. He felt his legs draining away. Too ill to register surprise, he was grateful for the arm coming about his waist, and thought *Elfwina,* but it was Lady Ella.

From across the hall, she had immediately taken in his wavering step, his pallor, and now saw the sweat standing greasily on his face. "Lean on me," she said quietly.

He moaned his gratitude through cold lips and dropped his arm heavily across her shoulders.

Back at the benches now, Mawer lifted his thumb toward the stair where Edward and Lady Ella were ascending, an arm around each other. The men seated about him turned to look.

"From a standing start, that's his fastest time," Aedred commented drily, and was disappointed he had not noticed the progress of things soon enough to take bets.

"What a fine piece," Mawer said, without it sounding offensive. "Be my witnesses, all of you--I slandered my prince." He paused. "He'll empty more horns tonight than I'll be able to fill in a month."

Chapter Thirty-One

[829] Ceolworth, Mercia. Lady Ella pushed the heavy door open. They came stumbling over the threshold, through the anteroom, and into the main chambers. "Help him into the chair," she told Tonberht, without the provocative tones she had used downstairs.

Tonberht had appeared the moment the door flew open. He gripped the prince's waist with his strong arm, half-lifting him to a chair. "Now what?" he asked the prince.

"Nothing much," Edward replied weakly, gulping air.

"They said you had no great injury. Why didn't you call for me?"

"God!" Edward moaned, the nearest he could come to a reprimand. Tonberht growled.

"Some water and soft clothes," Lady Ella told him, with a formidable look. Tonberht paused, assessing the prince's condition. He condescended to obey.

"A head wound, isn't it?" Lady Ella drew over a stool and swung Edward's legs onto it, watching his face.

"A battle axe on the helmet."

He felt her hands exploring his head with careful assurance. Discovering the swollen area, she did not touch it, but moved her fingers along the edges, defining it without causing pain.

Tonberht returned with cloths, a basin of water, and an air of tolerance. She dipped the cloths in the water, partially wrung them, and then laid them over the swelling. The water trickled soothingly over his scalp.

"The drenching's needed inside the skull," Tonberht said. "Sire."

Feeling slightly better now that he was half-reclining, Edward gazed up at him. "Mawer."

Tonberht closed his eyes and twisted his head in a downward shake. "There's no medical treatment for stupidity," he said.

The only response from Edward was a slight, wry smile.

Lady Ella looked again at Tonberht after this exchange, really seeing him now; a man in his early thirties, with a strong, well-cared for body, an ease of movement, a composed, trustworthy face. His hair and beard were dark, almost black, and neatly trimmed. His appearance, the modulation of his voice and its accent identified him as a member of the nobility. Her eyes cleared of authority and amusement took its place. Tonberht returned her look dispassionately.

What naughty sights have those eyes seen? she wondered. Turning away, she dipped a cloth into the water and continued her ministrations.

"You seem to know something about this," Edward said. She was standing close beside his chair as she changed the cloths. Her round breasts wobbled with her movements. His nostrils filled with her scent.

"I have four brothers who also think they're indestructible. You can thank Tiw your head wasn't split wide open."

"Tiw is Aedred's god," he mumbled, thinking he would like to push his face between those swaying breasts.

She drew back to look at him, and for a second he imaged she had read his thoughts. "What did you say?"

"I'm a Christian."

"I'd forgotten. You *were* lucky!"

His head was feeling better and the nausea was gone. The ale still swam in his veins, but it had lost its volatility, leaving only mellowness.

"You don't look quite so ghastly," Lady Ella told him. "How does your head feel now?"

"Good enough. You can take those away."

She removed the cloths and dropped them into the basin. Edward signaled for Tonberht to remove it and himself. Tonberht left with great dignity.

"I like your man," she said, when the handthegn was gone.

"Tonberht? He's a pain in the ass," he said with affection.

"I could see that," she smiled. "How long has he been with you--years?"

"Oh, Lord, yes--years. Since I was nine, I think . . . yes, since I was nine."

She was watching him and smiling gently. "Where's your comb?"

"Over there." He indicated a long carved chest near the window. "You aren't going to try to run a comb through my hair, are you?"

She found the comb and came back over to him. "Yes, I am. The wet rags have it every which way. It will be harder to comb once it's dried. I'll be careful." When he drew back with a grimace, she added, "It won't hurt, you big baby. It couldn't be nearly as bad as having a Dane bash your head."

"The Danes bash and have done with it. Combing borders on torture."

She huffed a small mocking laugh.

There was a period of silent concentration as the comb moved painlessly through his curls. Her hands touched him gently, hypnotically. He relaxed. "You'll have me asleep in a minute. I should thank the Danes; you'll make me a new man."

"Don't let the new man go rushing into another battle." She set the comb aside and pressed her hand against the curls at the side of his head.

"The last battle I rushed into was my first," he replied. "That was twelve years ago. The man may not be immortal, but I can guarantee he gives it his best effort."

She rose from his side, and he sat up.

"I would imagine you give everything your best effort."

"Everything's that's important."

She surveyed the room in a slow, supple turn. "Important to you?"

"It would have to be, wouldn't it?"

"Not necessarily. There's king and crown, etc. There's not much of you here, is there?" Her hand made a delicate sweep, including the entire, unadorned chamber. The sleeve fell back over her milky arm.

"I think there's more than enough of me here," he replied, amused, his eyes on that graceful arm. "But tell me what you mean by that."

"Bare walls, no personal effects. You spend most of your time at your father's court in Exeter, don't you?"

"Half the year."

"Half?" She seemed surprised. "And the other half here?"

"Unless the Danes are abroad in the south."

"How is it, I wonder, that I haven't seen you at Ceolworth before?"

"I've stayed longer, this time. Normally I'm here from May--from Thrilmilce to Blodmonath. Your father is here for three months beginning in Solmonath. We overlapped this time." He gave her a slow smile. "I may permanently shift my dates."

"That may not be necessary, Edward All-Fair. We're not far off Cyninges Street. Stop there. Father would be pleased to have you as our guest."

"Father would be? My life's ambition is to please Eorl Aldhune. What would please you?"

"Whatever pleases my father."

"A dutiful daughter." Edward couldn't help grinning.

Their eyes held. This silent exchange and her faint smile made a charming promise. Disappointment flickered at the edges of his interest.

She made another lazy turn and walked idly about while he watched her with lowered eyelids. When she came to a large table standing against one wall, she stopped and leaned over it. "Here's something more personal. What fine maps these are!"

He was enjoying the flow of her gown over her taut, round buttocks, how the material stretched and sheened as she leaned still farther to draw one of the rolled maps toward her. She glanced back over her shoulder at him. His eyes lifted to her face. She was smiling at him as if to say, *Go ahead; I've placed myself here for you to look at. We both know you like what you see.*

With disarming honesty, Edward replied, "Now, you've struck at the core of my vanity."

"Do you feel well enough to come here and explain these to me?"

Edward was held by conflicting motivations--the desire she had aroused in him and his reluctance to succumb to it. But he could think of no reasonable, civil way to end the sexual dance they had begun that would not be more difficult to perform than its expected conclusion. He wondered at his hesitation.

He raised his head with a smile that disturbed his lips but left his eyes unchanged. "What explanation does a fine map need?"

"Any you're willing to give." Her smile was again gentle. "I don't know very much about maps, but I have heard about yours."

He got up from the chair, found he was steady, and walked over to the table with a feeling of inevitability.

She gave him a side glance. "This one is of Mercia, isn't it? A military map of Mercia, I mean."

"You recognized that. Yes, it's military." He smoothed it out and placed on it small weights from a dish. He tapped his fingertip on a circle marked *Ceolworth*. His arm brushed hers, and she did not move it. He could feel her warmth through both their sleeves. "As you see, this is where we are now." He moved his finger along the parchment. "Here's the *Cilternsætna*."

"And Beorhhamstede." She turned her face up to him. "Not all that far from Wessex."

He felt himself closing to the intimacy she was offering. His amusement became brittle.

She bent her head over the map and traced a thin blue line that spiraled to a small circle near the point designated Farleah. Tiny precisely formed numbers marked each turn of the spiral. She looked at him again. "You've noted how high it is." She had recognized his sagging interest and considered it a challenge. "In relation to what? The surrounding countryside? What is your reference point?"

"I use the surrounding countryside," he replied, in some surprise, interested again. "That was an astute question."

"You are kind to admit it."

He stared at her, and then looked back down at the map. "It's not an altogether satisfactory system for several reasons. Only an approximation," he murmured, suddenly lost in this problem that had vexed him for a long time. "But it serves, until I can find a better method."

"Do you make these yourself, or does a clerk make them under your direction?"

"Hell, no! I'd hardly trust a clerk with them. I make them myself from diagrams and notes I make in the field."

"Remarkable," she said sincerely.

She encouraged him to go into his theory of map-making and, partly for his own enjoyment, partly to test her patience and the depth of her interest, he obliged. Her comments were intelligent and her attentiveness, as he knew she meant it to be, was flattering.

Her eyes are truly wonderful, he thought. *How could such a color mix arise?*

"You really must come to Beorhhamstede, Prince Edward." Her lips parted slightly, holding the shape of his name. It was artifice, but it was also effective. "But not solely to record the elevation. When was it you made your measurements?"

It was fascinating how the simplest statement from her mouth became suggestion. *I spent that night measuring the depth of a shepherd's daughter,* he laughed to himself. "A few years ago, when we were harrying the Danes through Waterperry. We camped there." *Oh, yes.*

"And you took your measurements?"

He couldn't help the grin, and she knew instantly what it was about. She reached up. Her fingers stirred his beard, and her eyes worked brightly over his face. "Come spend some time with us. The chase is excellent, the game plentiful." That crooked, knowing smile which matched his own, expanded. "Measure all our hills and valleys."

He lightly kissed her fingers. "A future time. I'm hunting Danes now."

Her smile dipped, pouted. "The invitation is open." Her face moved close to his, her voice low. "You can accept anytime you wish." The pupils of her eyes expanded as he looked down into them. He kissed her.

She pressed upward with her breasts as he put his arms around her. He kissed her again, slipping his tongue into her widening mouth. He allowed an erection to push up her belly. Her hips swayed to position her pelvis. His hand slid over the curve of her buttocks, pulling her closer, and their bodies moved against each other.

"Do we stand, Edward? Or do you have a bed?"

"I have a bed."

"I'm not a brood mare."

"I'll see to it."

Chapter Thirty-Two

[829] Ceolworth, Mercia. Her strange eyes glazed and withdrew. Her spasm thrust her pelvis bone up, counteracting his hard rhythm. As her orgasm began, he drew down the level of his own excitement, maintaining a rhythm without reaching coitus. It was something he did to perfection. She sighed, and he withdrew as life came back into her eyes. He touched her cheek with the back of his hand and bent to kiss her. Her lips curved and parted under his. He lifted his head inquiringly.

She was smiling at him. "How pleasing you are."

He smiled.

"I wasn't disappointed."

"Did you expect to be?"

"Rumors are seldom reliable," she murmured.

"Oh?" He gave her cheek a final tender stroke and sat up, looking at her as if he were unsure how to respond, or indeed, whether to respond at all. "You know gossip comes easy at court," he said finally. He began to dress.

She rose lazily and slipped on her gown. "Some small truth usually underlies it." She waited for him to catch the double meaning, but all he said was "Mmmm," without looking at her as he pulled on his trousers.

She fixed her hair and arranged her mantle, watching Edward pull his tunic carefully over his tousled head. When he looked at her again, his eyes seemed a darker blue, their expression closed, reflecting a distance not there before. But he smiled and put his arms around her. "What are you seeing?" he asked softly.

She decided not to give the answer rising truthfully to her lips: *Where is the man who has just made love to me with such sensitive anticipation of my needs?* Instead, she told him lightly, "A radiant man. An excellent lover." She felt his chest jump in a silent laugh and immediately regretted her decision, although what she had said was true enough. *Ah, well, one can't always hit the mark.*

"That sounds so good I'm sorry I didn't think to say it."

"I wish it *had* been you who said it," she laughed.

He kissed her, murmuring, "Can you stay?"

Polite form, of course: she answered with a wistful smile and a shake of her head.

At the door he took her face in his hands and told her softly, "You do have the most glorious eyes." With a sad and tender gesture, he kissed the lids. "Thank you."

He opened the door for her. "Goodnight, Prince Edward. Rest

well."

"I will have you to thank if I do." Empty, shallow, meaningless words. He stared blankly at the door. Then he turned away and padded about the room in his bare feet. For a while he stood at the window. Finally he sank into a chair and rested his head in his hands. A profound depression settled on him.

What is the matter with me?

It always ended in connection only. Intimacy became isolation as parchment became ash under flame. The body discovered, the essence unrevealed. He wasn't sure what it was he wanted, he only knew that every encounter left the same dissatisfaction, the same restlessness of soul. He groaned and sank his head lower into his hands.

There was a knock on his door, and he looked up, glanced about for Tonberht, remembered he had sent him off. He straightened in his chair, called, "Come in," thinking it was probably Mawer.

Elfwina entered from the anteroom and approached him slowly. He rose as she glanced around the room. He saw in her face she was aware of all that had transpired there.

"Aedred said you had been wounded. I didn't know. You seem all right, now." She glanced about, again.

"It wasn't serious."

She looked again around the room.

He said, "Just a thump. I had on my helmet." His lips felt unresponsive. "It knocked me silly . . . made me sick at my stomach for a time. That's all." He sank back into the chair.

"I see. Yet . . . it hasn't been that long since your other head wound."

She walked a few steps to the table and ran her hand along the edge where his maps lay, some in rolls against the wall, some upright in a stand. She bent her head as if she was studying the spread-out map of Mercia, but in fact she wasn't seeing it at all. "But you seem to be feeling better, now." It was a bitter statement.

"I'll live." He watched as she looked at the bed.

Through her eyes he saw its rumpled covers, the fur skins tossed aside, the pillows crushed. He could smell the warm musky after odor of intercourse. He saw his own disheveled appearance. He groaned, ashamed.

"Do you love her?"

"I hardly know her, Elfwina."

He sighed and pressed his cold fingers against his forehead. "It didn't mean anything." Then annoyed at his defensiveness, he said, harshly, "Grow up, Elfwina. Shut off your reproaches. These are my private quarters; what happens here is my business."

"Is this the sum of your manhood? Quick encounters that mean nothing?"

"As you say."

"Then I must have been one of the first quick encounters."

He looked up, his face shocked. "No! You must know it wasn't like that with us."

"How would I know, Edward?"

He took a breath, composing himself as he slowly rose. "I've wanted to talk to you about that--about that night in your chambers. I wanted to explain what you might not have understood."

"If you wish."

"Let's go into the other room," he said, wanting away from the revelations in the room. He led her through a door into the space he used for meetings. There was a large table, chairs, benches. She declined his offer to sit, and instead stood quietly regarding him, her hands folded into her sleeves.

He remained standing, too, his hand on his chest, the spread of his fingers unconscious protection as he pulled the words out. "I wasn't thinking coherently that night. I didn't expect all those things to come out. I had too much wine." When she made no response, he said, "You were right--we've never talked about it . . . what happened." When she still didn't respond, he said, "Look, you have to understand, boys sometimes adore someone they shouldn't. Someone forbidden to them. I--adored you that way. We were so close . . . our thoughts . . . so much that we shared. You remember. I wanted to be close in . . . every way. Physically, I mean. I know what I did was improper, but--" he looked away from her, cleared his throat, and met her eyes again "--but the contact, you know; it wasn't altogether . . . completed." He approached her, a supplicant, and she straightened, took one step backwards. He halted. "Elf, that was so long ago. Do you hate me for it?"

"Do you still adore me, Edward . . . in that way?"

He opened his mouth to speak, and then closed it and stood silent. Then he said, "I've outgrown adoration. I'm not that boy anymore."

"And the man? What about him?"

He said, "He is your brother."

"And of that love that was forbidden, nothing remains?"

"How could it?"

"No. How could it."

Elfwina's footfalls measured her room, crossed and recrossed, again and again, length to width, corner to corner as the night turned slowly above the hall. She could not stop pacing. And pacing did not help her think. Her thoughts tumbled, rolled around and she couldn't bring them into order. Nothing had coherence. She loved her husband. Unkindness or anger did not exist between them. There was only love, and she knew there would always be love. And yet--she felt she was dying. That part of her, long buried and unspeakable, had been ripped open and she was bleeding and Edward had abandoned her again.

Chapter Thirty-Three

[829] Ceolworth, Mercia. Most of the snow had melted except in the north shadow of the hall and in the deeper woods. The trees were still bare, the nights cold, the sun a thin disk. But the first blooms which suggested approaching spring were pushing through the ground, and the ceorls were readying the fields for the later planting. It was Solmonath, the Month of Cakes, when offerings were made to beg abundance from the earth.

The villagers were gathered at the edge of the open fields. Dressed in their best clothes, the children ran shouting through the groups of their elders and into the damp and weedy furrows of the yardlands, were reproved, and dodged back into the wet grass of the strip of land separating village from field. A little way into the field the ploughman waited with his hyacinth-garlanded oxen. Near the plough stood a table filled with cakes of barley and honey that were covered with an elaborately worked cloth.

For the occasion of the festival, Aedred wore a crimson mantle gathered at the right shoulder by a gold brooch intricately set with garnet and lapis lazuli. The yellow tunic beneath the mantle was embroidered with silver. His hose and bandings were purple. He looked resplendent. He sat with his arm along the back railing of the royal booth, his shoe resting on the edge of the bench where Edward sat in forbearance, the gold diadem of a prince around his brow, his concession to heathen ritual.

Looking as fragile as glass, Elfwina sat beside Aedred. Her green gown was girdled with a wide gold band, and a green mantle lined in purple draped from her shoulders. Her black hair was coiled and bound beneath a gauzy net sewn with pearls and strings of pale green peridot. Clutching her arms as if chilled, she gazed off toward the low hills rolling westward beyond the fields and the river. In the pale sunshine outside the booth, members of the court stood and talked and waited.

"These things always get off to a late start," Aedred said in a low voice.

Studying the problem, Edward replied, "I don't know. I don't mind waiting. You couldn't find a better seat than this to watch the crops grow. The turnips will rise there on our left; the cabbage will rise on our right, and ahead there in the fallow we'll watch the cow shit pile up for next year's ceremony."

Elfwina laughed, and Aedred pushed the prince with his boot. Without turning around, Edward shrugged and said, "Just an observation. Here comes Ceadda. Does he have anything to do with getting this thing going?"

Aedred looked toward his wife. "Does he?"

"My love, I don't arrange these things. I think he's a celebrant as we are."

Ceadda came toward them at an easy pace; giving the impression he could cover a long distance comfortably in a short time. He was dressed in grey, the tunic spun randomly with red threads. The colors suited him well. He came up to the booth and saluted them.

"You're welcome to join us, Ceadda," Aedred told him. "The thing hasn't begun yet."

Ceadda crooked his arm on the railing and leaned against the booth. "Thank you, Sire, but I believe I'll enjoy this sunshine." He laid his other hand over his forearm, and his sleeve dropped back, revealing a gold bracelet in the form of a snake biting its tail. Since he was closer to Ceadda than the others, Edward saw it clearly. Each golden scale that composed the snake's body was an interlocking link. Its fangs, cleverly embedded in the rings of the tail, were the clasp. One eye was ruby, the other an emerald. The workmanship was exquisite. Since Ceadda caught him examining it, Edward said, "That's a marvelous bit of work."

"It is beautifully crafted, isn't it? The World Serpent--do you know its significance?"

"His Majesty's standard bears the emblem--I think I remember the myth: the World Serpent lies beneath the ocean, encircling the earth." They were looking directly at each other, Edward with amusement, the magician with a point of intensity in the deep blackness of his eyes. "As long as the monster keeps hold of its tail, as I recall," Edward continued, "the world goes on about its business. Am I right, so far?"

"Your memory serves you well. Then, you did begin in our religion."

"Began, yes, but the right path was found for me, and I've moved steadily out of the darkness ever since." Edward smiled charmingly, refuting offense.

The magician's expression was congenial. "What else do you remember of the World Serpent?"

"Let's see--now we come to the direful part. If the tail of the terrible serpent is pulled from its mouth, there will be calamity such as the world has never seen." He gave the magician a guileless smile. "Keep its teeth secure, Ceadda."

The magician slowly returned the smile, his eyes depthless and shining. Then he looked out over the fields. His profile stood against the background of the great hall, its stone and timber walls and its fortifications, and seemed suddenly to be hewn from more substantial stuff and would be more enduring.

"In your mythology," Ceadda answered quietly, "the snake is a tempter of Woman. In turn, she shares with Man a fall from grace which brings fear, murder, and all sin to humanity." He looked back at the prince, who was staring at him. "A tempter is more vile, don't you think, than a simple worm whose function in keeping order is merely to keep its tail in its mouth?"

Aedred sighed, "Thank the Gods!" and both Ceadda and Edward, whose face had turned pale, looked around to see a procession coming from the village.

It was led by children, small boys and girls carefully groomed and governed by a grey-haired woman of imposing stature. She carried a long stick and walked with the procession, snapping the tip of the stick across any errant child.

Aedred leaned over the prince. "The woman is a demon with that stick," he told him. "Dead accuracy from fifteen paces through masses of arms and legs without touching any but the guilty."

"*You* marched in these?"

"Every year. I was black and blue."

Edward swiveled back to watch with a critical eye. "Splendid wrist . . . a mean, nasty sting to the purpose. Who the hell is this?" Edward suddenly doubled over with laughter. The next instant, Aedred, laughing, sank against the booth railing.

An important functionary was coming along behind the children, an old man, neatly but shabbily, dressed in a carefully patched tunic belted with a braided strap of gleaming leather. On his head a crown of hyacinths had sprung undone, and one long stock bobbed comically over one ear. He marched along on his bowed legs with determination, scowling at a man, apparently his son, who darted in repeatedly from the edges of the procession to grab at the front of the old man's tunic where it had gotten caught in the top of a stocking and gave an unrestricted view of his swaying testicles. Each time the son would put out his hand to pull at the cloth, the old man would slap at him. Frowning fiercely and stretching his mouth in ugly grimaces, he drove the younger man away only to have him circle back to grab at him again.

While this was going on, a signal was given to the children up ahead, who were being kept sternly in their places. They began in a high, ragged song: *Raise the cloth, raise the cloth . . .*

"What?" Edward sputtered. *"What* are they singing?"

Barely able to articulate, Aedred repeated the words. Edward roared. Laughing behind the screen of her mantle, Elfwina cried out to them, "Stop it! Stop it! Poor Wigmund will be humiliated if he sees you howling like this!"

Edward stretched out his legs and slid down below the level of the booth railing. He choked out, "I can't help it, Elf! 'Raise the cloth'! Oh, God--!"

Aedred had rammed his chin into his shoulder. His body shook as he stared with glazed and teary eyes toward the hall, whining inside his throat like a dog.

"Stop it, I say!" Elfwina squeezed his arm hard, barely able to control her own laughter. "There! Someone's managed to pull it down. Now! They're almost here. Up--both of you!"

Aedred recovered first. Pulling his crimson mantle about him, he was steely-eyed and regal by the time the singing children had passed the booth and the old man had come alongside. Edward surfaced with a sober face, but almost lost it again, for as the old man bowed to them, the hyacinth bobbing with him, the garland snapped altogether. As he came unsteadily upright, it uncoiled and slid down his face and off his chest to lie in a heap at his feet.

There was an embarrassing silence, embroidered by the tinny voices of the children as they marched on. The old man did not look down, but stared straight ahead with grim dignity. Then he turned stiffly to follow after the children.

Edward leaned to Aedred. "Is that garland necessary? Does he need it for the ceremony?"

Elfwina answered for him. "It doesn't have to be hyacinths, but tradition does require a chaplet."

"Poor old fellow," Edward murmured and stood up. "Hold!" he cried.

The old man halted. Edward went down out of the booth past Ceadda, who watched him with a faint smile, and up to where the old man stood waiting respectfully. Edward held his breath as Wigmund bowed, wavered, and came upright with a quick balancing step. The prince responded to this precarious bow with his best regal nod and tried to match the old man's solemn demeanor.

"I offer this for your ceremony," Edward said, and lifted the diadem from his head. He placed the gold band on Wigmund's head, praying silently it wouldn't slip over the old man's ears. The diadem was slightly large, but the man's hair was bushy enough to hold it. Edward stepped back. The old man blinked his eyes slowly in lieu of a bow which might have toppled the gold band. Edward acknowledged the gesture with a nod. With magnificent dignity, the old ceorl turned and moved along with the procession as it started up again.

Edward reached down and scooped up the garland of hyacinths and brought it back with him to the booth. "These may have some favor to them," he said, lowering the flowers into his sister's lap. He resumed his seat. Aedred leaned forward to briefly lay his hand on Edward's shoulder, and then sat back to watch the scene arranging before them.

The children had lined up along the verge. The ploughman was walking around his animals, running his hand along their necks, testing the traces. Most of the villagers clustered near the plough. Close by, and right at the edge of the field, four women stood behind the draped table facing two men who were holding baskets. Everyone waited as Wigmund lifted his feet carefully, testing the soil of the old furrows. He held his head erect, his movements involving his entire upper torso, insurance against a toppling crown. They all watched. He looked over at the children and raised his arm. They began to sing again: *Raise the cloth. . .* A smile flickered at the corners of Edward's mouth and then was gone.

Raise the cloth from our offerings--

The old man turned back to the table, flashing sunlight along the gold band. The women lifted the cloth away from the cakes. When the children sang *Our baskets fill with offerings to our Great Mother,* the women began to stack the cakes into the baskets held by the men. Then the children sang:

With cakes of barley and honey
We ask for your abundance
We are your children
We ask for your abundance

As the last verse faded, the old man held out his arms and, in a voice of startling purity, began to chant *We are the children,* and all the villagers and members of the court echoed *We are the children.*

Behind him, Edward could hear Aedred's formal tone and the sweet light voice of his sister singing with the rest of the assemblage in alternating lines with the old man:

We are the children
Who praise the name of their Great Mother
Whose abundance gives life
Without whose bounty we would perish
Look with favor upon the turning of our plough
And let your rich earth
Bless this year with your fruit.

The plough man called out to his oxen, the boy at their heads shook his stick, and the great beasts strained forward, the coulter cleaving the weeds and stagnant earth, breaking the way for the blade. As the plough pulled ahead, the old man walked to the side of the furrow it made, taking cakes from the baskets carried alongside him by the two men and dropping them into the dark groove. When he had emptied the baskets, he turned and came back up the furrow, chanting and making signs over the fresh ground. The ploughman called his oxen around and slowly followed, covering the cakes with the rich, dark loam.

When the old man and his assistants reached the starting point, he signaled for them to tip their baskets. They turned them over, and they sang:

Great Mother
Great Mother of all
Mother Erce accept our offerings.

With that solemn benediction there was a joyous cry from the children, and they ran laughing and shouting for the table. Food was being brought by men and women hurrying up from the village, and as the crowd shifted toward the table, Edward again found Ceadda beside the booth.

"If you were to go down there, Sire," he said, "it would be a sign of honor for Wigmund."

Edward came to his feet. "I would be glad to." He glanced back at the king and queen. Aedred was leaning over the booth railing speaking with Mawer and Grundl, and his sister was exchanging a word with several of the village women who clustered at the side. He went down the steps and into the sunlight.

Elfwina finished her conversation and seeing Aedred was still talking with Mawer, she sat looking out at Edward, where he stood near the table. With every movement of his head, the sunlight coiled brightly through his hair. He had been given a cake and was eating it as he talked with the villagers. From his gestures, she could tell he was asking questions about the ceremony. His manner was easy, and the people responded to that easiness. As she gazed at him, she ached with loss, with that wrenching away of love. Tears made a sudden flood. She pressed her fingers to her lips. As she watched her brother, one of the little village boys came bounding up to him and, so eager was he to speak to the prince he lost his balance and was laughingly recovered by Edward. She mourned at that kindly gesture.

The old man walked up to him, then, and held out the diadem. Elfwina felt her brother pause and knew he was deciding just how he would respond. The warm timbre of his voice drifted to her, the words undistinguishable. As she had so often in the past she knew his intent in those thoughts that moved between their skulls.

"By the Gods!" Aedred said close to her ear, "he's giving the band to Wigmund!"

"Not personally--for him to use in future ceremonies."

"Have we a convert?" Looking fondly down at Edward, he added, "I love that brother of yours."

"I know you do."

"What other prince in the world would salvage a ceorl's dignity with his crown?"

Ceadda walked back with them to the hall. Beside him, Queen Elfwina carried the purple garland of hyacinths looped over her arm. Their heavy fragrance filled his nostrils. At her side was Aedred and next to him, Edward. Ahead and behind them were the eorls and thegns of Mercia and their kinswomen. In the pale Solmonath afternoon, they all seemed immortal.

Chapter Thirty-Four

[829] Ceolworth, Mercia. The candles were guttering. Aedred glanced up, and Ceolric called for a fresh supply. The reeve sat back from his account books and said, "It promises well, Sire. When the cakes don't float on Ploughing Day, it's a fair sign."

Aedred chuckled and leaned back in his chair to give the servant with the candles room to work. "Always with the help of the gods. It looks in fine order, Ceolric."

He looked up briefly at the ceiling. His dark eyes were sparking when his glance fell back to the reeve's face.

"Sire?" But Ceolric recognized that look.

"I have a little experiment in mind I want to discuss with you."

"An experiment, Your Majesty?"

"If it seems feasible. Eorl Guthuf wants to get rid of one of his boars. He says it's too ungainly to survive in his woods. According to him, the animal's wide as a door and so low its belly rubs the ground. Take the swineherd and go have a look. Check him over. See if he could be raised in a small enclosure where short legs wouldn't be a detriment. If it's a deformity, I don't want him either. But if the boar's not elf-touched, I want it bred to our sows. The result could be domestic stock with more meat on their bones." He sat back and regarded Ceolric. "Are you following me?"

"Yes, Sire. If this boar is acceptable, you want to develop a new, heavier breed of domestic pig."

"There you go." Aedred looked at Ceolric with approval.

Ceolric's light brown eyes held a mild expression. "This is a wild boar, Your Majesty?"

"A pretty rough piece of pigskin by Guthuf's estimation. He figured the boar's a product of one of those Danish pigs slipping over from East Anglia to prick a wild Mercian sow. There's a treaty for you."

"And not an easy peace," Ceolric said solemnly, and then gave the king a slow smile.

Aedred was a moment taking in this humor from his serious reeve. Then he burst out laughing. "Probably the hardest piece a Danish pig ever got, Ceolric."

Aedred glanced up as a servant moved past the table to attend to a knock on the door. He grinned at the reeve. "Well, check him carefully." He became serious again. "Go on, then. Report back to me as soon as you've made your inspection. If it's workable, I'd want the project started right away. A few pounds of meat can make a difference over a bitter winter."

"Yes, Sire, immediately upon my return." The reeve began gathering his account books.

Aedred sat back, contented. "A good report, Ceolric. Efficient, as always."

"Thank you, Sire." Ceolric replied, pleased. He bowed and moved toward the anteroom where the servant was just reentering followed by a tall man with dark hair and a beard peppered with grey. The man had been on horseback for some time; his shoes were grooved with mud, his braccio and bandings spattered. Over a tunic of mail, he wore both sword and scramaseax. He came past the reeve with a nod. Ceolric returned the nod with a bow. Glancing briefly at the king, he saw no indication Aedred wished him to stay, so he continued on, a mask of discretion falling over his scholarly features.

Aedred sank back against his chair in amazement. "Eorl Teownor! You've been on a hard run. Not the Danes?"

Teownor bowed. "Not immediately, Your Majesty. King Brihtric sends his love."

"Sit down, you look all in." He turned to a servant. "Ale," he told him, "and food for the eorl. Then all of you leave us."

Teownor drank gratefully. When they were alone, the Saxon eorl leaned forward. "I was sent ahead, Sire. King Brihtric will arrive within the hour and Gryffn by daybreak. His Majesty thought it prudent to travel through Mercia unannounced."

Aedred stared at him. "I would like to know how that was accomplished," he said, considering his defenses and outposts. "Hel's gate!" he cried in exasperation. "But, go on--was Wessex overtaken? And Wales?"

"No, nothing like that, Sire. There's been no invasion. King Brihtric and Gryffn are coming to confer. After your couriers brought news of Tewkesbury, King Brihtric decided a meeting should take place without delay. We have a small entourage. We'll stay two days and return before the wind gets up."

"When did you leave Exeter?"

"Three days ago."

"Three days! There's a forced march the Danes could envy!"

"Have they harried further, Sire?"

"Not since their raid on Eorl Gyrth. We harried them a bit." He stood up, and Teownor rose with him. "Stay seated. Rest and eat. I'll set things in motion here and return shortly."

Aedred went first to the prince's rooms. He stood at the side of Edward's bed, his hands on his hips, looking down at the sleeping figure coiled, child-like, on its side.

"Ho! Edward," he called softly. "Come alive!"

Edward's eyes flashed open, glassy blue. He turned his head to look up at the king. "An attack?" He sat straight up and threw back the covers.

"No attack. Your father will be here within the hour. Teownor's in my quarters, now."

Edward came to his feet shedding his gown. "My God! Have they attacked Exeter?" He was scrambling into his clothes with the swift help of Tonberht, who had appeared in his nightshirt.

"No, the Danes are still sitting comfortably in Mercia."

The prince was looking at Aedred over Tonberht's busy shoulder and scowling, trying to make sense of it. "Did Father bring an army?"

"Only a few retainers, Teownor says. It's a conference."

"That's encouraging, anyway." Edward's brain was finally beginning to work. "Does Elf know Father's coming?"

"I'm going to tell her now." Aedred paused, watching Tonberht quickly cross-tying the bands on Edward's trouser legs.

"So it's a war council."

"That's the way it appears."

Aedred left Edward quietly swearing at a brooch he was trying to stab into his mantle and went on to Elfwina's chambers.

"She'll be dressing," Aedred quietly instructed Edyth. She went to open a wardrobe, and Aedred sat down on the bed. He gently pulled back the fur skins from his wife's head. She was curled up on her side in the same pose in which he had found Edward. *Twins,* he thought. He lifted the hair away from her face. It was Edward's profile wrought finer. Around her neck was the golden chain and jeweled ring of their mutual ancestor Offa, a talisman she never removed.

He leaned forward and murmured into her ear. She rolled over without opening her eyes and drew in a luxurious breath through her nostrils. Stretching her arms up, she took Aedred into her sleepy embrace.

"I was waiting for you," she told him, her eyes still shut. She kissed at his face, made contact with his nose, and closed her lips moistly over the tip. "That Ceolric is too thorough."

He ran his tongue over her lips. "What were you going to do when I got here?"

She smiled.

"Wina--"

"Come to bed."

He sighed. "I would, if your father weren't going to be here within the hour."

Her eyes popped open. "Father? Here?" She sat up abruptly, dumping him away.

With a laugh, he caught his balance. He told her of Teownor's arrival.

All business, now, Elfwina slipped into the robe Edyth held for her and said, "He knows this is no simple game, this time."

"Gryffn is on his way, too. He should be here soon." He knew what her reaction would be to that. "I know you don't like him, but he'll only be here two days. Will you put up with him for that space?"

"I'll put up with him, as you ask. I only wish you would see how dangerous he is."

"He's no more dangerous than any other leader Mercia deals with." He paused, and then said carefully, "It's personal with you, Wina. I'm not condemning it, but it clouds your perception of the man."

"His behavior toward me is not a clouded perception."

Aedred laughed. "He's in love with you, like every other male that comes to Ceolworth."

"Every other male knows how to behave regardless of their infatuation."

"Cut him short."

"I have. This is not an idle protest, Aedred."

"Yes, I know." He took her in his arms. "Put up with him, will you? He is our ally. We sorely need him. Besides, we'll all be busy these next few hours. He won't have time to pester you."

She was not satisfied, but this was not the time to pursue it. "I'll see that things are made ready," she said.

A slow file of horsemen came through the side gate and into the stable yard. They quietly dismounted. A number left the group and were led into the hall through the back passageway and up to the royal chambers. They spread slowly out into the room, nine men in battle dress, a tenth man wearing a heavy mantle and gold cap of a Christian archbishop. But the figure around whom the others moved was Brihtric. The Saxon king's blond hair and beard were now fading into grey. There was weariness in his face as he came forward to meet his son-in-law and kinsman.

"Welcome, King Brihtric," Aedred said warmly.

Brihtric embraced him. "I apologize for this lack of formality, but it is warranted."

"You are always welcome in Mercia--formally or informally."

"Thank you." Brihtric turned to Edward. "I believe this is my son, although I cannot say with any certainty, since I haven't seen his face for nine months."

Edward's cheeks blew suddenly rosy. "My intention was to return, Sire, but with the Danes assembling and the raids, it seemed better to remain here."

"This once, I will agree." Brihtric embraced him. Then, with his hands on the prince's shoulders, Brihtric glanced about. "Where is your sister?"

"Seeing to the details. She'll be along."

When Elfwina did arrive, she found the most trusted eorls of her father's council seated about the room talking quietly, their fatigue evident in their postures.

"Ah, Elfwina," Brihtric sighed and kissed her when she bent over him. He laid his hand along her cheek and whispered, "Beautiful child . . ." He took her hand and held it tightly. "Come, sit here beside me. You know everyone but his Excellency, Archbishop Ansel."

The archbishop bowed and murmured, "Ma'am," and retreated.

"Your chambers are ready, Father."

"Thank you, my dear. We'll go shortly. Even young Teownor is feeling the lack of sleep." He didn't look at the eorl, but Teownor's smile was wry.

After a short interval, Brihtric rose with a nod to Aedred. "We'll take a few hours' rest," he said. "With your permission, King Aedred, when Gryffn arrives, we'll get down to business."

Chapter Thirty-Five

[829] Ceolworth, Mercia. The winter sun lay low on the horizon, its light slanting directly into the chamber, brightening every corner. A large table had been brought in and placed against one wall. On it were rolled maps and stacks of parchment, quills and pots of ink. To one side, where he could write on the table's surface, the round-faced archbishop sat on a stool. Loosely grouped in a semi-circle were the rulers and their most trusted companions, and Queen Elfwina.

Listening to a summary of events, Gryffn sprawled in his chair at an angle, giving him full view of the queen. He was a man of small stature, with well-developed shoulders and arms. His chest was broad, his short legs sturdy. His skin was dark, his hair brown, long, and tied in the back. Except for a bushy, drooping mustache, he was clean-shaven. He was forty years old. He exuded a sinister energy recognized by everyone in the room.

He paid close attention to Aedred's narrative, but his smoky violet eyes, the only feature suggesting gentleness, kept returning to the queen. Each time this insolence happened, she met his gaze steadily, until his eyes slid away. Elfwina would never accept him as an ally, regardless of Mercia's need for the Welshman's help, but she would suffer him at her husband's request.

Having heard Aedred through, Gryffn was silent for a moment. When he did speak it was in a surprisingly melodic voice filled with the pitches and falls of the west.

"You tracked them out, Ma'am, and now we are confronted with thousands of Danes. Do we know who leads them?"

It was Brihtric who answered in his quiet tone, and Gryffn turned to him. "Urm is at their head."

The chieftain's laugh came from deep in his throat. "And who else?"

"Ingware and two of his sons."

"Which two?"

"Albann and Amund."

Gryffn's mustache pushed forward thoughtfully. "Ah, Albann, now . . . ." He lifted his hand to indicate only Albann was worthy of consideration.

"There's further news." Brihtric addressed it to Aedred. "Our fleet was able to drive off over thirty longships attempting to land at Cisseceaster, but at least that many had already unloaded their warriors and supplies. Now, there's word of a large assembly in East Anglia."

"Tilhere informed us of that." Aedred turned to the aide standing behind him. "At Maldon, wasn't it?"

"Yes, Sire, Maldon."

"And the ones marching through your kingdom . . . ?" Gryffn's mustache lifted faintly, and Aedred's eyes darkened. "How do you gauge their numbers?"

"At least three hundred, possibly more."

Gryffn chewed delicately at his mustache. He shook his head. "Peace always brings complacency. Shall we call it five and work with generous numbers?"

Aedred chose not to reply.

"So," Gryffn went on, "there are two thousand at the Severn, less the hikers who had Northumbria as their destination. With your figures, King Brihtric, we can count, say a thousand more? What was the estimate of the Maldon force?"

"Around a thousand," Aedred replied.

"With what Ædda and Osward can levy—another two thousand?" He looked around inquiringly. There were quiet agreements. "The force we may be reckoning with may be over six thousand strong, most of those seasoned warriors."

"That is the measure of it," Brihtric said wearily.

The discussion continued for hours. At some point of minor consequence being tediously argued, Elfwina got up and left the room. She went to her chambers and dropped into a chair by the window. She laid her head back and closed her eyes. Edyth came in and pulled up a stool in front of her. She placed the queen's feet in her lap and began to massage them, rubbing her strong thumbs up the soles, kneading the heels, stroking and drawing each toe.

"Ahh," Elfwina sighed.

"You're overtired. You've lost weight. You hardly slept last night."

"Great Mother! What is all this!"

"You're going to make yourself ill."

"I came over here to rest." She leaned toward Edyth and tapped her head affectionately. "You pounce on me like a cat. Put on my shoes, I must get back there."

"Eat something before you go."

"I'm not hungry--stop, they're snug. Let me put my feet down."

Edyth drew the queen up, opening her mouth to speak. Elfwina said crossly, "Oh, do be still!" and went out into the corridor.

Gryffn was standing close by. She jerked back, startled. He stared at her; his mouth softened, his eyes smoked and implored.

"You do not belong in this hallway," she said sharply. "Stand aside."

Instead of obeying her, he moved closer. "I would put myself at your feet, beautiful lady."

She was incensed. "You will not speak to me in this manner. Stand aside or I will call the guard."

"Why would you do that? Would you hurt one who loves you? That is why I am in Mercia. That is why I offer my help." He reached out his hand to touch her.

Appalled at the thought of contact with him and outraged that he would dare, she cried out, "Get away from me, Gryffn!"

The door behind them opened, and Edyth came into the hall. She stationed herself next to the queen.

Elfwina said again, "Stand aside."

"Your husband is in a predicament that my help would ease," he said. With a last smoky glance, he bowed, retreating so Elfwina and her woman could pass.

They walked silently down to the council room. Smiling, Gryffn trailed at a distance.

Elfwina entered the room, glancing at Edward as she took her chair. He was sitting relaxed, his legs stretched out in front of him as he listened to Mawer and Teownor, but he was watching her. Sensing something, he straightened. When Gryffn entered shortly after, Edward frowned, looked again at his sister. She was looking now at the council members.

Regardless of Gryffn's unwanted attentions, Elfwina had to concede the Welsh chieftain's point: Aedred did need him. He had the tools essential to any contest with the Danes--ferocity and small compassion. He was also a rule unto himself. While assuring the council of his willingness to aide them, he made it clear he was independent from both Wessex and Mercia.

During the earlier part of the session, Elfwina had merely listened. Knowing the way her father's advisors came to their decisions and how Aedred and Edward's men came to theirs, she had been more interested in the processes which moved Gryffn and his commanders to solutions. But her dislike of him continued to grow, and, in spite of the risk to his support, she attacked him.

He had put forth a plan concerning the defense of the northern border. She began to systematically undermine the support this plan had received. Using Edward's maps, she explained the terrain in detail. With her own knowledge of the topography and her ability to extrapolate an enemy's movements over it, she illustrated why it was unlikely enemy warriors would be able to defend it in the way Gryffn had suggested. Her methodical exposure of the weaknesses in his plan left it in ruins. His concession to her was honeyed, her acceptance gracious. Only Edward had caught her triumph.

The final plan required Gryffn to build and maintain a burh at Talacre at the mouth of the Dee. This was to be insurance against surprise reinforcements from the Norse in Ireland. He was also to levy an army of a thousand and march it to the Severn Valley. He accepted his part in the plan without protest. He turned to Brihtric. "And you, Sire, will join me at Tewkesbury with two thousand Saxons?"

"I will."

"This is the way it stands, then," Aedred said. "Eorl Heafwine will gather a thousand men from our southern provinces and join you at the Severn. The rest of the Mercian army will stand at Ceolworth and be prepared to move in any direction. Edward, you'll bring up another thousand men from Wessex, and you'll stay as commander."

Brihtric had argued strenuously against this role for Edward, but in the end had to abandon his opposition because he could not speak of the reasons for his objections. Edward listened in puzzlement, feeling the rise of old insecurities.

As the final link in the defense, the Mercian eorls of the borders would hold their fyrds ready in their provinces. In the event of attack in any province, the combined army from Ceolworth would respond and join with the local fyrds. This was the plan which would get its final acceptance from the witena soon to be convened. The company made their pledges, and Brihtric and Gryffn and their men went to their quarters to rest until their departure at daybreak.

Brihtric sent for his son. When Edward reached his father's quarters he found him with Archbishop Ansel.

"When was the last time you attended Mass, Edward? You took no priest with you."

"A long time, Father."

"Celebrate the Mass with me. It would please me to keep your soul intact."

"That could be a job. It has been a long time since I've been to Confession."

Brihtric smiled. "I'll take the time to nap. When you've finished, wake me."

Edward replied jauntily, "It may be a morning Mass."

He made his confession, a series of venial sins he dredged up to cover the months, and one or two more he knew Ansel would expect. Neither his confession nor his penance took long, and Mass was celebrated. Edward was relieved to have the task behind him.

Elfwina woke to something--a change in the rhythm of her heart? The movement of blood through her body? It was that elemental. Her chamber was flooded with moonlight, and she thought she must have been wakened by the slow passage of light over her eyelids.

Aedred was sleeping next to her, his face serene in the light from the window. The glass was a brilliant, compelling haze. For a moment the comfort of furs and quilts and the warmth of the musky body next to her overrode the mystic pull of that glow. Then she eased out into the cold room. She wriggled her feet into fur slippers and, pulling a heavy woolen mantle around her, went to the window.

The moon swam in the uneven glass. She pushed the window open to the night. Above her, the constellations hung palely in the sky. Creating silence from its cold glow, the full moon carved the countryside in black shadow and silver light. Frost glittered in the bare branches of the trees, in the dead grass, in the frozen tracks of horses.

She turned her face up to the moon. "Lady Litha, smile on me," she whispered.

"She does," Aedred said softly. He was raised on his elbow, looking at her. "How I love you," he said in the same soft tone. He rose naked from the bed and approached her in his graceful step. He glanced up at the moon, and then back to her face. "I think the light comes from you."

"A very small reflection." She had never seen him so beautiful. The light streamed off his bare skin and sank into the darkness of his hair and eyes, an eerie reassembling of the familiar into something strange and breathtaking.

"Enough to illuminate my life," he said, and then laughed at himself, becoming Aedred again. "No--it's true!"

He tugged open her mantle and she swooped the edges around him, covering his back as he hunched down and shook into her warmth. He nestled his bare toes into the furry tops of her slippers, and their weight felt good pressing on her feet.

"It's true." He laughed again, softly, self-consciously. "Sometimes I look at you for the sheer pleasure of it. Did you know I do that?"

"I've caught you looking at me. I've always liked it."

She tightened her arms so the mantle would keep him covered and warm. "You know I do." She kissed his nipples, and then laid her cheek on the smooth, cool skin of his chest.

His chuckle was low and pleased. "I thought you might."

He rested his head on hers, his face toward the window. "Look out there at our kingdom, Wina. So calm and undisturbed. What will it be like in a few months?"

He looked down at her. In the stark light, his mouth was composed, neutral. "I think war must be in our bones. In the bones of the Danes, in Ædda's, in mine. It's the curse of men, and I hate it. But it's beyond me not to rise to it. When the horn sounds, I'm so damned afraid my bowels turn to water. And yet, if I'm truthful, I'm exhilarated by it. There is a . . . rapture. I don't know, fear and exhilaration and the surpassing skill that comes of it. Death is all around me, and I feel immortal."

He had never spoken to her in just this way, in a low, vibrant voice that pricked her skin with cold. She felt the moonlight on them, felt his strangeness and knew it was a spell.

"And if you are not immortal?" she asked breathlessly.

"Would you mourn, Elfwina? Would you mourn that I was gone?"

She pressed herself against him, burrowing against that cold, stony body. "How can you ask such a terrible question?" she cried.

Chapter Thirty-Six

[829] Ceolworth, Mercia. Aedred and the prince had carefully selected two horses from the king's herd and were now beyond the walls training the animals in battle maneuvers.

Elfwina was in the building which housed the hall kitchen. It was a very large room with bins and shelves and a huge hearth hung with brackets and metal arms from which dangled cooking vessels and utensils. It had a fussy order to it. There was a large central table and a counter with a basin along one wall. Large water jugs were lined up on the top. An opening toward the back of the room revealed a long ramp that disappeared into darkness.

One of the cooks, a large woman with a dour expression, stood near Elfwina. The queen had her hands in a huge bowl filled with a mixture of wheat flour, barley, honey, and milk. Several young women and boys attended to their various jobs, but kept looking shyly at their queen.

"Burghild," Elfwina said to the cook, "some coriander, please."

Stepping to a rack of jars, the woman shot a ferocious look at her help. They dove away, tripping about as they settled back to their tasks. Elfwina went on kneading the contents of the bowl as she waited for the spice.

Edward stuck his head in at the door, paused, located his sister, and ducked on through the low doorway and into the room. There was a series of startled sounds, a flurry of curtseying and bowing, a gesture from Edward halting it all. He came up to where Elfwina was working.

"I thought I heard your voice, but couldn't believe it was coming from the kitchen. What are you doing here?"

She stared down at the sticky clump of dough in her hands, striving for normalcy, striving to accommodate that man who no longer loved.

"Is this a new duty for the queen? When do you mop the floors?"

"I'm making cakes to offer Mother Erce."

"You have a whole staff here; can't one of them to do it?"

"The ingredients have to be mixed by the petitioner."

"Really?" He looked at her curiously. "What are you petitioning for?"

"It's private, Edward. How can you have forgotten so much?" Before he could reply, she went on quickly, "Finished the training for today?"

"Mm-hm." He leaned over the bowl as he watched her mixing the dough. "We start again in the morning. You'll press these special offerings on a twig, I hope, or she'll spend the season stuck to the altar." He lifted his head and grinned at her. She shifted away from him, her eyes on the bowl.

"Sorry." He rested his hip on the counter and held his hands loosely on his upraised thigh.

The cook sidled up, staring at him, and it was hard to tell if she was in awe or annoyed. At Elfwina's nod, she dumped the contents of her palm into the bowl.

"Coriander," Elfwina said. Disturbed by his closeness she grasped for subjects. "Do the horses seem suitable?"

"I think so." He plucked one of the seeds from the dough, brought it up to his nose, sniffed, tried unsuccessfully to crush the seed between his fingers. "Aedred was satisfied. He went back to the hall. I wanted to try my horse on some tighter circles and reverses. I don't have his knack with horses." He tossed the seed back into the bowl. "I can't do without a bridle, and I like the security of a big, solid saddle under me. It limits my leg signals, and I never get those refined movements out of a horse that Aedred does, but I usually finish with an animal that answers well."

She nodded, and they fell silent. He watched her pat soft butter onto pieces of the dough, deftly mold them into cakes, and then place the cakes one at a time into a shallow basket lined with parchment. Near the basket a few grains of white barley lay scattered on the table. He rolled the grains into a circle with the tip of his finger, scattered them out, and then methodically rearranged them into a circle again. He saw that she had finished laying the cakes into the basket.

"Now what?"

"Wash my hands in the trough and put the cakes aside until tomorrow."

He glanced around. "What trough?"

"In the cooling room." She nodded toward the open doorway. A kitchen maid carrying a jar of milk came up the incline as she spoke. "Really, Edward, is this your first time at Ceolworth?"

"You can't expect me to know the intricacies of the kitchen. That's where the cakes go--down into the depths?"

"Yes. Would you carry them? My hands are sticky."

He picked up the basket. A boy came carrying another jar of milk and stepped quickly aside, bowing, as Edward followed his sister down the ramp. At each step, the air grew cooler. The ramp ended in a huge room hewn from the earth. The dark walls were lined with shelves filled with jars of butter, eggs bound in straw mats, great rounds of cheese, and crocks filled with rendered fat. Edward glimpsed in an adjoining room game pegged around the walls and carcasses of pig and venison hanging from gambrels. Barrels of salted meat stood all around the walls. From this room came a serving girl holding several plucked chickens by the feet. She curtsied and went away up the ramp.

Through the center of the room ran a wide trough built from hewn timbers. Water rushed through it, gurgling pleasantly as it swept around pitchers of milk and cream. The trough disappeared in a merry gush of water through an opening in the earthen wall. Along the trough on either side were shelves. On the near shelf a large yellow candle burned in a dish. A pleasant subterranean tang permeated the air.

"This is an education," Edward said, setting the basket on the shelf and looking around. "For as long as I've been coming to Ceolworth, I never knew this was here."

His eyes followed the motions of her hands as she dipped them into the water, smoothing off clinging bits of grain from her long fingers. He thought her hands beautiful, the motion soothing.

Elfwina was wondering why he was here, standing next to her in this place. She searched for something to cast between them. "Edward?"

"I'm here."

"What are your true thoughts on Gryffn?"

He gave her a quizzical look. "True thoughts? What do you mean?"

"Your impression of him. In all respects."

"Let's see--truly what I think . . . . He's excellent with the spear and the axe--never misses. He is an able leader--that goes without saying. Fierce, no compassion. As tough on his own men as he is with an enemy. Very harsh discipline. On the other hand, his men are extremely loyal, so they must think his punishments fair. Is this what you want?"

She had finished washing her hands, and they now stood with their backs against the shelf of the trough. In the distance came the faint sound of conversation and the clattering of pans.

"More or less. You describe him in military terms."

"That's my experience of him--military. He measures up well. Why are you asking? Are you changing your opinion of him?"

"He's an insolent bastard."

"He couldn't keep his eyes off you, if that's your complaint. You can't be surprised at that."

"I cannot abide his arrogance."

"You're not the first to say that; there are legions who feel the same. What happened to spark this?" Edward glanced up as another boy came in to pull a crock of butter from the shelf. He would have bowed, but the prince waved him on.

"I don't trust him, Edward. He's dangerous, I've told you that. He is not helping us in this endeavor out of love for Mercia. He would stab us in the back on a moment's whim."

"I don't know that I trust him, to be honest. But I think it's his manner that works against him. He certainly has done nothing to warrant mistrust. He's an uneasy friend, but Mercia needs him."

"Do you think I don't know that? Aedred is always defending him, too."

"I'm not defending him, if you're listening to my words. Look at it objectively--he's kept the treaty he made with Cenwulf years ago, and he's pledged his support now. If you put your prejudices about his temperament aside, you'll see he's done nothing to earn your suspicions." He leaned close, smiling. "Regardless of how your fur stands."

She jerked back from him, moving her hand from where it rested on the ledge behind her, and knocking the candle to the floor.

"Don't move, I'll get it." He took her arm, guiding himself in the darkness to bend down past her. He found the candle and lifted it back to the shelf. "Have you your strike-a-light?"

"Yes."

But she didn't move, and Edward, directly in front of her and still holding her arm, listened, heard her rapid breathing, smelled the faint scent of rosemary in her hair, a scent at once familiar and yet, in the darkness, intoxicating. He pulled her into his arms, bent her inward against his body, and pressed his lips against the curve of her throat. She did not resist.

"The boy adored you," he said, his lips moving against her soft skin. "The love he felt then is tripled in me now." He felt her draw in a sharp breath, and then a light flickered over his eyelids. He opened them, and, turning his head, saw a figure approaching down the ramp, illuminated by the kitchen's light. He released his sister and said in a voice that sounded loud in that space, "Your strike-a-light, please."

Elfwina pulled it from the girdle at her hips and struck it off. The candle wick sputtered. The serving girl, coming after a jar of cream, saw the sparks in the darkness and gave a little shriek.

"Wait a minute," the prince called to her.

She stood still.

"We'll have a light shortly, so you won't trip."

The candle flared. "Come ahead," Edward told her.

"There!" Elfwina said. She walked past the girl and on up the ramp; the prince followed a few paces behind.

They walked in silence across the enclosure yard, Edward looking straight ahead, Elfwina gazing at everything between earth and sky but her brother. But she could not shut out his steady breathing, the whisper of his clothing, the slight bumping of his sword at his leg, the soft brushing of his shoes over the grass; all the sounds funneled into her with no way to stop it.

From close behind them, a voice rumbled, "Sire!"

They halted, separating, to find Mawer at their heels. The big man saluted her, but his face was dark red and stormy.

"Is there something wrong, Eorl Mawer?" she asked, grateful for the distraction.

"I don't know if there is anything wrong, Your Majesty," Mawer said, barely controlling his high irritation. "And I don't want to trouble you anyway, may it please you. I beg you to ignore anything I say."

"I shall leave you to your prince, then." She smiled, and walked away toward the hall.

The prince watched her go, and then turned to the eorl. "What's got you so worked up?"

"There is a *pig* in my horse's stall!" His expression of distaste screwed the outrage on his features so comically, Edward had to choke back a laugh.

"A pig?" the prince echoed.

"A *pig!* I just came back from the village from--from--" stammered Mawer, "—an errand. I went to put my horse in its proper stall and found a great, surly, unnatural pig occupying it. Nobody in the stable can explain it--why there's a pig there or why he's in *my* horse's stall. I could bear with it for a time if there's a good reason, but the boar seems to have a permanent lease. And no one informed me at all."

"A boar, is it?"

"Massive thing, with beallucors you've never seen." He moved his big hands in a circle of impressive diameter.

Edward's eyebrows lifted. "I don't know anything about this remarkable pig, Eorl Mawer, but I'll have a look." He started for the stable.

"I would appreciate it, Sire," Mawer rumbled as if Edward had finally taken his point.

"Where is this pig?"

"Your nose will fucking find him for you."

As he spoke, the sharp, sour pig smell rammed into Edward's nostrils. "Wuow!" he exclaimed, with a quick snap of his head to one side.

"Didn't I tell you? Should a horse be put up with this?"

They approached the stall gate and as Edward looked over it, he got a glimpse of a massive brown form lunging toward him. He stepped back. The gate bowed outward with the impact of the pig's charge. "Nasty whore's son, isn't he?"

"If you're being kind."

They both approached the gate again. This time the boar stood still and stared at them with its tight red eyes. Its ears whipped back and forth. The wet snout was low and active.

Edward stared at him. "He's as wide as the stall!"

"And look at those legs, Sire. They barely clear his body from the ground. He's a monstrously unnatural beast."

Edward eyed the animal critically. "He doesn't have the look of deformity, Mawer. He may be the devil's own son, but his eyes are alert and intelligent--as boars go. And look at the meat on him!"

"But why's the fucking cocker in *my* horse's stall?"

"I can't answer that. Maybe the reeve can. Let's hunt him out--"

"Ho! Edward--Mawer!" Aedred came through the door, the reeve behind him. "So you've seen my pig. Grand fellow, isn't he?"

"Grand stench," Edward replied, standing aside with Mawer. "This is your enterprise, then."

They all grouped around the gate. The boar charged again, and Aedred laughed with admiration. "Just look at him!"

They looked at him. Edward threw a side glance at Mawer, who was staring down at the boar with a face cleared of expression. "It's like no pig I've ever seen," the eorl muttered.

"And there's his staggering value," Aedred said.

Mawer stared at him blankly. "He's got no legs. He couldn't run from a dead cat."

"Ah, but he won't have to run to protect himself. He'll stay enclosed and safe from anything that might cause him to run."

"In my horse's stall?"

Aedred grabbed Mawer's arm and held it. "Is this your stall? You must have had your horse out last night when I told them to put the boar in an empty space."

Edward turned with deliberation on Mawer. "*All* night?"

Mawer ignored him. "I was taking care of some business, Your Majesty. When I returned, here was this pig in my stall. I just wondered about it."

"Well, I am sorry, Eorl Mawer. Where's your horse now? Did you find a place for it?"

"All the stalls are taken, Sire. My horse is tethered outside."

Aedred looked about, saw a groom in the shadows near the line of stalls and motioned him forward. "Eorl Mawer's horse is outside. Find room for him in my stable."

The groom went off. "This is only a temporary pig roost, Mawer," Aedred said cheerfully. "As soon as his enclosure's finished, you can return your horse or leave it in my stable--your choice."

"Thank you, Sire," Mawer said, finally placated. He gazed now at the boar with generosity. "What exactly were you going to do with him, Your Majesty?"

"Why, breed a whole new line of pigs. The offspring of this boar will roll; they'll be so heavy with meat. The next step is to find a good fat sow to start the process."

"You needn't look for the perfect sow, Your Majesty," Ceolric told him. "Any sow could have offspring with the boar's characteristics. The best of the litter can be bred back, and so on and so on, until the strain proves true. I suggest breeding several sows to the boar."

"Several, eh?"

"Seems you have amusement planned for some years to come," said Edward, slapping the king on the back. "That is, if the Danes don't have him for breakfast some morning."

Aedred gave him a long and measured scrutiny, and Edward realized he was giving stock to his remark. So he added, "Danes love rashers, I hear."

Aedred stared distractedly at him. Then he turned abruptly to the reeve and said, with complete seriousness, "Ceolric, that needs to be considered."

Chapter Thirty-Seven

[829] Ceolworth, Mercia. Over forty magnates of the kingdom comprised the king's council. Summoned from all over Mercia, they had been arriving for the last several days. Now, with everyone gathered in the great hall, the meeting began.

The first day was spent apprising the witan of the situation and in getting an estimation of the kingdom's resources. Aedred had required the members to bring a list of their resources down to the last ox and axe handle, and all the foodstuffs to the last grain of wheat. The clerks were sent off with orders to compile for discussion the next morning the information they had been scribbling down. The meeting adjourned early. In a more jovial mood, the members reassembled for the evening meal.

The feast progressed at a leisurely pace, three musicians wandering along the benches playing pipes and a small drum providing a pleasant background to the conversation. Edward was seated on Elfwina's left, so close their arms touched. She was kept uncomfortably aware of him. They had not spoken since the encounter in the cooling room. Once again he had shaken her world to its core, wrenching her from the security of the lie they had been living so many years. When their eyes met, truth was there, and she feared it.

One of the pipers began a slow melody that drew attention to the floor. A woman who had been sitting far down the hall with servants of Wulfric of Benmarrow's company now stood before the assembly.

At the long table the thegn Wulfric sat directly across from the king. One of the wealthiest men in the kingdom, Wulfric was quiet, immaculate in his dress and person, his fastidiousness extending onto the battlefield, a subject of amazement for anyone serving with him for the first time. His brown hair and forked beard were stylishly dusted with blue woad, enhancing his aristocratic bearing. His wife Mildthryth sat on his left. She was as elegant as her husband, her gracious conversation flowing lightly among her table companions, until the woman came onto the floor.

The woman seemed at first to be of no particular beauty or distinction. She wore a long brown overdress with ridiculously long sleeves wrinkled back to her elbows, revealing a startling hint of the emerald-green gown beneath it.

"Ah!" cried the king amid the collective gasp of the guests when the woman's cloak rippled down to her feet, a chrysalis shed to reveal her gown in a dazzling swirl of green and blazing red-orange as fiery as her hair. Flashing out a sinuous message the silver and gold threads of her gown snaked along the curves of her body as she began to dance.

A slave! Elfwina thought, with surprise, watching the slow delicacy of motion that quieted the hall, all the people stilled, including Mildthryth, whose words trailed off. The thegn's wife touched her lips with her tongue, smiled, and then sat with perfect composure without once turning her head to look at the dancer.

As the piper quickened the tune, the dancer's speed increased with a surging energy and suburb control: in the midst of a spin came an infinitesimal pause, a spin, a pause, a spin; it was hypnotic. The toes of her bare feet gleamed with thin gold rings; several gold rings whirled and spun and stopped on her ankles. In the silence of the hall, she was a dazzle of movement and clear, bright chimes, dipping and whirling in one continuous flow of kinesis and music that brought her close to Wulfric's place.

The thegn sat half-turned on the bench to watch, and in that moment Elfwina focused on his profile. It was an astonishing revelation of love, pride, and tenderness. The emotions were so evident Elfwina knew instantly the reason for Mildthryth's deep composure. Then the dance ended; the woman curtsied gracefully, breathing heavily, smiling, her eyes flickering to Wulfric with the same sudden and quickly concealed expression that had been on his face. Elfwina looked at the thegn in disbelief.

Her attention was diverted by a sudden movement on her left. Edward was rising. She felt relief as she watched him walk down the benches to speak with Eorl Gyrth. Cuthred and his plump little wife sat just beyond the place vacated by Edward. The eorl leaned toward Elfwina and said, "I've only just heard about it, Ma'am. I'm going to have to see this boar His Majesty finds so valuable."

The Eorl of Chester was a portly, jovial nobleman who was a farmer in his heart. He talked at length about his pigs, while Elfwina attended with kindly interest, her mind again on the matter of Wulfric and the slave woman. She felt a sad disappointment with Wulfric, on whom she had always looked as exemplary: his loyalty to Aedred was unquestioned; he was an excellent administrator; he was a devoted father and husband whose name had never been touched by scandal. *I never would have expected this from Wulfric,* she thought, as if it had been a personal affront.

Once the captive had gone back to her place, Wulfric seemed indifferent. He did not look in her direction again, and Mildthryth took up her conversation vivaciously from the point from where she had left off. Elfwina sat sipping from a cup of mead, thinking it over. Aedred, she noticed, was drinking from the horn. She knew he would be sorry for it.

Suddenly, above the rumble of voices, several chords were struck on a harp, bright notes commanding attention to the instrument and the performer. It was Lady Ella sitting on a bench before the king and queen, her white fingers stroking skillfully across the strings of the instrument in her lap. Her clothes were white with golden trim. Her veil was a golden flow over her head and shoulders. Where the dancer had created beauty by her movements, Lady Ella was beauty in suspension. But for her hands passing effortlessly over the strings and levitating notes from the harp, her shining figure was still.

The vagrant notes dropped into a haunting minor key. In a crystalline soprano she began to sing:

The full-hearted king ruler of men
Lord of warriors leader of eorls

Hearing what the context of the song was to be, Aedred leaned forward with interest. Now there was no other sound in the great hall but the high, clear voice telling the king's story on the drifting notes of the harp. The melodious overture which had pulled their attention became burdened, uneasy, as she sang of war. Her fingers threw out arrows and clashed swords.

Behind Aedred, at his station near the hearth, Grundl stood impassive, his spear upright in his big hand, his dark eyes on the queen as the song told of bloody battles and fallen men. Lady Ella's voice sobbed the king's grief as he mourned the brave warriors fallen in battle, the sobbing echoed by the strings. The melody smoothed, then soared as her voice praised the good king, ring-giver to faithful friends, joyously gathered with his loyal companions in the shining hall.

There was a long silence in the great room, in this shining hall, approving, profound. Elfwina turned her head to Edward, sitting next to her again, and found him staring at her with an intensity that caused her to look away in confusion.

Aedred was saying, "Lady Ella, you have the power to move us all. Is that a song you composed?"

She rose and dropped into a curtsey at Aedred's words. She lifted her lovely head and answered him, "It is, Your Majesty."

"Have you others?"

She permitted herself the slightest smile. "Enough to fill a large basket, Sire."

"Well, then, a merry one this time, if you have one."

"Indeed I do. Will this please you, Sire?" She held the harp upright and plucked a series of careening notes she joggled into a sprightly tune.

Aedred smiled and nodded his head in rhythm with the music. He leaned over to Elfwina and said quietly, "If she'd sung another like the first, she'd have had us all in tears."

He had been in tears, of course. "Yes," she said.

"Don't look so sad," he whispered.

"Do I look sad?"

He smiled fondly at her, and then turned his attention back to Lady Ella. When she was roundly applauded, he spoke again to Elfwina. "I'll set us all to gaming, now. Maybe everyone will want to go to bed early." He leaned closer, his eyes soft as velvet. "I have that in mind for us. We'll leave within the hour."

When she smiled, he growled with satisfaction.

As soon as Aedred had redirected the company, Elfwina rose gratefully and, flanked by women of the court, moved about the room speaking with the guests and watching the games. As she neared the north fireplace she noticed the dancer, wrapped now in her dull brown cloak, standing alone beside the hearth. When the woman saw the queen and her entourage approaching, she dropped into a curtsey.

"We enjoyed your dancing very much."

"Thank you, Gracious Majesty," the woman answered in a rich contralto.

Her accent was heavy, the unusual inflections melodic and pleasant. Her eyes were light brown and seemed to glow with a warm and gentle light. There was a singular attractiveness in the contours of her face, the square shape and high cheek bones, the generous mouth.

Everything about her bespoke patience, which, to Elfwina, contrasted strangely to the bursting, energetic dance the woman had just performed. Her quiet assurance suggested she had been someone of substance in her homeland.

Elfwina said, "Tell us your name."

"Gytha Lothbrok, Ma'am."

"Then you are a Dane?"

"Yass, I am a Dane, Ma'am."

"Your dance was beautifully done, with natural grace. Your training must have started very early."

"Yass," she said again, this slowly spoken word of respect and agreement the apparent pause she needed to translate the queen's remark into Danish, and then to reply in English. "I danced first in my father's hall, and then in the hall of the great king Ineware."

"And your father's name?"

"Jarl Ubbi Lothbrok, Ma'am."

Elfwina hesitated at the name spoken with the Danish pronunciation, and then it finally rang true. "He was a brave warrior," she said. "Even his enemies respected him."

"Yass . . . . When he was killed his body was not defiled. Wulfric and his warriors treated him with honor." Her eyes moved and refocused to where Elfwina knew Wulfric was standing. "As I have been honorably treated in my captivity."

Elfwina turned her head and saw Wulfric casually avert his eyes. She looked back into the woman's patient gaze. "You have given us great pleasure by dancing for us tonight, Gytha Lothbrok."

She curtsied again. "Thank you, Your Majesty. It was a privilege for me to be able to dance before you."

Elfwina left her standing quietly beside the blazing hearth, a woman touched by circumstances that left her in dreadful isolation.

What the conversation had revealed disturbed Elfwina. A depressing domestic situation had now become a potential threat to the kingdom, and she wondered at Wulfric's boldness in bringing Gytha Lothbrok to Ceolworth.

Crossing the hall again, she found herself on a course that would intercept Lady Ella. The noblewoman was walking slowly along, accompanied by her father and Eorl Aethelred. She still carried her harp. It would have been an affront if Elfwina were to avoid speaking with the eorl's daughter, so she stopped. Smiling at the noblewoman, she said, "Your songs were delightful, Lady Ella, although the first one moved us to tears."

The men had halted on either side of Lady Ella, standing politely as the queen addressed her. Aldhune beamed at Elfwina's words. Aethelred gazed steadily down on Lady Ella.

"How kind of you, Your Majesty." Her eyes swept downward, and then back up to the queen's face as she made her curtsey. "I am sorry to have caused your tears, Ma'am, but I must confess satisfaction at my song's success."

Lady Ella was charming in her frankness, unaware of the reluctance of the queen to speak to her. Elfwina had never been this close to the woman, where the curious color of her eyes was evident. Edward had noticed those eyes with a very public comment. She shrank from that thought.

Having gotten the queen's attention, Lady Ella's father proudly told her, "She has loved music since she was a child."

"He would have preferred me to love the hunting bow, and I did try."

Aldhune said, "She is very good with the bow," as if he was shocked she was implying she might not be.

Elfwina looked directly at Lady Ella. "*Are* you good with the hunting bow?"

"Yes, Ma'am," she answered promptly, and then added with a slight turn of her lips, "Other hunting instruments, as well."

Elfwina thoughtfully held her gaze. Aedred had expressed his desire: "It would be our wish that you sing for us again tomorrow night."

"My pleasure, Ma'am. Something merry?" Lady Ella's mouth turned in a smile that was uneven and infectious.

"Perhaps a mixture weighted toward the merry," Elfwina replied with her own charming smile.

"I had been hoping to convince her to sing, myself," Aethelred said. His eyes still smoldered over Lady Ella. "I am glad you accomplished it, Ma'am."

"Not so difficult, really," Lady Ella answered in a cheery discouragement of the eorl's attention, which gained Elfwina's approval, "I lack the modesty to say no." She smiled again at the queen. "And I enjoy the sound of my compositions too much."

"It would be a shame to deny you the performance," the queen said in an echo of Edward's dry humor. The queen's smile as she passed on through the company was so like the smile of the prince, Lady Ella was thoroughly disconcerted.

True to his word, Aedred had seen to it they left the company before an hour had turned. He groaned as he lifted himself up onto Elfwina's high bed. "Did you see me at the horn?"

Elfwina deftly slipped pillows behind him. "Yes, I did and thought you would probably regret it."

"It's that Mawer of Edward's. Time and again I've seen him lay men under the benches, and time and again he manages to pull me into his contests."

"You contested with *Mawer!*"

"No, no. I've more brains than that! But officiating entails certain responsibilities . . . ." He groaned again.

"Keep your head up on the pillows, and you won't swim away."

He turned a regretful smile on her. "I had different plans for tonight."

"Did you!"

"First thing in the morning, I promise you." He puffed his breath out slowly and closed his eyes.

"Aedred, I want to talk with you about something I observed tonight."

His eyelids flipped open. "Oh?" His rosy eyeballs swiveled up to her. "From that tone, I don't think I'm in a condition to hear it. But go ahead."

"I think this is something you'll want to probe into."

"Well, let's hear it."

She told him of what she had seen between Wulfric and Gytha Lothbrok and of her misgivings about it. "There is always the chance I misinterpreted, but I don't believe I did. What passed was too plain, and poor Mildthryth was much too careful in her responses. She didn't look at Gytha Lothbrok once during the performance, just sat staring straight ahead. With great composure, naturally. There's trouble simmering there that could affect this kingdom."

He said slowly, "How is it you see these things, and I don't?"

"It was purely accidental."

"Well, I will need to see it for myself," he said. "I can't approach Wulfric on hearsay."

"Ask him outright why he hasn't ransomed her. The question is appropriate, and he'll not deny anything to you. Wulfric is the kind of man who will understand your interest is not in his personal affairs, per se, but rather in how his conduct will affect the safety of the kingdom."

"What if he does deny it?"

"Then he is a liar, and you will both know it. You'll at least be able to make intelligent plans knowing it."

He was silent for a long time. "I'll think about this," he said.

Chapter Thirty-Eight

[829] Ceolworth, Mercia. The second day of the council started off early, the information compiled the day before recorded on a large scale map of Mercia drawn up under Edward's supervision. The map was mounted on a frame where everyone could see the locations of the stores. Enough provisions for a thousand men were marked in red; correspondingly smaller stores were in blue, yellow, and green.

Elfwina sat in a chair on Aedred's left, looking out on the company. Edward sat next to his sister, his eyes on the map.

"We'll be watching two fronts," Aedred said. "North and south. Which will move first is anyone's guess. Or they could move simultaneously, once Ædda is up to strength."

Before a discussion could generate he said, "A few days ago, King Brihtric and Gryffn came here to personally pledge their support. The danger threatens them equal to the extent it threatens us, and none of us are willing to drain our treasuries for the king of Denmark."

The quiet at these remarks was speculative. Aedred nodded to his brother-in-law. There was a murmur as Edward rose.

"The outcome of that meeting--" he surveyed their faces "Was for Gryffn to maintain a garrison at Talacre to repel any support for Ædda from Ireland and to add numbers to Eorl Cuthred's defense. Gryffn also pledged to lead one thousand men to the Severn to join with two thousand Saxons led by King Brihtric and an army Eorl Heafwine will gather from the southern provinces. I'll bring up a thousand men from Kent and Wessex to stand here at Ceolworth with those summoned by King Aedred. That's the sum of it."

Edward paused. Wulfric spoke out. "Did I understand you to be suggesting a standing army, Sire?"

"For now. The plan can always be modified once we know what we're up against. Until we have a clear indication, we need to be able to move in any direction. That's what an army standing at Ceolworth would accomplish."

"Every time I call my fyrd," Aldhune remarked, "unless they're in the thick of it, I'm lucky to keep it to the end of the campaign. It's like trying to hold back the river out there with your fingers. They don't stand well to inactivity." That brought laughter. "We can gather the men, Prince Edward, but keeping them standing as an army is something no eorl I've ever known has accomplished. Maybe a prince can do it."

"Not alone," said Edward, smiling. He put his foot on the bench and leaned forward, his arm across his knee. "It happened that way in Wessex, too, but my father devised a new method. So far it has worked, and it's simple--half the eligible men stay home, while the other half stay in the field."

"I'm not sure that makes sense," Leodwald called out. "You'd only have half your strength."

There were noises of agreement.

Wulfric observed, "If thirty men stay through to the end of a campaign it is better than sixty who leave when you're in a corner. I'm surmising, Prince Edward, there is a rotation."

"There is."

"Then fresh troops would be an advantage in the middle of a campaign."

"You also have men coming up who don't know the battle plan!" Leodwald cried.

Mawer moved his big frame to call over his shoulder, "Just tell them to stick your spear in the nearest Dane. It's a plan that's worked for me." He winked at Edward, and then grinned bear-like at Grundl, standing silently behind the king.

After the rota system had been discussed at length, Leodwald conceded, "It sounds workable. I'll agree, providing they'll all fight within their own provinces."

"The idea is for them to serve *out* of their provinces," Aldhune said to his brother. "Didn't you get that?"

"Hell, that won't work. The only time you can get them to fight is *in* their provinces--I'll draw it closer than that--within their villages."

Aethelred and Cuthred would have jumped to the defense of the fyrds, but Eorl Penwahl, took the floor and looked with deliberation at all the faces now turned to him with varying degrees of impatience, except for the group of his loyal thegns. Penwahl ignored them all.

As Penwahl took his stance, Aedred heard Elfwina's faint sigh. Lifting his foot to the stool in front of him, he set his elbow on his knee, and rested his mouth against the knuckles of his hand. Edward looked over at him. Aedred's return gaze was neutral. There was the slightest lift to Edward's shoulders, and then he sat down on the bench. The witan rustled querulously.

"Years ago," Penwahl began richly, "when Mercia was first fighting for its very survival against the Welsh, we had a valiant group of eorls whose fe-al-ty--" he dragged out the word as his eyes swept the group "--whose fe-al-ty to their king was unquestioned. Those were perilous days and those were brave eorls . . . ."

He went on in this vein for some time, his white head tilted back as he paced with one hand on his hip, the other gesturing broadly. There was a distinct restlessness in the audience. But as long as Aedred was prepared to listen, no one dared do otherwise.

The eorl's final words to the witan was an admonition for them to speedily discharge their obligations. He swept his eyes over the roomful of men, and then resumed his seat.

In the silence that followed, filled only with the sound of expelling breaths, Aedred leaned back in his chair and turned his innocent gaze on Edward.

The prince rose slowly to his feet. "Thank you, Eorl Penwahl for that--those remarks." He brought them back to the point. "If you agree to the plan, it will be understood the men you levy will be rotated on a schedule. But every able-bodied man should keep his battle gear close at hand, for, like Wessex, every man in Mercia may be defending the kingdom."

The discussion continued at length. With a glance at Aedred, the queen got up and left the room. When she returned it was with women of her suite making a slow progress toward the back passageway. Because the witan were at that moment vigorously debating, hardly anyone but Aedred took notice that Gytha Lothbrok was walking beside Elfwina. He caught a glimpse of the prince's puzzled expression, and took enjoyment from knowing what Edward didn't.

As Aedred discreetly watched Wulfric, he saw Elfwina's suspicions take their proof. Unexpectedly seeing his slave with the queen, Wulfric was slow pulling himself together. Still, if Aedred had not been looking for precisely the reaction he saw, he would not have caught it, or the swift unspoken question that went from his face, and the soothing glance which was returned. Wulfric found Aedred looking at him. The king held his gaze. Wulfric's mouth tightened by slow degrees, and then he lowered his eyes.

When the mid-afternoon recess was called, Aedred invited Wulfric to walk with him. They strolled out into the enclosure and through the side gate and turned to walk along the path outside the wall. When Aedred was certain they were out of earshot of everyone, he broke across their superficial conversation.

"You have been a loyal friend, Wulfric. I hold your love dear."

Wulfric murmured, "Your Majesty," and inclined his head.

"You'll understand the question I put to you is not out of malice or idle curiosity."

Wulfric's manner was calm and attentive.

"I depend on your forthright answer."

"I will always answer you honestly, Your Majesty."

"Gytha Lothbrok is the daughter of a chieftain. Through her mother, she is the kinswoman of the king of Denmark. Why haven't you ransomed her?"

Wulfric looked ahead along the path. The thegn's profile was dignified and assured, framed by the frost-like blue hair and beard and the elegant drape of the dark green mantle about his shoulders and throat. But there was a slight tremor at the corner of his mouth.

He said, "I will not part with her."

They walked silently for a few paces, and then Wulfric added quietly, "It is not against her will. She does not want to leave me."

"I see."

They walked again without speaking until, with his eyes fixed thoughtfully on the slope of the mountains beyond which lay Wulfric's vast bookland, Aedred said, "The Danes will recognize her. Mercians could be killed trying to prevent her from being taken."

"She will go into hiding at the first sign of movement from the force, Sire."

Aedred saw the thegn's determination and knew it would not be productive to force him to obedience. *Wulfric has considered the hazards,* he thought. *He knows his men and his king are not going to put their lives at risk for a Danish woman.* Wulfric was neither stupid nor foolhardy.

"It will have to be a very deep hole you hide her in. They'll kill her if she refuses to go with them."

"They will not find her, Your Majesty."

They continued on. Aedred looked over at him. "If one man is harmed in defense of Gytha Lothbrok, I will exact the consequences from you."

"I understand that, Your Majesty. No Mercian will be harmed."

"Well, you've answered my question honestly, as you said you would. And now I will tell you honestly I don't agree with what you're planning. I think the course you've chosen will cause pain to people you care about, if it hasn't already, and I think you are going to regret it." It was as far as he felt he could intrude into Wulfric's private life.

They turned at the end of the wall and began walking back along the way they had come.

"A man does not always set the course, Your Majesty. Sometimes the gods have plans for him he cannot foresee or has any control over. He must be accepting. He must learn to praise their wisdom."

"May you continue to praise their wisdom," Aedred replied.

Chapter Thirty-Nine

[829] Ceolworth, Mercia. When Elfwina returned to her chambers from her walk through the hall, it was to a planned gathering of the women who had accompanied members of the witan. They had brought their needle boxes and needle work, so the afternoon was spent in this pursuit and in sharing news from over the kingdom and in speculation about the possibility of war.

Elfwina sat by the window, working on a panel of white silk she was embroidering. It was a race of fabulous animals entwined in leaves and vines. Through the thick paned window directly behind her, the lowering sun shone on the garment and sparkled along the gold and silver threads and flashed on the needle as it pierced the silk.

The room hummed with quiet conversation. In a far corner, Mildthryth's voice fluted brightly in counterpoint to Lady Penwahl's deeper murmur.

Eorl Penwahl's wife was thirty-four, petite, with black hair laced prematurely with grey. Her skin was baby-soft. Sweeping invisibly out, her energy pulled at everyone in her vicinity, so she was given ample room. An awed space, because she was a famous healer. She was the queen's closest friend. She had now seated herself near Elfwina, and the queen eased her needle as she listened to Lady Pen talking with Lady Ella.

"Our history is filled with war. We can ask ourselves whether they were good wars or bad wars, which is what men generally ask, meaning whether or not they won, but that question hardly addresses the real concern. The *result* of war is always the same--women and children die, rather grimly and with little opportunity to enjoy the glory of their dying for those noble causes of gold and prestige--your cup is empty."

"Is it?" Lady Ella paused at the small hand-loom she held in her lap, where her fingers had been playing as deftly over the warp as they had over the strings of her harp. She looked at her cup. "So, it is. No, I don't want anymore," she said, when Lady Pen started to call for a refill. She sat her loom aside abruptly, put her hands in her lap with a gesture of resignation, and stared at Lady Penwahl, who laughed at her.

Elfwina's needle continued rhythmically through the delicate silk. She looked at Lady Ella from under her brows. "Would you rather be hunting boar, than being bored?"

Lady Penwahl dumped her embroidery on the arm of her chair. "Answer her," she told Lady Ella, "unless you have a burning desire to fill your loom."

The queen smiled.

When the recess began, Edward went to his sister's chambers. He came through the anteroom and found Elfwina sitting alone near the window. When he entered, she drew in a quick breath and laid the embroidery hoops in her lap.

"Everyone gone?" he asked her, glancing around.

"Yes. Have you finished so soon today? I was going back for the end of the session."

"No," he replied, dropping into a chair across from her. "We're getting some fresh air."

"What went on this afternoon? Have you met with any opposition?"

"It's going well. Taxes were a touchy subject, but they all understood the necessity to raise them. I don't expect any trouble getting the complete plan through. They can't reasonably object to the offer Father and Gryffn have made. Aedred is with Wulfric right now, walking off any resistance, I suppose . . ." his voice trailed off thoughtfully. "What was going on earlier when you came through the hall with the dancer?"

She told him.

"So, that's how it is." Leaning back, he looked up at the ceiling.

Elfwina lifted her embroidery hoops and quietly began to work the needle in and out of the material. Sunlight concentrated in the gold thread. The stitches were tiny, overlapping, glinting through a rich uncoiling from serpent to bear to bird in a continuous dance of shining creatures running the length of the piece--gold and silver on lustrous white silk.

"This is magnificent," Edward said. He was standing beside her, looking down at the part of the pattern stretched tightly within the hoops. The needle stopped. "You do your best work when you're agitated," he told her, still gazing at the graceful upward movement of the animals that forced the eye to follow. Her head bent slightly as she moved the needle in one or two quick stitches, and then she stopped again.

"The jewels go here?" His finger touched the small round areas which were the empty eye sockets of the creatures.

"The goldsmith is making the settings now."

There was a silence. She had stopped breathing. He carefully lifted the hoops and fabric away and laid them on the table beside her chair. He took her hands and she looked at him as drew her up against him. She put her arms around his waist and lay her head against his chest. She could hear his heart beating strongly, a little fast, like her own. He held her close, his cheek resting against her hair.

"Don't leave me alone with this." He moved his mouth against her temple. "Tell me I'm not alone. Tell me we share it . . . please. "

It was barely a whisper. "Yes," she answered and felt the earth shift under her feet.

The witan agreed with the plan. All that was left was for the clerks to write it out for the parties to sign the next morning. Then it would be up to the Danes.

When everyone reassembled that evening in the great hall the atmosphere was relaxed, bawdy, and loud.

From the village, Edward had brought up an excellent juggler who was visiting kinsmen there. Aedred spent most of the evening tossing objects to the man, which odd assortments the juggler whirled about him, front and back and overhead. While this captivating act was going on, a dog that pissed on cue was brought in. Leaving royalty unscathed, it selected guests who leaped and dodged while the rest of the company roared. The king missed the performance.

When the wrestling contests began, even the king took notice, and when he awarded the winners and the entertainers with silver, the hall rocked with applause.

Late in the evening, Aedred had his bone whistle brought to him, and he played his favorite tunes for the guests with Lady Ella accompanying him on the harp. She laughed at his quick switches done purposefully to trip her up, but she never once lost the music. When the applause died down so they could speak, Lady Ella said, genuinely, "You have a talent, Your Majesty."

"I have a talent," he agreed. "But you, Lady Ella, have a gift."

Gytha Lothbrok danced again until she was close to exhaustion. Although he was not indiscreet, Wulfric watched her less guardedly than he had the night before, as if speaking with the king had released him from some internal stricture he had placed on himself. His wife sat next to him, carrying on a bright conversation with the men and women around them.

The entire company had become fluid, shifting among the tables and benches and moving in and out of the smoky hall. Edward stood laughing at Mawer: in drinking his horns with an eye to profit, the eorl had to make regular trips down the back passageway.

"I've got a grip on the hilt of a sword," Mawer whispered, when he saw the prince laughing at him. "I have to set this up just right. It takes a while to invest the prey with the thought he can win."

Edward didn't ask about this strategy, merely grinned and left Mawer to go about it. As for himself, he was not drinking.

As Edward walked by one of the tables, Cuthred leaned out from the group of men and cried, "Amazing animal!"

Edward stared blankly at him. Cuthred went on in an excited fashion, half-drunk, slurring his words passionately. "It was hard to feature from the description," he said, "but the glorious thing itself is an animal without peer—*without peer!*"

"A peerless pig," Edward said with a straight face.

"What? Yes, yes, peerless--that's it, you've said it. Peerless. The breadth of him! Why, one side would feed an army." His voice dropped, so Edward had to lean down to hear his confidence. "We've made an agreement that four of my best sows will be carted here and bred." He nodded his head vigorously, as if Edward might question the activity.

The prince studied him, and then said gravely, "Did he sign it with his hnocc or his trotter?"

Cuthred drew back with a startled look. Then he laughed in a gliding noise that ended in a high pitch. "The agreement's with King Aedred, you know that!"

"Even more amazing--"

"You! Now, now--listen to this--the king has choice of the litters, but out of the barrows I keep, I may breed back the promising ones." He leaned back against the table and gave Edward a triumphant look.

"The arrangement seems to suit you."

"Indeed, indeed! The pig's a wonder!"

Edward could think of little to answer to this, so he laid a firm hand to his Cuthred's shoulder and squeezed. "I wish my thegns would be half so pleased with twice as much," he said, and walked on through the scattered benches on a course which would eventually bring him to his sister.

Elfwina had seen him speak with Cuthred, and then seen him drawn aside by Mawer. As she watched, Eorl Waltheof laid a sword on the table. At that moment Mildthryth begged her attention, and when she looked back, Mawer was holding the sword and examining it with all the pride of possession, while Eorl Waltheof glowered. Edward was trying not to laugh and not being successful.

Above the merriment in the hall, Ceadda stood in the shadows of the balcony, his long scarlet mantle pulled around him. As the tides flowed in and out of the marsh, as the wind breathed through the sea grass, the sand was piling up one grain on another. He felt the onrush of disaster.

Chapter Forty

[829] Ceolworth, Mercia. Lady Penwahl and Lady Ella were standing in the mists of the stable yard overseeing the last tightening of their tack, when Elfwina came out into the early dawn. Her chestnut gelding stood ready. The huntsman waited with five of his assistants, all armed with boar spears. Nearby, the hounds milled about, pulling at their leashes and barking.

The mist now drifted upward into the trees beyond the eastern wall. Elfwina's glance came back to Lady Ella, to her strange, parti-colored eyes. The noblewoman bowed her head slightly.

Elfwina turned to Lady Penwahl, who was gazing at the sky and studying the general atmosphere. "It seems a morning for it," Lady Penwahl said. Then her sharp glance fell to the huntsman, who stood nearby adjusting the horn at his belt, but with his eyes fixed on her. She looked away.

"Cold and misty--could we ask for better?" Elfwina replied, and moved around and under her horse's neck to check the breast collar on the other side.

Lady Penwahl began tugging here and there at her horse's equipment aware of the huntsman approaching her. "You spend too much time indoors," she said to Elfwina, and retied the girth with quick, angry fingers.

"But, here I am outdoors, Lady Pen, obedient to you as always. You might give me credit for that."

Lady Penwahl glanced up as the huntsman came around the head of her horse and ran his brown hand along its cheek. He was twenty-one, a head taller than she with a bold stance and tilt of his head. He had moved closer, flashing a smile impossible not to answer it was so merry and honest.

"Was it not tight enough, My Lady?" As he spoke he rammed his fingers under the girth and looked at her in jovial inquiry. "She's on her tiptoes already--shall I cinch her more?"

Her laugh was soft, musical. "Go ahead, Ruthric, maybe she'll fly."

The huntsman's expression changed. He looked into her eyes and seemed suddenly confused. He flushed and his hands now dithered along the straps.

Lady Penwahl saw the grooms assisting the queen and Lady Ella into their saddles. "A hand, huntsman," she said, "and let's be off. We'll see the measure of your humor with the boar."

Ruthric, abashed, hid it behind an impudent grin as he helped her into the saddle. He mounted his own horse, and at the queen's signal, moved the party out single file through the side gate. The hounds were unleashed, and they streamed out, barking, as they ran discovering the ground ahead of the horses. Ruthric drew them back with short notes from the horn.

It was a fluid group of horses and riders and hounds, Ruthric at its head on a bay mare, the queen and the noblewomen behind him, and the five assistants positioned around them. The hounds ran alongside and ahead, every now and then called together by the curt blasts of Ruthric's horn.

They traveled southward along the wall and across the ditch into the great meadow and to the oak woods beyond. The low-lying mist rose swiftly through the bare branches at the first touch of the sun, while frost still glittered in the grass beneath the trees. The riders' breaths swam in the grey air. To their left, sheep took form in the parting mist, and the shepherd waved to Ruthric, who returned the salute.

The lifting mist haunted the bare branches of the beech and oak. Under the trees, the ground was soft with mast and sodden leaves from a hundred autumns. The horses padded among the mossy trees. With the casual motion of good riders, the women rode easy.

Now Ruthric let the hounds range ahead through the trees and low shrubbery. The party could hear their random barking as the hounds quartered the field, coursing deeper into the woods. Sunlight gilded the tops of the trees. Beneath the heavy interlace of branches, the air was losing its penetrating chill. The sunlight had reached halfway down the massive trees, when they came to a small stream. The party stopped to let the horses drink.

Ruthric brought his mare around and began talking quietly to three of his men. Lady Penwahl dismounted and retreated momentarily to the privacy of some bushes. The mare Lady Ella rode drifted toward Elfwina.

"Your hounds have been well-trained, Your Majesty. Even without seeing them work the boar, I have confidence in them. Who is the trainer?"

Elfwina stroked the neck of her horse. "Ruthric, with assistance from the handlers."

Lady Ella appraised the huntsman. He was listening to one of his assistants, his head turned slightly in an attitude of mild disagreement. Her eye was swift, judging the form beneath the short brown mantle and the dark green tunic, noted the confident way he carried himself, the bush of brown hair, the clean-shaven face with its wide impudent mouth and bold eyes. "I've heard about him," she said. "He is a prize, by all accounts." She turned back to meet Elfwina's faint smile.

"The king values Ruthric very highly."

"His Majesty is not much for the hunt, is he?"

"It's his favorite pastime in autumn," she said drily, meaning the Danes. "With your family the hunt is more than simple sport, isn't it?"

"Passion, Ma'am. We live for the hunt."

Lady Penwahl emerged from the brush and made her way over the spongy ground to where the queen and Lady Ella sat on their horses. She came between them, speaking in a low voice.

"I praise our Compassionate Mother who so wisely set our rhythms."

"Which rhythm do you address, Lady Pen?" asked Elfwina.

"I heard a plural," Lady Ella said, with her crooked smile.

"Nothing wrong with your ears, my dear. I had one uppermost in my mind, but there are two, with all the attendant rhythms."

Lady Ella leaned forward in her saddle. "Let's hear them all," she said.

"First, and from the heart, I praise the good female sense she had to end the menses. It never fails--on the day of the hunt you're either flowing like the Welland, or worrying because you're not. What a glorious relief not to have those anxieties and be able to piss in the woods without the hounds congregating at the spot."

Lady Ella's laugh cracked the air. The men's heads came around. "Is that the way it is today?"

"No, the Goddess smiled today. It was just an observation."

"I have to know this," Lady Ella said, leaning down inches from Lady Penwahl's face, "what do you do for cramps?"

She answered briskly, "That's easy--four fingers of wine in the morning and evening and time to indulge yourself without comment from the household. The latter being the most effective. Nothing works well, as you know. You must simply surround yourself with comfort in an uncomfortable time. Who wants to jolt about in a saddle when the cramp is on?"

"But there are times when the jolting can take your mind off it."

"One pain for another? Better to lie in bed with pillows and sweets and stab your hand with your dinner knife. There's much less effort involved, and the result is the same."

"My oath!" cried Lady Ella. "A clerk should write this down!"

From the distance came the sudden high baying of the hounds. Lady Penwahl, with no assistance at all, leaped onto the back of her horse, and, with the rest of the party, cleared the stream and struck into the thick humus of the forest floor. Ruthric made a quick survey of the party, and then, winding the horn, took the lead.

The hounds ahead were in full cry, surging at a large thicket. The brush heaved suddenly, and a boar charged from its center, flinging its head in a short half-arc that tossed one of the hounds yelping into the air.

The boar stood nearly three feet at the shoulder, with a long narrow body and legs as delicate as a deer. He turned swiftly about, slashing at the hounds with his long tusks as they darted in to tear at his shoulders and rump.

Lady Ella, intent on the boar, her eyes brilliant and her lips drawn back from her teeth, held her spear ready as her horse danced along. To the right, near the thicket, Lady Penwahl had moved into position with a long underhanded thrusting spear. Elfwina brought her chestnut through the milling horses of the men and poised with her spear balanced in her hand. The men shouted and the hounds swarmed at the boar, baying and yelping with each turn made by the wild swine.

With a sharp twist of his head, the boar ripped open the side of one of the hounds, sending it yowling to the ground. The boar plunged back into the shrubs with the rest of the hounds hard after it. The riders divided and swept around the thicket, regrouping in a clearing ringed by beeches. The hounds brought the boar to bay again.

"Ready!" Ruthric shouted, and blasted the horn. The hounds fell reluctantly back and would have left the way

clear for the hunters, but at that instant, the boar hurtled into the horses, cutting the front legs out from under Ruthric's mare. The mare fell forward, and Ruthric leaped away. But the boar came around and in one swift motion ripped the side of Ruthric's leg open from mid-calf to hip before he could gain his footing. He shrieked, grabbed his leg and stared wildly at the boar.

Lady Penwahl had swung her horse around when Ruthric's mare went down and was now bearing in on him. The assistants, forced outward, maneuvered clear and, roaring and shouting, began to reclose. Pushed to the side by Elfwina's gelding, Lady Ella was swinging back around. With an unexpected clear shot, Elfwina rammed her spear into the boar's shoulder. It screamed and wheeled and thrashed its tusks inches from Ruthric's back.

Lady Penwahl leaned down. Grasping Ruthric's arm as he reached up, she managed to pull him behind her. The boar slashed again, shaking its head and skipping forward on stiff legs, its tail straight up in the air. It whirled with a terrible grunt as Lady Ella's spear struck it deep in the side. It faltered. Elfwina bent low over her horse and drove her spear into the boar's throat. It fell to the ground in a shower of twigs and dead leaves, panted heavily for a brief moment, and then was still. Elfwina and Lady Ella exchanged a look of fierce satisfaction.

Lady Penwahl twisted in her saddle to judge the gash in Ruthric's leg. The banding had been severed from his calf to his knee and the hose ripped away. The leather banding had saved him from all but a superficial wound in that area, but from the knee to the hip, the flesh was laid open to the bone. Blood poured from the wound and ran down the horse's flank onto the ground.

"Easy," Lady Penwahl told the men crowding in.

As they lifted Ruthric to the ground, she slid off her horse and unclasped her mantle. She began wrapping it tightly around his leg as one of the men carefully lifted it.

Elfwina and Lady Ella had dismounted and joined the circle around the injured man. The queen turned to the assistant standing next to her, staring down at the huntsman. "Wind the injury call, fool!"

He dropped back with a bow and hastily blew the horn.

Up to this moment Ruthric had not spoken, only lay groaning and jerking his uninjured leg up and down in an agitated rhythm. Now, he flung his hands up to his face and cried, *"Oh, mercy!"*

The urgent winding of the injury call filled the wood.

The meeting was almost over. The mood was confident, full of camaraderie. Only the formal signing was left. Now, as they leaned around the table accomplishing this, there came the distant winding of the hunting horn. Edward glanced toward the windows.

Penwahl's head came up. "They've flushed one out."

"Who's hunting?" Edward asked.

"My wife, for one," Penwahl replied.

"Lady Ella is with the party, too," said Aldhune. "They're after boar."

Aedred pushed the parchment along to Edward and handed him the quill. "It's the queen's party," he told him.

Bending over the parchment to write his signature, Edward abruptly turned his head to the side and shot Aedred a blazing look. Aedred's eyes narrowed. Edward turned back to sign. Having taken that moment to pull himself together, he straightened. He swung away from the king and began a conversation with Leodwald. But with his anger at Aedred suppressed, he listened now for the call on the hunting horn that would signal an injury.

It came as they were moving away in small groups, the last conversations before the final breaking up of the witan. There was an abrupt silence, and then a movement toward the doors. Edward and the king turned and ran for the back passageway. Aldhune, Penwahl, and Leodwald were right behind them. They came out into the enclosure yard and saw Grundl directing the ready-wagon through the side gate. Aedred and the prince were into their saddles and swinging around the wagon as soon as it was clear.

They eased their mounts down the embankment and up the other side, gaining the top and turning to the south toward the oak woods. The urgent call sounded again, and the king and the prince let out their horses, pounding over the grassland and then under the wide-spreading branches of the oaks and beeches. They slowed their horses, shouted, and got an answering shout from nearby. One of the huntsman's assistants came loping his horse through the trees.

Aedred reined up next to him. "Who's injured?"

"Ruthric, Your Majesty. The boar broke the legs of his mare, and when they went down, the beast opened his thigh."

"Is everyone else all right?"

"Yes, Sire. The boar was brought down by Queen Elfwina and Lady Ella."

"Well, ride on, and give the eorls behind us your information." Aedred turned in the saddle to watch the man ride off. Then he looked at Edward.

"Thank God!" Edward said passionately.

"Yes, thank all of them," Aedred replied, and trotted his horse forward.

Chapter Forty-One

[829] Ceolworth, Mercia. When he heard the distress call, Ceadda had gone to the far end of the corridor where he could look down into the enclosure. He had stood watching the race leading from the hall on across the grassland and into the trees and had seen the return march with the wagon. When the procession was close enough for him to see what the situation was, he took a packet of powder and a small bowl from his leather bag, mixed ale and powder in the bowl, and went down into the courtyard.

Ruthric was barely sensible, his face chalky white. Under Aedred's instructions, his huntsman was carefully lifted down from the straw-filled bed of the wagon and carried forward. Lady Penwahl walked beside him. From her hip down, the right side of her garments was saturated with blood. Her right shoe made a bloody imprint behind her. With quick orders she sent a servant rushing off toward the hall, and then she led the men carrying Ruthric into the barracks.

Ceadda followed the crowd and stopped just inside the building. He could see Ruthric lying ashen and trembling on a narrow bed. While everyone else in the room ran about, and Lady Penwahl and Edward were issuing orders, the king was leaning down, speaking quietly to his huntsman. Materials were placed on a box set hastily next to the bed. The servant Lady Penwahl had sent running, returned with a small brass case. She took it from him and walked over to the bed and looked pointedly at Aedred. The king pressed his hand into the bushy mass of Ruthric's hair and straightened. He saw Ceadda standing by the door and came over to him.

"How serious is it, Your Majesty?"

"His leg's opened all the way to the hip bone. Treacherous damn boars. Good thing Lady Pen was along. What's this?" Aedred looked down at the bowl in Ceadda's hand.

"If you permit it, a concoction that will ease the huntsman's pain."

"What do you have there, Ceadda?" Edward said, coming up to them.

"Something for the pain," Aedred told him. "Take it over there, Ceadda. They'll welcome it, I'm sure."

The magician approached Lady Penwahl. The wound had been tightly rebandaged with clean cloths. Lady Penwahl was now opening the brass case, which held sewing articles. "I am Ceadda," he told her. "I have a mixture here that will ease his pain."

Her glance was penetrating. "What kind of mixture?"

Ruthric had been watching them. "Here," he said, lifting his hand to the magician.

Ceadda put the bowl into the huntsman's hand and elevated his head so he could drink.

Lady Penwahl watched. "I thought you wanted to supervise my stitching."

"Oh, I'll do that," Ruthric answered weakly. "This will help me count them." He flung the contents of the bowl down his throat, and then let his hand drop.

Ceadda gently lowered Ruthric's head back to the pillow and took the empty bowl from his fingers. "In a moment you will feel less pain."

"How long does it take?" Lady Penwahl asked Ceadda.

"Only moments."

She laid the hand with the needle in her lap and looked at Ruthric. He looked back at her. The sweat stood out on his white face and glistened on his neck.

In a voice heavy with pauses and intakes of breath, Ruthric said, "My Lady, I wanted to see you run that spear in underhand . . . . It was a thing I'd fixed my mind on the whole morning. I've seen you with the bow, and the stag doesn't live that could stand . . . after you've drawn on him. But the underhand spear--that's another thing entirely."

"You don't think I could do it, Ruthric? Is that what you're saying? Now you've shaken me. I'll sew a crooked seam." She was assessing his alertness. "So you lack confidence in my skill with the underhand."

His mouth moved in his impudent smile, and his eyelids drooped sleepily. "My Lady," he murmured thickly, "I have every confidence in you. You are perfect . . . perfectly desirable . . . ." His eyes closed and his head slipped to one side.

"Am I!" She shook her head. "He's a lad. Always has been--since he was old enough to know girls were different from boys." She frowned at Ceadda. "Your formula was potent. I've only seen poisons work that quickly. How long will he sleep?"

"For about an hour deeply. After that he will begin to waken."

"Good! That gives me time." As matter-of-factly as if she were seaming a garment, she pulled down a section of the bandaging that had become bloody, took her needle, and began to sew together the damaged tissues of the huntsman's leg.

"Would you mind if I watched?" he said.

"No. Sit down, though. Don't hover. Ceadda, you said?"

He pulled a box over and sat down. "Yes, Ceadda the Magician."

"Magician! That answers the question I was going to ask." She took several careful stitches, sewing the raw edges of the flesh together.

"What question, My Lady?"

"Whether your formula was secret. However . . . ."

"Allow me to decide the 'however', My Lady. I will consider it."

"It would only be used for purposes such as this," she said, pausing to look at him.

He watched her skillful hands resume their work. "I understand that," he replied.

Edward left the king answering questions from men unaware of the latest on Ruthric's injuries, and went looking for his sister. He caught up with her as she was passing one of the storage sheds and pulled her into the dim interior. She looked up at him, and then out at the sunlit enclosure yard.

"I want to talk to you."

"Not in here."

"Elf . . . a moment." He slowly stroked her cheek with the backs of his fingers as she looked into his eyes. "I was afraid the injury call was for you."

She wrapped her fingers around his hand and gazed silently at him. He stepped her deeper into the gloom of the shed. His hand trembled at her lips, and he felt her breath draw through his fingers.

"We can't do this," she said.

"What? Feel love? You answered yes when I asked you. Was that a lie?"

"No," she said, looking to this side and that, held by obedience, by the treachery of their past. "We can't do this," she repeated.

"We're finally being honest with each other." He ran his hands gently along her arms then took his hands away. "What's the harm in that?"

"You know there could be harm."

"Admitting it? Who else will hear it?" He said softly, "I've wanted to say it. Will you let say it? Now, in this place? You are the only one who will hear it."

She closed her eyes and was silent, held immobile by the heat of his body, the slow sway of his mantle against her arm.

"Let me say it." He paused. "Nothing more; just the words." He waited, touched her hair, and finally pulled her to him. "We've always loved each other, haven't we?" He heard her sigh. "Haven't we?"

"Yes."

"Saying that I love you isn't harmful; it's truth spoken. I love you. It would be a lie if I denied it. Can you deny you love me?"

She shook her head and tried to draw back, and he wrapped her against him. Her hands clawed at his sides, and then gripped his flesh. "Tell me you love me," he said, and it was a demand he repeated in the voice of time and events and years of dispossession.

"We cannot act on this."

His voice slid downward into a soft plea. "Tell me you love me."

It *was* true. She did love him. She had loved him from the time her memories began. His presence still filled her world. She felt trapped in his arms, yet she wanted to be there, belonged there. "I--"

Men's voices rolling past the doorway sprang Edward and Elfwina apart. The prince stood mute, watching as his sister walked to the bright rectangle of the open door. He saw her straighten, lift her head, and step into the sunlight, not the woman who loved him beyond all bounds, but the queen of Mercia.

"Well, this has been a morning," Aedred said, with a humorless laugh, when Edward came into his quarters. "We sign up for war, and in a totally unrelated casualty, as if to mark it, my chief huntsman is ripped by a boar. That wound is going to cripple him, I'm afraid. A bad omen."

"Lady Pen will make him right, if anyone can. They say she can work miracles."

"It will take one."

"He's young."

Aedred took a long drink from his cup, his eyes on Edward, who seemed distracted. He put the cup down.

"I have something to put to you."

Edward's gaze sharpened. "All right," he said slowly.

"I asked you to stay on after the attack on Gyrth because of the unsettled nature of things, but that's no longer the case. I know you need to start putting your portion of the army together, if you're going to move it here in the spring. So, I'm releasing you—with appreciation." He paused, turned his head slightly as he looked at the prince.

"Yes, of course, you're right--I have an army to levy." He agreed with the assessment, but was wary, an uneasiness at why Aedred brought this up on precisely *this* day.

The king was looking at him, his eyebrows slightly raised. He tilted his hand over, a question.

"No sense putting it off; I should leave."

Aedred nodded.

"Soon, I guess."

"Tomorrow?"

Edward looked closely at him; saw nothing but the polite pause for his question to be answered. He felt pushed along, but could think of no argument that would not arouse suspicion. "Tomorrow sounds right." He hesitated when there was only another nod.

"I'd like to leave my men here."

"You're not thinking of going alone!"

"Yes. Yes, I am. It will be faster. As you say, I'm behind in getting this together."

Aedred measured the prince's resolve and finally said, "You're certain about this? Mawer is surely going to protest."

"It will have to be a question of who's in charge, won't it? I think I'm still the prince and he's my minion."

Aedred snorted. "Well, you have the job of telling him that. What route will you be taking? Not Cyninges Street, I guess."

"No, that might be risky. I'll take the route Father did--through Coventry and Oxford."

Aedred nodded. "Take whatever you need from our stores."

"I will, thanks." He stood up.

"There are halls along the way."

"I'll take advantage of that."

"Daybreak is always a good time to start out," Aedred said.

Edward felt a little chill along his arms; what had Aedred sensed?

When Edward went to his sister's chambers that evening, he found Aedred there, comfortably settled in a chair in his dressing robe, evidently prepared to stay. He wanted to speak with Elfwina alone, but maybe that wasn't such a good idea. This would be better, less likely to raise suspicion. He swallowed. *Why am I worried? There was nothing . . . .*

He rested his arms over the ladder of one of the high-backed chairs and looked at Elfwina. She was standing by the hearth, her hair flared loose to her hips, the edges radiant in the firelight behind her. Framed in that glowing mass, her face appeared small and fragile. An erroneous picture, he knew only too well.

"We missed you at supper," she said, breaking a small silence in the room.

He glanced ever so briefly at his hands, and then back again to her face. "I had some arrangements to make," he replied, and some indefinable quality in the way he said it froze Elfwina momentarily. Sitting silently, his leg dangling over the arm of his chair, Aedred was listening with a certain scientific interest Edward's approach to the subject of his leaving, and missed his wife's reaction.

"Arrangements?"

"I'm leaving for Exeter in the morning." He glanced at Aedred and got a neutral gaze in return. Edward looked back at his sister. "There is nothing more for me to do here now that the witan agreed to the plan, and I have an army to assemble and equip for the march back here in the spring. I need to get started on it."

"I really don't see the reason for your leaving at this time, Edward," she replied, very calmly. She didn't understand this sudden decision, why Edward would do this. She was afraid, flailing, not knowing his motivation. "Father will not have been idle. He'd wonder at your thinking he would expect you to raise the thousand men yourself. You're needed here."

"I don't see why."

"No? As representative of Wessex and the pledge Father made, you help keep up the courage and spirit of our eorls."

"You can't seriously believe that. Confidence here has never been higher. I don't have anything to do with that."

She ignored that assessment. Clasping her hands tightly, she said, in a calm voice, "When the army is ready, Father will send word, and then you can go to Wessex and bring it back."

He could sense Aedred questioning Elfwina's tension, but he didn't know how to diffuse what was becoming a confrontation. "Why should I leave it all for Father to do when my being there would make the task easier? There's no good purpose for me to stay."

Elfwina drew a breath to speak, but Aedred said quietly, "Edward needs to make his own choice of captains; he needs to oversee the acquisitions of equip-ment and supplies. I agree with him; he should go."

She looked from one to the other. "This seems to be a joint decision. And carved in stone, no doubt, and without my consultation."

Aedred glanced at her in mild surprise. She returned it with a hard look she then swung to her brother. But by the time she had stopped in front of the chair he was leaning against, there was a panicked question in her eyes. Finding no response, she turned back to Aedred.

"I really don't understand this sudden rush."

"Hardly a rush," he replied. "We all agreed to it. It's what Edward needs to do."

"So!" She lifted her hands. "Tis done, then. At your command?"

He frowned slightly as he looked up at her.

"What time does he leave?"

"Daybreak."

She swung around to her brother. "On a fast horse?" she cried bitterly.

Aedred's voice cut hard through the room. "Elfwina, what the hell is going on?"

She turned to him and stood silent and startled before the cold warning in his eyes. "I'm sorry," she said. She looked back at Edward.

"I'm sorry. It upsets me when you leave. You know that. And now, with all this--" her head turned back to Aedred. "You know I get upset," she implored him. To Edward she said, "You are my brother, and I love you. I don't like to see you go--especially in this way. I apologize. I should have said so in the first place. My remarks were unkind. I'm sorry."

She went over to Aedred and sank down beside his chair. She laid her hands on his arm. "You are right to be impatient. Of course Edward should go. I won't say any more about it." She continued to look into his eyes with her hands resting on his arm.

"I get tired of this," he said.

"I know." She saw by his expression he had relented; she rose then and, with her fingertips balanced on the king's arm, faced her brother.

Edward had watched her undo the suspicions she had raised and quiet the dangerous lift of Aedred's temper. He was both proud of her and ashamed at himself. She had known in the face of Aedred's anger to be honest. He was confounded by the pull of his emotions and his lack of any clear-cut way to handle them.

"I have a number of things to do before morning. So, goodnight and goodbye until spring." He went quickly from the room, relieved she had not discovered he would be traveling alone.

At daybreak Edward rode out across the rolling expanse of grasslands that lay southward from Ceolworth, his horse dancing and eager in the growing light. The passage of its hooves dulled the silver glaze of frost. Edward rode erect with the easy motion of a good horseman who will be days in the saddle. His mantle was thrown back from his head. The rich yellow wool garment, designed to serve as blanket and cloak, draped his body and fell over the rump of his horse. In his bearing and in his manner, in the way his eyes boldly surveyed his surroundings, no observer would have needed an announcement to know he was a prince.

At the edge of the wood he stopped and swiveled around to take one last look at Ceolworth, and then disappeared along the faint trail leading into the woods.

Elfwina had been quiet the rest of the evening. Seeing her mood, Aedred had slept with her and tolerated the distance but had felt resentment at Edward, whose presence was as real as if he had been lying between them.

Chapter Forty-Two

[829] Ceolworth, Mercia. Early next morning, Aedred left his wife curled in his bed in a deep slumber, her arms crooked over her head as if she were warding off a blow. He knew she had lain awake for most of the night. He had finally dropped off to a dream-ladened sleep and had wakened before the sun was above the east wall.

He downed a quick breakfast of cold meat and ale, and then went directly to the small hut near the stables that was Ruthric's living quarters. The servant he had sent to attend the huntsman was not inside the hut. Ruthric lay asleep on his narrow bed, still and white-faced, his skin shining unnaturally. A candle burning on the small table in the center of the room dimly lit the meager furniture and the wealth of hunting equipment hanging from every wall.

To Aedred's surprise, Ceadda rose up from a pallet crowded next to the cot. "Well! I didn't expect to see you here. Where's Ruthric's attendant?"

"Good morning, Your Majesty," he said. "He's gone to the kitchen to fetch some broth. I gave your huntsman a potion that is tricky to administer. With your permission, Sire, I would rather not entrust it to anyone else."

"Of course you have my permission. I appreciate your interest in him."

Ceadda bowed.

"How is his leg this morning?"

"Swollen, but it doesn't fester. Lady Penwahl is remarkably creative in the healing arts. A fine woman."

"Yes, she is. I'll have to say, though, this is the first time I've heard her ministrations spoken of as creative; I've heard them evoke creative oaths."

"Creativity in healing, Sire."

Aedred nodded, curious at the animation in the magician's normally solemn face.

"Men are usually crippled by this much damage to the leg, making them fit only for begging. Lady Penwahl believes that rigorously exercising the leg will keep the muscles pliable and minimize any shrinking or stiffening. A simple theory, but it takes a gifted mind to perceive it."

Aedred's eyebrows shot up. "I don't think I agree with such measures. Exercising a leg as badly wounded as Ruthric's sounds like a way to cause further injury. When would these exercises begin? After the leg is healed?"

"Lady Penwahl began them before she left for Stafford. I'm to continue them."

"The man wasn't fully conscious when she left!"

"I can assure you he was by the time the exercises were over."

"That's a torture, not a cure. Even Mother Erce allows an injured animal to seek a quiet place to rest and heal."

"I had much the same objection, Sire. But, as Lady Penwahl explained, the animal does raise itself to change position, to seek water, and so forth, and in doing so uses all the motions it normally uses. She convinced me that if Ruthric follows her regime, he will be fit for more than a beggar's life."

The king looked down at Ruthric. "Well, I know she's too good a healer for me to argue with her methods. Let me know his progress, Ceadda. I want to see how this theory works out. I'd like this man on his feet again, whatever the means to accomplish it."

"You'll have word on him every day, Sire."

"You have a long project ahead of you."

"Time is something I have a great deal of, Your Majesty." The magician's eyes were on Ruthric. The solemn expression had once again composed his features.

"You are fortunate."

Still gazing at the huntsman, Ceadda replied, "No, Sire, I am not."

The month of Hretha arrived. The last furrow of the fields was turned over, and Aedred sent down three barrels of ale to mark the ceremonies for the vernal equinox, arriving just in time for the ritual dousing of the ploughman with the first bucketful. He was joined by his eorls, and they all stayed too long and too merrily at the celebration. Knowing the annual ritual well and its general conclusion, Elfwina occupied herself in her own pursuits.

She went down with Ceadda to the common paddock to watch Ruthric's first ride on his new horse. From her own stables, she had made Ruthric a gift of a silver-dappled filly at a time in his recuperation when his spirits were lowest and he was convincing himself he was never going to be able to hunt again. The filly had been the antidote for that slow poison. From the time he had received the animal, he had been making his way on crutches back and forth to the stable to oversee her care.

Ceadda still continued ruthlessly to direct Lady Penwahl's program of exercise. Facing mutiny at one point in Ruthric's convalescence, he had conjured up a monster to bring the huntsman back in line.

"What kind of monster?" Elfwina asked him, fascinated.

"A boar, Your Majesty," he had answered.

Appalled, she had responded, "That was wretched of you!"

"Would a crippled leg be kinder?" had been his mild reply.

Now they stood at the fence as a groom led the filly into the paddock and stood holding the rein as Ruthric approached. The huntsman had left one crutch leaning against the gate and was creeping toward the horse on the other, his hand pulling his leg along.

Ceadda called out in a quiet voice. "Let the leg lift itself, Ruthric."

"Wait till I get to the filly!"

"Let the leg lift itself," Ceadda repeated.

Ruthric made an abrupt, annoyed stop. With sweat beading out on his face, he awkwardly raised the leg and dropped it forward.

"Again," Ceadda told him.

The filly tossed her silver head and pranced sideways. The groom drew her back. Ruthric made another slow step and another until he had reached the horse. He flung his arm up, clutched the saddle and, dropping his forehead to the leather, hung there panting.

Elfwina looked over at Ceadda, and he gave her the ghost of a smile.

After the first two or three weeks, it appeared Elfwina had reconciled herself to her brother's absence as she always finally did, and life began to flow back into the space Edward had left. It wasn't long before Aedred was reminded about how much he had come to depend on Edward, how important the prince was to him, and, in truth, how much he missed him; these realizations coming in the interstices of the activities at Ceolworth and his preparation for war.

Aedred had ordered reinforcement of the walls surrounding the hall and the repair of the ditch. Over the five years' peace the side gate had been used more and more often and a trail broken into the embankment, an easy entrance for an enemy. The work was well under way, supervised in part by the king and in the main by the hall reeve Ceolric.

Aedred was in communication with his eorls whose preparations at their holdings were much the same as his--strengthening defenses. Additionally, they were grouping and supplying their portion of the army.

The first group of eighty men arrived around the first of Eostre in a downpour. The bivouac had been set up about a half-mile from the hall, out on the rolling, oak-starred hills between the hall and Cyninges Street. Edward's army, when it arrived, would camp in the great meadowland to the south between the hall enclosure and the woods. In both places buildings for stores had been raised and pavilions erected.

When the group arrived earlier than expected, Aedred rode over with Eorl Waltheof, Eorl Mawer, Grundl, and a number of thegns. They helped settle the men, pounding in stakes, lifting poles, maneuvering the oiled fabric into position, all in a drenching rain that wet them to the skin.

Aedred left Grundl in command, giving him orders to work out a plan to keep the men busy. Then he and the eorls returned to the hall and drank mulled wine as they dried out before the hearth.

Aedred sat with his back against the table, one foot propped up on a bench he had dragged out for the purpose. His arm lay along the table edge, a cup held loosely in his hand. He seemed half-asleep. Mawer rumbled a reply to Waltheof. The conversation drifted. After a while, Aedred stood up, and they all came to their feet. He waved them back down.

"If the rain quits tomorrow," he said, with a yawn, "I want to move our horses over to the bivouac. When our portion of the army is fully assembled, we're going to camp over there with the militia."

For the first time since Edward left, Mawer grinned.

Aedred went to his chambers, shed his water-stained clothes, and got into his dressing robe. He dismissed his handthegn for the night, propped himself up in bed, and lay there going over his strategies; what Ædda might do, the possible moves the Danes might make, and how he could counter all of them. With all the numbers Urm could have sifted north, he reasoned, the majority of the Danes still remained in the south at the Severn.

His first instinct had been to summon the Great Fyrd to reinforce the numbers of his allies at the Severn so it could be ended once and for all. That instinct still nagged him, running a thread of doubt through the plan to keep half his force at Ceolworth. But the clear possibility of Ædda gathering an army comparable to Urm's and marching out from the north, annexing what they would sweep over unresisted kept that instinct in check.

Where was it he felt most secure? The western border and all the area bordering Wessex. He thought all other points of vulnerability were covered; there was nowhere else the force could come from unless they dropped from the sky. And yet, he felt there was something he had overlooked . . . .

"Well, Edward, we think we've covered it all, but where's the crack?"

He started, coming awake at the sound of his own voice. He shook his head and laughed and sat up on the edge of his bed. He looked down at his bare feet. He wriggled his toes and waggled his feet, moving them in a circle as he stared at them. Would his huntsman ever be able to make these simple movements, again?

"Divining your toes, Aedred?"

He jumped when she spoke, not having heard her enter, and she laughed with great amusement that she had been able to startle him.

"I didn't hear you come in." He laughed, too, at his silly pursuit. "I was wondering if Ruthric would be able to walk normally again." His gaze sharpened. "Are you going to stay the night?"

"I would like to stay with the king, if I may--"

"*If* you may!" He came up from the bed to hug her vigorously. "Yes, you may stay the night with the king. He's missed you, do you know that?" He nuzzled her shoulder and neck, and kissed her soundly. "He's wanted you and la! Feel this creature--" He pushed the bulge in his gown up against her. "Such an impatient creature," he said.

He watched her lay her garments on the stand, and then unbind her hair. He sighed.

"I want that creature," she laughed and, leaping at him, hurled him backwards onto the bed. She slid her hands up his thighs, pushing his gown away to straddle him, pulling her knees along his sides and curving her body down so she could kiss him.

After some moments he murmured, "It's been too long; the creature is going to spout."

"Let him spout," she said, moving faster. "We have all night."

The next morning was brilliantly clear. In high spirits, Aedred ordered a paddock constructed beneath the trees at the edge of the bivouac and a shed for hay and tack erected. He spoke to Grundl about the schedule his captain had designed to keep the first militia from idleness, and then he went back to the hall purely on his own errand. As he had hoped, he found Elfwina still in his bed. He took advantage of the moment.

"Shall I stay here all day?" she asked in a drowsy question.

"Yes, stay here. There's no reason for you to get up." His mouth turned into a slow grin. "I'll come in now and then to serve your pleasure. Are you hungry?"

"Only sleepy. Nooo--" she protested in a little whimper when he started to get up. He was delighted. She began to kiss him again, slowly at first, tenderly, and then with an intensity and a hard pressure that bruised his lips and started an erotic spiral which had no part in the usual form of their lovemaking. She took hard from him and he gave fiercely, and when he had pumped himself dry, he looked down at her, expecting to see the soft satisfaction that was one of his rewards. Instead, her eyelids were squeezed shut, her lips drawn back in an expression so full of anger and so foreign and unwanted by him, he wrenched her arms away with a heave of his back and sat staring at her.

She opened her eyes.
"What was that?"
"It *was* intense," she said noncommittally.
"We haven't had anything like that before."
"You didn't like it?"
"Oh, I liked it. I'm not sure you did. You looked angry."
She laughed. "Why in the world would I be angry?"

Chapter Forty-Three

[829] Ceolworth, Mercia. A long time later, Elfwina left the hall. The gate had been thrown open for the convenience of the workers, and men with carts loaded with materials for the walls moved in and out of the enclosure. They shifted their carts out of her way, and then came upright to bow as she passed. She did not see Aedred.

Beyond the grouping of some seventy dwellings that was the village. Elfwina could see in the dark loam of the fields the first shoots of grain marking the furrows. A man walked slowly along one of the furrows, judging the appearance of the young plants.

She turned up the path which led to the sacred grove. The oaks on the hillside were beginning to leaf out in a haze of delicate greens and yellows, and the entrance to the grove itself was purple with lilacs. The perfume nearly smothered her as she pushed through the hanging blossoms.

Inside the grove, last year's dried grasses lay pushed into swirls and peaks by the receded winter snows. Here and there below the dead grass was an underlying greenness. Fallen branches and twigs lay everywhere. Dead weeds leaned against the stone figure and the altar.

She sat down the basket she had carried with her, and then began walking around the circle, dragging downed branches out of the sacred area, all the twigs and limbs that had broken under the weight of the snow. Once she had cleared the debris, she got down on her knees and began yanking the dead weeds and grass away from the base of the figure. When she had finished, she began at the altar, exposing the base stones. She stopped midway to rest.

Where her hand lay on one of the sun-warmed cornerstones, she felt a fine vibration, a tremor in the rough surface beneath her fingers and thought it was the rapid pulsing of her heart. There was another small movement against her palm, and then nothing more. She ran her fingers over the grain of the stone, feeling the pits and knobs, the minute and ancient textures.

"Please, Great Mother Erce," she whispered. "Take away this hunger. . . help me . . . heal me. Let it be as it was . . . ."

When she had finished her work, she wiped the altar stone, laid down a richly embroidered cloth, and mounded it with small cakes of barley and honey from the basket. She tied the four ends of the cloth together, pushed it to the center of the altar as she genuflected and murmured prayers.

She returned to the hall, coming up the incline as Aedred was approaching the gate tower on horseback from the direction of the bivouac. When he saw her, he stopped, dismounted, and, handing the reins to the nearest man, came back down the slope to meet her.

He walked in his long stride, his dark hair lifting back from his face and shoulders. His brown mantle rippled out from his body, showing the pale orange tunic he was wearing, the color repeated in the cross-bands on his legs. He looked brave and assured.

But his eyes are so solemn, she thought, with a sudden rush of love and guilt. *He laughs readily, but his eyes seldom reflect the laughter. He is more worried than he will say.*

"Were you in the village?" he asked.

"At the grove."

He fell in beside her.

"What's going on at the bivouac?"

"Nothing. Grundl's working their butts off."

"Will he be able to keep a thousand men busy without a revolt?"

"He'll manage."

A thegn came up from behind them, paced the king, waiting for permission to speak.

Aedred put up his hand. "A moment."

The thegn fell back.

"I'd like to talk with you once I've answered this. Will you be in your rooms?"

"I'll wait for you there."

When he came in, Aedred hurled himself into a chair, sprawled one leg over the arm, and told Edyth to bring him a cup of ale.

"One hundred fifty men, Wina, at Tuey Grange. They should reach here in the next couple of hours. Our good Penwahl's bringing them down." He drank deeply, his eyes on her all the while. "By the end of the week, two hundred more will be brought up from the south with Aldhune and Leodwald. That's half the army. When Gyrth and Wulfric and the others get here, we'll have the full army in the next fifteen days. How's that?"

"The *full* army?"

"Our portion of it, I mean. No word from Exeter, yet."

"Has Aethelred reported?"

"Yes. Nothing's stirring up there. If it does, he's ready for them." He drained the cup, signaled to one of the servants for another, and then leaned back and looked at her. He didn't say anything, just continued to look at her as he drank from the cup.

She finally said, "What is it, Aedred?"

He emptied the cup quickly and set it down. "Nothing. Just gathering my thoughts. Something's bothering me about our strategy, and I'd like to see if you can smoke it out."

"Of course, I'll try." She sat down. "What is it that bothers you?"

"The trouble is, I don't know. I've just a sense that something's been overlooked--something important."

"In the distribution of the forces?"

"Yes," he said slowly, marveling at her quick perception. As always, he was a little in awe of her abilities in military strategy. "Yes, I think that is where the center of it lies. But, when I go over the plan, there's no direction which can't be covered within hours."

"Let's review the distribution, then."

She got up and began to slowly pace the room. "In the southwest," she began, "at the Severn there will be a combined army of four thousand which will either engage the Danes or force a peace. In the west the border is being watched by the eorls of those provinces. Gryffn has been alerted. He is constructing defenses at Talacre to deal with any threat from Ireland--that *is* going on, isn't it?"

"So he informs me."

She nodded. "The garrison there will join with Cuthred's fyrd to stave off any attack from that quarter. Aethelred is responsible for the northern border, and Tilhere is our buffer from the Danish incursion from the Welland." She glanced over at him. "Back to the southern provinces--Ethelrad of London guards the Thames and Middlesex, the Gifla beyond that, while all the rest of our southern border is protected by Wessex. Our own army can meet an attack from any quarter, and the local fyrds can cause enough trouble to let the Danes know we aren't going to let them in easily."

She came to a stop in front of him. He had been sitting with his cheek resting against his fist, listening carefully to her summation. "Now, do you find a reason for your uneasiness anywhere in that?"

"It sounds a marvelous defense, doesn't it?"

Elfwina visualized the valleys and rivers, the hills, the passes an army could move through swiftly, the forests that offered protection and game, the villages, the promontories, all the aspects of terrain and settlement, the advantages of all for defense, for offense.

"I don't see anything wrong there, Aedred. Of course, any number of things can happen with battle plans. Events can benefit either side in the chance. But, as strategies go, it would be difficult to improve on this one."

He collapsed back into the chair. "You're right. I just felt the need to make sure nothing's been forgotten."

"There are few men as thorough as you, Aedred."

He looked up at her and smiled. "Or as tedious?"

"Are you begging a denial?"

"Yes! And a compliment to nail it down, if you have one."

"Hmm." She remembered the way he looked as he had come down the hill--indeed, how he looked now in the soft light from the windows. "You're very handsome--"

"You say that all the time."

"Oh, do I! So what point would you have your compliment take, since it's not to be freely given?"

He reached up and pulled her onto his lap. "Tell me you love me. That's the finest compliment I know."

She put her arms around his neck and kissed him. "I do love you." She kissed him again.

"I like this," he said.

"Me, too . . . Didn't we have such a lovely beginning?"

"Tell me about that beginning. I like being the hero. Start with when I came to Exeter." He settled her comfortably in his lap.

"That's ahead of the story."

"Well, then start where you please."

She laughed softly and nuzzled her head against his neck. "You had a mixed reputation," she began.

"You haven't said that before."

"A good storyteller always varies the details."

"As long as she bears witness to the truth."

"Of course."

"What exactly do you mean by 'mixed'?"

"Good and bad."

"Bad? That's never been part of the narrative."

"Affairs."

"Oh!" He laughed. "Those were the *good*--tell me what the *bad* were!"

"It could have been bad for you if I'd decided not to marry you--"

"Bad indeed!"

"I was *not* going to marry a man whose bedchamber had a door to the back stairs."

"My bedchamber had one door, and the world knew who came through it. But that was before I met you, if you'll give me proper credit."

"I give you credit."

"I see. You perceived the good and forgave me for--what was less than good, in *your* opinion, Madam."

"Men have lost kingdoms through their peccadilloes, my dear husband."

"Yes, you saved me from myself, I admit it. But we're stuck on this point. Get to the part where I am indisputably the hero."

"But, we must bear witness to the truth." She paused.

"I was ashes. You raised me from the dust." He laughed and squeezed her hard.

"Stop--stop! All right! Your London court was the talk of

everyone who came to Exeter."

"Interesting years. I liked London--"

"Pay attention! This is the part you've been waiting for."

"You've got my attention."

"When I came into your life your time in London was almost over."

"*Because* you came into my life."

"Shall I go on?"

"Please." He kissed her nose.

"When I was fifteen, you came to Exeter Hall--"

"I did." He kissed her ear and ran his tongue along the delicate fluting.

She shivered and murmured, "You were so bold . . . actually you were insolent."

Aedred laughed out loud.

"You knew all the women were buzzing about the handsome, *unmarried* king of Mercia."

"There you go--"

"You were swarmed and were patient with it. I made up my mind to have you for a husband--"

"Here it comes--"

"--*if* your nature continued to be as pleasant as your appearance."

He brushed his hand over her hair. "I wanted to topple into bed that evening and sleep for a week, regardless of the good ladies and their charming conversations, but that Edward insisted I hang about. And then I looked up and there you were at the top of the stairway, the most beautiful girl I had ever seen. You glowed. There was . . . radiance all about you."

He gripped her chin and tilting it up, kissed her noisily. "I was afraid you might be promised to someone. Like that Tilhere."

She laughed. "Not likely! Edward argued every suitor right out of existence." *He did,* she thought. *He did--why not Aedred?*

"But he did argue for me," Aedred said.

"Yes. He loved you and wanted me to love you, too." *But why?* But she knew why.

"And we were wed."

"And you left London and took me to live in the heart of your kingdom." She pressed his face in her hands. "I've never wanted to leave. I do love you so very much."

She kissed him, and this time they made love with immeasurable tenderness.

Chapter Forty-Four

[829] Ceolworth, Mercia. The numbers at the bivouac increased through the following week. Penwahl, Aldhune, and Leodwald set up their tents in the area, but Aedred decided to wait until the final group of men arrived with Wulfric before he joined them.

Everyone was busy. Repairs on the wall were going forward. Elfwina and Aedred inspected the progress, walking together with Ceolric and making suggestions where they thought more reinforcement was needed. The surrounding ditch and embankment was now fully repaired and the gate tower heavily retimbered. On the wide porch of the hall, spears leaned together like shocks of grain. Stores were being distributed into an area more convenient to the bivouac.

Although each man had been equipped and provisioned by his community for two month's duty, yet provisions had to be supplemented because of the change from a fyrd levy to a standing army. Because he wanted close control over the army's food supply, Aedred ordered rations issued each day for preparation by the men at their own campfires. Meat from the domestic supply and from game was roasted on spits in a common area and its division supervised by the captains.

One evening, as Aedred stood conferring with the eorls, Grundl was overseeing the distribution of rations to the men. Aedred was observing this, finding it running smoothly and more quickly than he had expected, and he was relieved that one more detail could be dismissed from the many holding his attention.

"That Grundl is a good man," Leodwald said. "He has a firm hand and a fair mind."

Before Aedred could reply, Penwahl intoned, "The man has always shown an admirable fe-al-ty to his king. A lesson well-given to us all." He looked pointedly at the other eorls. Leodwald went rigid in offense; Aedred had to cough to cover his laugh.

Grundl climbed the incline to the gate tower in thundering strides. He was on his way to confer with Ceolric about additional stores for the increasing numbers at the bivouac. Ceolric's dwelling was in the courtyard by the south parapet, so Grundl took a short cut through the hall, hammering up the steps and through the wide doors and into the relative dimness of the interior, his mind on what he was going to say to the reeve. He impacted with Lady Ella.

Rebounding from the collision, Lady Ella saw Grundl as if for the first time, found what she saw pleasing, and wondered why she had not paid more attention to Aedred's captain before this. She stared at him, still propelled backwards.

He grabbed her shoulders and stood holding her in his huge grip. A dark flush bloomed along his neck. *I've disconcerted him,* she thought. *I must keep the advantage.*

He released her and stood gazing at her from his scarred face, a face she found appealing because of its roughness. She drew herself up and demanded, with the degree of sharpness she thought he would expect from a woman of her rank, "What is your name?" She knew very well what it was.

"Grundl, My Lady," he told her in a deep, rumbling voice. "I do beg your pardon--"

She cut across his apologies. "Grundl, is it? Your recklessness is a menace, *Grundl,* not just to an unsuspecting guest of the hall, but to your own safety as well and certainly to the safety of your lord. If I had been an enemy and you so unaware of me coming into your path, I would have neatly had your melts, if not your head. Which eorl's militia do you serve?"

"I am not a militia man," he said tonelessly.

Having many brothers, she knew how to stretch her advantage to the maximum.

"If you're not serving an eorl, how it is you have the temerity to wear a sword?"

He answered her in a low rumble. "I am captain of the king's guard, My Lady."

I've distressed him severely, she thought. *I don't want to carry this too far.* She began to ease her manner without appearing to be impressed by his revelation.

"Are you indeed? I shall have to bow to the king's judgment in that." She began to turn away, flinched, and gave a gasp of pain.

"My Lady?" He reached out his hand.

"Your massive clumsy foot has bruised my ankle. Your arm, Grundl."

In the course of all this, a number of people had come and gone through the hall, slowing in curiosity. None of the observers, he noted, were of any consequence to him. He felt her cool hand lace up between his ribs and elbow and slide along his forearm to rest with the fingers pressing lightly on his wrist.

"There's a bench at the far end of the hall," she told him. "Take me there out of the way of this traffic."

She said nothing more to him as they slowly traversed the hall. He held his arm out awkwardly, a stiff brace for the light pushes she gave it as she walked along favoring her ankle. His sword clanked against his thigh; the scabbard of his scramaseax creaked against the belt around his waist. His shoes squeaked. *Like a thudding foot soldier,* he thought, and brought his hand down to keep the sword from banging against his leg.

He seated her at the bench she had indicated, one placed against the wall and far away from the activity near the doors. He backed off and stood looking down at her uncertainly. She looked back at him with the eyes he had heard about but had never been close enough to see for himself and, up until this instant, too distracted to clearly notice. It was an absorbing moment. Her lips twisted into a slight, uneven, and beautiful smile that tickled along his loins.

"Is it swelling?" she asked, in a voice that seemed without breath.

He swallowed. "What?"

"My ankle! Please look at it and tell me if you think it is swelling. You do know something about injuries, don't you, Captain of the Guards?"

"Yes, My Lady." He squatted down in front of her. He stared at her foot, which was sizable, although gracefully formed. The toes within the smooth stocking wiggled impatiently.

Oh, what the hell, he thought and took the foot in his hands and, willing it into a soldier's foot, drew down the woolen stocking and examined it in the rough way he would have handled a member of the army. She didn't flinch, and he discovered that it was indeed swollen.

"My Lady," he said, releasing her foot and sitting back on his heels, "I would suggest a warm herbal soak and that you keep off it for a day."

"I will take your advice on an herbal soak, Grundl, but my devotions will keep me on my feet tonight and tomorrow night."

"I thought devotions only affected the knees, My Lady."

A little trill of surprise burst from her lips. "Quite true, Grundl! You do have some wit."

He said nothing.

"I have to stay on my feet. You see, I've committed myself to a course of prayers to our Goddess Friga, which will not be concluded until tomorrow night." She paused, but again, he was silent. "Are you aware of the little wooden shelter about a quarter mile up the hill beyond the hall?"

"There is an old deer blind up there," he said. "Deep under an oak and hidden by branches that go clear to the ground. Is that the one?"

"Yes, that's it. It's a quiet place. Favored by the gods, I think. I have been going there every evening and must conclude the process."

There was a pause as she sat looking up at him.

"In that case," he said, "if you must continue, you need to add litter bearers to your retinue."

"I go alone, Grundl," she told him solemnly.

He straightened and looked down at her. "We've a new group about the hall, now, my lady. They're most of them honorable men, but with so many with time on their hands and the uncertainties, a few might forget themselves. Perhaps your devotions might be better made in the daytime."

"No, only at night." She added demurely, "It's the nature of the devotions."

"Then I urge you to take a guard. He can wait beyond the branches of the oak, giving you privacy but offering protection, if it's needed."

She seemed to give this deep thought, looking down for a long moment before raising her magnificent eyes to his face. "Possibly. But I don't think I could trust just anyone," she said.

After a delicate silence, Grundl cleared his throat. "I have an hour or two free this evening, My Lady. It would be a great honor for me to stand as your guard while you carry out your devotions."

"What hours do you have free?" she asked, allowing gratitude to hover in her expression.

"The two following sundown."

"But that is just the time I usually leave!"

"Then I will be here to fetch you at sundown. With your permission?"

She bowed her head slightly, and he turned and strode grandly away, his hand resting on the sword hilt to keep the scabbard steady.

When he had cleared the door, Lady Ella pressed her fingers over her mouth, smothering a little cry of laughter and accomplishment.

As the rim of the sun glinted through the oaks, Lady Ella, limping slightly, came to the wide doors of the hall and found Grundl waiting. He had on a fresh tunic, and his belt, the scabbard for his sword, his shoes, all gleamed, wiped of the dust from the bivouac. He carried his spear and shield and looked splendid and immensely reliable.

She nodded in solemn acknowledgement and proceeded down the stairs and through the gate. Grundl fell in a few paces behind her. She could hear the soldierly creaking of his various equipment, and she smiled.

She carried a small brass lantern with glass plates and a candle to illuminate the shelter and to light their way back to the hall. Her long mantle was draped voluminously around her and covered her head, hiding her face.

The noise and activity of the hall fell behind them as they slowly climbed the hill along a faint trail she had made herself, for she truly had been in a series of devotions to the Goddess Friga. Lady Ella could hear Grundl behind her, breathing steadily, not affected by the climb.

They reached a darkly spreading oak, one of the few in full leaf. The branches swept the ground. Grundl pushed some of the limbs aside so she could pass into the clear space beyond. Inside the enclosure formed by the tree stood a small structure of timber and rough poles. It had a door made of smaller poles that fitted haphazardly in their frame. In the wall opposite the door were two openings where a hunter could lean forward resting one knee on the long bench below the sill. The openings were now blanked by a frame of twigs and dried leaves.

Lady Ella had stopped to light the lamp as the darkness had grown on the upward path, and now she set it down on the bench beneath the windows. On the floor in a spot that had been cleared of forest debris, a long slender form of polished and rune-inscribed wood stood upright. In an automatic gesture, Grundl pressed the back of his hand against his lips and tilted the kiss toward the wooden form. He turned to Lady Ella, who was watching him closely from inside the darkness of her mantle.

"I'll be outside the circle of branches, My Lady." He bowed, ducked low to clear the top of the door frame, and walked into the darkness. She could hear him rustling through the branches to take his post.

She turned to the rune-form. "The man's too ardent in his duty," she said to it. "This will take some doing."

Grundl took his station beyond the branches of the oak where he could watch both the trail and the surrounding area and make periodic circuits of the blind. He stood with his feet apart in an attitude of easy alertness, holding the spear with its butt resting on the ground, prepared to stand and wait.

After a brief time, he heard the voice of Lady Ella at her devotions. It was a low and rhythmic sound. He couldn't distinguish the words and would not have wanted to anyway, for he was too scrupulous to have curiosity about the content. But the lovely sound of her voice rising and falling held him transfixed.

He had heard rumors of Lady Ella, and there were certain things he had observed from behind the king's shoulder, yet here she was in pious devotion. Her great musical gift was to be admired as well as her beauty, and in this place, and at this moment, he thought he could lay down his life for her. There was only one other woman he could feel this about, and she was an unreachable dream.

The sweet chanting continued. He was not inexperienced. In his thirty-one years he'd had his share of women. Nothing had ever seriously proceeded from any encounter and some encounters he had wished had never happened. He had never been unkind. He had at no time considered marriage.

He drew himself up, looked around him. It was time for a turn around the oak, and he made the circuit in a few minutes, realizing, as he returned to his original position, that the chanting had stopped. He lifted his head like a stag, turning it slightly, listening. He heard his name called and came swiftly through the branches to where Lady Ella stood in the doorway of the shelter, her shrouded figure dark in the light from behind her.

"I'm here, My Lady."

"Oh, Grundl," she said with dismay. She reached out and laid her cool hand on his arm. "I heard something outside--over there."

He glanced in the direction she indicated. "What kind of noise was it?"

"A crackling in the bushes. I think it may have been a large beast."

"A few minutes ago, My Lady?"

"Yes."

"That was me, Lady Ella, making a round. I'm sorry I frightened you."

"Oh." Her fingers tightened on his arm, and she looked up at him from the depths of her mantle, and then realized it was probably without effect because the light was behind her. She took her hand away. "Thank you, Grundl, for taking such care. I'll continue now." She went back into the hut, and he went back to his station.

About a quarter of an hour later, the chanting became more intense, and he found himself being caught up in it. He shifted balance and took another hold on his spear. Abruptly the chanting stopped. When there was no further sound at all for some moments, he grew uneasy and looked back over his shoulder, considering whether or not he should investigate. Then he heard her sigh, and he crashed back through the tree branches to where she leaned heavily against the door frame, her mantle back from her head, and her hair glowing gold in the light shining through it. When he reached her side, she looked up at him dazedly, her eyes huge. She laid both hands on his arm and dropped her head against his hard bicep.

She sighed again and said unsteadily, "You are so kind, Grundl, to accompany me. I won't be much longer. I must rest a moment."

She changed her position, shifting closer. "Sometimes I get so involved in my prayers to our Great Lady Friga, I'm afraid I tire myself."

"Please, My Lady, take all the time you need. I've fallen somewhat away from religious . . . activities."

He had become aware the warm mound resting against his hand was her breast. She looked up at him and murmured, "I'll return to it now," and slipped back inside and shut the door.

Grundl went back to his post and thought about that warm breast. He shoved his fist down on his erection, and with substantial discipline, wilted it.

Lady Ella walked carefully along the dark trail, holding the lamp so they both could see. She was more frustrated than she could ever remember being in her life, but she was also amused at this frustration, having taken such pains with such little success.

Could he be making a jest of me? The thought rang briefly and was soundly rejected. He had neither the sophistication nor the nature. She knew it as she knew men. She had one more night to carry her fable to a conclusion. Then she remembered he had volunteered as guard only for this night and not the next. She stopped and turned. Grundl stopped an appropriate number of steps behind her.

"You were patient, tonight, Grundl," she said. "And I am grateful you stood by as my guard. When I come alone tomorrow, I will remember the warnings you've given me and will be very watchful."

A puzzled frown just touched his brow as his eyes moved over her face. "You don't want me to stand guard tomorrow night, My Lady?"

Her face brightened. "Since you mentioned only this night as being free, I thought you had other duties for tomorrow night."

"Forgive me, My Lady, for not making it clear. I meant both nights. And whatever other service I can provide, I would be honored to perform it."

Oh, my! She thought in frantic amusement. *Dare I name the service?*

"You are too kind," she murmured, and led them back to the hall.

Chapter Forty-Five

[829] Ceolworth, Mercia. The next sunset found Lady Ella and Grundl moving up the trail from the hall as they had the night before. After inspecting the shelter, Grundl took up his post and settled himself to wait. Lady Ella began her chanting again, and he marveled at her commitment. He began to recognize a difference in the cadence. There was a new quality beyond the intensity of the evening before, a strong pulse in her song that repeated until he felt it echoing in his body and throbbing in his loins. He moved restlessly. There was a silence. The door creaked open, and then her voice directly behind him softly called his name. He found her standing at the screen of branches.

"Would you stay near the building?" she asked. "I think I would feel more comfortable knowing I can look out and see you."

They moved to the building.

"I'll stand just here, My Lady."

"Thank you," she said with feeling, lightly touching his arm.

She retreated into the shelter. She took up the disturbing chant again, and he tried to think of something else, but it pulsed at his body, and he began to wonder what rites she was performing and what shape they took. Did her body, her breasts sway with that pulse?

She suddenly appeared in the doorway again, her hair in golden dishevelment, her mantle loose about her shoulders. She leaned against the frame, looking at him, her hand at her breast. He came over to her. She didn't touch him, but said, "I would like to have you stand inside while I conclude my prayers. Would you do that?"

"Your privacy, My Lady--"

"You needn't be sensitive to that. I become so engrossed I won't even notice you." She added hastily, "But it will be comforting to me to know you're there."

He lowered his head and stepped into the shelter. She quickly closed the door.

"I think if you stand just over there--"

He walked to the space she had indicated in the far corner away from the goddess form and the lamp. She looked at him. "You'll have to put your weapons down," she told him and made a little motion with her hand that included the form and her reason for being in the shelter.

She stood quietly waiting for him to consider this, as she knew he would, having become aware of his priorities. But she had also seen his swift, automatic homage to Friga and knew he had some training in religious worship. It was a gamble, but she had no qualms about taking risks when the rewards could be so rich.

He leaned his spear in the corner, unbelted his sword and his scramaseax, and piled them at the end of the bench but still near at hand. She rewarded him with a warm smile. She took two steps away and, becoming solemn, told him, "The nature of my devotions--you understand--require that I perform them . . . unclothed."

She waited as he regarded her silently.

"I'll turn my back," he said.

"Oh, no," she cried softly, going over to him. "You've forgotten--it is an insult not to face the objects of Friga when prayers are being offered! But you can avert your eyes. You could pick a spot up there to look at."

His eyes moved to the point she indicated and held.

She walked back to the form and began the slow, pulsing chant. The dark mantle swept down; there was the rustle of another garment being removed. The seductive chant went on, then faltered and stopped.

"Grundl." Her voice was low.

He looked at her. She had rewrapped herself in the mantle and was leaning against the goddess form.

"You must disrobe," she said. "Friga demands that respect of even those who are not offering prayers. I cannot finish until you do."

For a long moment he looked at her without expression, his brown eyes considering, and then began removing his clothes. Lady Ella let out the breath she had been holding and fervently kissed the smooth wood of the form.

She laid her mantle back on the ground and softly began the chant again. From a soft beginning it began to rise and what had been intensity became sheer passion, and her voice moaned with the desire to be caught up by the goddess, to be held in the body of love, to flame, to burn, to be consumed. Her voice struck its clear highest note as she turned to face Grundl, whose eyes had never left her, his beard and mustache glinting copper, his scarred body shining in the golden light from the candle. He came to her as she lay back on the folds of the mantle, lowering himself next to her, his expression grave, with an underlying sadness that made her feel as though a spell was working on them both that would break if she spoke.

What is he thinking? How high has he placed me? The thought came suddenly to her that he would have to make this move himself and was surprised by her understanding of him.

And then he looked away to her breasts and, cupping one in his great hand, put his mouth over the nipple, gently tugging at it with the soft moist inside of his lips. He moved his hands slowly over her body, touching, not speaking, but with a soft question in his eyes as he learned the contours, the creases and folds, the silkiness of her skin. His hands stroked, and his mouth touched it all before he came back above her to gaze into her face and finally to kiss her voluptuously, and all the while she was saying to herself in complete astonishment, *This is no coarse soldier. This is no clumsy warrior. O Friga! O Beauteous, Kind Lady Friga! Not one prayer was empty!*

"Lady Ella," he said, in a deep, gentle voice that vibrated in her heart, "I am bigger than most men. I don't want to hurt you." And he took her hand and laid it on his penis.

It was in proportion to the rest of his body. But then, she thought, shocked, so is a stallion's hnocc. And his would be a joke, but one told with envy by men who would not consider what she had known instinctively from the way he had spoken, from the caution of his approach: his member had not always been a source of enjoyment for women.

"Dear Grundl," she answered, "put it in slowly, and I will tell you when it is enough."

He was skillful, and she guessed the skill came from rejection and perhaps even laughter and ridicule. I must be honest with him, she thought.

When she felt the pressure against her womb and it became uncomfortable, yet his stem remained uncovered, she took his face in her hands and told him in a quiet, lilting voice, "Enough. Now stroke me . . . ." She sank herself into the feeling of him, submerged, and heard his rapid, steady breathing.

When their breathing became more rapid, she said, "I don't want to get pregnant," remembering suddenly what had always been preamble.

"I'll pull it out when it's time," he said, and kissed her, drawing her back into his concentration, moving her with him, until he did start to withdraw.

Suddenly, positively, she did not want what she had asked for, and she locked herself around him.

He cried, "Push me away!" in an urgent supplication that belied his strength and mandated her power: she knew with certainty he had never impregnated a woman, and she knew as certainly that she wanted to break down every gram of restraint he had, and she answered, "No!" and felt the fluid surge against her womb as she held him fiercely and was elated when he sagged down, with a moan.

He raised his head. "Why did you do that? You said you didn't want to get pregnant."

"Grundl, lie down here beside me. What a beautiful and surprising man you are! Don't concern yourself. It was my doing."

"Lady Ella, I am only a soldier. If you were to get with child--"

"I won't." She laughed, with a light trill in her voice. "And if I did it wouldn't have to concern you."

He frowned. "A child I father would concern me. I've been careful to never put a woman in that predicament. If I had, I would have done what was required of me." He shook his head. "I'm only a soldier," he repeated. "The women I've bedded would have been able to keep a house and child on what I could give them. You are far beyond my means, Lady Ella, although I'm not without property. But I've never had the stomach for politicking to increase it."

She leaned back from him, pleased that she had guessed correctly, but with a look of mock amazement on her face. "Grundl, are you proposing? Or is it that you propose we marry if it turns out I'm pregnant?"

"I've never wanted to marry," he said.

She looked at him, uncertain. "Neither have I."

"I've never wanted to marry," he repeated, looking at her in wonder. "Until now, and it's impossible."

He was so sincere and so sincerely distressed and the whole situation was so far outside her past experience, that Lady Ella remained silent.

A short while later, he got up, saying, "I've an army to attend to. I'll want to see you back safely." He dressed quietly, and with each turn of the bands he wound on his legs, he became more a warrior. By the time he had belted his sword and scramaseax over his tunic and turned to face her, there was no trace of the lover.

Except in his eyes, Lady Ella thought, with gratitude. *Oh, yes, it's there in his eyes.*

Grundl returned to the bivouac and made his rounds through the camp before turning in at his tent. He leaned his spear against the tent pole nearest the door, and ducked inside. He lit his lantern. There was his pallet, his few utensils, his shield, and a stool. He laid his sword and scramaseax on the ground beside his bed and sat down on the stool to unwind his leg bands and pull off his shoes. He had one band halfway unwound when he slowly stopped and sat there with the partial coil of banding in his hand, staring into space.

He felt swept over and tossed about, spun around like dust on a plain. He felt bludgeoned and emotionally stunned, but he also wanted to roar like a bear or howl like a wolf or screech like a hawk to somehow release the joy that was expanding inside him by the minute.

He puzzled over the reasons she might have had for preventing him from pulling out of her when she knew he was coming. *By the gods, she is wonderful!* he thought. She had allowed him his pleasure, not joking or grunting with pain, yet letting him know what she could accept, and had taken her satisfaction from him within the limits his member posed.

He hardly knew what to think about himself, because, from the moment he had left her at the steps of the hall and seen her move into its smoky light, he was burning to see her again. He mused about what it would be like to settle down in Weardburh, his home village. He knew his father would give him land. If he were careful and thrifty, within a few years he might accumulate enough-- He began to sweat, a cold, uncomfortable wash of hopelessness. She was a noblewoman, young, beautiful, desired by men with titles and great stretches of land, men who were intimates of the king, Prince Edward, for instance.

His head sank. He wondered why he chose to love women he couldn't have. He began again to unwind his leg bands and completing that threw off his clothes and piled naked onto his pallet to stare at the ceiling of his tent until the morning glowed through it.

Lady Ella, composed outwardly, felt as though she might scream until her lungs turned inside out. What had begun as a clever frolic with the promise of great amusement and the usual physical rewards was now confounded and not amusing at all. She had expected him to leap, panting on her and to roll them around on the ground, clutching, clumsy, in the way she had supposed a soldier would behave, and she would have taken her crude pleasure and laughed about it later.

But something had happened. She was not sure what. The whole episode had been excruciatingly funny to begin with, but there had been a quiet dignity to this captain of the guards, and he had shown a scrupulous respect for her and what he understood her motives to be. The tenderness and concern he showed in his lovemaking was beyond anything she had experienced. It had not been some technique contrived to serve the moment with no shred of it beyond the purpose. She knew that to the center of her soul. She had been totally carried away by him. So carried away she had risked pregnancy, something she had never done before.

She put her hand on her belly and looked down at herself with a little rush of apprehension. What if that great whacking hnocc had done its work?

Lady Ella smiled.

Chapter Forty-Six

[829] Ceolworth, Mercia. Elfwina had been with Ceolric all morning, accompanied by her clerk Leofgyth. The three had inspected the buildings and checked items in the food stores. The hall was a refuge in times of invasion, but it had been decades since it had been used for that purpose. With the clear possibility of the hall becoming a refuge again, all the logistics of housing and feeding people of the surrounding area of the hall under siege conditions had to be reconsidered. They were working all this out when a commotion at the gate drew their attention.

Elfwina sent her clerk to investigate while she and Ceolric continued the inventory. Leofgyth did not return. Soon the noise and excitement and what was shaping up to be a necessity for some kind of action finally drove the queen to look into the matter herself. Followed by Ceolric and a train of servants, she had walked halfway to the gate, when Leofgyth started toward them out of the crowd, a young girl and boy beside her. The crowd trailed after them.

Leofgyth brought the children before the queen. Clinging together, they stared at her with frightened eyes. The girl was about eleven and the boy around nine years old. Both children were thin and appeared exhausted. Their bodies bore bruises and caked blood, and their clothing was torn and filthy. The boy was barefoot, and the girl wore shoes too large for her, the leather ripped in places and held together with strips of cloth. Elfwina looked at Leofgyth.

"The tale is difficult to put together, Your Majesty, but they're from Weardburh. Apparently a large force has occupied their village."

"What? When?" Elfwina turned to the children. "Is this a force of Danes?"

"Yes, Ma'am," the girl answered, nodding, not able to take her eyes from the queen's face.

"When did this happen?"

"Two days ago--almost three. In the afternoon--so, almost three days."

"How large is this force?"

"There are two forces--"

The boy interrupted. "First one came and then another--in two days."

"When did you leave Weardburh," Elfwina asked, seeking to clarify.

"Two days ago," the boy said firmly. "There are more than a hundred warriors," said the girl, still looking at Elfwina. "They killed our mum and daddy." She said it numbly, with no tears. The girl had dark, multi-colored bruises on her throat and all along her arms. Elfwina glanced at Leofgyth, whose eyes reflected sad disgust and anger.

"It's more than a hundred," the girl's brother said. He turned his face up to the queen. "I count the sheep," he said.

The boy looked about him and, judging the reaction of the adults, returned his gaze to the milky fairness of the queen's face and her dark eyes. He wondered why she was not wearing a crown. "I count the sheep," he repeated. "I know amounts. There were a hundred and fifty men with swords and spears and axes."

"Can you tell me from what direction they came? Was it from the south?"

"No.," they both said at once. The girl silenced her brother with a look. "It was from the east."

"From the east? Are you certain?"

"Yes, Ma'am. They came along the rise."

"I see. Do they have horses?"

The boy answered. "Some do. Maybe thirty horses altogether."

Elfwina was hearing alarm in the voices of the people who were beginning to crowd them. She glanced around at Ceolric, and he stepped forward.

"Inform the king. Tell him the children will be in my chambers." As Ceolric hurried off, Elfwina told her clerk, "Take them in and see they have food and drink. After the king speaks with them, have them bathed and give them a place to sleep. They're dead on their feet. Ask Edyth to see to their bruises." She took a breath. "And tell her the girl needs special attention."

Leofgyth moved off with the children and a large portion of the crowd that had been increasing as they stood talking. Elfwina followed slowly.

So, there was substance to Aedred's misgivings after all, she thought.

The village of Weardburh sprang to her mind--the wide valley with its rich soil, the broad sloping hillsides dotted with sheep that produced the highest grade of wool in Mercia and the finest cloth. The woods beyond the green hillsides were abundant with game, the small river filled with fish.

Two low rises ran from the far valley of the Welland, intersecting to form one gradually diminishing rise of ground at the western end of the vale. She had forgotten that contour. The Danes had passed undetected along those elevations. How had that been possible? Because they were not raiding as they came. Why? Because they had a point to reach before they could risk discovery.

Elfwina returned to the hall through the back passage and went up the staircase to her chambers. A table had been pulled out from one wall in the sitting room, and the children were seated at it on a padded bench. Edyth had attended to them. The other servants had been moved by their plight and were being solicitous. On the table was a cold joint, a loaf of bread, a small round of cheese, butter, a pot of honey, and a pitcher of cold milk.

Leofgyth joined the queen where she had quietly gone to stand by the window. "Would you like to speak with the children again, Ma'am?"

"No." She turned away from the window. "Let them take their nourishment. The king will need to hear everything they have to say, and they look ready to faint as it is. Will you make a list for me of all the items we discussed with Ceolric? My mind is getting cluttered with all that needs to be done, and I don't want to forget anything that might cause problems later. Also, make a note for me to inspect the cellar with Ceolric. We didn't get to that today. Here's the king. Have the list for me this evening, please."

Aedred had entered the sitting room with his eorls and Grundl. When the boy and girl, in the midst of eating, saw the men coming toward them, they shrank together in speechless terror. Edyth put her hands on their shoulders, and they glanced up at her. She smiled reassuringly, and then curtsied to Aedred and dropped back.

Aedred saw all this, looked back over his shoulder and raised his hand. The men with him stopped, and he came to the table the rest of the way by himself. "I am King Aedred," he said. The children stared at him. He pulled up a chair and sat down at the table. For a moment he returned their stares. "Have you enough to eat?"

The girl looked him all over and fixed her eyes on the brooch of lapis lazuli and gold holding the folds of his woolen mantle in place. Then she looked into his eyes and replied, "Yes, Sire." She hesitated. "Would you like some?" She glanced uncertainly at the faces around her. Should she do this? She looked back at the king. "The bread and honey is very good," she said earnestly.

"Is it?" He looked at her closely and saw as Elfwina had the nature of her bruises. "A slice of the bread, then." He watched her cut away a thick slice as Merefin hovered nearby. "What's your name?"

"Aethelberg, Sire, daughter of Trumberht. This is my brother Ordgar."

"Son of Trumberht," the boy added, his eyes shining at the king.

"Honey, Sire?" asked Aethelberg.

"Just bread." He politely took the piece from her. He lifted the pitcher of milk and refilled their cups. "Drink it up, Son of Trumberht. It washes down the bread and honey." He grinned at Ordgar. Giggling, the boy shrunk his neck into his shoulders.

Aedred chewed on a mouthful of bread as he watched the

children. "You've had a bad time of it," he finally said. "Tell me what happened."

There was an intense silence in the room as the children repeated their story. When they had finished, Aedred asked, "You know Grundl, don't you?"

Grundl stepped close to Aedred's shoulder and stood looking down at them. They silently consulted each other, and then shyly shook their heads.

"Sire, I haven't visited my village lately. They would know my father."

The boy and girl sat alertly, waiting.

"Edgar the Tall." It came from his chest a growl.

"Yes! We know him!" cried the girl. "He helped us run away. The second force lives in his house."

Grundl stiffened. "Have they harmed him?"

"They make him do the work of servants," the boy blurted out. "And they beat him. But he lives."

Aedred reached back for Grundl and gripped his arm. He released it slowly. "You're certain of this?" he asked the boy.

"Yes, Sire. At least he was when we ran away--" he stopped abruptly. After a glance at his sister, he went on in a low voice, "He helped us when they were--were doing what they did to my sister."

The girl's mouth drooped, and she put her head down. Edyth came up behind her and began stroking her hair. The girl turned her head and laid it against Edyth's arm.

Aedred kept his eyes on the boy. His tone held its note of gentle inquiry. "How did he help you?"

The boy sat up suddenly, and his voice was a harsh, ringing brightness in the quiet room. "He brought an axe down on the Dane that was on top of her and split his shoulder down to the ribs. The blood came out like that!" He flung his hands up in the air in two high arcs and cried out, "then he told us to run to the king's hall." He leaped to his feet, screaming, *"Run"*

Merefin swept up the little boy and held him. Ordgar braced his arms against the handthegn's chest and arched his body, flinging his head back in so rough a movement, Merefin almost dropped him. "Easy, easy--calm down, there now--" He kept his grip and the boy collapsed against Merefin's neck and began sobbing.

Aedred heard the breath pouring from Grundl's nostrils. He half-turned in his chair, and then surged to his feet and threw his arm around Grundl's neck, dragging the big man's head down as he stared into the flaming, blind eyes. *"Grundl!"* he yelled into that ferocious mask, "I give you my oath--they will die for it! *They will die for it!"*

Elfwina signaled to Edyth to take the children away and stood watching Aedred calming the big warrior.

Aedred was saying, "Grundl, we need your counsel. You know that area better than anyone here. Sit down, man, help us with your counsel. A decision must be made." As Grundl slowly lowered himself onto a bench, Aedred turned to his wife. "Join us."

Chapter Forty-Seven

[829] Ceolworth, Mercia. Lady Ella was coming up from the village with two of her companions when she saw the king and the eorls and Grundl leap down from their horses and walk rapidly into the hall with a singleness of purpose she recognized. Grundl did not see her. Ignoring the wails of her friends, she ran the rest of the way to the hall, stopping just within the enclosure to demand from one of the thegns gathered there what happened.

The information was succinct--a village was under occupation by a force of Danes. It was as she passed through the crowd that she overheard someone say a meeting was going on in the queen's chambers and the father of the king's captain had been injured. For perhaps the first time in her life, Lady Ella found herself held within the bounds of convention and propriety when she felt an intense need to act. But even if there had been no strictures she wasn't sure what she could have done for Grundl. But she fervently wanted to be with him. In great frustration, she sat down in the hall to wait for things to fall out.

There was a pause after the eorls all took their seats. Aldhune looked around the group and said, "It's damn bold of them to come harrying into the kingdom for the second time. Like they have the king's peace for their adventures. I say march on them now."

"Yes!" Leodwald struck the arm of his chair. "They've taken one of the richest valleys in Mercia. You can bet they're hauling away the wool. They'll make a fortune unloading it on the Continent." He looked at Grundl. "And then here's this man's father. Doesn't Grundl have the right of revenge? If that's the way it has gone. I say go now."

There was a storm of agreement.

Penwahl cleared his throat. "I agree." His resonant voice overrode and sank the other voices by its sheer weight. "I agree we should set out on them--" he paused, looking at every face while he held the last consonant with a lingering hum "--when the rest of the army has assembled."

Aldhune turned on Penwahl. "Are you saying wait for Prince Edward?"

"No," Penwahl answered. He looked at Aedred, who was quietly observing them all. "Have we news of Prince

Edward's army, Sire?" When Aedred shook his head, Penwahl turned coolly back to Aldhune. "I'm talking about the Mercian levy. When it assembles, then it is the time to handle the problem in Weardburh."

"Problem!" Aldhune snorted.

Leodwald bounced in his chair. "The longer the Danes are left to their own pleasure, the more people will suffer and the less there will be to salvage. We need to march now."

Penwahl turned toward him with an arch look. "How much do you think you'll salvage if they round us? You'd have us rushing off with five hundred men and leave Ceolworth and all this end of the countryside unprotected. Do we hold the battlefield or provide the Danes with the key to Mercia?"

There was an indignant protest from Leodwald, but Penwahl rolled over it. "Let us wait like reasonable men for a sufficient force to defend all the country in the manner we signed our names to not six weeks ago. You remember that, don't you Eorl Leodwald?"

"All right, Penwahl!" Aldhune flung out his arms in annoyance. "Let's do talk about this. The Dane's force is two hundred at most--allowing for some error on the boy's part--and we have five hundred here. We can take three hundred and leave the rest. When Wulfric and the others get here those numbers will be increased to a force that can protect all Mercia, as planned—and signed to."

Penwahl fixed him with a look of tired superiority. "If you think you're stalking game, Eorl Aldhune, you should know the hunt's a hazardous extravagance if you've only one spear against a multiplicity of boars."

"What the hell is that supposed to mean?"

"Penwahl!" Leodwald shouted. "The king's own lands are occupied! Can you think of a graver insult? For a man who harps on *fe-al-ty*, you're making a poor showing--"

Penwahl rose in a cold passion. "My fealty has never been questioned! Are you calling it into question, now?"

Rising hotly with him, Leodwald cried, "Take it as you like it!"

Mawer's deep voice cut through everything. "If you really put your minds to it, you can win the war for the Danes before you walk out from under your king's roof. Sit down, Eorl Penwahl. Everyone knows your loyalty to the king is unimpeachable, as is your courage. Eorl Leodwald, save your temper for the Danes. Now, then! Why don't we start this over?"

"A moment, Eorl Mawer," Aedred said quietly.

"Sire--I beg your pardon!" Mawer had been running along with the pack, seeing it bolt and the commander he was had leaped to the lead. He now regretted that headlong rush out of his own jurisdiction.

Aedred leaned behind Elfwina to rest his hand briefly on Mawer's broad shoulder.

Penwahl slowly resumed his seat. Aedred said to him, "Your concern is clear, Eorl Penwahl, and I share it. We want a sufficient force to meet the Danes, while keeping a large enough number here to defend the hall."

"That is the sum of it, Sire. A force here at Ceolworth large enough to handle any request for aid in other parts of the kingdom, as we all agreed." Penwahl's head was high, his back stiff. He looked at Leodwald with disdain. "If our numbers are split, that commitment would be extremely hard to fulfill."

"I note your concern," Aedred told him. "Now, Eorl Aldhune, you and Eorl Leodwald think our present force could be split three to two, the weight of it to go after the Danes at Weardburh. Based on the children's report, you believe that's a sufficient number to meet them. To answer Pen's objection, you don't foresee any problem arising that two hundred warriors couldn't meet before the rest of the levies arrive."

"Not in the two days before they get here, Sire," Leodwald replied, his eyes hard on Penwahl who was pointedly following the king's summation and ignoring the eorl.

Aldhune nodded to his brother. "I strongly agree with that assessment, Your Majesty."

The king turned to Mawer. "It's Prince Edward you serve, but join the discussion. How do you turn on it?"

Mawer gave him his awful grin. "Why, with you, Your Majesty."

"Your contribution, then . . . ?"

"I'm a cautious man," the West Saxon eorl replied slowly. "But I'm for moving now before the damage increases. I'm satisfied with the distribution of numbers."

Aedred said to his queen, "You've held a surprising silence."

Elfwina's smile was slow. "I've been considering a thorn that's stuck from the first we heard of all this."

"Well, let's see if we can tug it out."

"It may be a grievous mistake if we don't," she replied. "You had misgivings about our defenses that have proved out. We must ask why it is that the Danes, taking a route with a number of rich choices along it, moved straight to Weardburh? And as *two* forces, one joining the other. From what the children said, the Danes are sustaining their numbers, not sacking the region. Nor have they demanded their peace be bought--their usual method." Her gaze made a slow sweep of the men. "I believe this is the vanguard of a larger force meant to assemble at Weardburh. I feel this so strongly, in fact, that my advice is to wait until the remainder of our militia arrives, and then move with more substantial numbers ."

"There you have it!" exclaimed Penwahl, with a wondering look at his queen. Then he leaned back in his chair as if he would be amazed that anyone would dare to speak further.

"Ma'am," Aldhune said, "how is it you're convinced a large force is assembling? A part of one force might have been delayed and they are not two forces at all."

"That may well be true, Eorl Aldhune. My opinion is based on their behavior, which is not following their present raiding patterns. They moved straight to Weardburh. If they only wanted treasure, they could have enriched themselves any number of times along their way. To my mind, their behavior is understandable only if they are supplementing the forces now gathering in all directions. Keep in mind we would not have had wind of this if Grundl's father hadn't helped the children escape. Those ghost numbers we have been concerned with—Danes from East Anglia. This is the path they have taken."

"You think their strategy is to assemble in Weardburh and march on Ceolworth from there," Aedred said.

"Yes. They lessen the danger to themselves if they assemble close enough for them to take Ceolworth by surprise, capture the king, and take the whole country, and all with a minimum of effort. It could also be part of a plan to advance from three directions. We'd be held between Ædda's army and this force, while the majority of our defense fights on the Severn with our allies."

"That's a grim and evil picture, Ma'am," said Leodwald.

"Ma'am, may I speak?"

"Yes, Grundl."

"This group of Danes got through unseen, Your Majesty, but a force the size of the one you are talking about could not go undetected. If they are coming in smaller numbers to assemble, they need to be stopped before the whole is gathered. With all respect, Ma'am, I strongly advise leaving with three hundred men at daybreak."

"If the force has increased in the time since the children reached the hall, Grundl, then you have already been outnumbered." She looked at Aedred. "I suggest a count of the Danes before our warriors are committed to engagement."

Grundl leaned forward. "We can do both in the field, Sire."

Aedred had listened to the exchange between Elfwina and Grundl, with astonishment. Grundl was the same taciturn man he had always been, but a dimension of him was now being revealed: grief had made him articulate, and it was as though Grundl were stepping out from a shadow and Aedred was seeing him clearly for the first time.

The conference had reached a point where the group was waiting for the king's decision. Again, he weighed their comments. There was his own outrage; Leodwald had struck that rightly. On the basis of that alone, Aedred was for mounting now. But he had laid that aside, or imagined he had, and considered the arguments. As he sifted through them, and as much as he respected Elfwina's judgment, he could not put the weight of his decision with her argument or Penwahl's.

He looked at the faces around him. "We march at first light," he said.

Chapter Forty-Eight

[829] Weardburh, Mercia. Grundl made the announcement to the militia and directed preparations for the march to Weardburh. There had been an angry exchange between eorls as it was being decided who would stay behind to command the two hundred men remaining at Ceolworth. Leodwald told Penwahl he should be the one to stay at Ceolworth, since he had opposed the march. Penwahl took it as an accusation of cowardice, and the two eorls nearly came to blows.

Annoyed that Penwahl was being goaded, Aedred curtly told Leodwald he was to remain at the bivouac, ending all debate. Leodwald was quiet the rest of the day.

Grundl returned to his quarters. The sun had fallen below the tree line and left the interior of his tent dim. He looked aimlessly around. The camp noises so familiar to him faded away, leaving him in a thick silence that magnified the sound of his breathing until it seemed the tent itself was drawing and releasing air. With his body and his mind finally stilled, grief threatened him.

A voice directly outside called, "Is Grundl in there?"

He turned his head sharply and called, "Here!" short and loud. He stepped out into the growing darkness.

A hall servant waited for him. He handed Grundl a small scroll heavily sealed with wax.

"What is it?"

"A message from the Lady Ella."

Grundl glared at him, but took the scroll and slipped it inside his tunic. "You can go now," he said gruffly. He watched the servant walk rapidly away in the direction of the hall.

He turned slowly around and reentered his tent. He lit the lantern and then sat down on the stool. It was some minutes before he took the scroll from his tunic. He turned it over in his hands, studied the seal, which he made out to be a plummeting hawk, peered in at the ends where he could see writing, and then just sat there holding it in his big fingers, staring at it. Abruptly, he brought the scroll to his lips and held it there, his eyes closed.

Grundl rode out from the bivouac, letting his horse pace itself. Allowing neither grief nor curiosity, and numb with the discipline he exerted on himself, he watched the lighted windows of the hall drawing closer.

He was directed by one of the hall servants to Lady Ella's rooms on the east side of the upper hall. Her thegnestre answered his knock.

"Tell Lady Ella, Grundl wishes to speak with her," he said.

Lady Ella appeared directly behind the woman and quickly

dismissed her. "Come in, Grundl." She closed the door, looking at his broad back with concern. "This way." She led him from the little anteroom into a larger room that had a bed in the corner. He stood looking at her.

"Did you get my note?" she asked, when he didn't say anything.

"Yes," he answered.

She hesitated, and then said, "Please sit down."

He settled carefully on a bench and sat silently looking at her.

Lady Ella said, "Would you like ale, or--"

Grundl shook his head. "No." He looked steadily at her.

She said, "I was sorry to hear the force had occupied your village. As I said in my note--"

"Lady Ella," he interrupted. He took the unopened scroll from the breast of his tunic and handed it to her. "I don't know how to read."

She was stunned into silence at her blunder.

When she took the scroll but made no reply, Grundl said, "I didn't like sitting at a table for the best part of the day. My father wanted me to learn. He thought it would help advance me at court--" His voice broke, and he stopped and stared helplessly at her.

She rose swiftly and drew his head tightly against her breast. "Oh, my dear," she murmured, resting her cheek on his head. "My dear, dear Grundl." He was weeping, and she knew it was for his father.

Having given her best advice, Elfwina accepted, with silent misgivings, her husband's decision not to take it. She helped him prepare for the march to Weardburh, seeing nothing was forgotten and he could leave Ceolworth with a clear mind.

He held her with his wrists crossed at the small of her back, pulling her pelvis up against him. "The day my hnocc rises before a campaign, I'll abdicate and do nothing for the rest of my days but make love to you."

"Oh, that's a good idea."

He waggled his hips back and forth. "Feel that? Senseless as a dead crow." His hand went down to his crotch. He shook his head. "There's a subject with no fealty for his king."

He picked up the helmet and shield he had brought with him from the dressing room. "We'll be up and out of here by first light," he said. "I'll see you when we return. If Edward ever gets here, tell him we're so sorry we missed him." He put his helmet under the arm that held the shield and pulled her back against him. "I love you, you know."

"Oh, yes I do know."

"A little prayer to Tiw might help."

She kissed him tenderly. "Every day."

"Well . . . ." He stepped away. "Here goes the king."

"Yes," she replied. "Again."

He smiled at her, but his eyes were grave. "And yet again."

They moved out into the grey morning with eager steps. On his black war-horse, Aedred rode behind his standard at the center of a group of horsemen. Two hundred foot soldiers followed with the rest of the horsemen and, bringing up the rear, two supply wagons. They rested at noon, ate a cold meal each man had carried with him, and continued on. By sundown the second day, Grundl had brought them within six miles of Weardburh.

They made camp quickly and the watch was set. Aedred permitted no fires. Again, they had cold rations. Once the army had rolled out onto the ground to sleep as they could, Aedred and the eorls, with Grundl, sat conferring in the darkness before they wrapped themselves in their mantles to sleep an uneasy sleep.

They rose to a cold drizzle that beaded the grasses and dripped from the new leaves. The men sat hunched over their remaining rations, and then began to assemble for the march into Weardburh.

Grundl had sent two men familiar with the village to report on the movements and numbers of the Danes. Two miles from Weardburh the army met them returning. They reported one hundred seventy-five Danes moving about the village and many saddled horses in various locations. The village appeared quiet.

"We'll go straight in," Aedred told his commanders. "If the Danes aren't intimidated by our numbers into flight or a peace, we'll hit hard and fast and have done with it."

As they reached the last mile, they moved into battle order with Aedred at the center in the front lines of the horsemen, Penwahl, with his boar-crested helmet on his right, Grundl on his left. Aldhune and Mawer rode with the remainder of the men on horseback, forming a line down either side of the warriors on foot.

They moved without speaking, but the horses' hooves and the footsteps of the men created a vibration like a continuous roll of distant thunder, and they were heard long before they reached the village.

Aware of their approach, the Danes had gathered their arms and mounted their horses. They milled about when the Mercians appeared, then turned in a disorderly rush and streamed in full flight from the village toward the eastern end of the valley.

Aedred drove his horse forward. Grundl and Penwahl shouted back at the foot soldiers. Aldhune and his thegns took up the cry, and the whole army moved ahead at a run, the horsemen thundering in the wake of the king, Aedred and the thegns sifting through the running Danes to engage the mounted warriors, leaving the Danish foot soldiers for their militia.

In a rounding turn, the Danes swiftly dismounted and sent their horses scattering as they took to the ground, driving back into the oncoming horses with their spears and swords and battle axes.

Aedred swung his horse about, laying down into the crowd with his sword. The swarm of Danes, by their sudden ferocity, pressed the advantage, and the Mercian horsemen gave ground. But Aedred danced his stallion through the melee without harm.

With concentrated savagery Grundl was off his horse and fighting on the ground, his spear a deadly force. Aedred spun his horse around. A Dane slashed at him, hit him in the side. Without wounding him, the warrior's sword rent Aedred's mail, leaving it hanging shredded below his ribs. The Dane then tried to leap onto the black stallion, dragging the animal into a stumble with the heavy shift in balance. It recovered, throwing itself up as Aedred's sword sliced into the warrior's arm, striking bone with a dull violence. The man dropped away. Aedred's horse came around.

Nearby, Penwahl was leading his thegns forward in a solid push against a line of Danes. Aedred shouted for his men to close, and they drove the Danes back over the territory they had just won. There was a lull, then, and Aedred called to Aldhune and Penwahl to draw in the warriors who had begun to scatter over the grazing land. He looked around for Grundl; saw him acting on the order.

Aedred rode into the midst of the gathering Mercians. "This is too small a force to keep us so busy," he told his eorls. "We need to put an end to it now. Aldhune, bring your men up and take their right flank. Pen, take the left." To Grundl, he said, "Mawer and I will drive up through the middle. You bring the militia behind us."

Grundl's calm eyes met his from behind the mask of his helmet. "Yes, Sire."

"Away, then." Aedred trotted his horse forward as his men raced to their positions.

Their pace was moderate until Aedred saw they were ready, and then he gave the battle cry and heard it repeated all around him. They plunged into the Danes, and the Danes fell back. With a sudden bitter instinct, Aedred knew something was wrong, but in that instant, not what it was. He swung his head around. At the low western rim of the valley, he saw scores of horsemen and foot soldiers pouring down toward the valley's mouth.

"*Mawer!*" he bellowed. He flung his arm toward the hillside as the eorl turned to look at him.

Because they rode full speed at the head of the force, they could not abruptly change their direction without endangering themselves or the men behind them. So, at Aedred's lead, they urged their horses faster, cutting toward the left as they shouted and gestured. The maneuver slowed the onrush of the militia. Grundl, seeing immediately what the situation was, roared back the order to retreat. By this time the horsemen had become aware of the danger and were swinging around, and then it was a desperate race to reach the mouth of the valley before the new force of Danes could close it, trapping them.

Aedred urged his horse still faster, yelling encouragement to his eorls, directing them toward the gathering force, intent on breaking through the closing gap. They hit the Danes head on, crashing the weight of their horses into them. But the line held, and they piled up against the ever-growing numbers from the hillside. The Danes who had lured them out into the valley were returning to attack them from behind.

Now the Danes had identified Aedred. He was fighting for his life, trying to keep them off, whirling his horse in a circle, his shield close to his body, his sword hedging and flashing as the warriors closed in on him, the sheer weight of numbers bringing his horse to a plunging standstill. Then from behind, Grundl charged the ranks, sending one of the attackers to the ground to be trampled under the lunging war-horse and freeing Aedred from having to defend himself from that quarter. Penwahl, on foot, swooped in to protect his right side.

The king twisted in the saddle as a Dane grasped his left ankle with one hand, the other thrown back to hurl his battle axe. Aedred's sword came down. The axe flew out of the warrior's hand, and he bounced forward along the shoulder of the war-horse, clawing for a hold and spraying blood over the black neck. With a cry, he sank abruptly out of sight.

A new attack came at Aedred from the rear. As he swung about to meet it, he saw the arm draw back, the spear poise. He saw the steadiness of the hand, the acute balance, the spark of his life reflected in the eye. His fingers jerked tight on the grip of his shield, the knuckles bulging. The muscles of his left forearm roped and raised the shield, pulled the shield along the curve of his torso, his sword arm lowering as he rose on the stirrups, twisting, turning, leaning his

body away, leaning out from the point hurtling toward him. He felt his horse shift loyally against the imbalance.

The spear struck him in the side, driving deep into his body through the rent in his mail. The impact of the spear arched him back over the saddle at the same time the horse's rebalancing flung him sideways. He struggled to come upright but was dragged from his horse by the Danish warriors and thrown down head first. The spear shaft jabbed into the ground and broke off, leaving a length of it jutting from his side. He tried to rise, to slash out with his sword, but it was torn from his hand. He was buffeted and kicked, his limbs yanked outward as he tried to curl into a ball. He heard Penwahl shout, heard the wild fizz of blade sliding against blade, the resounding thunk! of sword against wooden shield. Grundl's roar filled his ears, and Mawer's answering yell. A weight fell across him, and all he could perceive was pain in a crushing pressure across his ribs which would not allow his lungs to expand. His head was bent toward his belly, his arms shoved inward under that dead weight.

The pain seemed less. The shouting and the ringing of metal began to fade. Too weak to grip the spear shaft, his hands only caressed it. His fingers seemed huge and vaporous, cloud-like and unmanageable. He could hear the madness going on above him, but he was folding into himself, pulling inward. *I am dying,* he thought, and the words as if taking material form dropped slowly all around him, like ashes.

I am the son of your loins, My Father, he began the prayer. *I am the son of your loins through Cenwulf through Wulfhere through Agel through Alweo . . . .* The prayer unreeled, not consciously, so well-known and recited it moved of its own swift accord too fast for the reasoning mind to follow. But he knew he was offering it.

I rise from the field of slaughter. Accept me, AllFather. I am the son of your loins. . . . But he was murmuring aloud, "Protect them, Mighty Tiw . . . ."

He drifted without pain. *I am ready,* he thought. *I will rise without shame, without dishonor. . . .* He drifted and wondered when and how. After a while the pressure eased and he had to fill his lungs and the breaths were deep and painful and tore at his side like a new wound each time his chest expanded.

He heard voices again, speaking with tension and excitement, Grundl and Mawer and then--*Edward!* Edward, speaking close to his ear, his voice as golden as a god's saying, "Don't move, Aedred, don't move." He felt rain falling on his face as his helmet was pulled away and Edward's beard was against his cheek and he did not want to die he wanted to live and he reached out with complete faith that Edward would pull him up from the darkness.

Chapter Forty-Nine

[829] Weardburh, Mercia. They had been several days on the march and were within sight of the valley of Weardburh, when the men he had sent ahead to notify the town of their impending arrival came pounding back along the road to report the battle raging there between a large force of Danes and an army of Mercians which was heavily outnumbered and led by the king himself.

Edward halted the Saxon army. In the relative quiet, they could hear the sound of battle. At once, Edward divided his army into horsemen and foot soldiers. With Edward leading the horsemen, they galloped toward the village, the foot soldiers following at a steady trot.

At the narrow opening at the western end of the valley, the Danes presented a solid barrier to the Mercians struggling at the center of a force which surrounded them. But when the Danes saw the Saxons descending on them, they had to turn from the Mercians to defend themselves and then were under attack from both sides.

Over the heads of the warriors, Edward saw Grundl and Penwahl holding away the surge of Danes trying to reach the king where he lay motionless at their feet. Edward slammed his horse into the warriors. With horror, he glimpsed Penwahl going down, the eorl's head nearly severed from his body by the rounding swing of a battle axe. Several feet away, Aldhune and a group of Mercians were struggling forward.

Routed now, the Danes tried to retreat. Edward sent a number of Saxons in pursuit, and then swung back. He flung himself from his horse and came staggering down beside Aedred just as Grundl was pulling off the king's helmet. Aedred's face was ashen and slack. The broken spear in his belly shuddered.

"Is he alive?" Edward cried.

In a sudden convulsion, Aedred kicked his legs and struck out with his arms. Edward grabbed his wrists, pinning him down as he pressed his cheek against the king's face, his mouth close to his ear. "Don't move, Aedred. Don't fight me. Lie still." He felt Aedred yield. Like a drowning man, Aedred reached up to clasp his neck. Edward crouched over him, holding him in his arms until Aedred's grip loosened and he sank into merciful unconsciousness.

Edward laid him back on the ground. Aedred's face was waxy. The bluish under shadow of his beard, normally disguised by his dark complexion, appeared smutty and rough. He looked strange, a diminished, ravaged man, his vitality turned to white stone.

Oh, dear God! Edward thought.

Mawer crouched down next to the prince. He embraced Edward,

crushing him against his chest. Tears ran along his broad nose and into his mouth. "Mother of God--Mother of God!" He looked into Edward's eyes. The prince squeezed his arm hard. He took a breath, and then looked down again at Aedred.

Grundl leaned down to him. "He's cutting himself up every time he moves, Sire. Before we lift him, the spear has to come out."

Edward examined the villainous rent in the mail. The links had been severed, the stiff backing-cloth cut as neatly as if by shears. The spearhead was buried up to the lugs in Aedred's flesh. Blood that had saturated his tunic and trousers and run over his leather greaves was still welling up out of the wound. "Right," he said. "Hold onto his legs, Mawer. That's it--Grundl, go ahead with it."

Grundl stood to grip the broken end of the shaft in both hands. He braced his feet and drew the spear upward with a steady pull. Aedred screamed and tried to throw himself to one side, but they held him down. When the blade pulled free, Grundl flung the spear away and dropped to his knees to press both hands over the wide gash. The blood poured around his fingers.

"There's a house over there," Mawer said.

Edward looked around in the direction Mawer had indicated and saw the large dwelling that stood some two hundred feet away. "God, I wish we didn't have to joggle him for that distance. But it's the best we can do." He glanced at Grundl and then at Mawer. "Let's lift together, now."

They brought the king up and carried him forward as Grundl held his hands over the wound, taking small steps, one foot lifting over the other in an intricate dance. As he looked from his bloody hands to the ground ahead, his face dark with concentration, he told them, "To the left. The door is in the front--around the corner."

They were approaching the house from the side, and so they adjusted their direction, coming around the house to the entrance. Above the door, a human head hung by its golden brown hair, the eyes closed, the broad face dull. Ropes of clotted blood swayed from the severed neck.

Grundl flung back his head and roared like an animal. He shouted to Edward and Mawer to go on into the house. *"Move on! Move on!"* he yelled. His hands pressed into Aedred's side. Aedred's blood was running through his fingers and pooling on the ground. He screamed at them to carry the king into the house. They dove through the door and rushed back to the room where the high, huge bed of Edgar the Tall was neatly made and ready.

They laid Aedred hastily down on a bright wool spread that made his pallor all the more dreadful by its contrast. Grundl was still holding his hands over the wound, but writhing as if he was in pain, his breath heaving in his chest.

Edward said, "Go take it down--"

"No!" he roared.

Mawer started around the side of the bed, his face alarmed.

"No!" Grundl shouted again, looking at him with a ferocious grimace. "The living first! Cloths! Give me cloths! The bleeding has to be stopped."

Mawer looked uncertainly at Edward.

"Go find Cuthrac," the prince told him.

Edward pulled out the edge of a blanket and hacked it into strips with his scramaseax, handing the pieces to Grundl as the big warrior packed them into the wound with his gory hands.

"That seems to be stopping it," Edward said, leaning over Aedred while gauging Grundl's emotional state.

"That's all I can do," Grundl said. He laid his bloody hand over the king's heart with a gentle touch. He looked up and took his hand away as Mawer came through the door with a short, wiry man whose garments were blood-spattered. He carried a squared leather bag with a flap. Grundl said, "I'll go now."

Edward nodded.

Cuthrac came over to the bed, threw an inquiring glance at the prince. He set the bag next to the king and began exploring around the cloth-packed wound.

"What can be done for him, Cuthrac? The spear went deep."

"We'll see." He examined the king with swift, experienced hands. When he was finished, he looked up and sighed. "I can sew him, but his gut was pierced. It could be very bad."

Edward stared down at Aedred's white face. "Are you sure it pierced the gut?"

"Yes, I am, Sire," he replied unhappily.

Edward looked hard at Cuthrac, and then lowered his eyes to the king. "Do what you can. Will you need any help?"

"Yes, Sire. Someone in case he wakes."

Edward glanced at Mawer, who nodded. Edward left them and walked back through the house and found a group of men standing just inside the door.

One of them stepped forward. "Sire, how is the king?"

"He lives."

The man shook his head several times. "I am Lyfing, Sire, thegn to Eorl Penwahl--" his mouth jerked uncontrollably and tears rolled down from his eyes. He took a breath and started again. "We have our brave eorl just outside, Sire. We ask permission to return him to his hall."

Edward could see the body of Penwahl draped with a long mantle and resting on a litter made from another mantle stretched between spear shafts. Four warriors held the litter. A number of men behind the litter stood solemnly watching as Edward came forward. For a long moment the prince stood over the covered figure, his head bowed. Then he crossed himself and spoke to the leader.

"Yes . . . take him home. And when you've buried him with honors and mourned him, return to Ceolworth. King Aedred will need you."

Edward watched the slow march away of the litter bearers and the silent warriors. He turned to look above the door, saw that the severed head of Grundl's father had been removed, and again made the sign of the cross. As he was starting into the house, two of his thegns came loping up on their horses. He waited as they reined in and dropped from their saddles in front of him.

"Sire, we've gathered the Danes near the mill down there. There's about sixty left alive. The leaders have been questioned but gave no information. Their commander has a keen desire to talk with you."

"I'll bet he does. He can wait. Don't make them too comfortable."

"We heard King Aedred was wounded, Sire."

"We can praise God he lives. Keep a close watch on the prisoners and see that our men have a decent camp. I'll come down there presently."

The townspeople had gradually been coming out of their hiding places and were silently watching the proceedings. Edward searched their faces for a sign of a leader, realized that with his father's death, Grundl would probably have to assume that role. He returned to the house.

Cuthrac had finished and was deftly rolling soft woolen cloth around the king's waist as Mawer gently lifted that part of his torso. Aedred remained unconscious.

There was the sound of running footsteps, and Aldhune appeared in the doorway. Right behind him were several Mercian thegns. Aldhune hesitated, and then came toward the bed. The men crowded around beside him, staring down in distress at the figure lying there. "How bad is the wound?" the eorl asked.

"The spear pierced his intestines," Edward replied.

Aldhune grimaced. "How is he now?"

"You can see for yourself."

Aldhune moved all the way to the side of the bed. He stared down at Aedred. "I couldn't reach him," he said. "I couldn't move a step from where they had us." He swung suddenly around to Edward. "Not a step! They told me Penwahl is dead."

Edward nodded slowly. "His men just left with his body."

Mawer's voice rumbled out coolly. "A Dane struck off his head as he defended your king." He stared at the Mercian eorl.

Aldhune replied in a low voice, "You were all for it, too."

There was a silence.

"I'm going down to the mill," Edward said.

Aldhune looked down at the bed; thrust his hand out suddenly, as if to touch Aedred, and then he pressed the hand softly into the woolen cover. "I'll follow shortly."

"Cuthrac needs a man to stay . . .?"

"I'll stay."

Edward nodded to Mawer, and the eorl got up and followed the prince out of the house.

"What's the story in there?"

"Penwahl was for waiting until all the Mercian army was in place before coming here," Mawer replied. "The brothers and the rest of us were of the other mind. Leodwald taunted Penwahl for a coward. The king left Leodwald to watch the landscape at Ceolworth."

Edward was quietly regarding him. "This was an ill-advised adventure. I'm surprised Aedred undertook it."

"We know it was ill-advised now! That's easy. But what the hell--the fucking Danes were raiding as they pleased and holding a village near the king's own hall, for Christ's sake! Two little ones came in beaten and abused and scared to death. That's how we found out. Grundl's father had bought time for them with his own life. That was his head up there. Feeling ran high, Sire. It argued well, then." He looked away from Edward's steady gaze. "Queen Elfwina was the other dissenter," he muttered.

Edward's lips parted involuntarily, and then closed again. "The story's been told. Let it rest."

Mawer nodded gravely. When Edward's hand pressed his shoulder, he said, "I don't feel good about it."

"Don't ride yourself. There's no useful function in that."

Mawer gazed unhappily after him as the prince headed toward the mill.

Chapter Fifty

[829] Weardburh, Mercia. The rain had become a drizzle again from thick clouds low above the valley. Small groups of Mercian soldiers were gathered outside the house at a respectful distance, watching the prince and the eorl. Edward looked toward the east. Beyond the village, his army camped on the open land. On the periphery of the bivouac area, horses tugged lazily at their tethers. Not seeing his own mount there, he glanced about him, and then whistled sharply twice. The men watched him silently. There was an answering neigh from nearby; Edward whistled again. With an impatient, tossing head, the bay gelding trotted out from behind the house and with him Aedred's black stallion. He caught the reins of his horse and the breast collar of the war-horse. "You can go on down," he told Mawer. "I'll be along in a minute."

Edward led the horses to a trough under a huge elm. He tied both horses where they could drink and called over a militia man and gave him orders to stand at the front door of the house and to pass on to him any word from inside.

Just then Grundl came up a path that led to the trough from a stand of young oaks. His hands were covered with dirt. He washed them in the trough, glancing now and then at the prince with a grim face.

"Are you going down there now, Prince Edward?"

Edward looked toward a high narrow building sunk in the foliage of enormous linden trees. It was set in a depression filled with vegetation marking the stream. "Yes. That's the mill, isn't it?"

"Yes, Sire. Sire, I have the right--"

"Come along."

Grundl fell silently in beside him.

"It depends on what we find down there. Until I've determined what we're facing, no action is to be taken. Is that understood?"

"Yes, Sire," Grundl replied, tonelessly.

They walked on for a few paces.

"Do you have any idea why your father's body was treated in that way?"

Succinctly and without emotion, Grundl told him about the children.

"I see."

As they continued down the slope toward the mill, Edward spoke again. "We have no idea what is going on at Ceolworth. There could be another force gathered there right now. There needs haste. When we're through here, I want you to take a few men and go directly to

Ceolworth. If there has been a rout there, send back immediately for reinforcements. If not, inform Queen Elfwina of what has happened here and that we'll start for Ceolworth as soon as the king is ready to travel. Tell her I will send four hundred men from my army tomorrow under Eorl Mawer's command. Unless the queen directs you otherwise, I want you to remain there. You may tell her it is my opinion the kingdom would best be served if she stays at the hall."

"I understand, Prince Edward."

"Gryffn should be apprised of this. See that a message goes off to him right away. There may be something moving on his edge."

"Yes, Sire."

They were nearing the mill site. In a large cleared area beneath the trees, they could see several hundred Saxons and most of the Mercian army keeping guard over the Danes. The captives had been herded into a tight mass. Some were sitting, others standing, all watching their captors with a wary fatigue. Their weapons lay in a massive pile against the stone side of the mill, guarded by a line of Mercians.

Those Danes sitting or squatting on the ground stood up as Edward approached; those already standing straightened and grew watchful. Eorl Waltheof and Eorl Gyrth were near the mill door. As Edward approached them, Grundl dropped back a few paces.

Eorl Gyrth asked the prince, "Has there been a change?" His features were pinched, his mouth white.

"No change. Cuthrac is doing what he can. I didn't see you come down," he said to Waltheof.

"You were tending the horses, Sire."

Edward turned to look at the prisoners. The mill was on sloping ground above where the Danes were penned. He could see the angry Mercians strung out like a squall line along the perimeter of the encircling Saxons.

Gyrth's wild eyes followed his glance. "We should march them away from Weardburh before we bring them down--out there beyond the woodlands where the ravens can pluck them clean before the stench fouls the air."

Waltheof was nodding. "We could spread them out. Twenty or so every quarter mile so the scavengers can do their work. The less competition, the quicker it's cleaned away from the townsfolk."

"Who's the commander, there?" Edward asked, ignoring their remarks.

Gyrth pointed. "The big blond bastard with the peaked cap."

Aldhune joined them.

"How is he?" Gyrth asked him.

Aldhune frowned and tilted his head. "It's hard to tell. Not worse. He hasn't wakened. But he's uneasy." His head turned to the restless crowd below them. His eyes bulged with hatred. "Those fucking bastards! I could rip every one of them apart with my bare hands!"

Edward could see exactly what was going on with Aldhune and knew he could use it to control the eorl. He had to go carefully; in spite of his favored position and that he was generally well-liked, he was still a Saxon and this was not his country. He might take over now and meet no resistance, but later, when they had time to think it through, the Mercians would remember and resent it. Still, he had no intention of letting these men make the decisions. He had leverage as head of the majority force, but he would have to walk the beam between command and consent.

"Have any of you talked to their leaders?" Edward asked.

"I don't know what you mean, Sire," Gyrth replied. "What is there to talk about? They know we're going to kill them."

"You could do that, but why not get all the information from them you can, first? What's their plan? Are there more forces? How many of them are there? You've got nothing to bargain with after they're dead."

"What kind of a damn would that information be worth?" Aldhune said, not looking directly at Edward. "They could tell us anything."

"That's right," Gyrth said.

"Wait a minute," Waltheof said. "Let's not slip the nock. This will all have to be accounted to His Majesty. We'll need a fair presentation to give him."

"Since the leader asked for me," Edward put in judiciously, "no doubt he has something to say. Are we to hear it?"

There was a pause.

"If King Aedred dies . . . ." Gyrth was looking at him with his head lowered, his eyes blazing.

"Then we'll kill them all," Edward said, without hesitation.

"Where's the bargain, then?" Aldhune finally met his eyes. "They know where they are in this scheme and what's on. Where's the bargain for them?"

"We'll lie to them," answered Waltheof. "Tell them we'll let them go and then slaughter the lot. It's no more than they would do to us if things were reversed."

Edward refrained from saying anything, waiting first to see what the other responses were before he refused.

"Let's hear what the asshole Dane has to say," Aldhune finally said. "We know and they know we can kill them anytime we want. It might give them an incentive."

"Grundl has a right, here . . . ." said Edward in a tentative reminder.

They all looked around at Grundl, who stood like a monolith a few paces off.

"If it comes out who did it, he's entitled," Waltheof said.

The rest agreed.

"Then I talk to the Dane?" the prince asked.

"As long as the outcome of it is they die," Aldhune told him.

"I can't agree to that. I don't know what he's got to tell me. We need to know their plan. Did it include an attack on Ceolworth? They could have the hall under siege right now, for all we know. Or breached the defenses. If the queen were hostage right now, we'd hardly be ahead if we killed our captives. There are always unforeseen circumstances that won't be answered by restrictions. If I'm going to talk to him, I have to have a free hand. I am not going to automatically order them put to death."

They were silent, considering where Edward stood in the king's esteem and kinship. They knew he was extending them a courtesy. But they were not happy.

"Why is he asking for you, anyway?" Aldhune was uncomfortable, angry, and off balance. Edward did not want to press his advantage. He wanted the others to do it.

Gyrth took Aldhune's arm. "I want to quarter every one of them," he said. "But Prince Edward has a point. We do the best revenge at this moment by baffling their plans. This Dane bastard probably thinks he has a better chance to stay alive by offering something. What chance can he think he has otherwise?"

Aldhune laid his hand over the eorl's wrist. "All right, all right. I can see you are for this. But when I look at them, I see blood." He turned to Edward. "I don't like it--I think they should be slaughtered to the last man. Our king lies in mortal danger of his life, and it is no way certain they have anything to tell us. It could be a stall while reinforcements gather. I don't like it," he repeated passionately, "but I won't oppose it."

"I note that," Edward said. "You'll have your revenge."

The Saxons gave way as they came down the slope, making a wide path opening directly on the Danish prisoners. Edward's thegns and the Mercian eorls gathered in behind him. He came to a halt within the zone separating the Danes and their guards. As he stood there, his eyes moving over the faces of the warriors, the man who had earlier been pointed out to him as the leader came forward. He was older than most of the warriors. He had long blond hair, as blond as Edward's but straight and held back from his face by a pointed leather cap. His blond beard was full and his eyes were not green, not blue, but somewhere in between. He met Edward's gaze calmly. Four men grouped themselves closely behind him.

"I am Edward, son of Brihtric of Wessex. You asked to speak with me."

"I am Ingware, chief of these brave men." He swung his arm out to include all his men, a slow and graceful gesture. He did not look away from Edward. His voice was deep, with a thick, lilting accent. "I wish the release of my men."

There was the sound of derisive laughter from the surrounding Saxons and Mercians. Neither Edward nor the Danish chief made any sign they had heard it.

Looking beyond Ingware's shoulder to the four men who stood stony-faced behind him, Edward said, "Those are your captains?"

"My jarls, yass."

"Only four?"

There was the faintest flicker of amusement in Ingware's eyes. "It does not take many to lead brave men."

Now there was laughter from the Danes.

"You couldn't have led them better," Edward said, very clearly.

The laughter slackened. Ingware continued to look at him, unperturbed.

"You've invaded the Mercian kingdom, murdered and pillaged and raped in this town. You've taken to the field of battle with the Mercian army. You've wounded the king of Mercia. Do you think it likely your men will be released? Be serious, Ingware. These deeds require execution."

Edward had spoken loudly enough to be heard in all but the most distant ranks of the men. What he had said was quickly passed on. There was agreement, with an under swell of hostility. The Danish warriors, hedged in on all sides by Saxons and Mercians, remained watchful.

"You are not a man unused to the consequences of warfare, Prince Edward." Ingware was calm, direct, but not bold. He had also raised his voice so his words would be heard by the men encircling him.

"You are going to know the consequences, Ingware. So listen--if the king dies, you, your leaders, and your men will all die. If the king lives, you and your jarls will be hostage for your men. They will be allowed to leave, without horses or arms, forced march into East Anglia. If your warriors leave the line of march to enter any village or any dwelling, or if one Mercian is harmed on their way, you will be killed, and they will be killed. Further: a man was murdered in this village and his head placed above his door. The guilty man must stand to answer to that murder before anyone leaves, or the punishment will fall to you and your jarls, and your men will find an uncertain future with the Welsh or the Hwicce or on the Thames embankment."

Ingware's eyes never wavered from Edward's face. "Many men are killed in war."

"The killing was not honorably done in a fair battle. It was a cowardly murder."

The villagers had been gathering at the top of the incline and were watching as Edward spoke to the Danes. The Danish warriors, who could hear what was being said, exchanged glances and then looked to their leaders. They were watching Edward without expression. Behind Edward, Grundl scanned the faces for that fleeting and unguarded sign marking the guilty man.

For the first time, Ingware spoke with visible emotion. "There *was* an act of cowardice: the man killed one of our warriors with an axe from behind."

Edward sensed his caution and wondered if Ingware himself had struck the blow. "You speak a half truth," Edward replied. "The villager struck in defense of a child being assaulted by one of your men. We want the man who killed that villager."

"What is the punishment if this man is found?"

Edward turned to Grundl.

The Mercian came forward, drawing his sword and holding it straight up. "His head with this sword," Grundl replied.

Ingware studied the scarred, immobile face. "Your father," he said.

There was a long silence. Then, from the ranks, one of the prisoners stepped forward and spoke loudly in Danish. Another man quickly came up to stand beside him shouting the same phrase. Other men joined the line with the same loud cry, until it was apparent half the company was confessing to the crime. Ingware looked at Edward, waiting.

Edward stretched his arm to the side. "Send the first ten men over here," he said, not taking his eyes from Ingware's face.

There was no hesitation from the warriors. They came directly to where Edward had indicated. Grundl stepped to the line.

"Tell the first man to kneel," Edward told Ingware.

He replied, "I am the man you want."

It was instinct, perhaps, because Ingware had given no sign when he spoke, but Edward turned abruptly and called up three of his men. "Take him," he said, pointing toward one of the Danish commanders.

The man was as blond as Ingware, but younger, more handsome, with clear blue eyes. A coarse bandage wrapped around his bare arm was seeping blood. He looked surprised, and then angry. He side-stepped the quick reach Ingware made for him and came forward before the men reached him. He regarded Grundl unflinchingly. Grundl stared back, stolid, impassive; his feet spread apart, both hands resting on the hilt of his sword, the point to the ground.

The jarl addressed him in English. "I killed him and put his head above the door as a warning to those who would dare kill any Danish warrior. I would do the same again. It was a clean blow. He felt no pain. Be as accurate with me."

As Ingware lunged forward and was held by the Mercians, the jarl took off his mantle, laid it on the ground in front of him, knelt gracefully, and almost before the eye could follow, Grundl's sword rose and fell. He stepped aside. Without looking back, he moved through the groups of Mercian warriors jostling to get a glimpse of the corpse and walked on up the incline and out of sight.

In a slow, stiff gait, Ingware walked to the jerking body and covered it with his mantle. With the help of his remaining commanders, he gathered the head in the bloody mantle it had rolled onto and, holding it with both hands tightly against his chest; he came to stand in front of Edward. He was weeping silently. "I will want a pyre."

Edward's face did not change expression. He inclined his head to Ingware. It was all the compassion he could give this enemy.

Chapter Fifty-One

[829] Weardburh, Mercia. Edward sat next to the bed watching Aedred's face in the gentle lamplight. Pain crossed it often, and occasionally he would moan. His skin was hot and greasy and his pallor was taking on a dead whiteness that alarmed Edward. The king's hands lay beside his body, limp, the fingers translucent, the nails colorless. It was the second night Edward had sat this way, watching, praying, trying to hold away what he knew was rapidly nearing.

On a table by the door were quantities of food brought in by the women of the village. Edward had expressed his gratitude, but had not been able to eat. Occasionally lying across the foot of the huge bed of Edgar the Tall, he would try to sleep. But always the slightest sound or movement from Aedred would bring him upright. The king's pain seemed to be increasing, but there was nothing that could be done by anyone, and Edward knew it. For this moment, however, the king lay still.

Edward walked out past where Cuthrac lay sleeping in the next room and on through the front room to the door and stood on the threshold, looking into the darkness.

Above him the low-hanging clouds seemed faintly illuminated by an interior light, but there was no moon. Somewhere in the village, a dog barked. On the green a cow late to be brought into her stall lowed and shook her bell. A nighthawk called briefly from the luminous air. To the east, the camp was quiet, a few cooking fires wavering in the darkness. The air was cold and refreshing, so Edward lingered, leaning on the frame of the door, the dim light from the far room silhouetting his figure.

Please, Heavenly Father, don't let him die . . . .

Edward folded his arms and looked down at his feet as he changed position. He took a long, audible breath and looked up at the sky again.

Please, Merciful Father . . . .

He looked again at the quiet village, the dark shapes making up this community he had brought his army to unaware--

Aedred screamed in a high, piercing cry that sent Edward careening back through the rooms. Dangerously close to the edge of the high bed, Aedred flailed about, his eyes wide open and bulging from his head. Edward flung himself across the king's chest, holding him down, trying not to hurt him, trying to keep Aedred from tearing himself open.

Cuthrac had leaped up from his bed when the prince ran past, and now he grabbed Aedred's legs, and together they finally subdued him. The two men rose from the bed, both breathing heavily from exertion and alarm, intent on Aedred, who had dropped again into unconsciousness.

"My God!" Edward panted.

"I'd better have a look, Sire. He may have broken his wound."

While Cuthrac unwound the bandages, Edward dipped a cloth in water and swabbed Aedred's burning face. "Did he open it?" He looked over as Cuthrac lifted the woolen pad.

A fetid odor rose from the suppurating wound. Edward looked away.

"No, Sire." Cuthrac replaced the cloth. The king moaned. "Sire," Cuthrac said in a low voice, "I think it's only a matter of hours. The infection--"

Aedred's face contorted, and he cried out again and lay panting, his body moving restlessly.

Edward turned on Cuthrac in sudden rage. "Goddamn it! Haven't you anything to relieve his pain?"

Tired and plagued with his own sense of helplessness, Cuthrac lowered his head like a bull, sinking his wide neck into his shoulders. Looking directly into the prince's angry stare, he said harshly, "The pain is everywhere in his body. Nothing is strong enough to ease that."

Edward wiped at the white face, again. Recognizing his unfairness, he dropped his voice. "Go on and lie down, Cuthrac. I'll call you if he starts thrashing around again."

Cuthrac cleared his throat. With humility, he said, "Sire, it would be better if we were to tie him down. Better for him if you happen to drop off and not reach him in time to keep him from rolling off the bed; better for us, because as the pain increases, so will his strength. I've seen this myself. The two of us might not be able to hold him."

It was something Edward recoiled from doing, but he wasn't sure he could prevail against a strength Cuthrac described. As it was, it had taken the two of them to bring Aedred under control.

Cuthrac obtained a rope from somewhere, and they drew it over the king, handing it back and forth across his shoulders, chest, thighs, and ankles. White and shrunken, Aedred lay in his bonds. Cuthrac returned to his corner in the adjoining room, and Edward took up his vigil again. He began his silent prayers, aware now of the foul odor rising from the bandage over the king's abdomen.

"Edward?"

Edward opened his eyes from his prayers and was startled to find Aedred looking at him, his face distorted by pain, but his eyes clear and focused. When he saw this recognition, Edward nearly wept.

"Yes, I'm here."

"Why am I bound like this? There are ropes across me."

"You were wounded. You've been moving about. It's to keep you from breaking open your wound. Are the bonds too tight?"

Aedred did not answer. As if he had nothing further to say to Edward, he turned his eyes to the ceiling. His hands lifted spasmodically as far as the ropes across his wrists would allow, and as Edward watched helplessly, Aedred moaning, cried out, *"Great Mother Erce . . . ease me . . . ease me!"*

He slipped back into a fretful unconsciousness. Now, Edward laid his forehead against his tightly clasped hands, his lips moving silently. He prayed passionately with no other thoughts coming into his mind, driving out everything that wasn't a plea for the man lying in a room filling with the smell of death.

He heard the watch call out from the distance the deepest hour of the night, a call from the darkness where life shifted and turned and renewed itself. The fragrance of small flowers twined in summer grasses breathed into the room, and from that sweet-scented darkness the figure of a woman emerged, a woman shrouded in umber, the face unseen.

His unspoken question: *Who are you?*

The answer in a voice warm, intimate, familiar and loved, yet only a collection of beloved voices: *The brother of your heart is near death.*

I want him to live.

I will heal him.

Aedred spoke to that form, his head tilted up, answered that voice in a language unheard before by Edward, the strange words winding about the prince, lulling him. In his drowsy haze, he saw Aedred's face splashed with light, his eyes brilliant and knowing.

Edward lifted his head from the coverlet and saw the sun streaming in the windows. Cuthrac had taken the ropes from around Aedred and was cleaning the wound. Edward shook his head and breathed deeply. There was no foulness in the air.

"Good morning, Sire," Cuthrac said cheerfully.

"How is he?" Edward, fully awake now, stood up and stared intently at Aedred.

The king's eyes were closed. For the first time in days, his face appeared relaxed. A faint flush of color showed through the dark stubble on his chin and around his mouth. As Edward gazed down at him, the mouth twisted a little into an expression Edward recognized.

The eyelids opened. "Weak as a fledgling." Aedred tried a laugh, winced, and settled on a smile. "By the gods, I'm still here, and curious about how you come to be in my bed."

Edward gasped, managing, "As the story goes: 'I was passing by with my army' and it continues from there. The tale can be long or short."

"Well, the long one. I think a few details have escaped me." He lifted his head to peer down at Cuthrac's ministrations. "Not much of a gash," he said. Still weak, he dropped his head back down.

Edward met Cuthrac's wondering gaze. "It looks much better than last night."

"Mercians are all hardy," Aedred replied. "With this good physician and the help of the gods, I'll heal fast."

After exacting a ransom, Edward had sent Ingware and his jarls away. The Mercians were not entirely happy with this, but they did accept it. With Aedred's agreement, the prince had left a contingent of Saxons at the valley to help refortify the ancient burh. There would be no surprise from that quarter again.

Fourteen days after he had been wounded, Aedred returned to Ceolworth and a wild welcome that brought out the countryside and cheers from the entire Mercian army, which had assembled during his absence.

Aedred had been deeply grieved over the death of Penwahl, holding himself responsible. He had not heeded the eorl's advice and as a result of his pique with Leodwald, had brought about Penwahl's death. He said nothing to anyone about this, and no one guessed how harshly he judged himself.

Thus the days were taken up and the month of Thrilmilci began--the lush and opulent month when cows yield milk three times a day. As everyone had agreed at the council, there was a periodic shifting of troops as groups went home and others came newly into the force and Grundl's stern discipline.

Aedred's early plan had been to live at the bivouac, and he carried it through once he had spent two weeks' recuperation time in the hall with Elfwina, although love-making was as yet not possible for him.

He had not said very much about his wounding to Elfwina, partly because he did not want to make a deal of it after the fact and partly because the scar hardly substantiated how close he had been to death, it was so thin and unnoticeable. Nor did he tell her whom he had summoned to heal him, or why, with profound reverence, he was building a new temple to Mother Erce.

Unaware of the severity of his wounding, Elfwina assumed his delayed return was his interest in refortifying the burh. So the queen's thoughts were again taken up with the agony she was experiencing over her brother: for no reason she could understand, after the declarations of love, Edward was avoiding her. It had so often been this way--he would disapprove of something, often she hadn't known what, and he would withdraw, leaving her to spend agonizing hours, sometimes days, in trying to pull herself from that emptiness and again feel his love and approval. After Aedred fell asleep, Elfwina would go quietly into the sitting room and pace up and down until night gave way to dawn.

God had granted his prayers, and having had those prayers granted, Edward had been compelled to evaluate the turn taken in his relationship with his sister. Now Edward was following a rigorous schedule he had devised which purposely left him little time in her company. He went infrequently to the hall and only on business. His quarters were now at the northwest edge of his army's encampment in a tent doubling as a meeting place where he could confer with his commanders or with Aedred, when the king came down to talk with him, although more often it was he who went to Aedred's encampment. He felt secure in his resolve to maintain distance from his sister.

At the hall a constant stream of men from one army or the other and people from the village and countryside coming and going through the gates and shuffling in and out of the building seemed endless. By the end of each day, Elfwina was ready to sleep but sleep always evaded her. She would stand at her chamber window, looking out on the night with its flickering orange fires to the west and south. She would hear the restless sound of human voices and the sound of horses, all blending with the incessant voice of the river. When she did sleep, it was fitfully and without depth. She lay on the surface of sleep, submerging now and then, only to rise again to the reality of the night and its thousand voices.

One evening she sent for Ceadda. He was brought into her sitting room, an arresting figure in silver and blue. Tonight he looked like a magician.

"How is Ruthric, these days?" she asked, reminded by his presence that she had not followed the huntsman's recuperation.

"His leg is healed, Your Majesty, and it has shrunk very little. Lady Penwahl's regime has saved him from permanent disability."

"So this method has impressed you."

"Completely, Ma'am."

"Do you think this remarkable treatment could be repeated with others?"

"I'm convinced of it. Your Majesty--"

"Yes?"

"I was very saddened to hear of Eorl Penwahl's death. I understand he and Lady Penwahl had been married for a number of years."

"Twenty-four, I believe."

"A long time." He hesitated. "When an association of that length ends unexpectedly--tragically--grief can be debilitating."

"Have you heard that Lady Penwahl is debilitated by her loss?" Elfwina asked in surprise.

"It has come to me that she is withdrawing, becoming reclusive, not available to even her closest friends."

"You're sure of this?"

"Yes, Ma'am, I am."

"What about her son?"

"Her son is in Flanders."

"Yes, I'd forgotten he was only here for his father's funeral." She studied his face. "I saw her when she came to escort Eorl Penwahl's body back to Stafford. She was handling her grief well at that time. But your sources indicate that is not the case?"

"Yes, Ma'am, to an alarming degree."

"Lady Penwahl is very dear to me. Perhaps I'll make a visit to Stafford . . . ." Her voice trailed off as she gazed briefly into space.

"Forgive me, Your Majesty. You sent for me, and I've caused a digression."

"No digression, Ceadda. I am always interested in Lady Penwahl. The matter I sent for you for--I can't seem to sleep at night. I don't quite know how to account for it, but I need to have a full night's rest. Have you a potion that might help me?"

"Of course, Ma'am, I will do what I can." He was sympathetic, but his eyes were watchful. "Perhaps all the activity . . . and there was the concern about your husband. These things can keep sleep at bay."

"Possibly."

When she said nothing more, only gazed at him with her dark eyes, he said, "I will get a remedy for you immediately."

"You needn't come all the way back from your room, Ceadda. I'll send someone with you."

He left with two of the queen's maids following him. They waited in the corridor while he dug into his leather bag. He took a small packet to the waiting women. "Tell the queen to take a pinch mixed in wine each night before she goes to bed."

With a sad gaze he watched the women walk away. "Sleep is not the answer," he said softly.

Chapter Fifty-Two

[829] Ceolworth, Mercia. Although there was some respite for Elfwina in the potion given her by Ceadda, it was not enough. After two or three nights and she was still unable to sleep, she told Edyth it might be the noise, the incessant comings and goings beneath her chamber that was keeping her awake.

"Why don't you sleep in your brother's chambers," Edyth said. "He's staying with his army and his rooms are empty. It's farther from the doors and the great hall. There'll be much less noise there."

She wondered why she hadn't thought of that herself. "If the king should come," Elfwina told her, "tell him where I am."

Some of Edward's belongings were still in the room; he had not entirely moved to the bivouac yet, and she was comforted by their familiarity. She fell asleep with her face on his pillow, breathing the faint, fresh scent of his hair. The next morning she awoke rested and with new energy.

Edward spent most of the same day with Aedred and the eorls, riding out over the immediate countryside and inspecting with them the repairs recently completed on the roads and bridges.

"Either we'll have an easy way out," he told the company at large, "or the Danes will have an easy way in."

"We'll win in any case," Aedred replied.

By the time they had returned to their own camps, it was late evening. On the way back, they had all entered into a noisy debate about routes into and out of Ceolworth, and Edward had offered his maps to settle it, since his opinion was most in question. They all agreed to meet in the morning at Aedred's tent and, with those maps, determine who was correct.

Mawer followed Edward into his tent for a cup of ale and sat drinking it and watching Edward go through his packs for the maps.

Edward straightened and stood musing. He murmured, "I must have left them at the hall."

Mawer took a great swallow from his cup. "We can ride up there in the morning and get them before we go on to the meeting."

"No, I want to show you what I was talking about. If there's a hole in my argument you can help me plug it before I make an ass of myself."

"I've never known you to go wrong on questions of terrain," Mawer said, yawning.

Edward laughed. "I can see you've no interest in this tonight. Finish your ale and be off to your bed. I'm going to get the maps."

He left Mawer to his ale and decided to walk rather than wait to have his horse resaddled. He met a small number of his thegns returning from the hall, and then he overtook another group on their way to the village. They urged him to go with them, and after a brief consideration, he declined but walked with them as far as the hall gates.

The lamps in the great room were lit and the hearth was glowing. It was getting late, and the few men clustered at the benches were preparing to rise. Before anyone could notice him, Edward sprinted up the stairs and into the corridor. He slowed as he passed the huge double doors of the queen's chamber but then, with resolve, continued down the hallway.

There was a lighted sconce on the wall beside the door to his rooms. He pulled it free of the bracket and then entered, holding up the torch as he went from the small anteroom into the larger room which served as both sitting room and bedchamber. He walked to his map table. The light illuminated the table and threw the rest of the room in shadow. Edward propped the sconce carefully against the wall and drew one of the maps out of the stand and unrolled it, scanning it as he weighted the corners with objects from the table. He bent forward to study it more closely.

Elfwina lay buried in quilts and fur skins. She had not moved since the door first opened, not knowing who it was entering. Now she twisted the dark mass of hair from her face and looked at Edward where he stood quite still staring down at his map, unaware of her. The wavering light shed gold over his head, gleamed in the hair curled around his face, which was in profile to her. Gold caught in his mustache and beard; gold poured down the folds of his white mantle where it draped along one arm. The quiet concentration in his posture, the view of him in this state of unawareness lay like a vow in her heart.

With a deep breath, she rose up, and her movement and the sound she made brought him suddenly upright and turning toward her, his eyes wide, his right hand automatically crossing to his sword, stopping with the blade half-drawn when he saw who it was.

"Elf!" He relaxed, shoved the sword back in place, and laughed. "You scared the hell out of me! What are you doing here? Don't you have a bed of your own?"

She stumbled over the words. "I--I haven't been able to sleep--"

"No? You haven't? That's not like you. You sleep like a winter bear." A smile spun across his lips and was lost.

They looked at each other.

"I can't explain it. I even went to Ceadda--"

"To Ceadda?"

"For a sleeping potion."

"You needed that? Did it help?"

"No." She looked away from him. The light gilded her face and was absorbed into the blackness of her hair where it spilled over the cover she had pulled around her bare shoulders.

He said, "And you came naked to my bed as a final remedy."

She took a breath that outlined the hollow in her throat. "It was quiet here."

His eyes turned away to the burning sconce, to the table, to the unseen door beyond the anteroom. "It is quiet."

They both listened and heard nothing.

"It's late," he said, still looking toward the door. "Everyone has settled down for the night. There's no one about."

She didn't reply, only watched him silently. His head turned back and his eyes came once again to her face.

"I came after a map," he said. "I'll take it now and go."

He turned back to the table. *I came here innocent.* One by one, from each corner, he took off the weights, set them carefully aside. *This is not my doing.* He rolled the map, squared it, tapped the ends, and then stood there with his hand resting on the scroll, looking down at it. *Fate has determined this.*

She remained silent, watching him.

He closed his eyes. "Let me lie beside you," he began in a low voice. "Nothing more. Just lie beside you." He stood motionless, looking down at the scroll, at his shaking hand.

"No." She had barely been able to speak the word as the air drained out of the room. "We can't do that."

His hand pressed down on the map. "It's not lust. I just need to touch you. Nothing else. Please!"

She moaned, dropped her head on her arms and rocked it slowly back and forth.

For a long time he stared at her. Then he turned back to the table and set the scroll down. He unfastened the belt that held his sword and knife and laid them next to the scroll. He removed the clasp at his shoulder and folded the white mantle over his weapons.

She had been listening to his movements. "Don't do this," she said from the cradle of her arms.

As if he were alone in the room, he sat down on the bench near the bed where she sat huddled, her head still on her arms. He carefully unwound the banding on his legs and pulled off his shoes. He drew the tunic over his head, stood to take off the loose braccio he wore. He laid them all on the bench. He said, "Look at me."

She raised her head obediently.

She had never before seen him naked, and he looked so beautiful she caught her breath. He was at the prime of his manhood, trim, his hips supple and smooth-skinned, the legs firm and well-molded. His chest hair was thick and fair, the mass thinning to a silken line marking the center of his belly down to the nest of dark golden hair. He was not aroused.

"It is not lust," he said. "I only want to feel you next to me. Nothing more."

He came slowly into the bed, easing down beside her, and then he gathered her against him. For a long time he held her, adjusting his position now and then so their bodies aligned and touched the entire length. Each time he moved he sighed softly, a small tension and release. She heard the sighs and her eyes filled with tears. There was no wrong in this--this sweetness of contact, this easing of her yearning to be again in the warmth of his love. And yet, it was more than she had ever expected, this sweet knowledge of him.

And in that ease, she pressed the soles of her feet against the bones of his insteps and thought how strange and marvelous it was that she could feel those fine bones, strange she and he could have sprung from the same parentage, grown side by side, lived in each other's thoughts, and yet this was the first time she had ever touched his bare feet.

He stroked her cheek and the hair at her temples with the backs of his fingers. "I feel such peace," he said, and was at once filled with a feeling of exaltation so compelling he could do nothing but give himself up to it in joy and relief--this freedom from physical desire, this purity, this very essence of love.

"I want you to feel my bones," she whispered.

He was unsure of what she meant.

"Does anyone know us better than we know each other? Yet, I've never touched your feet before. The bones in your feet are mysteries. I want you to touch every bone in my body. I want you to feel the bones beneath my skin . . . ."

He said nothing, now understanding what she was asking. He rose up and came gently astride her, felt her shift and relax.

"Feel inside the skin," she murmured. "Feel inside the skin."

His fingers closed around her skull and felt its ridges, circled the caverns of her eyes, rounded on the cheeks, and pressed at the union of her jaw and skull. His fingers explored the vertebrae of her neck, and he remembered how those bones looked with her head bent forward, her hair parted on either side.

"Only the bones," she sighed.

"Yes," he murmured.

The skeleton took form in his mind. The delicacy of the bones, and yet their strength, their incredible strength doubled in his own. His own finger bones traced what was his from the seed of their father. He saw himself in death, cradled in her bones.

Edward rose before daylight to make his way back to the camp under a lightening sky. The watch, startled by his sudden approach out of the mist, spoke sharply. "Sire! All's well!"

"Glad to hear it," Edward said, and ducked into his tent.

Mawer was in his own tent, shifting on a tunic, when he heard Edward come in. He pulled the garment down and gave the wall of his tent a hard stare. He sat down on his cot with a grunt.

The sun was well up when Edward came out of his tent, dressed in Saxon green. Just coming from the paddock leading his own horse and Edward's bay, Mawer saw him standing before the tent, his hair bright in the sunlight, one hand resting easily on the hilt of his sword, the other on his hip, looking toward the western camp. Mawer gazed at him with appreciation of his manhood and an intense feeling of love. As he neared the prince, Mawer saw him glance toward the hall, his face turning grave and thoughtful. At that moment, Edward heard the eorl's approach, and he gave him a broad smile.

"Are you learning the craft of a good groom?" he asked, coming to meet Mawer and taking the rein of his bay gelding. "This saddle looks well-cinched. I'll give you five silver pennies if you stay out the month."

Mawer laughed. "If your grooms hear this, you'll have a riot."

"I'll direct them to the father of it." Edward mounted his horse and paced it around Mawer, who was swinging up into his saddle. The eorl guided his horse next to Edward's, and they rode out of camp, striking out across the grassland toward the western bivouac.

"Where's the map?" Mawer asked him.

For an instant, Edward stared at him blankly. Then he said, "I stayed too late at the hall with a good companion. I completely forgot. We'll get it now." He changed his horse's direction toward the hall.

Mawer fell in beside him again. "It must have been a very good companion to keep you until dawn."

"You heard me come in? Ah, someone has to lift the sun over the horizon," Edward said cheerfully.

"Are you holding to your original idea this morning," Mawer asked, "or have you changed your view?"

"I hold firm to my opinion, which I'll happily express to one and all with conviction and the solid evidence."

They had come through the gate and up to the steps of the hall. Edward swung off his horse and looked up at Mawer with a grin. He handed him the rein. "Five silver pennies," he said, and ran lightly up the steps with Mawer's loud snort following him.

Edward's head hummed from lack of sleep. At the same time he felt buoyant, elated. He glanced around the great hall, and then went up the stairs two at a time and on down the corridor past the doors of his sister's chambers to his own rooms. The covers lay in a heap to one side of the bed. He spread his fingers over the soft fabric. *Nothing happened. In all those beautiful hours, nothing happened that shouldn't have happened. I can face him. There was nothing wrong in what we did. Nothing.*

He came out into the sunlight to find Mawer holding the rein of his horse and staring gloomily off toward the south. "Here it is," Edward said brightly, with a wave of the map. He tucked the roll inside his tunic and got back on his horse. "I'm ready for some of the king's ale; how does that sound to you?"

Mawer brightened. "I can just tolerate that. It's damned hot today, sitting out here holding the fucking reins of a horse."

"And you so well-paid for it."

The king and his eorls and their thegns were gathered under a gigantic oak, shaded from the unseasonable heat. It was easy to see how the morning had been taken up. Aedred sat with his leg hooked over one arm of his chair, balancing a horn of ale on the other. His dark head lifted when he saw the prince and Mawer approaching. His eyes caught Edward's, and he gave him a smile which told him *Take a look at how the morning's been progressing.*

The recognition of what had occurred since he had last seen Aedred only hours before struck Edward at the pit of his stomach and flashed hotly to his face. Knowing he had reddened, nevertheless, he was able to meet Aedred's eyes and return his smile.

Leodwald shouted out, "Comes Prince Edward and his minions!"

"Only one minion," rumbled Mawer, rocking horse and saddle as he dismounted. But his eyes had lit up when he had seen the horns and heard Leodwald's drunken yell. "By God," he cried, "you've moved on us!"

"You'll have no trouble catching up, Eorl Mawer," Aedred said.

"I'll be pleased to prove you right, Your Majesty," he replied, accepting a horn from a servant appearing at his side. As the man started to walk away, Mawer's great hand came down on his shoulder, keeping him stationary. Mawer's eyes made a circuit of the group. Leodwald nodded fuzzily at his bench. Aldhune was exchanging a look with Gyrth. Wulfric watched calmly, amusement faintly curving his mouth. Mawer's awful grin stretched his face. He raised the horn to his lips.

"Make me proud, minion," Edward told him.

Mawer tilted the horn and drank and did not bring it down until it was finished. He tipped it over to show it was empty and took the approving laughter with a modest expression. "Now you can go," he said to the servant and shoved the horn into his hand. "Fill it up and be quick. Every swallow they take puts them ahead." He laughed as the servant ran off, and then he ambled over like a great bear to sit down beside Wulfric.

Chapter Fifty-Three

[829] Ceolworth, Mercia. Edward had watched Mawer's exhibition with the rest, smiling indulgently, while still probing his reaction to Aedred. He realized he felt no guilt. He felt no guilt, he told himself, because he had committed no offense. Brother and sister had simply lain in a chaste and sinless embrace, an embrace that was their right, the entitlement of their blood.

He stood smiling at Mawer, who winked up at him, and in that instant a sudden understanding opened to Edward like a broad door opening onto a sunny, brilliant world: he saw that his confused longing for his sister was not some perverted desire, for lust had been no part of it. The physical closeness he had wanted so desperately for as long as he could remember, the need to have her body touching his, was only the outward manifestation of the interior, familial bond of blood and brain; no one on earth knew him as she did--without pretenses. She knew who lay naked beneath the hundred protective disguises he wore, and she loved who it was. In that symbolic and actual nakedness, in that chaste communion, God had been a witness and known his heart, and Edward's relief at discovering this was profound. He looked at Aedred with a sudden warm and deep affection.

Aedred called out to him, "Well, we've waited half the morning for your defense, Edward. Where's the map? Or are you ready to forfeit?"

"Forfeit!" cried Edward. "You'll all be paying homage as if I wore a bishop's ring." He paused and glanced around. "That's a Christian joke."

"It's wasted on us," Aedred replied. "Stop stalling. Where's that proof you boasted of yesterday? Or do you think you'll charm us away from the matter with your Christian wit? I decree here and now you're not to raise a horn until your proof's laid out."

"That's a sorry lack of trust." Edward pulled the rolled map from his tunic.

"Now, we're at it!" Aedred leaned forward. "Bring up a bench so we can settle this squabble."

Aldhune and Leodwald lifted a bench and set it down in front of Aedred, and they all gathered around as Edward unrolled the map. He held the parchment open so they could study it, but didn't look at it himself. Mawer glanced down, grunted, and turned away with a wink at Edward. He called for another horn and, straddling the bench with his thick legs, sat down to drink his ale.

"Shit!" Aldhune drawled in disgust. "I would have given my oath this was the route." He drew his finger along the map and looked up at Edward, who smiled at him angelically and shook his head.

"You're truly right on this one, Prince Edward. I'll give you that," said Leodwald, squinting at the map. "I'll fuck a goose if you're not." Leodwald stumbled away and sat down heavily on the nearest bench.

"I'd like to witness that," Mawer rumbled.

Leodwald did not hear him. "Now that I see it there, Sire, I can see you're right. I'll give you that."

Edward grinned benevolently at the eorl's silliness. "You think I'm right, then, eh, Leodwald?"

"Right as the tide."

"Leodwald and Aldhune agree I'm right," Edward said to the remaining skeptics.

"I can't quarrel with the evidence," Wulfric said, straightening away from the map. "But I wouldn't relish bringing an army through there."

Aedred had been carefully studying the map. "But neither would an enemy," he said. "That would be the advantage." He looked up at Edward. "Elfwina would know this one, too."

"I expect so, although I haven't spoken with her about it."

Aedred turned his head. "Gyrth, are you a hold out, or do you concede with the rest of us?"

"Sorry, Your Majesty," Gyrth replied with a start. "Yes, I concede. I'm just wondering how someone from Wessex would know Mercia better than we do?"

"That's easy," Leodwald mumbled, "he's never in Wessex."

Edward's annoyed reply was less diplomatic than it might have been. "I know Mercia better than most of you because I don't think of myself only as a West Saxon; I'm a man of Angelcynn. Whatever the boundaries we've made to suit our various purposes, we're all of us on one island. Claiming that island as my homeland, I'm not bound to know only one kingdom well."

Aedred heard this testy answer with some amazement and saw the others had responded much the same way. He laughed, but his eyes speculated. "The ramifications march out in armies from that proposition," he said.

The moment he had uttered it, Edward had also seen its imperialistic overtones. "See what comes of depriving a man of ale on a hot day? He becomes philosophical. In pity, undo your decree."

"Less in pity than in defense of the kingdom," Leodwald said loudly, with the random accuracy of drunkenness.

There was an uncomfortable silence.

"If you'll clarify your meaning, Eorl Leodwald," Edward said evenly, coming to stand in front of him, "I'll know how to answer."

He leaned down and spoke directly into Leodwald's face. "And answer you, I surely will."

Wavering drunk but never a coward, Leodwald nonetheless scented unexpected political danger in Edward's challenge. Although not able to get a grip on the whole situation and genuinely not having meant to offend him, still Leodwald did not retreat from Edward, but made a comical grimace and answered, "Philosophy is an ale curdler."

Edward drew back with a frown from what at first seemed a non sequitur. Then he laughed. "That's nearly clear enough," he said, and laughed again.

Leodwald laughed; too, pleased he had effected a satisfactory end to the moment. He buried his nose in the horn he had been balancing precariously on his knee.

Aedred had closely followed this exchange as had the others. Although he had started off so early on the horn the edges of his perception were dulled, yet the king did wonder at his kinsman's statement. "Give him ale," he told a servant, vaguely concerned he might have offended Edward with his jest. But as time went by, it was Edward's response to Gyrth which remained in Aedred's mind to agitate and leave a ripple where the waters should have been calm.

The rest of the morning passed uneventfully. Leodwald drank himself into a near stupor, bowing forward out of the general talk, with his chin on his chest.

Grundl appeared. Aedred had him seated and a horn placed in his hand. Edward observed this with interest. Grundl was no longer a simple captain, but had been promoted to a generalship that was just below Aedred himself. From what Edward knew of Grundl, he was glad to see it. *How long,* he thought, *before Aedred makes him an eorl?*

The bench moved as Mawer suddenly shifted his weight. Edward glanced over at him and saw he was concentrating on Grundl with a shrewd look in his eye that Edward recognized too well. *Ho!* he thought, *that would be a match.*

"Damn me!" Mawer thundered at Grundl, who sat near the king, one hand resting on his knee, the other raising the horn to his lips. "You grasp that like a man who knows how to drink!"

Grundl lowered the horn and held Mawer's eyes across the space. His deep voice rolled out. "Are you thinking to set me up, Eorl Mawer? You forget I've stood at the king's back for ten years. Time enough to watch you increasing your treasure hoard with the belongings of foolish men. You must be the richest man in Wessex. Approach me if you dare, Sire, but don't think me a victim, for if you contest with me, you will be the loser."

A guttural howl of astonishment wound out of the spectators.

Mawer laughed loudly with his teeth and gums exposed; a dangerous bear. "A straight forward man! I like that. No arriving at the point around a timid circle, but straight on--like a spear."

He loudly addressed the company that had suddenly come alert. "He may have stood at the king's back, but he's in front when there's a battle. We've all seen him, haven't we? There on his feet, disdaining the comfort of a horse, jabbing away with his spear--*Dane-Skewer,* I'd call it. He's a bold warrior in any man's estimation. But, look here, Grundl," he cried, centering again on the big Mercian, who was taking all this flattery without a change of expression, "you are absolutely right! We've seen a great deal of each other over the years, but--and how can you credit a world like this?--*never on the bench!* Well, till now. And here we are, and since you've thrown out such a bold challenge, boasting you'll win, because I respect you, I'll give you the chance to make it good. *Fill the horns!*"

The noisy approval to this contest was abruptly halted. Seated beside Mawer, with his back to the road, Edward saw first a curious expression cross Grundl's stoic face, and then he saw warmth brighten the king's features. He turned.

The queen and five women attending her rode into the gathering. There was Lady Ella, Lady Mildthryth, and three others with whom Edward had little acquaintance but whose presence sparked interest in the other men.

"We don't wish to interrupt you," Elfwina said, with a smile for all the company, although it was Aedred she addressed. Her eyes touched Edward briefly. Aedred had sunk back into his chair and was smiling up at her. "We're merely passing through."

"Why not join us? We were just about to witness a contest among giants."

"How so?"

"Giants?" echoed Lady Ella, looking toward Grundl.

"Grundl challenged Mawer to the horn. We're about to see the awful clash."

Unaccountably, Grundl seemed extremely embarrassed. Aedred mildly noted his captain's neck was dark red beneath his beard.

Elfwina looked from Grundl to Mawer. "My," she said, "won't that be exciting." It was graciously uttered, yet suddenly gave the whole affair an air of childishness. She addressed Aedred again. "We were hoping you would join *us*. We've brought lunch and wine to have beyond the Street. Perhaps after your contest, you might meet us there."

"The contest can wait," Aedred said. "We'll join you now." And that was that. He called for horses.

Gyrth had other business and so declined the invitation and went on his way. Aedred noticed Grundl edging away in the general disorder, plainly not considering he was part of the group.

It may have been the ale he had drunk, or his general mood, but whatever the authorship, Aedred felt a sudden tightening in his throat that after all these years Grundl felt he did not belong. Aedred caught his shoulder. "Grundl," he said in a voice that reached only the ears of his chief commander, "you needn't move in and out in shadow fashion any more. You belong in this company. On my crown, my good friend, I am going to make you an eorl."

That Grundl's face was expressionless did not fool Aedred. "Come to my tent, tonight," he told him, "and we'll settle the matter."

Aedred stepped away to mount his horse. Grundl stared after him numbly. A horse came up close to him, and he stepped aside.

"Are you coming Giant Grundl?

Lady Ella was gazing at him from her horse, the crooked smile which was such a delight to him, playing at the corners of her mouth. He felt the blood rush to his head. He got on his horse and started out with the rest of the riders, falling in next to Mawer, a man he did like and respect. They talked all the distance, a conversation he would not have been able to recall if his life had depended on it.

The company arrived at their destination, a cool glade, green with new grass and a fresh overhang of leaves. A spring made a clear pool, and then wandered away down the sloping ground. They tethered their horses near the stream, and then the party spread out at the upper end of the glade under the trees near the little pool and ate and drank companionably in the warm afternoon.

Elfwina sat in half-shade. With her pale yellow mantle about her head and body, she looked draped in sunshine. She was placidly watching Aedred where he stood a distance away down the slope, talking with Wulfric and Aldhune. Still farther down the gently sloping ground, Lady Ella was sitting gracefully on the grass, smiling at Grundl. He sat in a casual posture, one leg drawn under him, the other raised, his forearm resting on the knee. His elbow braced his body; the hand spread in the grass. His head was tilted thoughtfully down. For the first time, Elfwina saw him as someone more than a form representing security. She suddenly realized he was quite attractive. Not handsome, but his appearance compelled a need to look beyond the scarred features and see what lay within the warm, quiet eyes. She saw Lady Ella was doing this, and Grundl, like a large and powerful beast held captive for the moment, was allowing it.

Mawer, Leodwald, and Ladies Godgifu, Osthryth, and Hildelith were performing an elaborate and fluid dance of advance and retreat. Elfwina watched with amusement, and then glanced toward the edge of the glade and saw Mildthryth, speaking in a soliloquy, it seemed, until Edward's green figure, invisible at first against the background of shadowed woods and grassy slope, emerged as he turned and the sunlight illuminated his head.

All dressed in green, my love,
My love all dressed in Saxon green . . . .

The song came to her as clearly as if a piper stood at the edge of the glade. She drew her breath.

Aedred appeared in front of her. "I've been trying to get to you all afternoon," he said. He sank down with a contented sigh and put his head in her lap. "Look at that sky," he told her.

She looked up and saw the green leaves standing freshly against the cobalt sky. Just above the western canopy of trees, a few shredded clouds tended eastward, their edges softened with dove grey. A kestrel held the air for a moment, and then slid away over the treetops.

"Listen," he said softly, "the beauty's not only in the sky . . . ."

The sound of laughter drifted up the hill. Laughter and teasing, frivolous banter, shifts and eddies of human voices mingling with the cascading notes of a nearby bird. A slight breeze dropping down from the heights that bore the clouds, hissed pleasantly through the grass. Aedred's voice identified the theme and wound a minor key through it. "Do you think it will ever be possible to have afternoons like this that aren't stolen in the trances of war?"

She gazed down at him. *I love this good man. He is my husband and my dear friend. But we did nothing wrong. There was no harm.* "It does seem as if there has never been a time when there wasn't either war pending or the recent end of a battle." She looked back into the serene afternoon. "Perhaps it's possible. Perhaps it could be accomplished somehow. You accomplished it for a while."

They looked on the scene in companionable silence. Then Aedred said, "Edward made a curious remark this morning before you came."

Her heart turned over. "Oh? What was it?"

"It was in answer to a comment Gyrth made to the effect that Edward, A West Saxon, knew more about the terrain of Mercia than the Mercians did. We'd had a friendly disagreement about routes in and out of Ceolworth. Edward brought his map to prove his contention, which was valid, and Gyrth wondered how that could be. It was Edward's answer that struck me."

"And that was . . . ?"

"It followed his old arguments. He said he didn't think of himself as a West Saxon or a man bound to a single kingdom, but that he felt himself a man of Angelcynn and on that basis claimed the island as his own. It was too boldly stated for the occasion."

Elfwina was astonished. Edward's long-standing theory that the many kingdoms should one day be united under one ruler was no secret. He and Aedred had debated the issue for years, but always in abstract terms. As a debate topic it was acceptable, but in the context in which this remark had been made there was the suggestion Edward saw himself as that ruler. It was not like him to speak so incautiously. She carefully replied, "Did you respond?"

"Hell, yes! I could hardly let that pass without comment, since the silence following it was heavy as a rock. But I wasn't quite sure about the reason he spoke as he did, so I let him know the statement was full of thorns and left it open for him to explain."

"And did he?"

"He turned it into a joke. But drunk as Leodwald was he wouldn't hold it that way, and there very nearly was a collision over it. Edward can be stupidly tactless." His laugh was humorless. "If he survives long enough to rise to the throne himself, his view will change and damn quick. It's one thing to mouth off about a united country under one ruler when you're a prince; it's a totally different perspective when you're a king that might be deposed." He frowned at the sky.

"You don't really think he was suggesting he would take over Mercia, do you?"

"No, but he needs to watch his mouth."

"You know Edward."

"Oh, yes, I know Edward!"

She rubbed her fingers over his eyebrows. "This is not what you want to think about on this beautiful afternoon."

He smiled then. "No, it's not." He was quiet for a moment. "Is anyone looking this way?"

She glanced around. "No."

"Lean down and kiss me."

The witty conversation with Mildthryth had gone on joined now by Wulfric and Aldhune and one of the court women. Edward had stepped back, free now to move away. He saw that Aedred was with Elfwina, his long legs stretched out in the grass, his ankles crossed, perfectly at ease with his head resting in her lap. He watched as she leaned down to kiss him and jealousy flared inside Edward with a violence so intense he staggered. It was there, and then it was gone. He swung around and stared blindly into the deep shadows of the wood, sickened by what he had found in himself.

Aedred sat up and turned to his wife. "I'm not too happy with the arrangement I've made to stay in the camp," he said to her. "I hardly see you at all. I'd come up to the hall tonight, but I've some business with Grundl that will probably take most of the evening. And then tomorrow night there's something else--" He raised his hand in a gesture of resignation. "I really am disgusted, you know." He looked disgusted.

She smiled at him, not daring to say anything.

"I'll try to get up there sometime tomorrow morning. Will you be free?"

"I am sorry. There are some things scheduled." She felt wretched, realizing in a panic, she did not want to lie with him.

"Maybe in a few days, then . . . ." He gave her a wistful smile.

She looked away to hide her misery. Her gaze moved down the slope to Lady Ella and Grundl. He was rising now. He stretched out his big hand to help her to her feet. Their fingers lingered together and then parted. They began to stroll through the glade.

"I've decided on something," Aedred said, as he watched the two figures move in and out of the shadows. "I'm making Grundl an eorl."

"That's wonderful, Aedred! Oh, I agree with that!"

"I told him about it back at the camp before we left." His eyes glittered. "I know it was a shock, but he didn't show it. I wanted to see a reaction, but the big bastard wouldn't give it up." He reseated himself so they were side by side. They gazed down on the fluid groupings of the party.

"I really am glad you're doing this."

"He deserves it, doesn't he? He gives Penwahl the full credit for saving me from the Danes before Edward showed up, and the Gods know I am grateful to poor, brave Penwahl, but it was Grundl who protected me when Penwahl fell. It's not the first time Grundl's stood for me. And after all these years, I'm just realizing his talents. So! We'll thrash it all out tonight, and then make it formal." He smiled at her. "I'd like a feast for him tomorrow night. Can you manage it on such short order? These days there seems no appropriate time for anything."

"Yes, we can do it."

"Good!" He looked immensely pleased.

"You are a good king, Aedred. A good and generous king."

The sudden deep warmth in her voice flustered him. He said off-handedly, "Aren't I!"

Because she knew his manner well, she smiled in a way that let him know he had not fooled her. They both began to laugh, adding to the bright magic of an afternoon between wars.

Chapter Fifty-Four

[829] Ceolworth, Mercia. "And these are the boundaries," Aedred said. "Fifty surrounding hides added to your holdings in Weardburh." Aedred took his chair again and sat looking up at Grundl.

The torch light flickered briefly up the walls of the tent, and then steadied. Grundl was leaning over the map Aedred's clerk had made up earlier that evening, his hands spread in two big fans at the edge of the parchment. He shook his head slightly. "Sire--" he began and stopped.

Aedred sat watching this struggle, one curled finger pressed against his lips.

"Things are happening very fast, Sire. This--"

Aedred waited, and then because Grundl seemed stuck again, he pushed on. "The food-rents normally due me will pass to you. I reserve the right to levy the fyrd, which you would command, and to exact repairs of bridges and roads and the burh fortifications just completed. You will keep a third of all taxes you collect. I think that covers it."

"I see."

"And I would command your loyalty," Aedred added quietly, watching his face.

Grundl straightened abruptly. "Sire! Loyalty is all I truly have to give you! And I give it freely, as I have these past many years."

"Indeed you have, Grundl; well-said. So, now. You agree to all this then, do you?"

"Yes--I--yes, Your Majesty."

"Then I'll have a charter drawn up, which we'll both sign tomorrow with my council's approval and witness."

He walked with Grundl out into the night. For a few moments they stood breathing the night air, looking out at the watch fires and listening to the familiar camp sounds: a cough, an interrupted snore, a quiet conversation somewhere in the darkened tents, the stomp and restless neigh of a horse.

"There'll be a feast tomorrow night at the hall for you, Grundl." Aedred slapped him on the back. "Wear your finest," he said, and then he laughed. "I'll put you up against Mawer any day, Eorl Grundl. Any day."

In a fine humor, Aedred watched Grundl walk off toward his quarters, a huge and looming shape that disappeared into the dark geometry of the camp.

Edward had been profoundly ashamed of his jealousy of Aedred. In his distress, he had told Elfwina, revealing it as he sat with his head bent, his shoulders slumped. She had watched him with great compassion, being aware all the time of how vibrant and immediate he seemed in his Saxon colors, how fantastic, in his forest-green mantle and tunic, the green hose and gold banding. Again the song ran at the edges of his low voice: *All in Saxon green, my love . . . .*

"I love Aedred--" he had not been able to finish his words. After a time, he said roughly, "He *is* the brother of my heart. But this terrible feeling . . . . I don't understand it!"

She fell to her knees and spread her hands over his. "I know you love Aedred. We both love him. But don't you see? What we have is separate and apart from the love we have for Aedred. There is no reason for you to feel jealous of him."

She pressed his face, and he raised his eyes to her. "No reason," she repeated.

"Yes," he said. "Yes, you're right. It is a separate world. And there's no harm to him. That jealousy--I smothered it quickly. I don't feel it now."

"No, I knew it was a momentary thing."

He touched her face and murmured, "You were mine long before Aedred."

"Yes."

He smiled. "That separate world--it was our kingdom. Remember? Yours and mine."

Her lips parted in a deep breath as a little shock ran through her. He took her hands and kissed the fingers, and then he pulled her up and into his arms.

They lay together as they had the night before; coiled together, learning textures of their flesh with innocent fingers, speaking as if one were inside the brain of the other where there could be no secrets, no omissions. The deep sense of peace Edward had felt the night before returned, that freedom which opened him to a miraculous understanding of himself, of her; that release from the unsatisfied wanting.

A faint change in the density of the night framed in the window was a signal. Edward stirred. "It's nearly dawn," he whispered.

They slowly drew apart, a mystic sorting out. Whose flesh was whose? He raised himself on his arm and looked down at her, at her breasts, her soft, flat belly, the line of her hips and legs, faintly luminous, dawn focusing in this pearly form, night still reigning at her cloudy head.

She tucked her head toward her shoulder, the movement, slow, sleepy, like a small animal nuzzling. The smell of her--warm, a mixture of her and him--rose into his nostrils, into his mouth; something he could taste, something dissolving and entering, creating a delicate turbulence, disturbing a balance.

He smiled and leaned down to kiss her forehead, a tender kiss. When she closed her eyes, he kissed the lids softly. And then, what he had not done before, he touched his mouth to hers. She went very still. He hovered, stunned. She spoke his name against his lips; it slid through and touched the back of his throat. He flushed white-hot and went erect. He swayed down on her, his mouth covering hers, diving below the surface, rolling, tasting, suddenly drinking at the well of his deepest longing, his thirst unquenchable. Her arms came around him, her fingers pulling at his ribs, dragging him closer. He was melting like candle wax, pouring down over himself, over her, this dispersion of the million particles of himself all disconnecting and sinking into her body. His chest, belly, the bones of his hips, all his flesh burning, adhering to her, becoming one flesh, immersion, something . . . killing him. Their hearts stopped and in starting up again took on a single beat. The signals of their brains fled along one nervous system in their perfect joining.

He was changed forever. He had been burned alive, had fallen to ashes, and had been recreated whole out of her fiber, the scaffolding of her bone. And now, as Edward rode through the lightening air of the morning toward the camp, joy spiraled up in him, and it was so exquisite he began to cry. He stopped his horse. Bending forward in the saddle, he buried his face in his hands and wept.

Every aspect of her life had been woven by Edward's hand. His presence had been the heavens surrounding it. She could not have denied him. And now he had wrenched her from her boundaries and in that terrifying freedom she had embraced the sun.

Grundl appeared at Lady Ella's door at daybreak, with no apologies and no explanation until she pulled it out of him.

Her thegnestre, hastily arisen, admitted Grundl into the small anteroom and told him to stay there. Lady Ella had awakened immediately at the rumble of his voice and started to get out of bed but changed her mind. "Any clue?" she asked her thegnestre, who was a kinswoman and confidant.

"It's hard to tell from his features."

"It's sure to be something unusual or he wouldn't be here, not at this hour. Prop me up, will you? I'll receive him from my bed. I may as well be comfortable."

She heard Grundl rattle restlessly in the other room and stifled a laugh. "Go on, go on," she whispered. "Bring that extraordinary man here. And then you go back to bed." She added, "And stay there until I call you."

"I don't have much time," he said, when the handmaid had left.

"Why?" She sat up quickly. "Are the Danes upon us?"

"No," he said with astonishment. "Would I be here if they were?"

"I don't know. Why *are* you here?"

He looked at her in distress, his hands on his knees. "There is no one else I can go to in this circumstance."

"Great Mother, what have you done?"

"I'm not sure. I think I might have been too good at warfare." He looked worried now, and sank into his own thoughts.

She waited. When his meditative silence lengthened, she threw herself impatiently back against her pillows. "Grundl!"

He looked up at her. "King Aedred is making me an eorl tonight, and I don't know what I'm supposed to do."

Her mouth flew open. "An eorl! Grundl! But that's marvelous. How very wise of the king. Congratulations!"

He nodded his head. "Yes. But what am I supposed to do at this feast tonight? I've seen these things go on over the years, but there was no need for me to notice the form, never expecting to be in this situation myself. If I had, I might have watched more closely. But I was a body guard, and how many body guards can expect to become an eorl?

"He said to wear my finest but, as I live, Lady Ella, the finest I have is what I wear from day to day--the garments I've always worn in the king's service. They're to the purpose, but no one would call them fine. And when do I stand? And when sit?" He put his head in his hands and cried out miserably, "And am I to make a speech?"

She looked at him with fondness, pity, and a dash of wry amusement. "Does this seem insurmountable now, Grundl? I can assure you, it's not."

Hope glimmered briefly in his posture, and then he slumped forward again.

"Look, my dear," she said kindly, "we can dispense with one thing right away--I'll see to it you have the proper clothes to wear. Is that understood?"

"How can you--?"

"I will do it. Now, the next thing--you must be yourself. Behave perfectly Grundl and everything will go beautifully. After all, the king is doing this because of who you are--a person who is honorable, loyal, and reliable. You are acceptable to him and that's what matters. So be yourself, and you will feel quite easy tonight."

"Who else could I be," he said dejectedly.

"It will be all right, truly."

He remained staring unhappily at the floor.

"Oh, dear. Shall we talk about form?"

He grunted.

"It varies from court to court, of course, but from what I've seen and what I know of Aedred's court, he really doesn't care much for formality, although if he told you to dress that probably means he and the queen will wear their crowns."

He was listening intently, and she felt like going over and kissing him, but she also thought that if she could ease his mind about the ceremony, he might be receptive to spending an hour or so in her bed. Offering that reward to herself, she continued her instruction.

"Since the king doesn't emphasize formality, I think he would get the ceremonies over with early so we can feast." She gave him a smile meant to be comforting within its amusement. "You're less likely to suffer indigestion."

She could tell by his look he had taken her seriously. "So . . . you will be at the hall on time, in your finest, looking terribly splendid. Now, more or less, this is the way it will go--I may have it out of order, but these things I mention are always part of the ceremony. The king and queen will enter. You'll be seated across the table directly in front of them because you are the guest of honor. You needn't do anything at this stage but bow and murmur politely.

"At some point, mead will be passed around, and I caution you not to drink more than one cup. If you take more than that you may run the risk of making a supreme ass of yourself. Later you may drink as much as you like. Everyone expects a newly minted eorl to make an ass of himself after the ceremonies are over."

She paused, but he was silent, his gaze not moving from her face.

"So," she continued, "most of this time will be taken up by the king saying wonderful things about you. You must endure it with good grace. Soon after, the king will start giving you gifts. I have no idea what they'll be, but to everyone they'll represent the regard in which he holds you. This is always the most interesting part for the spectators. Everyone is calculating what a new eorl's elevation will be."

"I've never liked that idea," Grundl told her with a heavy frown. "A measure shouldn't be put to generosity."

An inveterate calculator herself, Lady Ella felt a twinge. "Nevertheless, it's a game played at these affairs."

"Not by me."

"You *are* a paragon."

"I try to be an honest man."

She smiled. "Yes, I know. You're very successful at it."

He basked a moment in that smile. "Lady Ella?"

"Yes?"

"I want to kiss you."

She straightened. "Do you! Come ahead."

He got up from the chair, walked over to her, kissed her passionately, and returned to his seat. Laughing, she shook her head. "That was very nice."

"What I want more is to bed you, but I have to get this off my mind first."

"Then let's get it over as quickly as possible. In the meantime, you could take your clothes off and get in here beside me. You can learn as easily here as you can over there."

When he was comfortably established against a mass of pillows and was discreetly holding her hand on top of the covers, she continued.

"If he gives you a gift you can put in front of you on the table, do so. If not, if it's a horse, for instance, have one of your ceorls there to lead it away--you're looking distressed. What's the matter?"

"I don't have any ceorls."

"None at all?"

"Why would I have ceorls? I'm a warrior."

"Don't worry. I'll take care of it. There'll be one or two men at your call. They will know what to do." She put her hand over his. "We're moving along. How do you feel about all this, so far?"

He let out a sigh. "Much better." He gave her a rare smile that transformed his face. "You are very good to me, Lady Ella."

"Am I?"

"You're wise about many things. I'm not very knowledgeable about anything but war." He smiled again, and her shoulder melted against his. "They stand me against the wall between battles."

"How charming you can be."

He kissed her again with great ardor. When she found they were sinking down into the bed, she said breathlessly, "One thing more about the ceremony, Grundl, and then we can concentrate on this."

"All right." He pulled them both back to the pillows. "I forget what you told me last."

"That you will be given gifts. Possibly the final gift will be your arm ring. As I said, the order varies. At any rate, when the last gift is given, then it will be time for your speech of gratitude and fealty."

He dropped back against the pillows and lay staring up at the ceiling. "I knew there'd have to be a speech!"

"It's not difficult, Grundl. All you have to do is lavishly praise the king and promise fealty to him. You won't have any trouble doing that, will you?"

"*Yes!* How do I say it? You tell me to praise him, but how do I go about it? What words do I use?"

She took his hand. "Tell me about King Aedred. What do you admire about him? What is there about him that's made you serve him so faithfully for so long?"

"I love him. He's my sovereign."

"That's not the whole answer, though. *Why* do you love him? What is special about him that makes you feel this way?"

Grundl was silent for a long time. "He's the finest warrior in Mercia. Astride a horse, no one can match him. His leadership can't be matched. Not even his father could command as well as he does. I trust him completely."

She nodded encouragingly.

He thought some more. "I've never seen a braver man."

"Ah," she said.

"Brave . . . and willing to stand for his men down to the last old ceorl. And there is not a man anywhere in Angelcynn who is as fair. He never makes a judgment until he has heard all sides. When the judgment is made, it is carried out. You can depend on his word. If he says it, he will do it. He is not afraid of what other men think, whatever their rank. He's a virtuous man. He doesn't mouth one thing in public and do another in secret. He is faithful to everyone who places their faith in him."

Lady Ella listened to all this in amazement. *He really could be talking about himself. Can I possibly live up to a man this virtuous? He has selected those things most esteemed by him. From what I've observed, Aedred also has a bawdy sense of humor and enjoys women, while staying faithful to his queen. The king has a temper, and I think he could be dangerous. Grundl would only be dangerous on a battlefield . . . .*

Grundl was looking expectantly at her.

"That is what you'll be saying tonight, only a little more flowery, to fit the style of these occasions. You have a marvelous speaking voice. You'll have them in thrall. Now, we'll go through this again, and I'll show you how to arrange it."

They went over the speech several times, Lady Ella becoming so fascinated by what was emerging that she completely forgot their earlier agreement until Grundl firmly and ardently put an end to the rehearsal.

Chapter Fifty-Five

[829] Ceolworth, Mercia. Elfwina had just finished dressing when Aedred came in dusty and sweaty and full of apology. She turned toward him, her head lifting, the light flashing along the delicately worked gold of her crown. He stopped dead and stared at her. "How is it after all these years you can still take my breath away?"

A soft groan barely moved her throat as she looked at him. The deep red of her overdress reflected on her cheeks, belying her pallor. Beneath the overdress the heavily embroidered gown beamed a vibrant purple, the folds of the skirt just touching the floor; the purple sleeves hung long and full. The ensemble was cumbersome, hot, and weighty for her to wear, but she looked magnificent.

"There is no woman on earth like you," he said, coming closer to stand gazing at her. He suddenly wrinkled his face. "I'd kiss you, but I'm worse than my grand pig. I just came in to tell you I'll be as quick as I can."

"You have time. Has Grundl and the others signed the charter?"

"Yes, and I had him measured for his arm ring. He seems a little overwhelmed by all this."

"You may be surprised."

"By what? Do you know something I don't?"

She adjusted the folds of her gown. "Lady Ella took him in tow. She's training him in deportment and will see he's dressed appropriately."

"Damn! I didn't think about that. The poor fellow must have been in a state."

"At first. Lady Ella calmed him down."

"It usually works the other way with her, doesn't it?" He laughed. "She's gifted, but strikingly forward. I thought she had Edward, but he's an eel, and I've heard she's just as slippery. Too bad, they made a handsome pair."

"She's not a Christian."

"She might have switched." He was teasing her.

"She's interested in Grundl--seriously interested."

"Is she!" A smile flickered. During long campaigns he'd seen the blankets rise in the early morning over Grundl's hnocc, and he thought he knew the locus of her interest. "Well, let's hope it's a satisfaction to them both. The man's not used to women as sophisticated as Lady Ella. I don't want him moping around on a battlefield."

"Do you think that would happen?"

"It's hard to say what a man will do over a woman." He retracted.

"No, he's too damn level-headed to fall apart over a love affair." He looked at her with a suddenly warm expression. "You glow, Elfwina. You dazzle me."

She looked away.

"The gifts," he said. "Did Ceolric get those arranged?"

"Everything is ready. You've been quite generous."

"When everyone starts tallying, I don't want them to find Grundl short."

"You do love, Grundl, don't you?"

"Yes, I do. The man is absolutely faithful to me--total, unqualified faithfulness. I should have made him an eorl a long time ago. He will sit at my right hand, you know."

"Yes, I thought that you might do that."

He put up his hands. "If I'm going to complete the process, I'd better get dressed."

She waited for his return, numbly, sitting on an upholstered bench, her skirts in careful folds around her body, her eyes on the grain in one of the broad planks of the floor, a figure which seemed to suggest a solitary bird with outstretched wings.

Aedred's voice spoke briefly in the corridor, and she rose as he swept in from the anteroom. He came to stop before her, his purple mantle settling in a graceful drape around his body. He wore a dove-grey gown that reached to his ankles, his ceremonial sword with the gold hilt and gold decorated scabbard hanging at his side, the gold repeated in his treflèd crown and in the long scepter in his hand.

Her lips parted in a quick breath.

"Well?" He spread his arms, holding the gold scepter out from his body.

"You look . . . heroic."

"Merefin thought so too." He leaned close and kissed her gently. Then slipping his arm around her, he kissed her again. He held her arm with an easy grip as he propped the scepter against a chair. He took her by the shoulders. "When the damned Danes settle in for the winter, I want us to go to the vill at Thornwald--just the two of us, no retainers, and no servants beyond what is absolutely necessary. We'll have no interruptions, no guests, and no wars to keep us from each other. Would you like that?"

Surprised by what was an entreaty made with no surety of the answer, she said, "If you want to spend the winter at Thornwald, of course we'll go." But she noted that Edward was purposely excluded, and that made her uneasy.

"Good! That's what we'll do. Well, are we ready to put Grundl through his noble paces?"

The eorls, all gorgeously dressed and gleaming with silver

armament, waited for them in the corridor. They bowed as the royal couple came through the door, and then fell silently in behind them. The company moved slowly down the staircase as the whole glittering assembly below came to its feet.

With motionless lips and the low voice he used on these occasions, Aedred said to her, "Look at Grundl! Just look at the man!"

She was looking. The crowd had opened all the way to where Grundl stood in solitary magnificence near the table.

Earlier in the day, Lady Ella had appealed to Elfwina for help in finding a suitable garment for Grundl, and together they had hit on the white silk piece Elfwina had embroidered. She gave it as a gift to Grundl, and Lady Ella carried it swiftly away to be made into a garment for him.

Now he waited in this garment with great composure, the jewels sparking in the eyes of the silver and gold beasts spiraling up the front of the tunic and around the neck. His mantle was white, as were his trousers and bandings. His hair looked burnished, and his beard had been fashionably forked. He wore no weapons and, knowing what gifts he was to be given, Elfwina suspected Aedred had sent word for him not to wear his own. But Grundl, even without weapons looked every inch an eorl.

"By the Gods . . . !" Aedred breathed.

In a group standing farther down the table, Lady Ella gave herself away only by the shining of her fabulous eyes.

The king and queen moved through the channel of people, who dipped and rose as they passed. They reached the dais, erected for this occasion, and took their seats facing the crowd. The guests seated themselves at the benches. Grundl turned so he stood before the king.

Raising his gold scepter, Aedred called out, "*Hwæt!*" and when the crowd grew quiet, he addressed Grundl in a formal manner.

"Grundl, son of Edgar the Tall, faithful shielder of the king, you've stood many an hour at our shoulder in this hall. While we took our leisure and our ale with our good companions, you kept a quiet guard, watchful through the night so no harm would come on us unaware. All could see, but few noticed, you were such a skillful shadow. But as a shadow announces a presence in a stream of light, so your presence announced our safety to those who might have had a wicked intent. . . ."

He is so good at this, Elfwina thought, as she looked out at the attentive faces. Edward sat beside Mawer. Because he had given his diadem to the villagers, he wore no band, but jewels flashed in the wide collar of gold that encircled his neck and lay partway down his chest. The royal blue of his mantle reflected brilliantly in his eyes as he lifted his head and found her gazing at him.

"Yet, for all of this," Aedred continued, "a man's true worth can be told on the battlefield in the sweep of a sword and the whisper of a spear. Your own face, Grundl, attests to your courage and each scar tells a singular bravery . . . ."

Grundl stood in an agony of discomfort, sweating, but with the sweat being absorbed by the undergarment Lady Ella had insisted he wear. He was glad of it, for the fine silk tunic would have been drenched. He listened intently to the king, astounded at what he was saying about him before all the company. He had not imagined the ceremony would be like this. The king was speaking a long list of deeds which were true--he had performed them--but when recounted by the king, they took on an aspect he himself would never have given them. He was a warrior, and these were the things warriors did. In the recounting, the king was specific. He created a string of pictures for the listeners, some humorous that made them laugh, but never at Grundl, only at the situation which Grundl always rescued.

His discomfort grew. Uncomfortable as he was it would have surprised him to learn that outwardly he appeared calm and attentive, with a great natural dignity in his bearing, his glistening face only enhancing his rough features.

Aedred was saying, "All these incidents and more we've not related would have made you an eorl. But one stands out above all. In Weardburh, we were surrounded by an overpowering force. Many brave Mercians were struck down. Among them, our own dear Penwahl, that brave eorl, died defending his king." Aedred's voice shook. He paused, took a breath, and then went on. "We lay gravely wounded. You stood over us and held off the rush of warriors that would have ended our life. When help arrived, and the Danes fell back, you pulled the spear from our side and with your own hands staunched the blood . . . ."

It was the first time Elfwina had heard the actual events of his wounding, and she turned to look at him as he spoke in the deep silence of the hall. She felt a sudden, overwhelming guilt.

Edward looked toward her and knew what she was thinking.

Aedred stood, and everyone in the hall came to their feet. He placed his scepter in its stand and beckoned Grundl to the dais. Eorl Aldhune came up with a folded cloth and presented it to the king and then stepped away.

"Hold out your arm, Grundl." He opened the cloth and lifted out a wide gold bracelet with a lip sculptured to deflect a weapon. Aedred opened the hinges, closed the large ring on Grundl's upper left arm, and slipped in the gold hinge pin. Then Aedred drew his sword and sat back down, his feet flat on the floor, the sword lying across his thighs. Grundl knelt and, resting his forehead on the king's knees, gripped the blade with both hands.

"The king wills it," Aedred pronounced. "You are in fact what you are in truth--Grundl, Eorl of Weardburh."

Grundl stood again. There was a rustle of movement as everyone took their seats. Aedred gazed calmly at Grundl who looked down.

For a breathless moment, Lady Ella thought he had forgotten what to say. But no, in his deliberate way, he was only collecting his thoughts. His deep voice rolled out in a low vibration.

"Gracious Majesty, lord of eorls, ring-giver to men, you have praised my exploits and given me great honor by the love you have shown me. In your service I did, indeed, stand behind your right shoulder. I saw from there all that men are and the show of what they would like to be. But you, gracious lord, exhibited your public integrity through all the years and through all events, great and small, and I saw with my own eyes this public statement was also your private creed.

"You never waver in your commitment to your people. You are generous and faithful to those who are your friends and your subjects, and relentless and uncompromising with your enemies. There never was a more courageous leader of men, or a more wise and just king. Those things you have found to praise in me were learned and practiced through your good example. Before you and this company, I swear my fealty to you. I will serve you faithfully and well for as long as I shall live and breathe the air of Mercia."

There was a long, swelling uproar that was both approval and the collected astonishment of men who had known Grundl for years. Aedred rose and went laughing tearfully from the dais to embrace Grundl. Knowing the strength of her husband's emotion, Elfwina went down to stand beside him.

"Hwæt!" Aedred called out again, and there was surprised silence. "Eorl Grundl, from this time forward you will sit at my right hand."

It was the ultimate gift for an eorl. A buzz of excitement spun through the guests. From out of nowhere the thought came very clearly to Elfwina: *One day this eorl will be a great man*. She gazed at him in the wonder that comes with presentiment.

Seated now at Aedred's right hand, Grundl was hugged and pounded by well-wishers, until Elfwina was certain he would be black and blue. Aedred leaned against him, his arm around the big man's neck, as his subjects honored the new eorl.

The cupbearer came to Elfwina, and she drew Aedred back to inform him. He nodded.

Elfwina came to her feet. Taking the king's cup, she returned it filled with mead. "Drink this, Sire, in celebration of another good companion added to the many who serve you in love and loyalty."

Aedred drank from the cup and winked at her over the rim. Another cup was handed to her, one chased with gold over the silver bowl. The cupbearer filled it with golden mead.

"Eorl Grundl," she said, offering him the cup, "Take this vessel made with precious metals; drink in good health and prosperity." When he hesitated, she smiled at him. "Take it, Eorl Grundl, and drink. The cup is yours."

Looking into her eyes, he reached for the cup and his big fingers rested on her hand. In that instant, the pupils of his eyes expanded, opening to her the warmth and its long guarded meaning in their depths. Stunned, she let her fingers slid away.

When he had emptied the cup, she signaled, and a woman came forward with a cloth and gently shook out the folds. An appreciative sigh swept down the table. It was a mantle of fine russet wool so cleverly interwoven with gold threads it shimmered as if it had been spun of bronze.

"A garment worthy of you, bold Eorl Grundl, with a clasp that suits it; its teeth will hold through any conflict." She laid the clasp in his hand. It was of bronze, a simple design, but in its simplicity, elegant. As he listened to her, his eyes retained their natural warmth, but without suggestion, and she wondered if she had really seen that honesty. But the gentle remainder in his eyes still warmed her skin. "Wear these, good eorl, and please us." She returned to her seat.

Aedred raised his eyes to Ceolric, who stood nearby. Ceolric nodded, and a servant stepped forward with a gleaming byrnie. An audible murmur rumbled up and down the table as the warriors appraised the bright interlocking chains of metal forming the tunic. The servant laid it on the table in front of Grundl. Aedred smiled with pleasure as Grundl's big hand briefly stroked the mail.

"Now," the king said, "you must stand."

Grundl came up from the bench. A man approached him with a long sword lying across his outstretched hands. It was an old weapon of beauty and service, with a bronze hilt. Grundl took it by the grip and felt it fit his hand like the hand of an old friend. "Sire--" he began, but Aedred, smiling, shook his head.

The scabbard was brought up and put around Grundl's waist. He slipped the point to the etched leather and pushed it home. Grundl took his seat again.

Aedred told him, "This next is a work of art and balance."

A spear was brought forward. Made to the new eorl's size and grip, the shaft was of the finest fire-hardened ash. The point had been honed by a craftsman and balanced to a breath. Runes were inscribed on its surface. "A spear is what you most favor," Aedred said. "This one should truly bear the name *Dane-Skewer*."

There was a deep rumble of laughter from down the table. It was Mawer. And all who had been in the gathering that day when Grundl had challenged him to the horn, joined in. Aedred was laughing, too. With a slow smile, Grundl said, "*Dane-Skewer* it will be."

At that moment, there came a clattering from outside. The great doors to the hall were swung wide, and five grooms, each leading a horse, moved forward across the floor. There was a startled cry of envy and appreciation from the crowd. All the horses were large but their gaits were nimble and spirited. The first was a magnificent roan with leather tack polished against the elements. It was obvious the most skillful leather maker had constructed the saddle and bridle. The next three horses were all sound and well-trained with intelligent eyes and calm behavior. The last horse brought several of the thegns to their feet to get a better look. It was a chestnut stallion with a flowing mane and tail and a gait suggesting power and speed. It had been outfitted with a bridle adorned with brass and a gleaming saddle that matched the color of the horse.

Grundl turned to the king, and the look they exchanged left Aedred beaming. "Eorl Grundl," he said in a rich, vibrant tone, "accept all these gifts, for you are a brave and faithful friend to a king who holds your loyalty as treasure more precious than gold."

Chapter Fifty-Six

[829] Ceolworth, Mercia. At his proclamation, the feast began. The hall servants began carrying in whole roasted animals and fowl, steaming dishes of grain and vegetables, fruit tarts sweetened with honey and dappled with cheese and clotted cream. Aedred remained in his place, giving the honored guest his attention, using all his skill in getting Grundl to laugh frequently, a pleasant rumble that drew Lady Ella's head around with a look of delight.

"Do I recognize the garment Grundl is wearing?" Edward's voice was at her ear.

She turned her head. "Yes."

"It's a beautiful piece of work, Elf. He's spectacular in it."

"It was a surprising transformation, wasn't it? An eorl in hiding all these years."

"Take a turn around the hall with me, will you?"

She rose, and Edward took her arm to guide her out of the crowd into the relatively clear space next to the walls. His hand slid from her arm, and they walked a few steps in silence.

"Grundl's taking on the role with style," Edward said. "He looks more the part than any of the others, except for Wulfric, who's not an eorl." He glanced over at her with a smile.

"Aedred is very happy with this."

"I can see that he is."

They fell silent again.

"I haven't seen Ceadda lately," Edward said. "Is he still around?"

"He went to visit Lady Pen."

"Lady Pen?"

"He feels she is grieving too deeply over the loss of Penwahl."

"That doesn't sound like her. She's too sensible to bury herself in that kind of grief."

"No, it doesn't seem something she would do. But others have confirmed it. I thought I might go up and see her myself."

"When?"

"I'm not sure," she answered vaguely. "Soon."

They stopped for a moment to speak with Aldhune, and then continued their slow circuit of the hall. To avoid walking through a group of guests assembled in their path, they passed to either side of one of the huge supporting timbers of the hall. They came together where the great hanging lamp threw a shadow over them.

Edward said, "Wait."

She stopped, and he moved her backwards into the deeper shadows. He touched her face. "Am I dreaming? Are we lovers?"

She shook her head and cried in a low voice, "The runes have come true."

"The runes? I don't--"

"The runes said I would wear a second crown. You said, Our kingdom. It is a *Saxon* crown. And the spear of Aedred's rune is poised at his heart."

"Don't talk this nonsense!" He calmed the sudden black fear rising through him, and touched her cheek again. "Don't talk like this," he said more gently. "Not now. Not when we've finally been truthful with each other."

"It was . . . horribly wrong."

"Stop!" He grabbed her arms, leaning over her trying to expel the fear. "It wasn't wrong." He glanced around, saw no particular notice had been taken of them where they stood in the shadows. But he was wary, the habit of a lifetime. "You said it yourself, we love each other. We always have--"

"What God bound us together this way?" she cried.

He caught her face with his hands, not permitting her to turn away. "Your gods and mine," he whispered savagely. "Bound us by blood. Blood more sacred, more eternal than any marriage."

"Please . . . ."

"You love me--say it, Elfwina. Say it to me now!"

She was shaking her head. "I won't betray him again."

There were people approaching, and she was too agitated. "We'll talk about this. I'll stay here tonight--"

"No!"

He drew back. "No?"

She pressed her hands together in distress. "Aedred may spend the night."

Edward looked away, not seeing anything, not able to think. "All right," he finally said. He took her arm, moving them forward into the light.

They walked along, struggling to maintain a façade, stopping to exchange meaningless words with the guests as they slowly returned to their starting point. Just before they reached the tables, he whispered, "I'll be here tomorrow night." At that moment there was a loud shout of laughter from the benches and a general commotion. They looked around.

"What the hell is that all about?" Edward said. He saw then a space had been made around Grundl and Mawer. They sat on a bench opposite each other, with drinking horns in their hands. A cupbearer stood ready by each of the men.

Aedred was straddling the bench on Grundl's side, and when he saw Edward, he called out, "Where did you get to, Prince Edward?

What wager will you lay on this side? Make it good. Let's hear the evidence of your faith."

Edward felt his sister step away. He turned his head to her. "Tomorrow night," he said.

She nodded, and he turned again to the benches. Walking up to the Saxon eorl, he exchanged a look with him, and then propped his shoe on the bench and crossed his wrists over his upraised knee in a show of casual deliberation. "Eorl Grundl is a good man," Edward said to the king, "and has the volume, but Eorl Mawer has had years of practice. Too bad a fresh eorl is to be outdone at the start of his career--"

"Is this smoke to cover Mawer's retreat? Come on; what's your wager?"

"Give me time. When I know I'm going to win I need a moment to consider the amount of the treasure."

"It will have to be a moment, the game's started. They've already emptied a horn apiece. Come on, come on! Your lack of boldness is holding things up and depressing Eorl Mawer." Aedred swung around to call out to the surrounding crowd, "Look here how Prince Edward stalls." He turned, smiling, back to Edward. "Maybe this will stir you: what is there of mine you'd like of your own? A sword? A horse? Or do you think in grander terms?"

Edward stared at him. The deep circle of onlookers was laughing with the king. "It should have enough value to make it worth the trouble," he answered through numb lips.

"Well, what then? I'm waiting."

Edward took his foot off the bench and straightened. "How's this? You put up a year's feorm from your vill at Donnewich, and I'll do the same with my estate at Leatherhead."

Aedred slapped the table. "Done! Now, men, let's get at it!"

Elfwina had drifted away toward the hearth. Behind her, she heard Edward and Aedred's light bantering in a lull of the noisy crowd. She was nearly overcome by shame at the deception Edward was practicing, and then felt the shame of her own unholy deceit.

Two servants came with a log. For a long time she sat staring at the sparks flying up in the vortex and the flames spreading brightly around the bark.

Suddenly there was a startled whoop from the crowd. She walked back to the guests and found Aedred grasping his heavy crown by his side in one hand and doubled up with laughter. Beside him, Edward was roaring, his head thrown back.

Both Grundl and Mawer were lying senseless on the floor. Four men were at each of the contenders, trying to lift them. After a struggle, the limp bodies were manhandled to a wide bench and laid down, foot to head. The crowd paraded over. Stumbling with laughter, Aedred pulled Elfwina along with him. Lady Ella was calmly covering Grundl with his new bronze mantle. And so, even in his cups, Grundl looked a splendid eorl.

The hour was late and the conversation subdued. They had laughed themselves out over Grundl and Mawer and the contest which both the king and the prince (and the crowd) had agreed was a draw, since both men had toppled to the floor at the same time. Aedred had given his crown into Ceolric's care and removed the purple mantle. His shoes were off, and he sat with one stocking foot under him, leaning heavily against one arm of his chair. Edward sat across from him, relaxed, his jeweled collar throwing off small brilliant points of light as he breathed. In a dressing gown, Elfwina slowly paced the room. When she passed near Aedred, he reached out and pulled her down onto the padded bench next to his chair. He put his arm around her and drew her head close to his.

"Shall we tell Edward?" he asked her.

Having no idea what he meant, she merely replied, "If you want to."

Addressing Edward, but looking at her, he said, "When the Danes go to ground this winter, we're going to Thornwald." He ran his finger down her cheek. "Just the two of us." Now, he looked at Edward. He leaned back. His hand dropped over her shoulder and rested carelessly on her breast. "We need a respite from everything."

Edward showed interest. "A retreat?"

"Yes, that's it--a retreat. A retreat from the world. Thornwald is a fine place for it. Have you been up there? I don't remember."

"No."

Aedred stared into space. "The snow lies unbroken for miles. There's a sting in the air, and the falling snow lays such a peaceful silence on the night . . . ." His eyes came back to Edward. He laughed and flung the image away. "I've developed a longing for the place. So, that's where we'll spend the winter."

Edward seemed to cordially accept this. "Sounds appealing. Who'll run the kingdom while you're both gone from the world?"

"Well, you've hit on the troublesome aspect of the plan. My administrators will handle things as they normally do, but if an untoward occasion arises, I'll return to the world. I'm hoping it will be a dull winter in Mercia this year. He gazed at Edward. "Where are you going to spend the winter?"

Edward gave him a mild look. "Exeter, possibly London."

"London, eh? The winter there won't be dull."

Elfwina's voice came softly in. "It's only Thrilmilci; who knows what may happen between now and winter that may change all our plans?"

Chapter Fifty-Seven

[829] Ceolworth, Mercia. For the greater part of the day, Elfwina worked with Ceolric on finishing the inventory begun some weeks before. They had been in the low cellar under the hall where barrels of beer and ale and crocks of wine and mead were stored. A servant held a torch for them as Leofgyth made notations and compiled her lists. It was dusty down there and, after a time, cold. Their final count was taken in the underground rooms of the kitchen where the perishable stores were kept. When they were finished they retired to Elfwina's chambers for mulled wine and sat drinking it by the fire while they discussed the inventory.

Under the best possible conditions, they could endure a siege of thirty days, under the worst conditions, eighteen days. The hall would provide sanctuary and sustenance for all living in the hall and the village and surrounding countryside, about 600 people plus most of their animals. They devised a plan. Ceolric was to have a location map of the stores made up by one of the clerks. By the time they broke up, it was evening.

Elfwina stood by the window until the fires of the fading sunset had given way to the watch fires of the encampments to the west and south. A wind had sprung up and the fires laid their flames toward the north in long, twisting blows of glittering embers.

She began to pace, slowly circling the room to stop at the window and look out again toward the west. Edyth entered and started to turn down Elfwina's covers, but she said, "No, I'm not going to sleep here tonight." She looked out toward the west again, then lowered her eyes and turned back into the room.

"If His Majesty comes . . . ?"

"He decided to stay at the encampment. Please go to bed. I won't need anything more tonight."

Edyth silently curtsied.

Elfwina changed into her dressing gown, left her chambers, and walked to the far rooms. A torch burned in its sconce in the wall, and she lifted it out and went through the door.

"Don't be alarmed." Edward's gentle warning came from the darkness beyond the anteroom, but Elfwina started uneasily at his voice.

She walked on into the room and then stood stiffly, the sconce lowered, as she silently watched her brother come toward her.

"I thought it better not to show a light under the door." He took the sconce from her and placed it above the bed. "There were people about."

"Were you seen?"

"Yes, but no one will think anything of it. Come sit down, Elfwina. I want to talk to you."

"You can only stay a few minutes. Then you have to go."

He gazed at her until she looked away. She sat down on the edge of the bed and closed her eyes.

Pulling up a bench in front of her, he said, "You didn't tell me about Thornwald."

"I'd forgotten with . . . everything else."

"It was plain I was excluded."

"I know."

"You'll go with him, then?"

"Of course. You heard him. He needs to get away for a time--" she drew back when he took her hands but didn't try to pull them away. "He hasn't fully recovered from his wound."

Edward looked surprised. "He seems recovered to me."

"He remains . . . unable . . . ." She lifted her hand slightly and looked away.

"And he wants to test it out over the winter at Thornwald?"

"Edward!" Now, she did pull her hands away.

"I'm sorry. That was--I'm sorry."

"He almost died," she said darkly. "No one told me he almost died. He needs time away from all these *endless* preparations for war. *No one* should criticize that."

"He's a king, Elfwina! By birth and by choice. He knows the risks and the responsibilities, and he certainly has reaped the rewards. Can't you see? He doesn't need a holiday; he's separating us."

Her eyes widened. "Why would he do that?" Her hand went to her throat. He reached over and gently took the hand and stilled the fingers.

"He doesn't know anything," he told her.

"Then, why did you--?"

"Maybe he senses something. He's wrapped up in so much hocus pocus." But Edward did not disdain Aedred's uncanny instincts, his involvement in things outside the prince's experience. "He doesn't know anything."

"I won't betray him again."

She had begun to shake, and he sat down next to her. "Come here." He cradled her against his chest. "We can call it betrayal. We can beat ourselves to death with the word. But it doesn't serve Aedred, who doesn't know and will never know if we're careful." He smoothed her hair and let his fingertips slide along her cheek with an increasing pressure that drew her head around to face him. "We've fought this for most of our lives, but it has happened and it is beautiful and I can finally say I love you. That doesn't harm Aedred, does it?" He kissed her softly. "This doesn't harm him, does it? After all the years and the misery, these few moments we have together belong to us and no harm comes to anyone."

The hoof beats woke Grundl, pounding him out of a dream of helplessness and fear, then bringing him to his feet and reaching for his clothes as he recognized the stumbling lope of a horse pushed to exhaustion. He came out of his tent and grabbed up his spear, arriving at the watch fire as the rider, as weary as his horse, was beginning his explanation.

The watchman yielded as Grundl strode up to them. In the firelight, the eorl saw the green Saxon mantle. He said, "Who has sent you?" At the answer, "King Brihtric," Grundl said, "Come with me." And to the watchman, "See to that horse."

He led the courier away from the watch fire and toward the great oak that spread above the king's tent. Inside a light flickered and held. A shadow moved on the wall, and they heard the low murmur of the king's voice.

"It's Grundl, Your Majesty," he called out quietly, "with a courier from King Brihtric."

"Bring him in."

Aedred had also heard the horseman as he lay awake on his pallet. He had heard the hoof beats first at the edge of his thoughts and then as the focus of his attention as he heard the animal falter. He had called out to Merefin to get the lamp. Rising from the bed, he had flung a mantle carelessly around him as the handthegn lit the lamp.

The courier came in and swayed into a bow.

"Get him a chair," Aedred said.

Grundl caught the man, easing him into the chair Merefin quickly placed behind him. The eorl took up a position near the tent flap. Aedred seated himself on a stool, his mantle falling open to his bare chest and belly. He gazed thoughtfully at the courier, giving him a moment to collect himself. The man stared back, his body sagging into itself.

"What is your message?"

The man straightened. "Sire, the message is from King Brihtric. He begs for support as soon as possible. Gryffn's force has been pulled away by an invasion of his coast, and a large force of some forty longships landed on the Severn--"

"When was this?"

"I left early this morning; the events occurred yesterday."

"You've run a swift course."

"Yes, Sire," he replied. "The Danes moved unexpectedly, shifting their numbers so a large section of our army was separated from the main body. Eorl Teownor fell and five of his thegns."

Aedred frowned and raised his eyes briefly to Grundl. "Send for Prince Edward."

Grundl turned immediately and left the tent.

"The king has fallen back to the southernmost edge of the Eardene Forest," the messenger continued. "The men serving Eorl Teownor have fallen into disarray, most of the leaders killed. They're scattered all over between Gloucester and Wincelcumb. The force is advancing on King Brihtric. He thinks he can hold them off for a time, but the Danes have the superior numbers. The king asks that Prince Edward move his force in along the eastern edge of the forest. Their combined numbers would serve to drive the Danes back."

"He wants only Edward's force?"

"Yes, Sire. He strongly feels this movement of the Danes may be a coordinated effort involving an invasion from the north. He says to keep your army in readiness against the possibility."

Aedred sat looking at him thoughtfully, one hand on a bare knee. He glanced up at Grundl, who had come back into the tent. "We're changing that order. Have someone wake the eorls and get our horses. We'll council at Edward's bivouac."

Grundl ducked back out of the tent. The messenger quickly rose when Aedred stood up. "We'll want you with us," the king said. "Go after Grundl and have him get you a fresh horse. From the sound of your arrival, yours must be half-dead."

"Yes, Sire, but he only faltered at the last."

"Go on, then, and get another."

By the time Aedred had quickly dressed, Grundl was having the horses brought up. In a few minutes the eorls were assembling. He gave them a quiet summation. "We'll go to Prince Edward's camp and hold our council there," he told them.

They mounted their horses. Carrying torches, they moved out of the camp, setting out at a trot across the rolling grassland toward the far watch fire of Edward's camp.

"Who goes there?" called the guard. He stood near the fire, his shield raised, his spear leaning against his collarbone.

"The king," Aedred answered, moving his horse into the ruddy light. The eorls came up around him, holding up the torches.

"Sire!" the watchman cried and snapped his spear upright.

"Let us pass to Prince Edward's tent."

"Yes, Sire," he replied, stepping aside. "But Prince Edward is not here."

"Where is he?"

"At the hall, Your Majesty."

Mawer had heard the horses approaching and the watchman's

challenge. He had clearly heard Aedred's answer and the exchange that followed. He leaped from his cot and threw on his tunic.

Aedred had turned in his saddle to look toward the hall. His eyes picked out its dark outline, the surrounding walls, and the lighted gate tower. He turned back. "A late appointment," he said in a neutral tone. "When is he expected back?"

"He's been coming in just before dawn, Sire."

Aedred regarded him silently. The man shifted his weight and stared back.

Mawer's voice boomed out, "Sire! Do you come to see Prince Edward?" He came into the firelight, tousled and barefoot.

Aedred's gaze moved to him. "Yes, but it seems he's at the hall."

"Yes, Sire, I believe he is. Come in. I'll send a man for him. Better yet, I'll go for him myself, right now."

"You'll need your shoes," Aedred said.

Mawer looked down at his feet.

"Tell him there's a war council in his tent." Aedred signaled for the horsemen to follow, and they went on into camp.

As Grundl passed Mawer he saw the anxious expression on the Saxon's face and swung around in his saddle to look at him again. He saw the eorl give a swift, harsh command to one of the men of the watch and then hobble off on his bare feet toward his tent. Grundl turned back around, a slight frown drawing his brows.

Chapter Fifty-Eight

[829] Ceolworth, Mercia. Mawer galloped his horse recklessly along the wide path. He was out of breath far out of proportion to his exertion, hurtling along in the darkness and driven by his anxieties to make a fool of himself before the king. But he didn't know, and he wasn't sure, and there were an infinite number of ways to protect one's lord.

Mawer glanced hastily around the darkened hall. The only light came from the red bank of coals gleaming in the hearth like a malevolent eye. He moved swiftly up the staircase and down the darkened corridor to Edward's chambers. He paused at the door with his fist raised, and then knocked forcefully and called, "Prince Edward! Prince Edward!"

Edward shoved himself backward, twisted away to the side of the bed, and sat there staring toward the dark anteroom, one foot pressed against the floor, the other foot and leg tangled in the covers. He murmured hoarsely, "It's Mawer. Something's happened."

Elfwina rose on one elbow and groped for his arm. "You can't answer. My servants know I'm here."

There was another volley on the door. Edward untangled himself from the bedclothes and got to his feet. Elfwina came up beside him and threw on her mantle.

"Prince Edward!" Mawer knocked again. "It's Eorl Mawer!"

"Damn the man!" Edward grabbed his braccio and quickly drew them on.

"He's going to wake the hall," she told him. "I'll go to the door."

"God damn this!" he grated through his teeth. But he moved back against the wall, while continuing to dress.

Elfwina opened the door to Mawer. His face went blank. "Yes, Eorl Mawer?"

"Ma'am," he saluted her. He kept his eyes on her face, not letting himself look beyond her into the dark interior where he felt Edward's presence as surely as if a door to a burning room had been thrown open. *Holy Mother of God,* he thought in horror. *This can't be!*

He raised his voice so it would carry into the next room. "I have an urgent message for Prince Edward from the king." He hesitated fractionally. "I thought he might be in his chambers. I'm sorry I disturbed you." He bowed, made as if to leave.

"Have you looked for him downstairs?"

"Yes, Ma'am."

"And the chambers on the other side of the hall?"

"I'll go there now." He turned uncertainly.

She said quietly, "What is the message, Eorl Mawer?"

His reply was quick. "The king has urgent need of him at a war council in the southern bivouac."

"A war council!"

"That was the king's message, Ma'am. I don't know any more about it than its urgency."

"Go back to the king, Eorl Mawer. I'll see Prince Edward is found and the message given to him."

Mawer's eyes touched her face, veered off. "Yes, Ma'am," he said, and walked away down the corridor.

When Elfwina came back into the room, Edward had nearly finished dressing. He was seated on a bench, cross-tying his bandings. Elfwina stood in front of him, clutching her mantle around her. "Do you think the Danes have broken through?"

"I don't know. Anything might have happened. I'll find out." He stood up.

"I'd go with you, but--"

"No, not unless Aedred sends for you. We can't risk--"

"Mawer knew you were here."

"I know," he replied grimly, "I could hear it in his voice." He adjusted his weapons and fastened his mantle at his shoulder so his right arm swung free. He put that arm around her.

"Mawer is your friend. This is more than friendship can forgive."

"Don't," he told her. "I'll find out what this is all about and get word to you, if Aedred doesn't."

"I'm going to my chambers. Have word sent there."

He opened the door and glanced down the corridor. The dim light from the stairway was gathered in Elfwina's dark eyes. "I don't know what's going to come out of this, or how long it's going to take. I'll try to be here tonight, but . . . ."

"I know. Please be careful."

He came out onto the wide porch and found Mawer sitting on his horse and holding the reins of another. Edward silently mounted, and they swung away from the hall and through the gate. They struck off down the pathway that curved palely through the black landscape toward the sprawling southern bivouac. Edward glanced at the eorl once or twice, but Mawer was staring straight ahead, his profile stern.

The watch fire blazed up as if new fuel had been added; numerous small fires sprinkled the darkness.

"Everyone's stirring," Edward commented.

Mawer made no reply.

As they neared the area, they could see the horses tethered near the prince's large tent. Figures moved against the glowing walls. Warriors, recognizing something in the air, were finding reasons to linger near the center of activity. Edward entered the tent to find it crowded with his commanders and Aedred and his eorls.

"Ah, Edward," the king said.

The prince angled away from Aedred to a chair vacated for him. "What's going on?" He sat down. Mawer pulled up a stool beside him, and then there was a subtle movement as Edward's men shifted toward him.

"We've just got word that Urm holds your father in durance in the Eardene--"

"What?"

"Here's the way it has gone . . . ."

Edward listened intently. After he asked a few questions of the messenger, he looked over at Mawer. "Cyninges Street and Fosse Way straight to the Eardene?"

"By way of Warwick," the eorl corrected. With the wind at our back, two and a half days." Mawer still did not look directly at the prince.

Edward gazed at him. "All right, then, as you say, by way of Warwick, and we'll pray for a steady breeze." Edward leaned back in his chair and looked about at his commanders. "What's our strength?"

Edbriht of Canterbury replied, "Nine hundred eighty, Sire. Twenty men are down for various reasons."

"All too serious for them to march?"

"Two or three could possibly make it, but the others would give more problems than they'd help."

"We'll leave the whole twenty, then. When they recover they can add strength to the hall force. Horses?"

The horse-thegn answered, "One hundred seventy-five mounts; thirty transport animals."

Edward nodded. "We'll take five wagons that will follow us at their own pace. Let's plan the march . . . ."

Their schedule was devised to move the army at its fastest pace. Edward told his commanders, "I want to be at least sixteen miles from here by evening. We move out in one hour."

He looked at Mawer, who rose heavily and went out of the tent followed by Edbriht and the rest of the commanders. Edward went over to Aedred's chair and stood looking down at him, his hands resting easy on his hips. "I feel uncomfortable about pulling away from Ceolworth now," he said.

"I can levy another thousand, if it comes to that. I've sent word to Cuthred and Aethelred about a possible movement out of the north," he added, anticipating Edward.

"Look, I'm going to send messengers to you once a day, so you'll know what's going on with us. Keep me informed, too, will you? If we lose communication, we're at the mercy of them all."

"I'd planned to do that, Edward."

"I know you'll keep abreast of it, it's just that I've a broad uneasiness--"

"--when you can't control it all?"

Edward was amazed that the mild question reached back to the careless reply he had made to Gyrth about being a man of Angelcynn. Aedred was still rankled by it. The eorls stood curiously silent around the king.

Aedred laughed. "We have that in common, Prince Edward. All the reins have to be between our fingers. But for this exercise, put your energy into the problem at the Severn. Leave the rest to me. Mercian kings have held the Northumbrians to their own territory for centuries. We'll be ready to meet whatever Ædda and Osward have planned for us."

The talk went on from there, more now between the king and his eorls. Held wary by what had just passed, Edward did not mention Elfwina, but instead sat quietly at a small table and wrote a quick note to her. Aedred glanced at him once, but paid no further attention.

Elf, wrote Edward. *The matter here is that Urm has separated the royal army and forced Father's portion to retreat into the Eardene. Aedred will give you the details. A courier brought Father's urgent plea for my army to reinforce him. We will leave within the hour. We'll move as fast as we reasonably can and should reach Father within three days.*

There is no telling the length of the engagement or my participation in it, since time will have to be spent in reassembling the portion under Eorl Teownor that was scattered at his death. Not only good Teownor died, but five of his thegns with him. The Danes have the advantage now. I pray we reach Father in time. I ask God's Gracious Will in preserving Mercia and its rulers and to keep them safe. Until I see you again, Your loving brother, Edward.

Edward sealed the note and sent it by messenger to the hall. Then he went to see how the decampment was progressing. At the end of the hour he had set, they were ready to go.

High above the treetops of the eastern sky, silver light was spreading upward. The Saxon foot soldiers were in a casual order that stretched their numbers back toward the most distant campfires, which were being systematically doused. The horses were gathered in front of the troops. Mawer had already mounted and was holding the rein of Edward's bay gelding. Edward took it from him as Mawer looked away.

Edward lay the rein over his horse's neck, preparing to swing up onto its back, when he heard Aedred call his name. He turned; the king stepped forward and stood face to face with him, looking silently into his eyes. Then he took another step and put his arms around Edward. Taken by surprise, Edward brought up his free hand and pressed it against Aedred's shoulder.

"You be careful," Aedred told him in a harsh voice.

Aedred had pulled the prince's head so tightly against his Edward felt the words vibrate through his cheek bones. He would have replied but did not trust his voice. His eyes filled with sudden tears.

Aedred stood watching as Edward rose away from him and settled gracefully into his saddle. The prince looked all around, saw his men were ready, and gave the signal to march. The horsemen paced slowly by the king, followed by the infantry and finally the wagons. Aedred could feel the vibration of Edward's army long after he had ceased to hear their passing.

Chapter Fifty-Nine

[829] Eardene Forest, Mercia. The march had been uneventful, and by evening of the third day, they had come within five miles of their destination. Edward had sent couriers ahead of his army, informing his father of his progress. The returning couriers had brought the information that the Danes still held their position and had made no threatening moves beyond creating a few skirmishes. Edward had brought his army close enough to the Saxon position that he now believed he could ensure his father's safety. He relaxed from the keen sense of urgency he had felt since he had been made aware of the king's predicament.

At a meal of cold rations, Edward sat down with his commanders, and they went over their plans again. Aedred's messenger arrived with a letter from Elfwina. Edward retired a little distance away and sat down to read it.

Dearest Edward, I have grave misgivings about the withdrawal of Gryffn. It could have been as he said it was: the necessity for a quick response to a force attacking his coast. However, unless there were trusted eyewitnesses to that landing and their numbers, I would be cautious about accepting his account. As a result of Gryffn's despicable retreat, loyal Teownor and his thegns were killed. Yet, through his cunning, Gryffn remains a friend because there was no total Saxon disaster. But he is no friend. I fear treachery. The man is dangerous because his motivations are always unclear.

I beg you to consider what I've said when Gryffn appears again with his willingness to help, which he will surely offer soon.

This letter comes to you with my love and my prayers for your safety and for the safety of our father. Your loving sister, Elfwina.

Edward reread the letter. He hadn't expected an intimate message; it was enough that her hand had written it. She had been succinct and, like she often did, offered a new perspective. He would carry this assessment with him into any future encounter with the Welsh overlord.

He carefully rolled the parchment and tucked it inside his tunic. He rejoined his commanders for a time, then, like the rest of the army, he rolled up in his mantle on a rough piece of ground and slept.

Three hours later, Edward woke instantly at a challenge called out by the watch. Grabbing his spear, he jumped up. Mawer came up beside him, his fair hair tousled and his clothing twisted around his heavy body. In the light of the watch fires, they could see figures in Saxon colors approaching. Edward dropped his spear, buckled on his sword, and walked quickly to where some forty Saxons were grouped to the warmth of the fires.

There were shouts of recognition and greeting when he came up. Edward was astonished; these men were a remnant of Teownor's force. They had been trying to make their way back to the main army, when they stumbled onto Edward's warriors. As they told their story, he was thinking of Elfwina's analysis.

Gryffn, they said, had gotten Brihtric's permission for him to leave, but then had pulled out so abruptly the king had not been able to relay the information quickly enough to save Teownor. The eorl had acted on what he saw as an immediate need to close ranks. In doing so, he shifted away from his own position, creating a momentary break in the line. The Danes wedged in and widened that advantage. As a result, Teownor's army fragmented, and he and the thegns rallying around him were quickly picked off. Brihtric had seen the calamity and had ordered a retreat into the forest where the Danes were reluctant to follow. Clearly resentful of Gryffn's action, Teownor's men were not appeased even after they were told the reason for it.

They were hungry. What food they had eaten had been foraged from the countryside, already well-picked over by the Danes. Edward had rations given to them. Everyone had just settled down when another group of about fifty Saxons appeared, and the previous scene was repeated. By morning, the number of Teownor's men sifting into Edward's camp had increased to seven hundred.

With the morning came the couriers Edward had dispatched the afternoon before. Two men had been sent back with them by Brihtric to quickly guide Edward and his army to their meeting point in the Eardene forest. In a grassy clearing three miles from the force of two thousand Danish warriors on the Severn, Edward met his father with an uneasy heart.

Edward's army halted at the edge of the clearing and settled down to wait. The numbers stretched away through the trees, becoming part of the forest, as suddenly intimate with the play of light among the leaves and dark green shadows as the trees themselves. The clearing was dappled with light filtered through the over lacing branches of ash and beech. Somewhere nearby the blossoms of a linden released its perfume.

Edward paced his horse out into the open area and saw his father move from the deep shadows and approach him. He was shocked by how fatigued the king appeared, by his grim expression, and by the weariness showing in the unsynchronized movements of his body as it adjusted to the motions of the horse.

Edward slowly dismounted, composing himself as he went forward to receive his father's kiss and embrace. He said softly, "You look exhausted, Father."

"I am--I am," the king replied in the same soft manner as his son. Then, more loudly, he said, "Thank you for answering my summons so promptly." He looked over Edward's shoulder and his eyes widened. "Are those Teownor's warriors with you?"

"Seven hundred, Sire. Ready to fight again."

King Brihtric's eyes, heavy with tears, came slowly back to Edward's face.

"Teownor--a great loss." He dragged air through his nostrils. "You know our circumstances. Is everything quiet in the north?"

"Unless there has been a change in the past few hours. The courier you sent to Ceolworth said you felt an attack from the north might be imminent. Aedred acted on it. But we wondered, of course, just what was the reason for it."

"We intercepted a courier. Let's sit down. I'm unsteady . . . ."

Edward leaped to assist his father as he swayed and then recovered himself.

"It's all right--momentary--a lack of sleep."

"Yes," Edward murmured, alarmed. "That can do it."

"I'm all right. Sit down. How is your sister?"

"Fine. Concerned, naturally. I didn't see her directly before we left, but I sent her a note." He glanced up as they were joined by their commanders and Eorl Heafwine, who was commanding the Mercian contingent assigned to Brihtric's force.

"Always good to see another Saxon." Heafwine smiled and sat down in the grass next to Edward.

Brihtric began in a tired voice, "Here is the situation we are faced with . . . ."

After their retreat into the forest, the Saxons and Mercians had thrown up an earthen and timber defense work on the southern perimeter and now faced the Danes across this earthwork.

"Urm has led skirmishes and demanded for us to surrender," Heafwine said. "It was going to be either stand or comply. We hoped you'd arrive in time to weigh the odds in our favor."

Brihtric's idea was to have Edward, in a show of force, come down around the forest's eastern edge to swing around the Danes' right flank as they advanced to the ramparts.

"That plan will still serve, I think," Brihtric said. "And with good Teownor's men we now have a division to attack the left flank. That prospect should give Urm second thoughts on our vulnerability."

There was disturbance at the edge of the clearing. They all looked in that direction and saw a large number of men gathering there. The nearest Saxon and Mercian warriors rose in a defensive posture.

The newcomers were dressed in animal skins and carried bows

and spears. Their legs were bare, but they wore soft leather boots that came halfway up their calves. Their blue hair was long and unkempt and hung in greasy strands around their bearded faces. They glanced at the menacing soldiers but seemed unimpressed.

"It's the Hwicce," Edward said.

His father nodded, gestured, and the protective circle their retainers had quickly thrown up around them opened out. Mawer called an order, and the soldiers pulled in their spears. Seven of the fierce-looking warriors came up to the group. The leader was a man of remarkable ugliness, with a broad pitted face and one white and rolling eye.

"Take a seat with us, Baldan," Brihtric told him. "The grass is reasonably comfortable."

The man scraped Edward with his stony eye in acknowledgement, sat easily down on his haunches, saying, "War provides humble accommodations."

Brihtric laughed. "We would be the first to agree. We accommodate ourselves on your territory, but only briefly, we hope."

"We have observed your efforts at comfort," Baldan answered drily. "An interesting entertainment. The wagers were evenly divided, until the wily Gryffn lifted his bony wings and fled down the wind. The odds dropped then, and the game was no longer interesting." He paused and seemed to study Brihtric with his milky eye but found only wry acknowledgement of the facts brutally cited. Edward had listened carefully and noted the disdain of Gryffn in Baldan's words.

"Since we were not consulted," Baldan continued, "even though the action was on our doorstep, we were content to watch how it all fell out: no fox stays underfoot when wolves contend. So we saw how our old friend Brihtric lost favor with the gods and took refuge in a Hwicce wood. Then la! Here comes the son of Brihtric to his aid. Not only the son, but also the common soldiers of the unfortunate Eorl Teownor, gathered from pieces to rally around their king. Carefully observing all this, we thought our offer to join this effort might not be refused, for even though our bellies lie close to the earth and our manner may not be suited to the court or the town, we are very familiar with the etiquette of the battlefield."

"You've always been too modest, Baldan," Brihtric replied, with perfect seriousness. "Every man who has had the good fortune to have the Hwicce fight with him knows they strike terror into the enemy, and the battle is already half-won when the enemy learns the Hwicce are in the ranks. And you, Baldan, what man hasn't heard of your courage?"

Brihtric went on at length enumerating the deeds of Baldan loudly enough for his words to be heard by the nearest groupings of soldiers and relayed by them to the rest. Baldan sat listening alertly, sometimes nodding gravely at his men, who were animated by the account Brihtric was giving.

"In any engagement, we would be proud to have a Hwicce fighting with us. But we hadn't intended to fight on Hwicce ground, so why bother the Hwicce with our quarrels? But you've seen too clearly how intentions sometimes go. We would be grateful for your help, and we can promise you rich rewards."

"We've always known Brihtric to be a generous king," Baldan smoothly replied.

"As we will always be with our friends," Brihtric said.

The discussion the arrival of the Hwicce had interrupted now went on again with the tribesmen included. Brihtric advanced the possibility of a peace being bought, explaining, "Urm could have launched a full attack anytime in the past few days; he doesn't behave like a man who wants to fight.."

"Urm is known for his flexibility," Baldan said with a cold smile. His sinister eye rolled in its socket, taking in each of the commanders. "Ingware would have attacked before you had cut down the first tree for your rampart. But with Urm . . . ."

Mawer leaned toward the king. "With the force we have now, he may decide a peace is just what he wanted."

They arrived at a figure in the event a peace could be bought, and then returned to the formation of a battle plan. Baldan and his chiefs listened as the battle plan took its final form, adding a comment now and then but, for the most part, merely indicating their agreement. The final plan was for Edward's army to form the left wing and Teownor's force and the Hwicce, to form the right.

They finally rose from their meeting, agreeing to bring the elements of the army together before dawn.

Chapter Sixty

[829] Cardene Forest, Mercia. In the cold hours before daybreak, Edward moved his army quietly out of the forest to take a position to the left of his father's earth-work, while Edbriht of Canterbury brought up the thousand men of the combined force of Teownor's army and the Hwicce out on the right.

So when the sentries woke the Danish camp the leaders saw the silent array of troops stretched toward their position from either side of Brihtric's earthwork, the Hwicce facing them on one end, and on the other, his green mantle rippling back over the flanks of his horse with the fresh breeze, Prince Edward sitting at the head an army that had appeared as if by sorcery.

The army they had scattered the Danes now saw drawn together and standing fast in disciplined rows, the fearsome Hwicce prominent in their midst. Between these two wings, Brihtric's two thousand beleaguered Saxons and Mercians presented a shield wall spanning the distance.

Brihtric's commanders were holding their positions as they waited for the sun to clear the horizon. Facing the rising sun, Edward watched its blazing rim lift above the treetops. He looked toward his father. The king raised his hand, and the high mellow note of the horn gave the call to advance. Restraining his excitement, Edward began to shake. He paced his horse forward and then turned it to the right. He was followed by Mawer and the rest of his commanders and the horsemen and then the foot soldiers.

Now the second call sounded. The Hwicce began a blood-chilling hum. Edward moved his horse into a trot, shifting closer to the foot soldiers as he urged them forward, shouting down the wrath of God on the Danes as he listened for the third instruction from the horn.

They could clearly see the Danes, now, dodging about behind their earthworks, the sun flashing off their helmets and weapons. Beyond them, the empty longships rode gracefully in the river.

Too long still and now eager to join, the men of Brihtric's army took up the Hwicce's chilling hum and sent it reverberating across the narrowing distance. Edward, caught up now in that impetus, reined hard to keep his horse at a trot, holding it in, measuring the speed of his commanders, saw they were maintaining the positions of the men, and got from Mawer just before the eorl pulled down his face mask, a slow and awful grin, which Edward returned as a full-throated laugh and found he wasn't shaking anymore.

The pace was picking up in spite of the restraint of the commanders. *We won't be able to hold them back much longer,* Edward thought.

A small number of Danish warriors suddenly appeared from behind their rampart. The banner of their chief floated above the iron standard they carried. Leaning forward on his straining horse, Edward thought, *Do they think they're going to stop this charge?*

The breeze abruptly lowered. The banner rippled fitfully and folded against the pole. From behind him, Edward heard the sudden call to halt. In a frenzy of disappointment, he reined in his horse, saw his men had heard and were complying with a similar truculence. He looked toward his father. Brihtric was advancing slowly from his army with a group of eorls, one of which was bearing the king's standard. From the Mercian contingent, Heafwine was moving toward the group.

"Stay here," Edward told Mawer. Wheeling his horse about, he cantered to meet his father and reached him at the same time as Eorl Heafwine. "They waited long enough," the prince said to his father, "another two minutes and there'd been no stopping the thing."

"Urm was testing our resolve."

Still feeling deprived, Edward replied angrily, "He almost tested our swords."

"This is far enough," the king said. "Let them come to us."

They halted about one hundred fifty feet out from their army and dismounted. They removed their helmets and weapons. Leaving their horses with a groom, they walked a short distance, and then stood waiting for the group of Danes to come the rest of the way. Beyond these men, they could see Danish warriors climbing up onto the ramparts to watch.

"I've never seen Urm," Edward said. "Is he the tall one?"

Goda answered, "That's the bloody bastard."

The chieftain was walking at the center of the men coming toward them. He had a long, angular face with a clean-shaven jaw thrust forward so far the lower lip protruded full and slack beyond the upper lip, which appeared shrunken because of this alignment. His long face was surrounded by a bush of reddish hair, a color repeated in his heavy eyebrows. He had set a moderate pace and maintained it in an easy, long-limbed stride. He and his men came to a stop a few feet away from Brihtric's group. His nearly colorless eyes made a complete survey of the men in front of him before he spoke in a rich voice in heavily accented English.

"I am Urm, son of Guthfrith. I am the leader of this army. These are my commanders." He formally named each one.

Brihtric gave them the same dispassionate survey, holding the eyes of each man in turn. Then he said, "I am Brihtric, king of the West Saxons. These are my trusted commanders." He formally introduced them, including Edward. "What do you want to parley about, Urm?"

A curious look of indifference, almost of boredom, settled on the Danish chieftain's face as he passed his gaze over his enemies again as if he were considering whether he would answer so tedious a question. But he finally did, bringing his eyes back to Brihtric. "We will leave the battlefield, if you will pay for the needs of my men."

If Brihtric was surprised at this preambleless offer, he did not reveal it. His eorls, however, by the restless changing of stance suggested they were unprepared for the matter to be so quickly presented.

"The needs can't be many, Urm," Brihtric said in a mild tone, "since you've cleaned out the countryside and look like you've been fed well enough. But putting an easy end to this is agreeable to us, if you don't mean to be outrageous. What do you have in mind?"

"Six hundred pounds of silver would be barely adequate."

Brihtric laughed and his eorls joined in.

Urm raised his eyebrows.

"We'll give you two hundred pounds of silver for your immediate withdrawal and your oaths not to return to the Severn Valley."

Urm turned his head in a languid movement to the men on either side of him. His lower lip glistened with saliva. When he looked again at Brihtric, he said, "You'll have our oaths, but the price for us to leave is six hundred pounds--five hundred for my warriors; one hundred for the king of Denmark."

"The Saxons and Mercians have paid enough into the treasury of the king of Denmark. We'll not pay one gram more. Two hundred fifty for your men. If it suits you, pay your king from that."

"You seem more ready to fight than to make a peace, Brihtric. We can accommodate that." He stared at the king, and then pulled at his moist lower lip with a scarred hand. "Good men will die on both sides," he said. Then, "No army can move for less than five hundred."

"How many pounds of silver does it take to pull an oar, Urm? You're playing with me. I'm losing interest. Three hundred and that's the game."

Urm stared again at Brihtric, and then glanced once more from side to side. His commanders returned his gaze with expressionless faces. "We'll consider this," he said.

They drew back several paces and stood conferring. During this period, the Saxons and Eorl Heafwine did not speak. Brihtric exchanged a brief and significant glance with his son. The Danes returned.

"Four hundred pounds of silver," Urm said.

"Three hundred twenty-five, Urm, for your immediate departure and your oaths not to return to this valley, and not one shilling more." Brihtric said it quietly, but there was no mistaking its finality in either his manner or the manner of his commanders, who slowly drew themselves into wary attentiveness.

There was a long silent moment as the two groups confronted each other. "There will be another time and another place," Urm said. "We accept."

Brihtric turned immediately to Eorl Eadnoth and nodded. The eorl walked back to where the groom stood with the horses and swung up on his mount. He trotted back toward the Saxon lines. The groups of Urm and Brihtric moved apart from each other and stood quietly talking among themselves.

"They took it!" Eorl Sigeric said with relish.

The same expression of restrained triumph was on one or two faces in the Danish group. It was clear both sides felt they had won.

"They had already decided they weren't going to fight," Brihtric was saying, and Edward looked at him.

"Their strategy escapes me," Edward said, annoyed.

Brihtric's eyebrows rose. "It was to get as much as they could for doing what they were going to do anyway. Ah, here is Eadnoth."

The two groups came together again as the eorl rode up with a horse pulling a cart bearing a metal strapped wooden chest. Eorl Goda and one of Urm's commanders wrestled it to the ground and then stepped back into their own groups. Brihtric opened the chest. Inside were silver ingots and coins. He stood away while Urm's commanders checked the depth of the box and examined the silver. When they were satisfied Urm and his commanders gave their oaths to the conditions they had agreed upon while the Saxons listened carefully. Then, as each group turned to go back to their armies, Urm called out, "Prince Edward!"

Edward turned around.

Urm measured him insolently with his eyes, brought his tongue out to the edge of his lower lip and withdrew it. "Ingware sends you his regards. He is looking forward to meeting you again."

"We'll all meet again, Urm."

"He found you so engaging he prays daily for the opportunity. He wonders if you have a son."

Edward made no reply, merely turned and joined the king and the eorls in the walk back to where the horses were waiting.

"What did he mean?" his father asked.

"Ingware was at Weardburh. I ordered his son's head struck off."

Brihtric understood this grim reply and said nothing further. They remounted their horses and went back to Brihtric's line.

"It's getting hot out there," Edward said. "I'd like to move my men back into the woods."

"See to it," his father said. "And then come back here."

"Yes, Sire," Edward replied, and went off to see to the comfort of his army.

Chapter Sixty-One

[829] Winchester, Wessex. Edward had been at the royal hall at Winchester for over two months. After Urm's withdrawal, the danger of attack had lessened and Edward, at his father's request, had allowed his army to disperse back to their villages. Couriers ran regularly north and south, keeping Edward and his father informed of events in Mercia and keeping Aedred abreast of the status of things in Wessex. In the last few days the West Saxon levies were again being assembled as a result of recent intelligence. Two raids had taken place in Aethelred's district on the Mercian northern border, and there appeared to be a movement of Danes within Northumbria just across from Stofe. Edward was relieved at the prospect of returning to Ceolworth.

During the two months he had spent with his father, the old marriage question had surfaced. Edward knew it all by heart. He repeated the vague assurances he had always given to this question and found his father pressing him for something more specific. He wondered at his father's persistence. His uneasiness grew.

"I've made discreet inquiries about Lady Aelfthryth. You remember that charming girl, don't you? Eorl Eadnoth's youngest daughter? She reached marriage age this year."

While Edward stared silently at him, his father went on to explain the advantages: Eorl Eadnoth was loyal, had sound economic sense, and was in charge of the West Saxon treasury.

"Lady Aelfthryth has inherited her father's economic ability which is a value in a queen, certainly. She is well-liked by her peers, respected by her elders. She has a sympathetic attitude toward the people, and shows intelligence. She has good breeding and has traveled widely with her parents. An altogether lovely girl, well-suited to be a queen." It was obvious his father saw this as a perfect union.

Edward was furious and so suddenly afraid he would be commanded to marry this girl that he stalked out of his father's presence and did not return to the hall for two days. With a feeling of sorrow, Brihtric had let him go: Edward knew who would prevail.

Appalled at himself, Edward came back and apologized to his father for his behavior and begged his forgiveness. He duly met Lady Aelfthryth and escorted her to two or three functions, found her to be young, charming, and no doubt a reasonable choice for a future queen. But not once did he make any commitment, or suggest he would make one. He was attentive, courteous, and noninvolved. But his father seemed satisfied at these meager efforts.

The army was nearly assembled. For the past four days Edward had spent most of his time at the camp. This evening he was eating at the common campfire with the militia, listening to Mawer carrying on a good-natured argument with some of the men, when a Mercian courier rode into camp. He found Edward and gave him a letter from Elfwina. The prince sat back down where he could read the letter by the firelight.

She had written in English, which immediately gave him misgivings.

Dearest Edward, he read, *this comes to you by trusted courier from Stafford. I urge you to destroy it as soon as you've read it.*

"My God," he muttered. "Now, what?"

Edward glanced up from the letter. The messenger had found someone he knew in the group around the campfire and was speaking with friendly animation as he sat down with a plate in his hands. No alarm there. Edward went back to the letter.

I'm here with Lady Penwahl, partly for the reasons we discussed at Grundl's ceremony, but also because I have been so sick lately, and Aedred insisted that I see someone--if not Lady Pen, then another physician he threatened to have brought up from London. There was no avoiding the scrutiny. I thought I knew the cause for my illness but dared not believe it. Today Lady Pen has confirmed it. I am with child.

It is the final betrayal in the number of betrayals my lack of resolve in anything to do with you allowed. I am not blaming you. I am a grown woman, and I will accept the consequences of what I have done. But this innocent child must be spared.

I've thought this through very carefully. There is only one course for me to take and that is to tell Aedred I am pregnant. It will be a terrible blow to him. He will want to know the identity of the father, and I will tell him it was a visitor to the hall, not someone of the kingdom. I don't want him to torture himself with suspicions about the men who surround him. I will tell him it happened but once, and then the man left the country. Distance, I think, will make it easier for him to bear. I will put myself on his mercy. I think he will forgive me. I do not believe he will have me exposed as an adulteress.

We are both aware of his secret. Once the pain has eased, I think he will accept this child and raise it as his own. I believe he will consider what is good for the kingdom, rather than revenge his private humiliation.

I feel a strange mixture of fear and guilt and joy. In spite of everything, this child seems so precious. I have the deepest faith it will thrive in love and grace as is its right by birth and heredity.

I must close. The courier is at the door. Lady Pen says the morning sickness making me feel so wretched should be gone in another week. At that time, I will return to Ceolworth. Don't be unduly concerned for me. I am well enough for the course of these things. I pray you remain safe. Your loving sister, Elfwina.

Edward's hands were shaking as he finished the letter. He stood up abruptly, turned, and walked away from the fire, away from the light, out past the edge of the encampment. In the pale light from a rising quarter moon, he made his way along to where a stream meandered through a dark meadow. Where he stumbled and fell, he remained.

Mawer saw him rise from the fireside and grew alarmed at the stunned expression on the prince's face. He followed him at a distance. For a moment the eorl thought he had lost him, but as he came to the edge of the meadow he saw Edward lying full length in the dark grass, his arms over his face, sobbing as a man will do only when he knows he is alone. Mawer retreated silently, with great misgivings about what it might mean.

After arranging to have the men follow later who were still due to report, Edward ordered the army to be ready to march at daybreak. Then he went to the hall to speak with his father.

"This seems quickly decided, Edward."

"I hardly think so, Sire. There's a force building in the north, as the messengers have been telling us, and there have been raids. Urm and Ingware could move within a few days to reinforce Ædda. We'll be six days on the march as it is--long enough in this uncertainty. Nothing is served by our staying here. I want to get them out on the road."

The king sat regarding his son while carefully putting together what he was going to say. He did not question Edward's military judgment. His doubts lay in another dimension, in his fear that in spite of his efforts the relationship between his son and daughter held danger to them both. It was too close; he had always known that and strived to restrain it. They were adults, now, but still the fear remained. And he suffered because of his suspicions. Who wanted to think such a thing of their children? Uneasiness remained, a nebulous something filling him with a sense of urgency. And so he now said to Edward, "I would like an agreement with you before you leave."

"About Lady Aelfthyrth? How far will you go, Father? Will you command my marriage?"

"I will."

Edward was a long time replying. When he did speak, it was carefully, evenly. "Allow me to finish this campaign. Then, I will open negotiations myself with Eorl Eadnoth."

It was a bitter resignation, and Brihtric knew it. The king inclined his head but said nothing. His son left without embracing him.

Edward drove the army like cattle back toward Ceolworth,

oblivious to everything but his need to get there as soon as possible. He knew for an absolute certainty that he had to stop her from telling Aedred. And over the days of that march, he devised a solution that would finally allow him and Elfwina to be together, a solution best for them all. Edward forced the Saxons on, pushing men and horses to their limit, until Mawer convinced him to slacken the pace.

A day out from Ceolworth, Edward left Mawer in charge of the march and rode on by himself through the night and arrived at Aedred's encampment at sun up. He was told the king had been in the north assessing the threat from Northumbria but was expected back that evening. The queen had not returned from Stafford.

Edward made arrangements for his army to be billeted again in the southern meadow. Then, completely thwarted and near exhaustion, he went to his chambers and, dropping across his bed, swayed into a fatigued and motionless sleep.

He awoke not knowing where he was or the hour of the day. He sat up slowly and pieced things together. It was evening. He got up and pushed open the window and looked out on the countryside. His window faced south, but he could see the smoke drifting from the western bivouac where supper campfires had been lit. He breathed in the pleasant, smoke-tinged air, still trying to clear his head. Finally, he went to the cabinet which held the water supply for the room, stripped down, bathed in the cold water, which revived him, and put on clean clothes. Then he went downstairs to find out if any word had come of Aedred's expected arrival.

The wide doors stood open to the balmy evening. The western horizon was silvery green, fading upwards into black. One brilliant star hung above the treetops. From the dark river banks, a choir of frogs sawed amid the reeds. Mercia was rolling into the last quarter of the double month of Litha. The earth was warm, the evening calm.

July, he thought. *The year is beyond the halfway mark. February will bring her to term. February--Solmonath, the month of cakes.*

He turned from the doors. At the southern end of the great room, away from the enormous black mouth of the central hearth, a number of Aedred's thegns sat drinking ale under the smoky lamp at that end of the hall. When they saw Edward coming, they shouted greetings and scraped back from the table, rising to bow and then make a place for him.

"Here come the Saxons to share the entertainment," one cried out.

"Those Saxons are a quiet bunch," another observed.

"You'll hear them well enough tomorrow," Edward replied. A servant came up to him with a cup of ale. Edward told him, "Bring me cold meat and bread." He looked back at the thegns. "Have you had any news from the border? I hear the king comes back tonight."

While he ate the first meal he had eaten in two days, the prince listened to the accounts of the skirmishes that had taken place near Stofe. Eorl Aethelred was never taken by surprise. Prevented from doing little more than brandishing weapons and yelling obscenities, the Northumbrians had been run scornfully back across the border. Apparently Ædda had risked this foolishness because of the support of a large gathering force of Danes that had not participated in these exercises. This gathering force was the reason Aedred had gone to the border with his eorls. Had Elfwina told her husband she was pregnant? That was information no one at the table could give him. He shoved away the half-eaten plate of food.

The Mercians wanted to know how things had gone in the south. He told them over a second cup of ale. They were amused by the Hwicce joining with the army.

"The Hwicce's," one thegn said, a red-faced, round-cheeked man with a sense of humor, "are butt-ugly. They can scare the shit out of you, coming out of the dark with those blue faces and animal skins."

A thegn from down the table called out, "Are those bear hides they wear?"

The man sitting across from Edward said, "I hear they've bred up hares—big ones."

"Yeah, for the skins."

"Bunny fur," another man sneered.

"You'll think bunny fur if one of their hares runs up your ass."

In the midst of their laughter, they heard the arrival of the king.

Edward followed the thegns across the hall and out onto the porch, seeing Aedred before the king saw him. He looked tired and dusty and was showing an unusual impatience at the servants he was directing up the stairs loaded with clothing cases and other objects. A chill fingered Edward's spine; his indrawn breath hissed between his teeth. He took another, deeper breath. At that moment, Aedred saw him. At first the king looked dumbfounded, and then he let out an oath and swam toward the prince through the men who instantly gave way. Edward took a quick step backward but was grabbed by the shoulders. Aedred hugged him fiercely, and then held him at arm's length.

"Where's your army? What are you doing here? There's nothing afoot, is there?"

Edward let out his breath. In that instant he knew there would be a confrontation between them, that it was going to happen, and that it would be catastrophic. But, for this moment, he clung to Aedred's love and his ignorance and felt shame.

"No," he said, "there's nothing afoot."

Aedred had come back through Stafford on his way from the border; Elfwina was to join him for the return journey to Ceolworth. He had been preoccupied, going over with his eorls again and again all possible responses to all possible advances by the Danes.

On the night before their return, the royal couple were together in a room overlooking the rich valley that was the boundary between the Penwahl and Aethelred earldoms.

"You're looking much better now," he had said and tightened his arms around her waist. "I was worried about you. Did Lady Pen dose you with herbs?"

"She gave me some remedies."

He kissed her, and then stood with his arm around her for a moment before he let her go. Then he flung himself on the bed.

She studied him carefully. Sitting down beside him, she asked, "Just how bad is it up there?"

He reached for her hand and interlaced his fingers with hers, brown and white, brown and white. "How bad is it? It's bad."

"What is the size of the force, now?"

He looked up at her. "Around a thousand."

"And the Northumbrians?"

"Unknown as yet. A rough guess from what they've managed in the past--five hundred or so. But with Osward . . . that would put them more or less at the strength of the Danes." He sat up and released her hand. "The last report from Wessex has Ingware still in East Anglia. But that was four days ago. Who knows?"

She watched him get up from the bed and walk to the dark fireplace. He hooked one arm on the mantel and stared down into the empty grate. "Maybe fifteen hundred more there." He held out his hand as if he were warming it at a fire.

She felt such pity for him her throat ached, and she stroked it with her fingers until she could speak. "With Ingware's army that makes eight thousand. Even with all our allies, we have little over half that number--"

"There's Gryffn."

"I would advise you never to count on Gryffn again. His treachery on the Severn has shown how trustworthy he is. There is only one way you can act, Aedred, and that is to take the offensive. You must take your army into Northumbria before Ædda can fully assemble and act on his own plans."

He turned his head slightly, listening as he looked steadily at her from the corners of his eyes. When she finished, he straightened and came full around to face her.

"I didn't go to all the trouble to make a treaty with Ædda so I would be the first to break it. I've never been an aggressor. I maintain my borders, but I also respect them."

"Yes, I know that. You have always been careful in that regard."

"I do not respond to threats, Elfwina. Only actions."

She gazed at him silently. He stepped away from the hearth and came back to where she sat quietly on the edge of the bed.

"Even if there were ten thousand warriors, until Ædda violates the border it remains only a threat." He smiled. "Skirmishes don't count."

He sat back down on the bed and looked over at her. "There's a civil structure I'm bound by oath to preserve, and it rests on non-aggression." He laid his hand on hers where they rested in her lap. "I appreciate your advice, and I recognize it is sound military strategy. It is just not one I can employ. I'm sorry."

"No," she said, feeling as if she were losing touch with him completely, "of course you can't." She took a breath. "What is your strategy?"

He got up and seated himself in the chair. He told her about what he and his eorls had been discussing without let up since they had surveyed the force from the Mercian side of the border.

"I haven't made any decisions, because I want to hear Edward's opinions on the situation."

That was the first she knew the Saxon army was now enroute to Ceolworth.

When they had reached the western bivouac it was evident the Saxons had not yet arrived. The eorls stayed on at the camp, while Aedred and the few servants came on with Elfwina to the hall. She was extremely tired and wanted to get to her chambers. She was standing beside the baggage wagon when she heard Aedred's loud oath and the sudden pleasure and relief in his voice. She sensed Edward's presence before she saw him.

Edward could see she was exhausted. They spoke briefly, and then he numbly watched her go up the stairs, solicitously aided by her husband, who soon returned.

"She hasn't been well lately, an unpleasant illness that's kept her in bed for most of a month."

"Oh? That must be why she looks so tired."

"The journey from Stafford did that. She made most of the distance on foot. Riding upset her stomach again." Aedred laughed. "I'm worn out, too. I walked with her most of the way." He gripped the prince's arm. "Look here, Edward, come out to the camp with me. I need your opinion on what we learned in the north."

"I'm always ready to give an opinion," Edward replied.

"You say your army's due tomorrow?"

They were walking out to where Aedred's horse was tied to a

post. He told the groom, "Get us another horse."

"They should get here about mid-afternoon."

"I can't tell you how glad I am to see you," Aedred told him, and flung his arm around the prince's neck.

Chapter Sixty-Two

[829] Ceolworth, Mercia. Elfwina woke early, without nausea, but the same sense of apprehension which had dogged her waking hours for days still lingered. It was the awareness of what still had to be done, something onerous and painful. She had not been able to tell Aedred at Stafford; there were too many things he was already juggling, too many pressures building up. She had decided to wait a day or two, perhaps at a time less hectic when she could sit down with him in a quiet place and tell him this thing that would tear his heart. Added to this anxiety was Edward's sudden appearance ahead of his army.

Edyth brought her a light breakfast and then helped her dress. "You're putting on weight," she said. "It's about time."

"Oh," replied Elfwina.

She paced about the room, waiting for Edward. When he did arrive, she dismissed Edyth quickly and for a moment was unable to do anything further. Then she groped for Edward and he held her, his face against her hair.

"I didn't expect you," she said.

"I drove the army like a madman, then finally left it and came on alone."

"I knew the letter would upset you."

He caressed her cheek. "It's really true? You're with child?"

"Yes."

She trembled, and he gathered her closer, holding her with a swaying, comforting motion. When he felt her ease he said, "Come," and sat her down in a chair. He pulled another chair up in front of her and took hold of her hands, but when they looked at each other, she began to cry. He put his arms around her, and they hung awkwardly, bridged together over their knees.

She said against his cheek, "Can there be any happiness in this?"

He took her hands again and studied the fingers, the pale pink nails, the bones beneath the flesh. "I don't know. There's no measure that fits us. Maybe we can. Maybe it's possible. If you leave here."

"Leave—no--what do you mean?"

"I just thank God I got here before you told Aedred. I have a solution to all this."

"There is no other way--"

"Yes, there is. Go to Winchester and stay with Father. As soon as I've finished my commitments here, I'll join you. Then we'll go to Exeter to live." He gripped her hands. "That's where our child will be born."

"I can't do that."

"Of course, you can. The longer you wait the more difficult it will be for you to leave. You don't have to explain anything to Aedred now. Tell him you want to visit Father while you recuperate. He'll understand that. He'll be glad to get you out of all this. Tell him. I'll make arrangements for you to leave tomorrow."

"He doesn't deserve this, Edward."

"What's the alternative? Throw everything in upheaval? Aedred needs a clear head now. Spare him the turmoil. Don't make it--"

She threw up her hands. "Stop! You're confusing me! I need time to think . . . ." But what he said was true; the same thoughts had governed her decision at Stafford to delay telling Aedred. She put her palms against her eyes and pressed hard. "What would we tell Father if I stay on? You know where he'd feel I should be. If we go to Exeter, what reason would we give?"

"For God's sake, Elf, tell them both you're ill! Act as if you're ill. You can do that." He caught up her hands. "Our child's life depends on you doing this."

"No, our child's life depends on Aedred accepting it for his own!"

He shook his head. "You're not being rational. You know the penalty for adultery." He knew the penalty. He had witnessed it, witnessed Aedred passing the sentence and watching as it was carried out. "You don't know how Aedred is going to react when he finds out. I'm not going to let you take a risk like that."

"If I go to Wessex, Aedred will never--" she faltered.

"Never what?"

She looked at him sadly. "Call the child his own." She leaned forward and pressed her hands against his knees. "This is the only way it can be done, Edward. What kind of future will a child have if its father can't be named?"

He rubbed his fingers hard across his brows.

"You see?" she said gently.

"Don't you want to be with me?"

"For how long? Father will have you marry, you know that. And what then?"

Edward stood up. He put his hand into his curls and strode about the room, thinking of the agreement he had made with his father, of the impossibility of everything. He stopped in front of her. "If the child is raised at Exeter, it won't matter if I have a wife or not; it will have all it will ever need, including its father's love--"

"But not his name! And Aedred would never give it his if I leave."

"Being a bastard is not automatically a handicap. Sometimes just the opposite."

"Yes! Where the father is known to everybody; where he admits responsibility. But this child's father can never be known--never! No nobleman is going to take a young woman to wife when it's uncertain whether her father is an eorl or a swineherd. And what kind of life would a boy have in court where it's whispered the mother had lain with a groom--a boy whose birthright was to wear a crown?"

She began to cry, but shook her head violently and fanned her hands at him so he would not interrupt her. He sighed and took her hands between his, quieting them.

"I don't think Aedred would have me exposed as an adulteress . . . I think he would give the child his name . . . I believe he would do that--" when she saw the tears coursing down his cheeks she clutched his head, drawing it hard against her neck. She sat rocking him back and forth, sobbing.

A heavy knock sounded on the outer door beyond the anteroom. They both straightened as Edyth opened the door to her room. She advanced into the chamber to answer the door and then hesitated at the sight of Edward's tear-stained face as he rose from the chair and turned toward her.

He said, "Send them away, Edyth."

Edyth glanced toward the queen, but Elfwina had turned her head aside. The woman continued on into the anteroom.

Edward drew a hard breath and stood blinking at the floor. Elfwina got up. They stood facing each other, their fingertips touching as if that small contact were vital to them both. Their startled glances met as Aedred's voice rang into the chamber from the anteroom.

Edward said, "It may as well be now," and heard his sister moan, "Not yet!"

Aedred swung into the room, saw their faces, saw both had been crying, noted their falling glances. He stopped dead. "What's the matter?"

He walked straight to Elfwina and would have touched her, but she drew back slightly. His hand stopped in mid-air. He brought it back down to his side. "Are you ill, again?"

She moved away.

Aedred turned to the prince. "Tell me what's going on here."

Edward pulled his fingers down his wet mustache, looking at him through swollen eyes. He sniffed once or twice, cleared his throat. "Edyth, leave us, please," he said, watching Aedred's narrowed gaze rest briefly on the woman before swinging back to his face. "Let's sit down," Edward said, with a deep sigh.

Aedred looked closely at him, and then glanced again at Elfwina. She had dropped down onto a bench and was faced away from them. "All right," he said, and went over to one of the chairs and sat down with his arms on the rests, his head bowed slightly. "Let's hear it," he said quietly.

Edward took a chair near him, looked at his sister, trying to decide what to say, how much to say, struggling for words that would persuade her to leave. "This will be difficult," he began, and turned to look directly into Aedred's eyes.

"Edward--wait!" Elfwina had risen swiftly from the bench and come toward them. "I'll tell him."

Aedred lifted his eyes to her with the same guarded expression Edward had seen. She paused, staring down into his dark gaze. "Oh," she breathed. Turning, she took a few aimless steps away.

He was sitting motionless, watching her. He felt his lungs constrict and slid the fingers of one hand beneath his mantle to rest them in the furrows of his ribs. His heart pounded against his hand. Something dark and unwanted began to rise, and he was unable to stop it.

"Aedred--" she began, and then stopped, driven again to silence by that wary, unfamiliar gaze.

Edward grabbed her arms from behind and pulled her back against him. "She's trying to tell you that she *is* ill. She needs to have quiet where she'll be safe to recuperate. I think she should go to Winchester and stay there with Father--out of this murderous atmosphere--"

"No!" she cried, pulling away. "I belong here. This is not a time for me to leave!"

"Good Jesus, Elfwina!" Edward said.

She clasped her arms, hugging them to her sides, rubbing her hands nervously along her sleeves. The hands suddenly stopped. "There is no easy way to say this," she told Aedred, who was frowning, trying to understand what was unfolding in all the discord between her and Edward. "I'm going to have a child."

Aedred did not move, neither did he say anything nor indicate he had even heard her. He slowly exhaled and lowered his eyes to stare at some remote point away from her face.

Elfwina could not look away from him. *I've said it. He's sitting there trying to believe it, trying to understand why. Should I have gone to Wessex? Did I make the wrong decision?*

When Aedred's eyes came back to her again, she was stunned by their lack of expression. His words were measured, clear, and toneless. "Who is the father?"

She did not answer.

He looked at Edward. The prince was frowning as he stared at his sister, his eyes still red from weeping. *He knows,* Aedred thought. *He would, of course.*

"Who is the father?" he said to Edward.

Edward glanced at his sister, and then at Aedred. He looked away without speaking.

"Was this a brief affair?" he asked Elfwina. "Or will it continue?"

She remained silent.

"I see," he said. "Someone in the hall? Someone I see every day?" His voice trembled, and he flattened his lips against his teeth to control it. "A man hiding in my ignorance, pretending loyalty and friendship?"

Edward took two steps toward the king. He had broken into a sweat that bathed his forehead and glistened in his beard. He stood looking down at Aedred, his face flushed, his chest moving rapidly up and down.

"I will find out who he is," Aedred said.

"He's not a Mercian!" Elfwina cried out, desperately reaching for her original plan. "It only happened once. He came from . . . another country." She had begun to shake. She clasped her hands so tightly the fingers were white.

"What country?"

She was not able to keep the fear out of her voice. "I beg you, let this child live."

He was stunned, not realizing how his face had appeared, what violence his voice had suggested. "You think I would put you to death? Who is this man?"

But the possibility she had glimpsed still frightened her, evident in her face and in her voice. "Will you give me your oath you won't harm the child?"

Edward groaned. "Lord . . . ." He felt the world slipping out from beneath him, whirling away.

Aedred glanced briefly at him, looked back at Elfwina. He faltered, stumbling over his question. "You need my oa--oath?"

"Will you swear it?' she whispered.

His voice faltered again as he replied, "I give it—my oath. I won't harm the child--or you."

She was so visibly relieved that his pain on seeing it drove him to his feet. He tried to put his arms around her. "Why do you need me to swear it? Why do you think I would harm you?" It seemed unreal that she was trying to slide out of his embrace. He held on, attempting to bring her face around to his. "Elfwina . . . !"

They struggled, and then she pulled away from him helped, he realized, by Edward. The prince was holding one of his arms.

"Great Mother," she cried, staggering back, "help us!"

"We can't get any where this way," Edward said, loosening his grip.

Aedred turned on him. "Where are you in this? Did you know all along and not give me a hint?"

"It was not that way," Edward said.

"What way, then? You know who the father is. Give me his name."

Elfwina cried, "It's over and done!"

"Is he alive?"

She opened her mouth but made no sound.

"If he is alive, he is a *coward* to leave you to suffer the consequences. *Who is this man?"*

Edward raked his fingers into his curls as he stared at the king. "There are circumstances--"

"Edward!"

"There are things you don't know. Things that happened over years--"

"Over years?" Aedred swung around to Elfwina. "You said once. Are you a liar? How long has this gone on?"

"Leave her alone," Edward said. "It wasn't her fault."

"No? Whose fault was it?"

"I'm going to tell you."

Elfwina threw her hands out with a cry. "Edward! *Don't!"*

Aedred focused wholly on Edward, but the prince did not speak. Instead, he squeezed his eyes shut as he slowly brought his hand up and, with a low groan, dragged his palm across his forehead. The gesture was a revelation.

Elfwina began to sob, her body shaking, as she huddled down, shrinking into herself.

A chill began at the base of Aedred's skull and the dark thing that had lain silent in his blood rose with a roar that deafened him. He stared at her in bewilderment before his stricken gaze turned to Edward. He moved stiffly forward a few steps past the prince, as if he were going to the door. He drew in a hard breath and with it Edward's familiar smell. Everything in the room was at once familiar, yet suddenly foreign and sharp with pain. He did not know why he was going toward the door. He stopped, turned around, and with his gaze anchored on Edward's shocked and brimming eyes, rolled his head slowly to the side.

"Aahh . . .no . . . ." It was a low and terrible sound. "Only the beasts do that."

"For God's sake, Aedred!" Edward said it in great agitation, but Aedred did not hear him; he had turned and was moving toward Elfwina. She was bent over double on the bench, still sobbing, her hands covering her face.

He stopped abruptly. His head tilted back and his eyes rolled and searched the ceiling. "Ah, no," he said again. "Not you." He slowly bent forward, his hands on his thighs, his head down, breathing deeply, strenuously. Then he straightened. "How could you do that? How--how could you do that?"

There was no answer, and he walked back to his chair, lowered himself into it, half-lying on the rest, his eyes closed. When he opened them, he looked at Edward. "Your blood is too close. It will die or live a monster."

The prince stood a few paces away. His lips were white. His hands shook where they rested on his scabbard belt. His forearms jumped spasmodically. With one cold and active portion of his brain, Aedred was thinking he had never seen Edward so disabled. He did not recognize his own dissolution.

"We didn't mean for it to happen this way," Edward told him. "It was not the way it began--" Edward was struck into silence by the sudden black hatred in Aedred's face.

Elfwina came to her feet. Aedred turned his head toward her. She was no longer crying, but stood motionless with her hands clamped together in front of her, her face white. She was staring at him with a wariness that made him feel suddenly isolated, cast across a distance on a cold, dark plain and as mad and as dangerous as her expression suggested.

Edward was floundering, attempting to go on with an explanation he instinctively knew was all wrong, but he could not think clearly. "We tried to stay away from each other--"

Aedred's heart began to pound violently. The room glared white, the blinding light flattening objects, taking away their depth until the whole interior seemed painted on a shield.

"I love her--and we--"

Aedred held up his hand. "I don't want to hear the rest, Edward," he said quietly.

Edward abruptly stopped talking. He dropped into a chair and sat with his arms across his knees, his head hanging down as he stared at the floor with tear-filled eyes.

In the silence that followed, Aedred slowly straightened in his chair. He spoke with gentleness, "You look done in, Edward."

Edward could not answer.

I have been blind, Aedred thought. Edward, how could you do this evil thing?

The prince looked up at him, and Aedred realized he had spoken the question aloud.

"What do you want from me, Edward?" he asked, without hostility. "I mean, besides what you've already taken."

"He has not taken anything from you," the queen said.

Edward said, "Please, Elfwina." It was a warning.

"He hasn't?" Aedred addressed her in a mild tone, still watching

Edward and speaking as if she was a casual acquaintance. Then his eyes blazed and his voice cracked in sudden wrath as he moved abruptly forward. "You are the vilest creature in the world, Edward," Edward froze. Slowly easing back in his chair, the king said, "You haven't answered my question."

Edward did not speak.

"I'll answer the question," Elfwina said. She came gracefully across the floor, without sound, except for the soft swish of her silken gown against her legs.

"All right," he said, but did not look at her.

She was so restrained and fearful her words and the manner in which she spoke seemed cold. "Three actions are possible: "You could have me exposed as an adulteress and have me put to death. But you have already said you would not do that. You can--" she paused because her voice had begun to shake. She breathed deeply. "You could declare Edward and me . . . incestuous--" she lifted her head and swallowed.

Aedred remained in profile to her, listening as he gazed at the prince. She realized he could not bring himself to look at her, and shame burned inside her. "You swore your oath you would not harm my child, isn't that so?"

"Or you. Yes, I swore that."

"Then you can't declare us incestuous because that would mean I would be put to death."

"Yes."

Her eyes flickered in relief.

"Is this the answer to my question, then? The third possibility? Do you and Edward--are you going to Wessex?"

He had repressed everything as he had spoken, yet what he feared most to hear from her had broken free and was immediately recognized by her. She drew in a ragged breath. "No," she replied, half-crying again. "No, that is not one of the possibilities."

Edward's head came up, his eyes brilliant with pain.

Aedred sighed, but said nothing.

"The other possibility, and it is the only solution if there is to be no scandal, if you are to keep your oath, and if everything is to remain intact--" she paused and the word seemed to circle the room and expand around them "--then the only solution is for you--is for you to . . . accept this child as your own . . . ." She had offered it brokenly, crying, stopping and starting. Both men had kept absolutely still, Aedred staring at the prince, Edward with his gaze on the floor.

Unable to absorb all that was being inflicted on him, Aedred could not respond to her immediately. He was being stabbed again and again, and there was no escape from his attackers. They had ambushed him; fallen on him in the darkness of his ignorance. Coming unarmed among friends, he had offered no resistance, and they had poured his blood on the ground. Defeated and without hope, he groaned aloud. Edward lifted his head to look at him.

"This is what you want, Edward?"

"No, this isn't what I want. I want her with me. I always have. I did before you even knew her." He clawed his fingers through his hair. "This is what Elfwina wants." His head sagged into his hands. "It seems the only way now."

It was clear to Aedred that the prince was unnerved. Out of the turmoil in which they were struggling, the one fact emerging was that Elfwina did not want to go to Wessex as they had obviously discussed and Edward wanted. Her choice was to stay here with him. He did not know if that was a consolation or not, or even if he wanted to live to the end of the day.

Like a predator, he smelled blood and realized a sudden sense of his power to wound Edward. But his own wounds had weakened him, draining him of a desire for vengeance. And he could not understand why he had not risen in the fury gripping him to strike Edward down. He found instead a pain so great he longed to be generous, thinking generosity would salve him with its curative power. He saw Edward's demoralization as if it were his own and felt like weeping because he depended on Edward's strength, the assurance of his presence. And then it all seemed like such nonsense in this context, but he knew the loss and felt like weeping anyway.

"Then it is what you ask of me," he said to Edward, ending his long silence.

"What are your conditions?" Edward asked him.

It had not crossed Aedred's mind there naturally should be conditions to such a pact, and he realized what a ruin had been made of his will. He took a moment before he answered, drawing on the most obvious, "The child is never to know its natural father."

Edward dropped his forehead against his clenched hands and sighed deeply. "Yes, I knew that would be one."

There was silence again. "There will be state matters, business between our kingdoms, which must go on; aside from those occasions, during which you and Elfwina will never arrange to be alone together, neither of you is to make any attempt to see the other again."

Edward nodded without lifting his head. Aedred heard a low murmur of agreement from Elfwina.

"Elfwina," the king said, "the child is never to be taken to Wessex, and you are never to go to Wessex again."

"Never? May I never visit my father?"

"You are never to go to Wessex again," he repeated.

"Is that . . . all the conditions?" she asked, after a pause.

He thought carefully. "If the child is normal and a male, he will be my successor. He will be the future king of Mercia. That is what you are demanding of me in this vile alliance. This is what I demand of you: your oaths will not be discharged at my death. They will stand for all time. Do you agree to this?" He saw they did, and he said, "Now, both of you swear to it."

Elfwina gave her oath, standing beside him, looking down at the dark head with its fine hair flowing smoothly from the center part. She wanted to touch that soft hair, tell him she was sorry, that she loved him, but she knew that would never be possible again.

"Now you, Edward."

Edward was slow answering him, but he finally said, "I swear I will never tell the child I'm its father. I swear I will never see my sister again, except under the conditions you named. For all time."

Aedred said, "I give my oath the child will be raised as my own."

No one spoke for a long time, and then Edward asked, "What do you want me to do now?"

"Right now? Go to your camp and stay there."

Edward swayed wearily to his feet. He did not look at his sister or at the king, but simply turned and left the room as Aedred had commanded.

The king and queen did not speak, but they both listened. Through the open window they heard Edward's footsteps in the general noise of the yard below, his calm voice speaking with a groom, the sound of his horse moving away from the hall to the gate, and then his departure was lost in the mingling of other familiar sounds of the enclosure.

Aedred sat with his head bent to his chest, his arms along the chair rests. "I don't know what's going to happen up at the border, but before I go, I'll write a document and have it witnessed that I know you are pregnant and the child is mine. I'll name you as regent should I die before a male child comes of age. I'll leave it with Ceolric, so if something happens to me, there'll be no question. I will trust you to raise the child as a Mercian of royal blood."

"Aedred--"

He made a weary gesture. "Don't--please."

And in silence he considered the irony of preparing to war with enemies surrounding his realm, while, in his own hall, without a drop of blood being spilled, he had given away his kingdom, its future, and the legacy of the Mercian kings to an abomination created by a betrayal he could never avenge.

When another moment or so passed, he rose. After a long and

tortured look at his wife, which ended somewhere in space, he walked from the room.

Elfwina watched him go, the debris of her life scattered all about her.

ABOUT THE AUTHOR

Francine Mezo is the author of three science fiction novels: *The Fall of Worlds, Unless She Burn, and No Earthly Shore,* all published by Avon Books. Her short story "At a Cove on a Distant Planet" was published in an anthology by Fivebadgers. She was editor of the magazine *Dakota Harvest,* a teaching tool for students in English at the University of North Dakota.

Ms. Mezo lives in a forested, frontier county in Northern California with a large, friendly dog and a surly cat.

Printed in Great Britain
by Amazon

38817049R00209